FAERIE PATH
LAMIA'S REVENGE
VOL. 1: THE SERPENT AWAKES

Created by Frewin Jones
Written by Leigh Dragoon
Art by Alison Acton

HAMBURG // LONDON // LOS ANGELES // TOKYO

Faerie Path Volume 1: Lamia's Revenge: The Serpent Awakes

Created by Frewin Jones
Written by Leigh Dragoon
Art by Alison Acton

Lettering - Lucas Rivera
Cover Design - James Lee

Editor - Jenna Winterberg
Contributing Editor - Tim Beedle
Pre-Production Supervisor - Vicente Rivera, Jr.
Print-Production Specialist - Lucas Rivera
Managing Editor - Vy Nguyen
Senior Designer - Louis Csontos
Senior Designer - James Lee
Senior Editor - Bryce P. Coleman
Senior Editor - Jenna Winterberg
Associate Publisher - Marco F. Pavia
President and C.O.O. - John Parker
C.E.O. and Chief Creative Officer - Stu Levy

A TOKYOPOP Manga

TOKYOPOP Inc.
5900 Wilshire Blvd. Suite 2000
Los Angeles, CA 90036

E-mail: info@TOKYOPOP.com
Come visit us online at www.TOKYOPOP.com

For information address HarperCollins Children's Books, a division of HarperCollins Publishers, 1350 Avenue of the Americas, New York, NY 10019.
www.harperteen.com

ISBN 978-0-06-145694-7
Library of Congress catalog card number: 2008904273

1 2 3 4 5 6 7 8 9 10

❖

First Edition

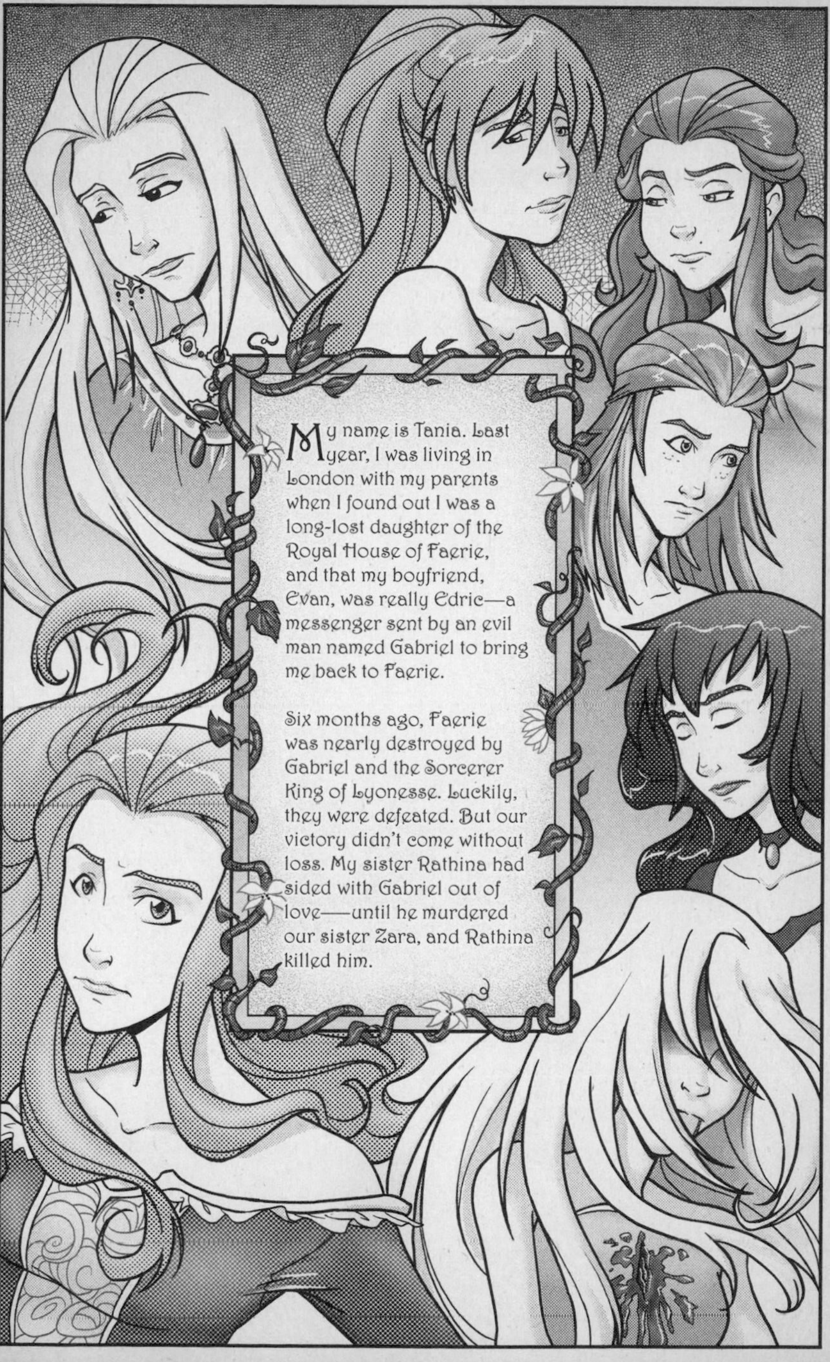
My name is Tania. Last year, I was living in London with my parents when I found out I was a long-lost daughter of the Royal House of Faerie, and that my boyfriend, Evan, was really Edric—a messenger sent by an evil man named Gabriel to bring me back to Faerie.
Six months ago, Faerie was nearly destroyed by Gabriel and the Sorcerer King of Lyonesse. Luckily, they were defeated. But our victory didn't come without loss. My sister Rathina had sided with Gabriel out of love—until he murdered our sister Zara, and Rathina killed him.

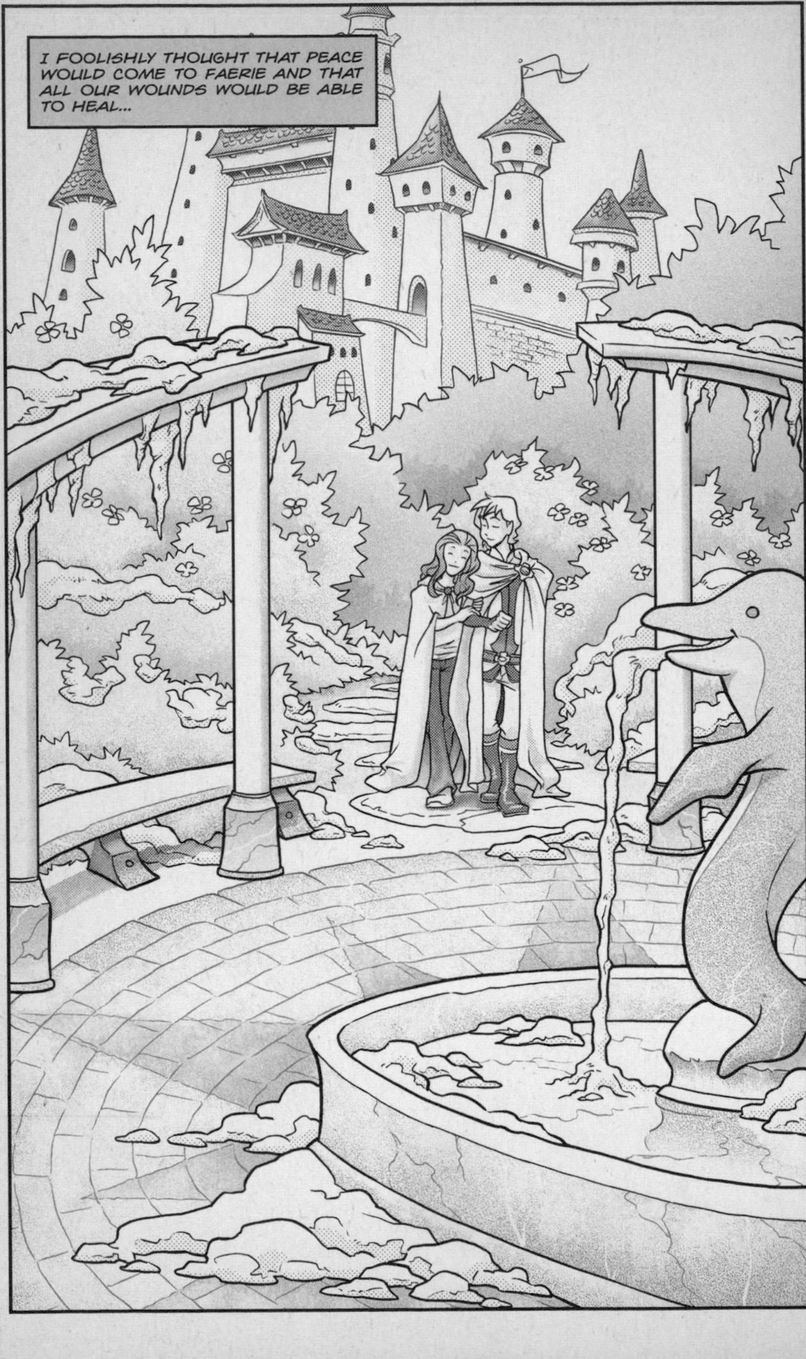
I FOOLISHLY THOUGHT THAT PEACE WOULD COME TO FAERIE AND THAT ALL OUR WOUNDS WOULD BE ABLE TO HEAL...

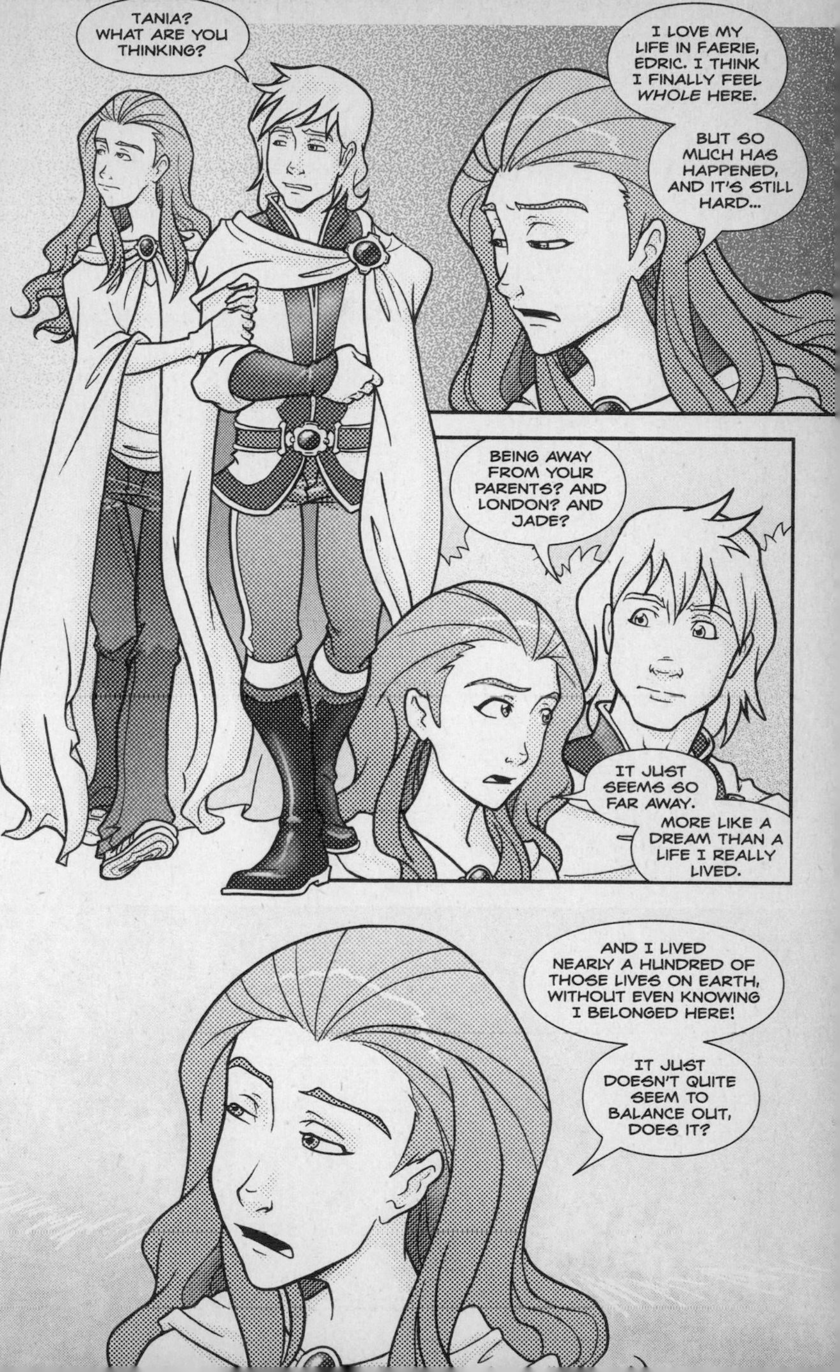
TANIA? WHAT ARE YOU THINKING?
I LOVE MY LIFE IN FAERIE, EDRIC. I THINK I FINALLY FEEL *WHOLE* HERE.
BUT SO MUCH HAS HAPPENED, AND IT'S STILL HARD...
BEING AWAY FROM YOUR PARENTS? AND LONDON? AND JADE?
IT JUST SEEMS SO FAR AWAY.
MORE LIKE A DREAM THAN A LIFE I REALLY LIVED.
AND I LIVED NEARLY A HUNDRED OF THOSE LIVES ON EARTH, WITHOUT EVEN KNOWING I BELONGED HERE!
IT JUST DOESN'T QUITE SEEM TO BALANCE OUT, DOES IT?

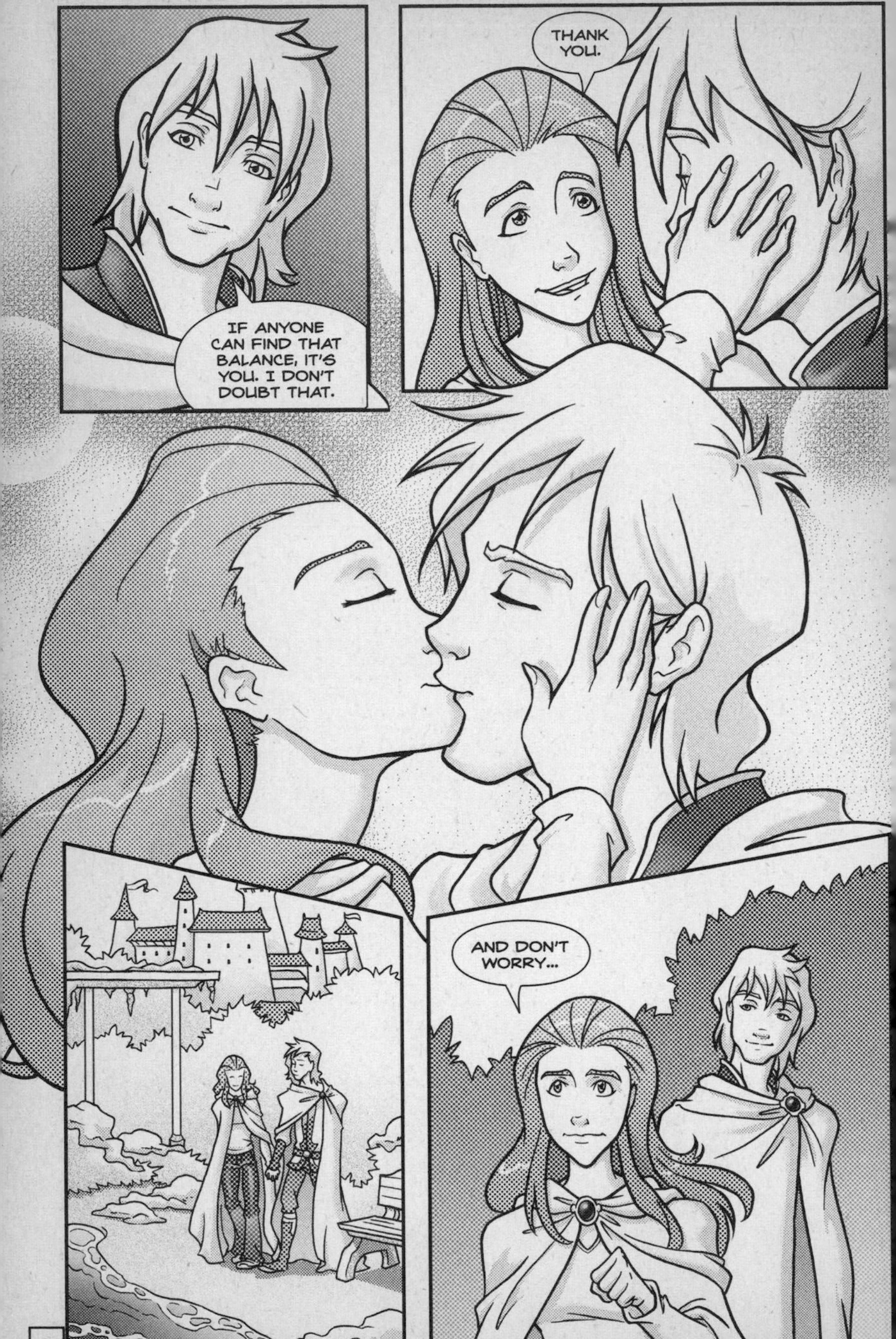
IF ANYONE CAN FIND THAT BALANCE, IT'S YOU. I DON'T DOUBT THAT.
THANK YOU.
AND DON'T WORRY...

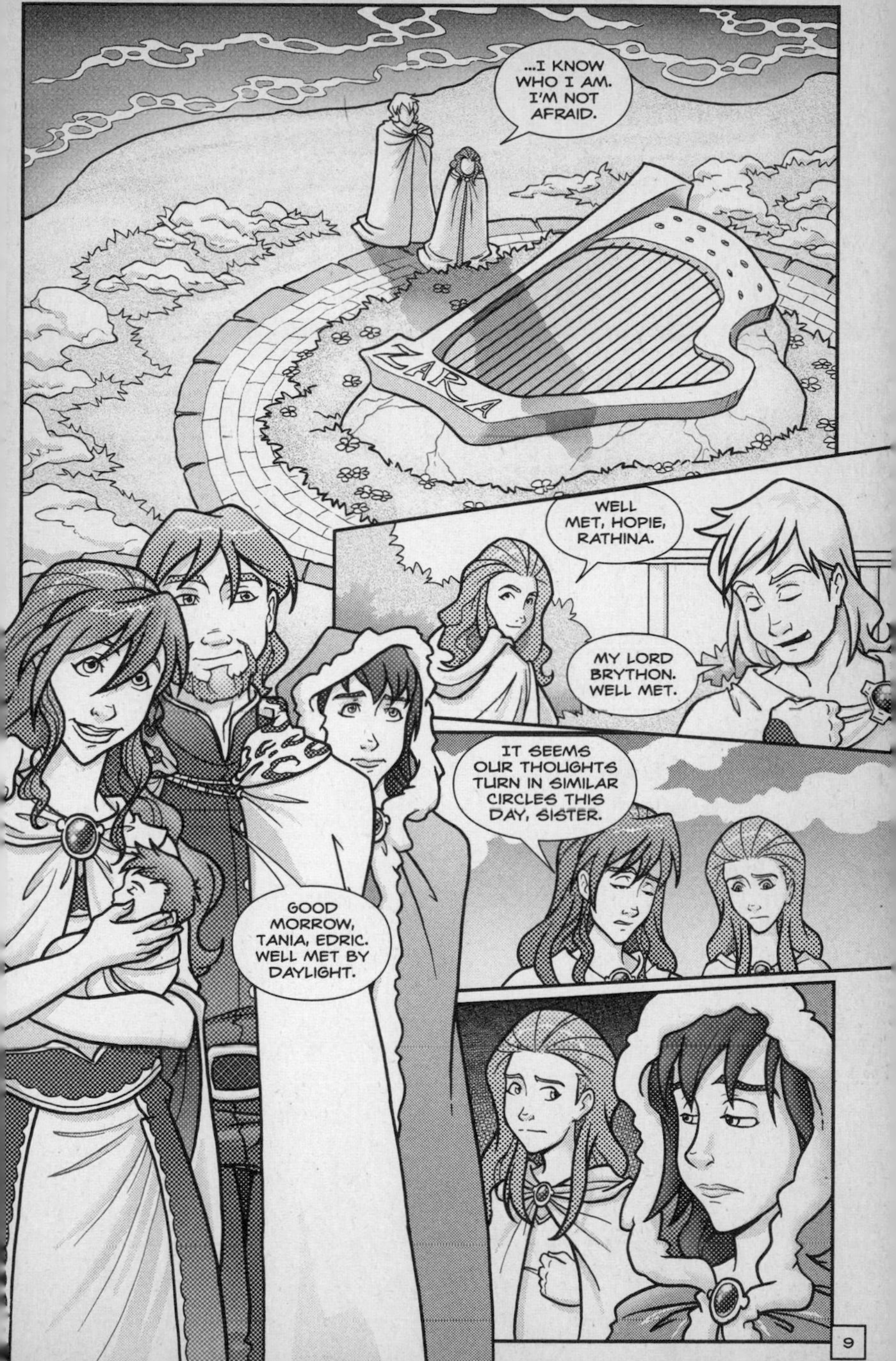
...I KNOW WHO I AM. I'M NOT AFRAID.
ZARA
WELL MET, HOPIE, RATHINA.
MY LORD BRYTHON. WELL MET.
IT SEEMS OUR THOUGHTS TURN IN SIMILAR CIRCLES THIS DAY, SISTER.
GOOD MORROW, TANIA, EDRIC. WELL MET BY DAYLIGHT.

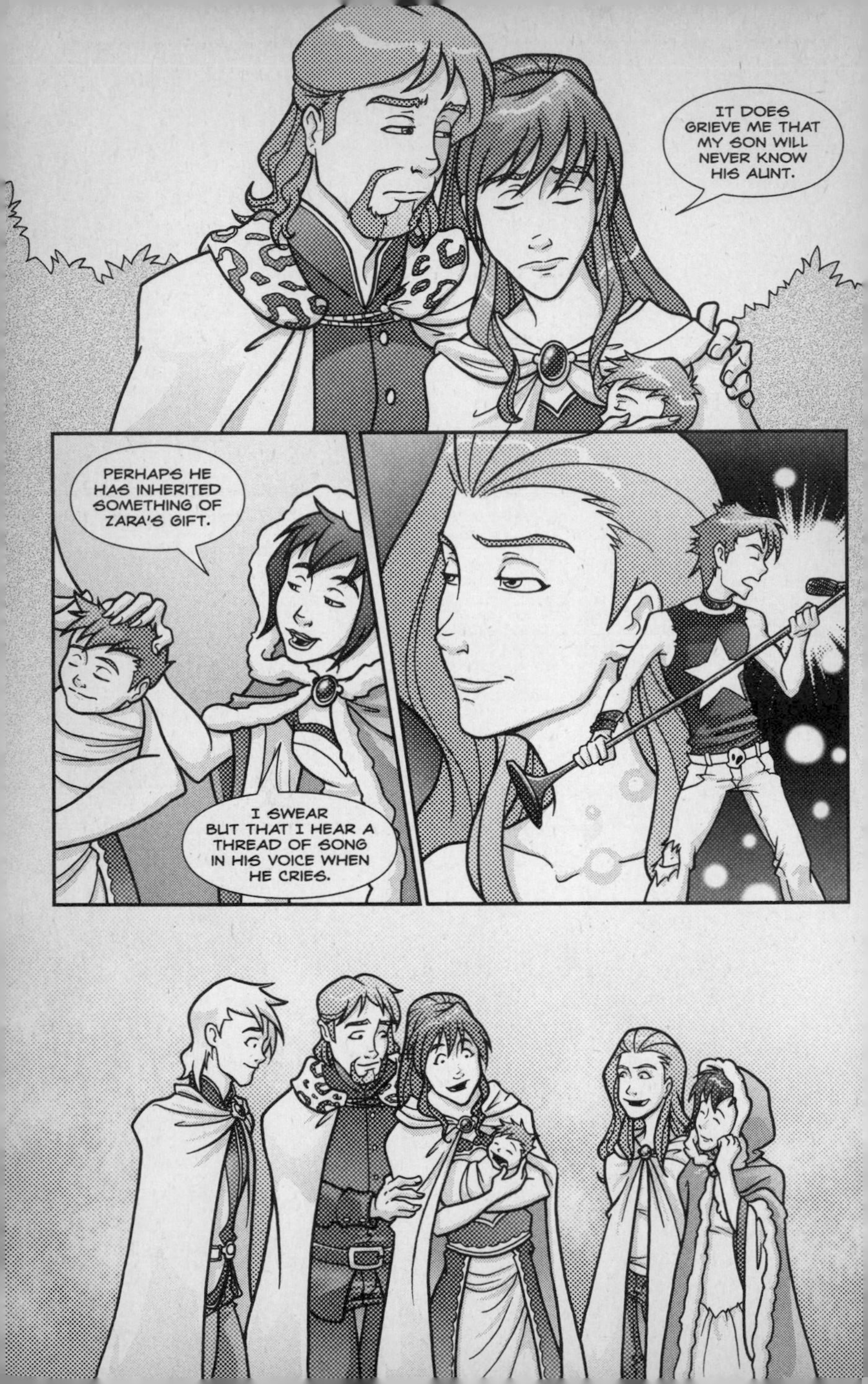
IT DOES GRIEVE ME THAT MY SON WILL NEVER KNOW HIS AUNT.
PERHAPS HE HAS INHERITED SOMETHING OF ZARA'S GIFT.
I SWEAR BUT THAT I HEAR A THREAD OF SONG IN HIS VOICE WHEN HE CRIES.

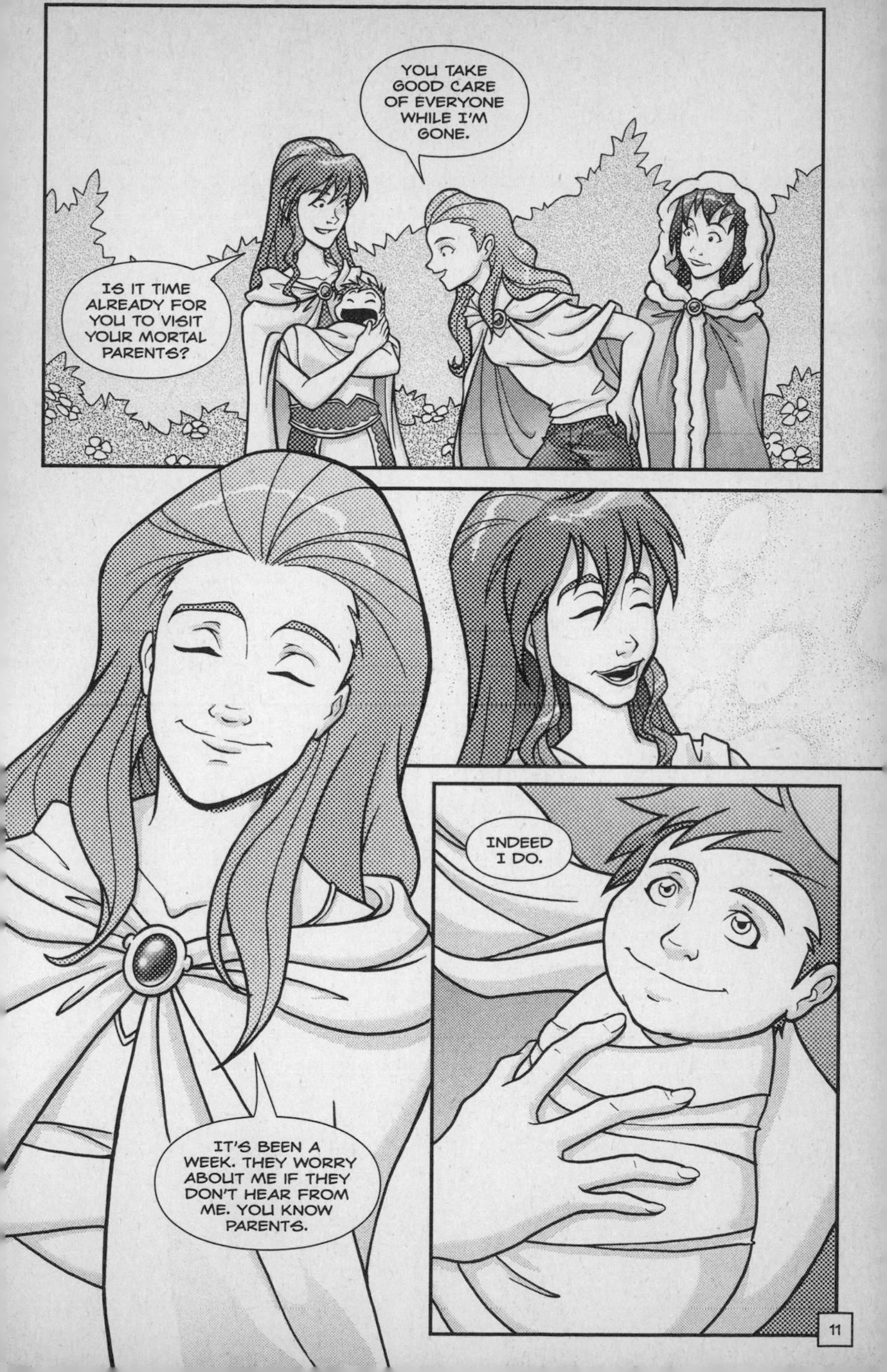
YOU TAKE GOOD CARE OF EVERYONE WHILE I'M GONE.
IS IT TIME ALREADY FOR YOU TO VISIT YOUR MORTAL PARENTS?
IT'S BEEN A WEEK. THEY WORRY ABOUT ME IF THEY DON'T HEAR FROM ME. YOU KNOW PARENTS.
INDEED I DO.

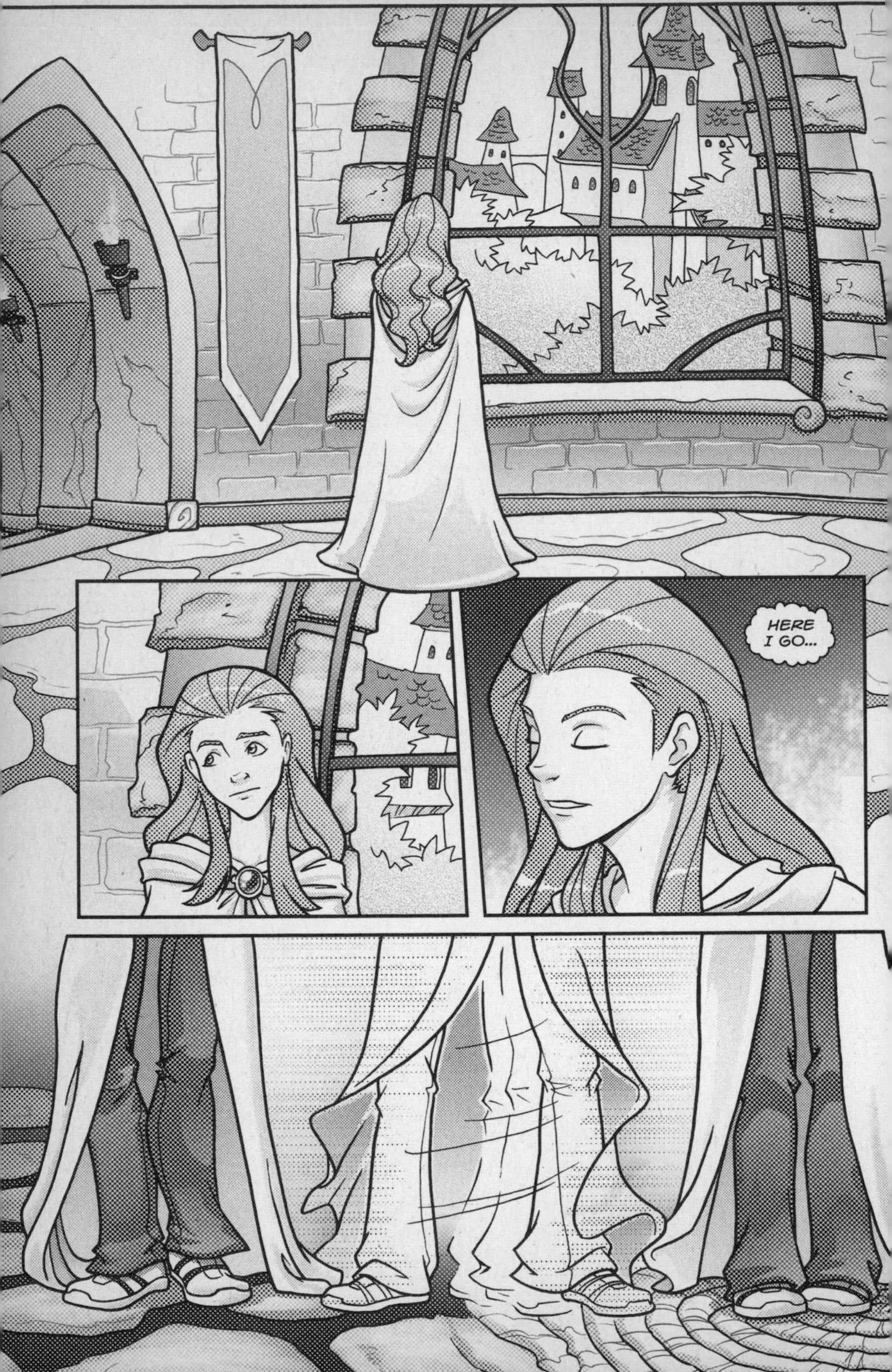
HERE I GO...

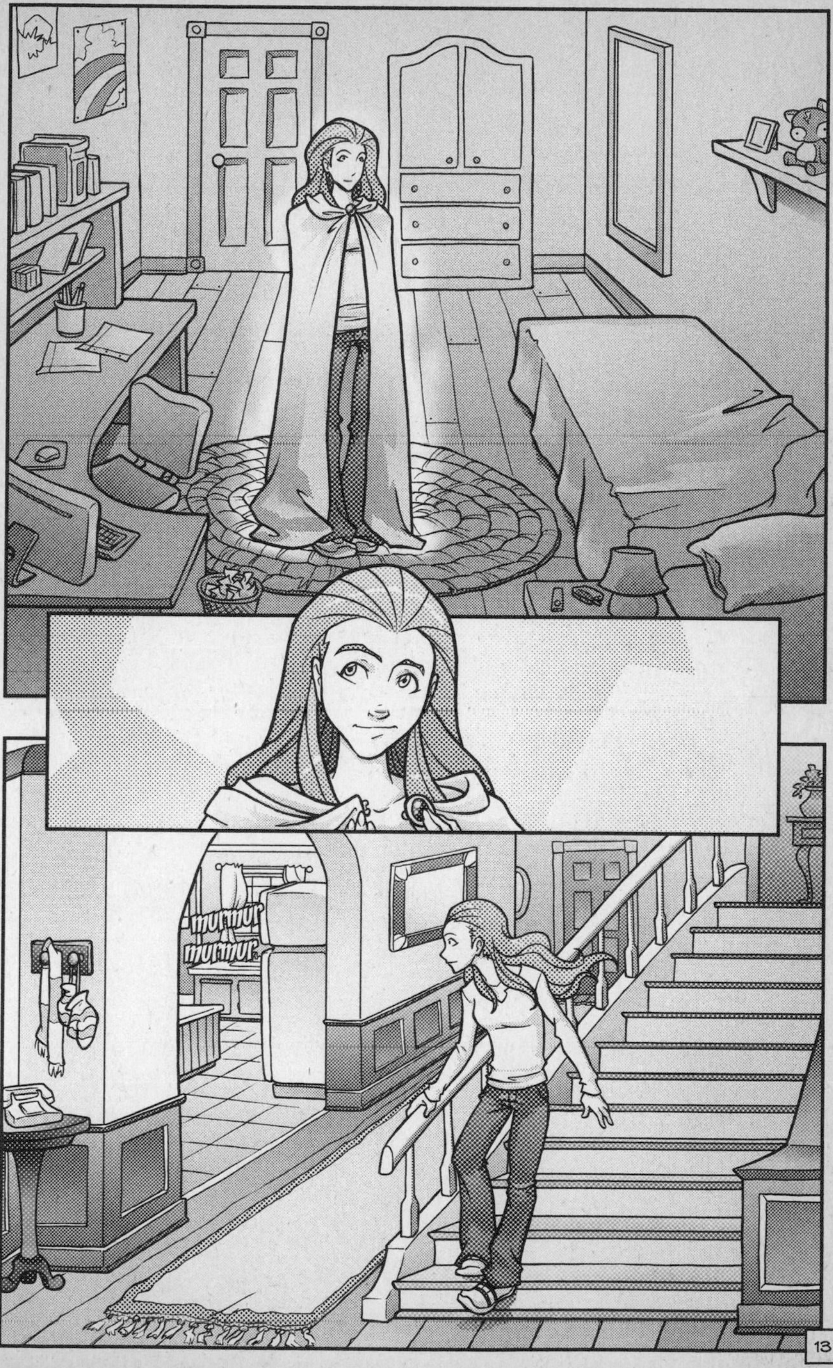

murmur
murmur

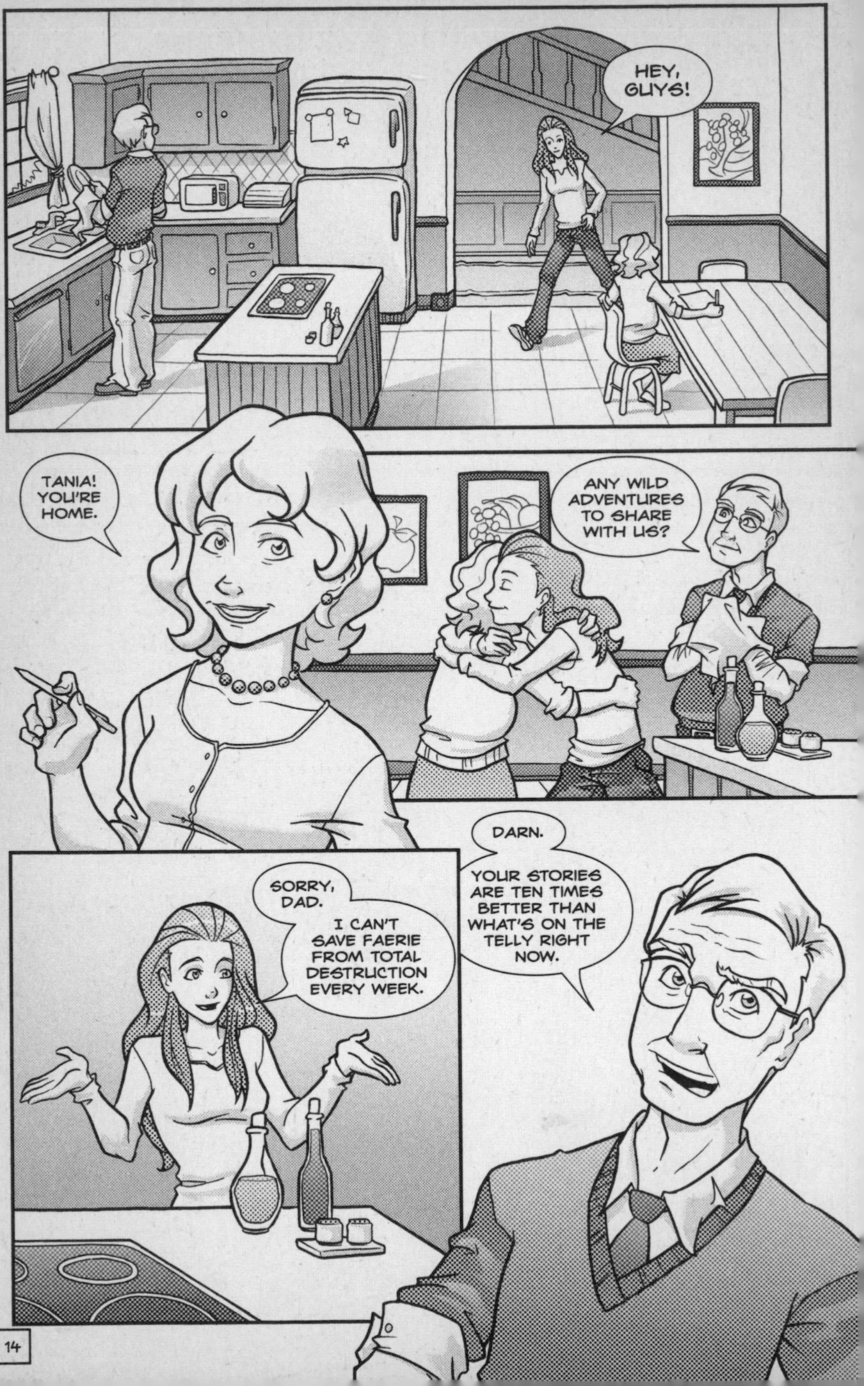
HEY, GUYS!
TANIA! YOU'RE HOME.
ANY WILD ADVENTURES TO SHARE WITH US?
SORRY, DAD.
I CAN'T SAVE FAERIE FROM TOTAL DESTRUCTION EVERY WEEK.
DARN.
YOUR STORIES ARE TEN TIMES BETTER THAN WHAT'S ON THE TELLY RIGHT NOW.

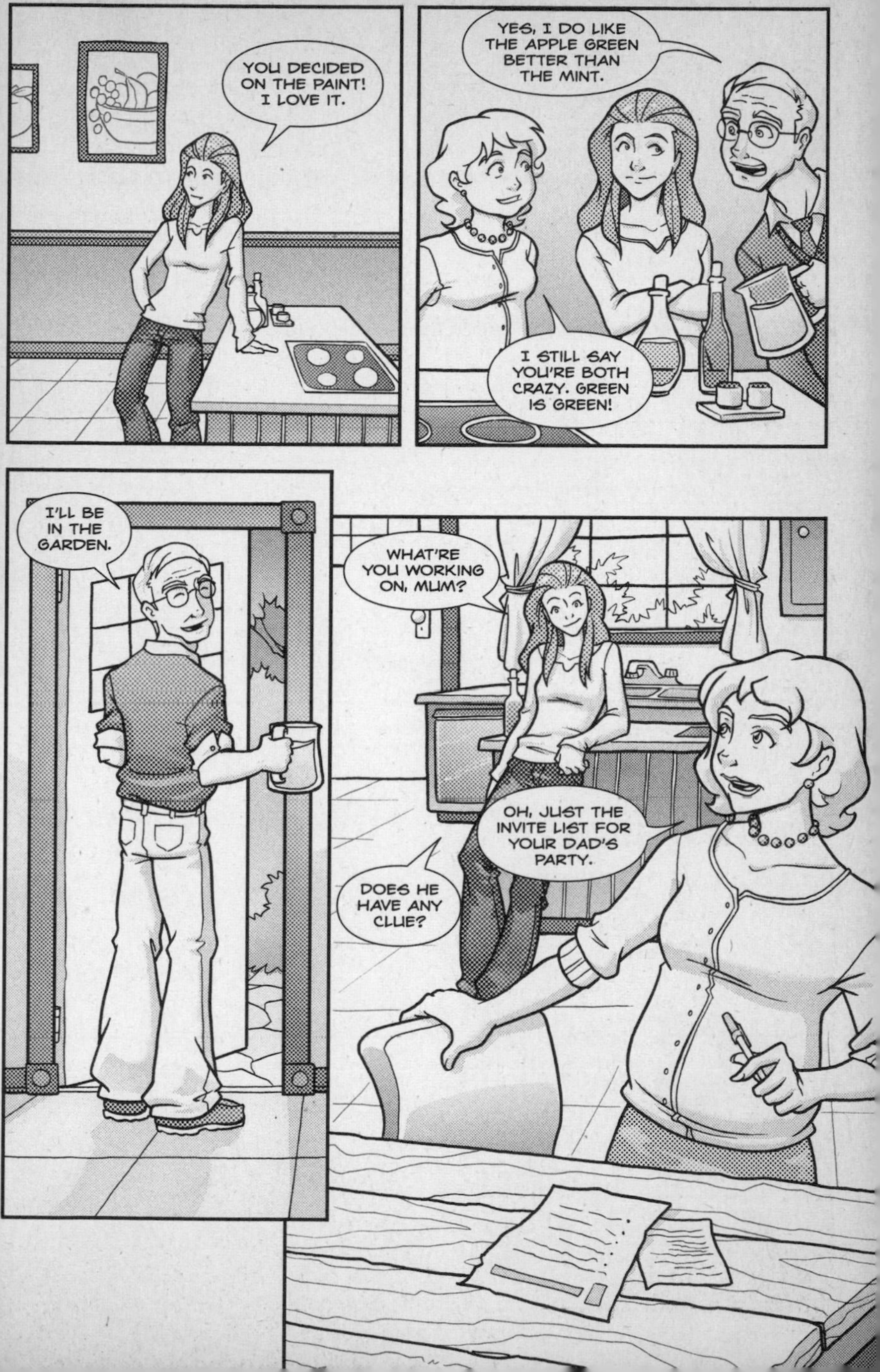
YOU DECIDED ON THE PAINT! I LOVE IT.
YES, I DO LIKE THE APPLE GREEN BETTER THAN THE MINT.
I STILL SAY YOU'RE BOTH CRAZY. GREEN IS GREEN!
I'LL BE IN THE GARDEN.
WHAT'RE YOU WORKING ON, MUM?
OH, JUST THE INVITE LIST FOR YOUR DAD'S PARTY.
DOES HE HAVE ANY CLUE?

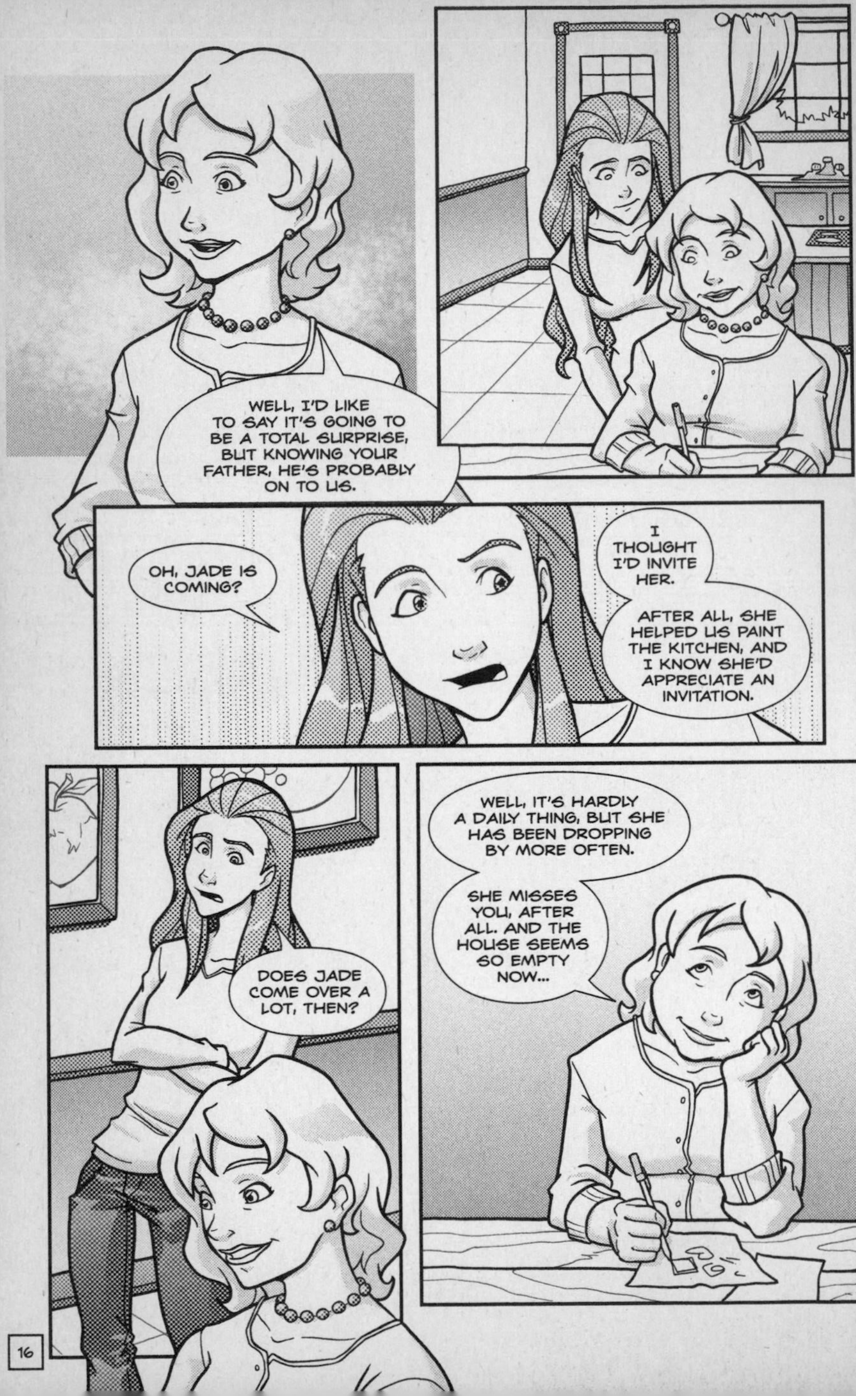
WELL, I'D LIKE TO SAY IT'S GOING TO BE A TOTAL SURPRISE, BUT KNOWING YOUR FATHER, HE'S PROBABLY ON TO US.
OH, JADE IS COMING?
I THOUGHT I'D INVITE HER.
AFTER ALL, SHE HELPED US PAINT THE KITCHEN, AND I KNOW SHE'D APPRECIATE AN INVITATION.
DOES JADE COME OVER A LOT, THEN?
WELL, IT'S HARDLY A DAILY THING, BUT SHE HAS BEEN DROPPING BY MORE OFTEN.
SHE MISSES YOU, AFTER ALL. AND THE HOUSE SEEMS SO EMPTY NOW...

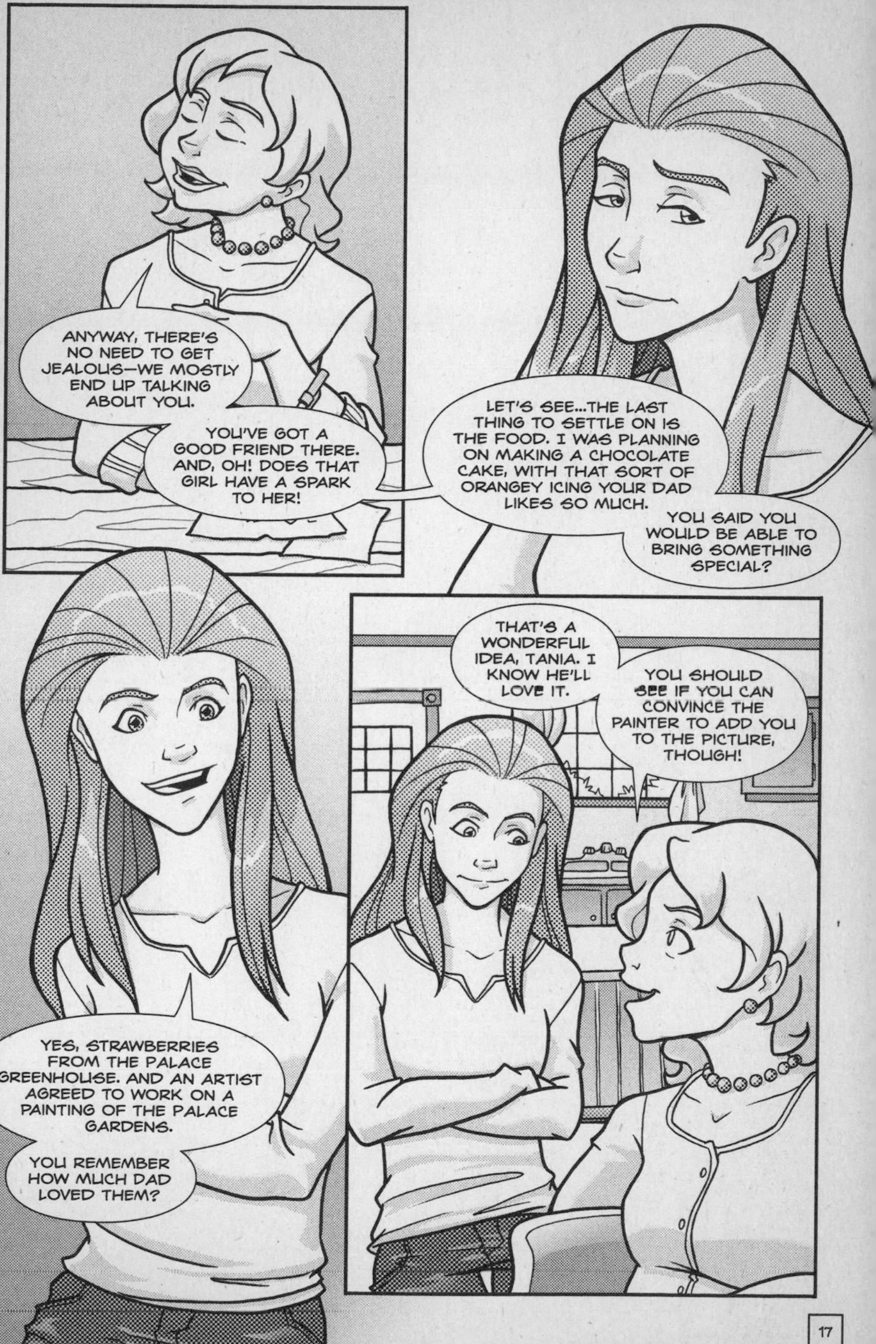
ANYWAY, THERE'S NO NEED TO GET JEALOUS—WE MOSTLY END UP TALKING ABOUT YOU.
YOU'VE GOT A GOOD FRIEND THERE. AND, OH! DOES THAT GIRL HAVE A SPARK TO HER!
LET'S SEE...THE LAST THING TO SETTLE ON IS THE FOOD. I WAS PLANNING ON MAKING A CHOCOLATE CAKE, WITH THAT SORT OF ORANGEY ICING YOUR DAD LIKES SO MUCH.
YOU SAID YOU WOULD BE ABLE TO BRING SOMETHING SPECIAL?
YES, STRAWBERRIES FROM THE PALACE GREENHOUSE. AND AN ARTIST AGREED TO WORK ON A PAINTING OF THE PALACE GARDENS.
YOU REMEMBER HOW MUCH DAD LOVED THEM?
THAT'S A WONDERFUL IDEA, TANIA. I KNOW HE'LL LOVE IT.
YOU SHOULD SEE IF YOU CAN CONVINCE THE PAINTER TO ADD YOU TO THE PICTURE, THOUGH!

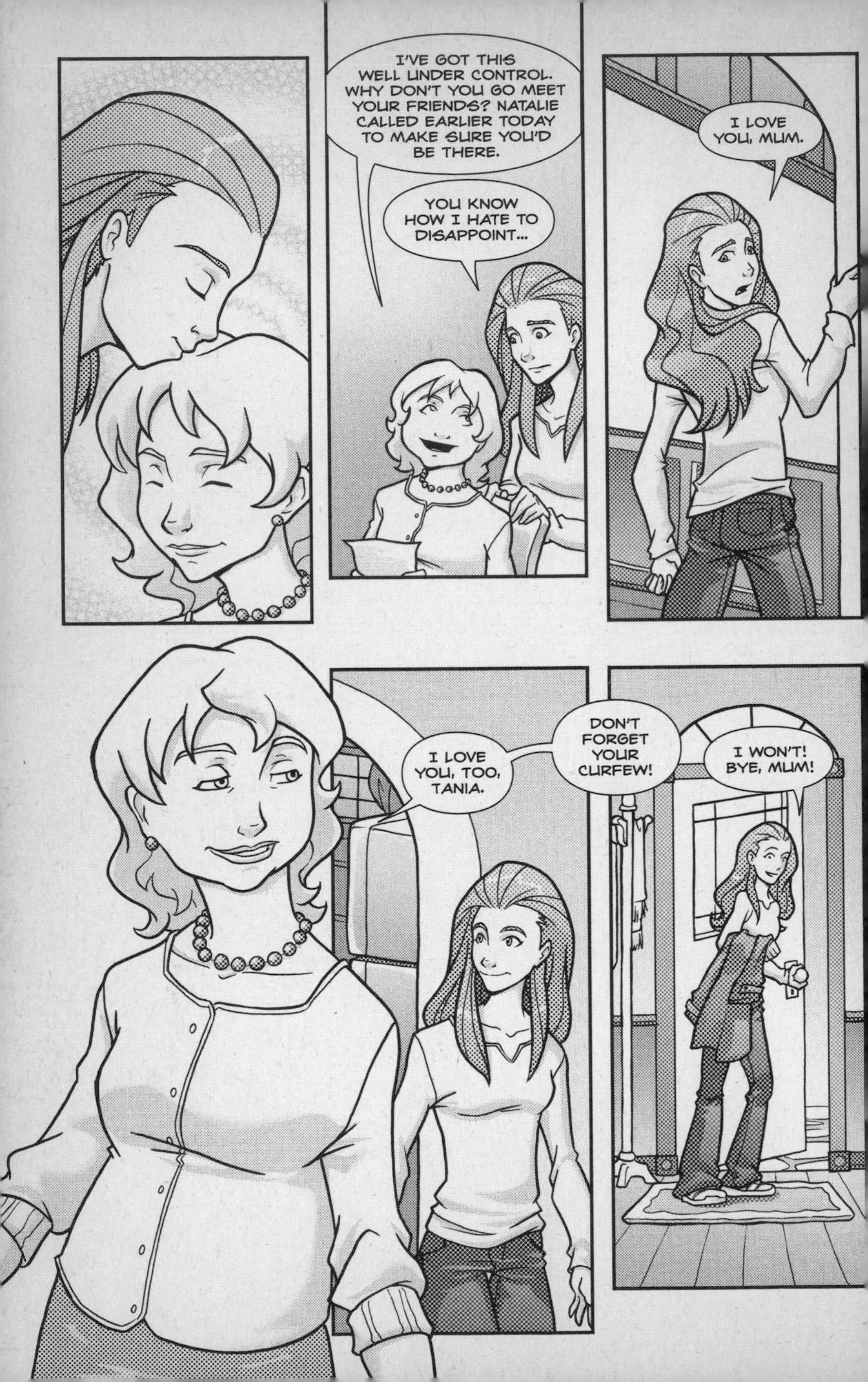
I'VE GOT THIS WELL UNDER CONTROL. WHY DON'T YOU GO MEET YOUR FRIENDS? NATALIE CALLED EARLIER TODAY TO MAKE SURE YOU'D BE THERE.
YOU KNOW HOW I HATE TO DISAPPOINT...
I LOVE YOU, MUM.
I LOVE YOU, TOO, TANIA.
DON'T FORGET YOUR CURFEW!
I WON'T! BYE, MUM!

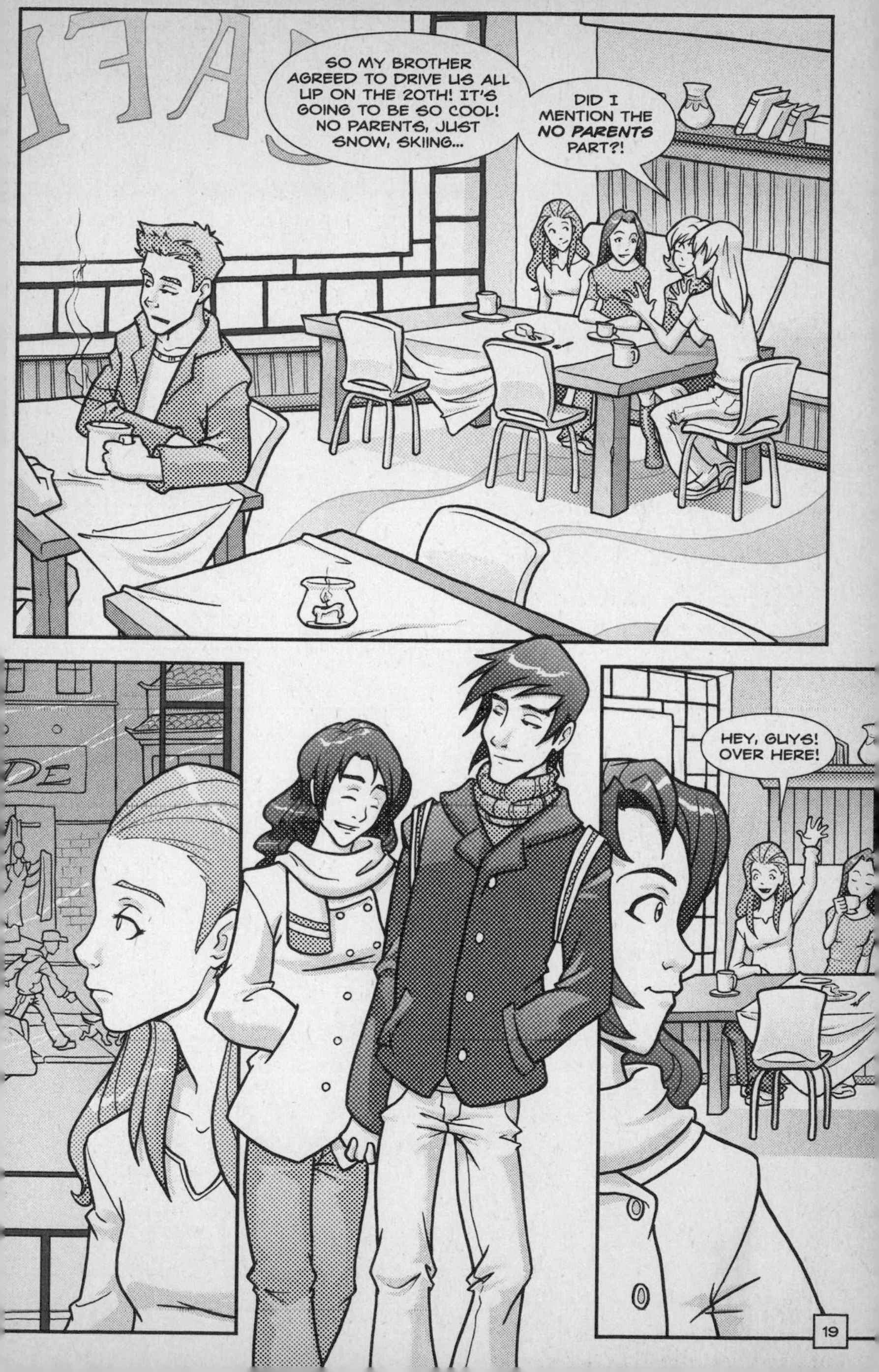
SO MY BROTHER AGREED TO DRIVE US ALL UP ON THE 20TH! IT'S GOING TO BE SO COOL! NO PARENTS, JUST SNOW, SKIING...
DID I MENTION THE ***NO PARENTS*** PART?!
HEY, GUYS! OVER HERE!

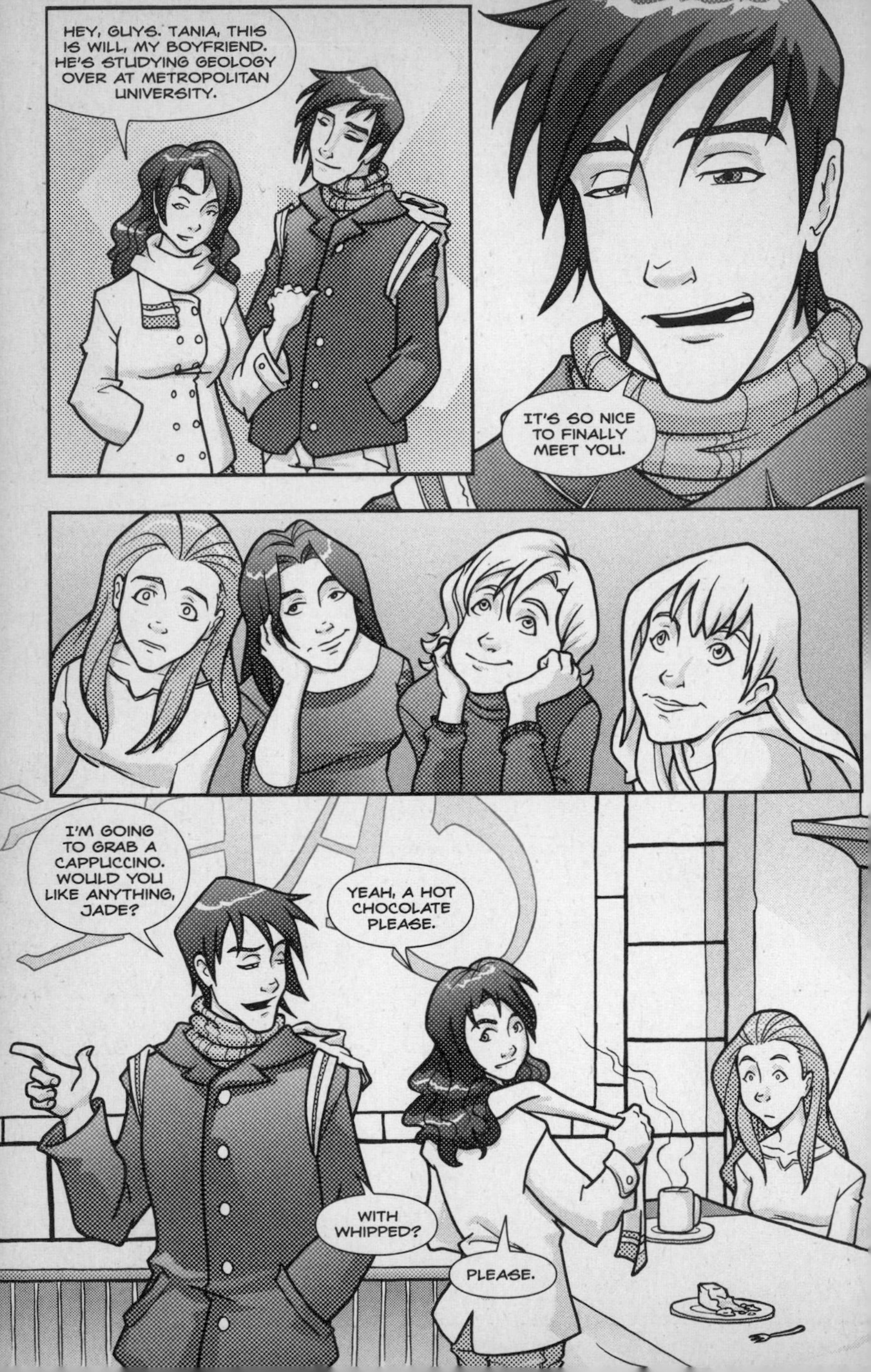
HEY, GUYS. TANIA, THIS IS WILL, MY BOYFRIEND. HE'S STUDYING GEOLOGY OVER AT METROPOLITAN UNIVERSITY.
IT'S SO NICE TO FINALLY MEET YOU.
I'M GOING TO GRAB A CAPPUCCINO. WOULD YOU LIKE ANYTHING, JADE?
YEAH, A HOT CHOCOLATE PLEASE.
WITH WHIPPED?
PLEASE.

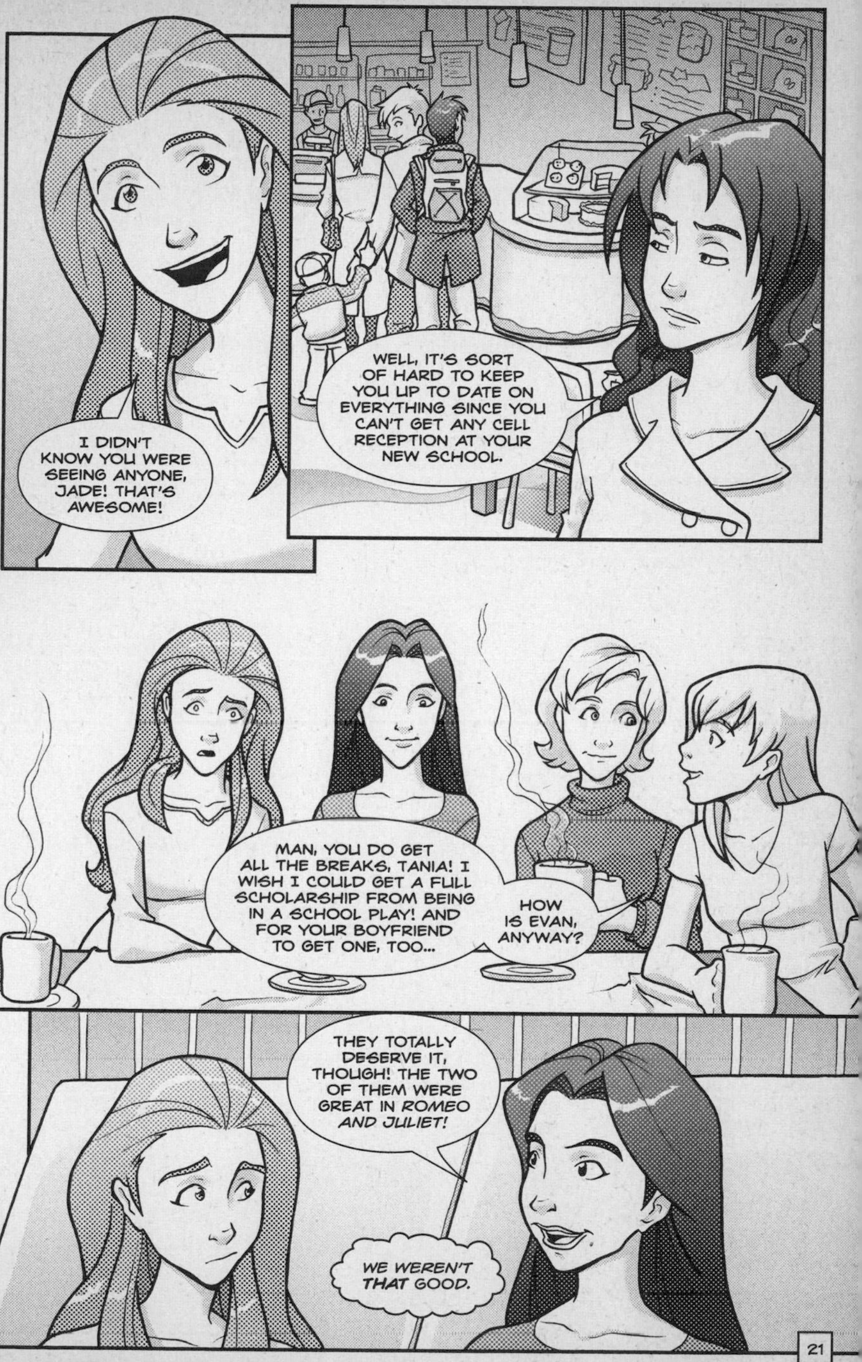
I DIDN'T KNOW YOU WERE SEEING ANYONE, JADE! THAT'S AWESOME!
WELL, IT'S SORT OF HARD TO KEEP YOU UP TO DATE ON EVERYTHING SINCE YOU CAN'T GET ANY CELL RECEPTION AT YOUR NEW SCHOOL.
MAN, YOU DO GET ALL THE BREAKS, TANIA! I WISH I COULD GET A FULL SCHOLARSHIP FROM BEING IN A SCHOOL PLAY! AND FOR YOUR BOYFRIEND TO GET ONE, TOO...
HOW IS EVAN, ANYWAY?
THEY TOTALLY DESERVE IT, THOUGH! THE TWO OF THEM WERE GREAT IN *ROMEO AND JULIET*!
WE WEREN'T ***THAT*** *GOOD.*

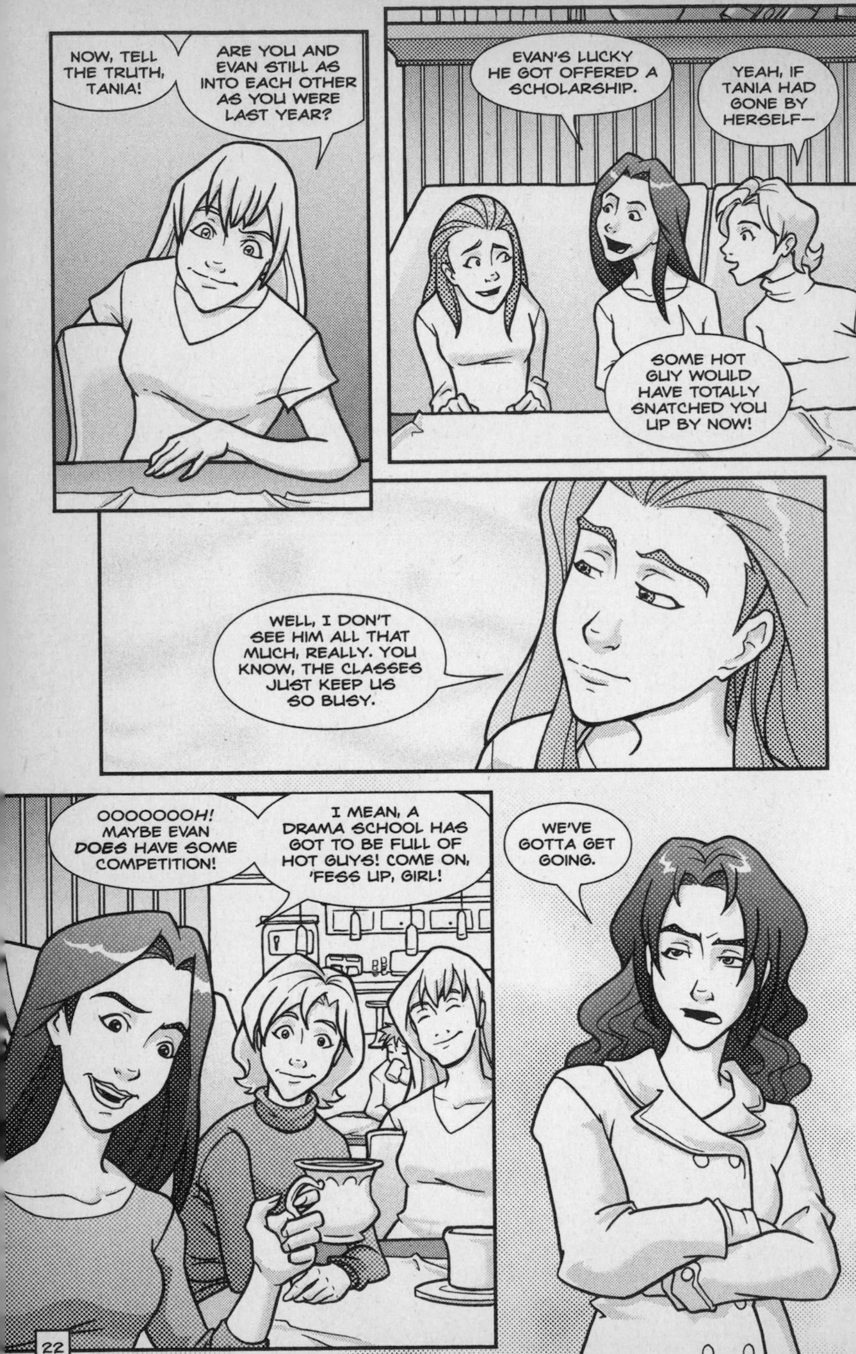
NOW, TELL THE TRUTH, TANIA!
ARE YOU AND EVAN STILL AS INTO EACH OTHER AS YOU WERE LAST YEAR?
EVAN'S LUCKY HE GOT OFFERED A SCHOLARSHIP.
YEAH, IF TANIA HAD GONE BY HERSELF—
SOME HOT GUY WOULD HAVE TOTALLY SNATCHED YOU UP BY NOW!
WELL, I DON'T SEE HIM ALL THAT MUCH, REALLY. YOU KNOW, THE CLASSES JUST KEEP US SO BUSY.
OOOOOOOH! MAYBE EVAN *DOES* HAVE SOME COMPETITION!
I MEAN, A DRAMA SCHOOL HAS GOT TO BE FULL OF HOT GUYS! COME ON, 'FESS UP, GIRL!
WE'VE GOTTA GET GOING.

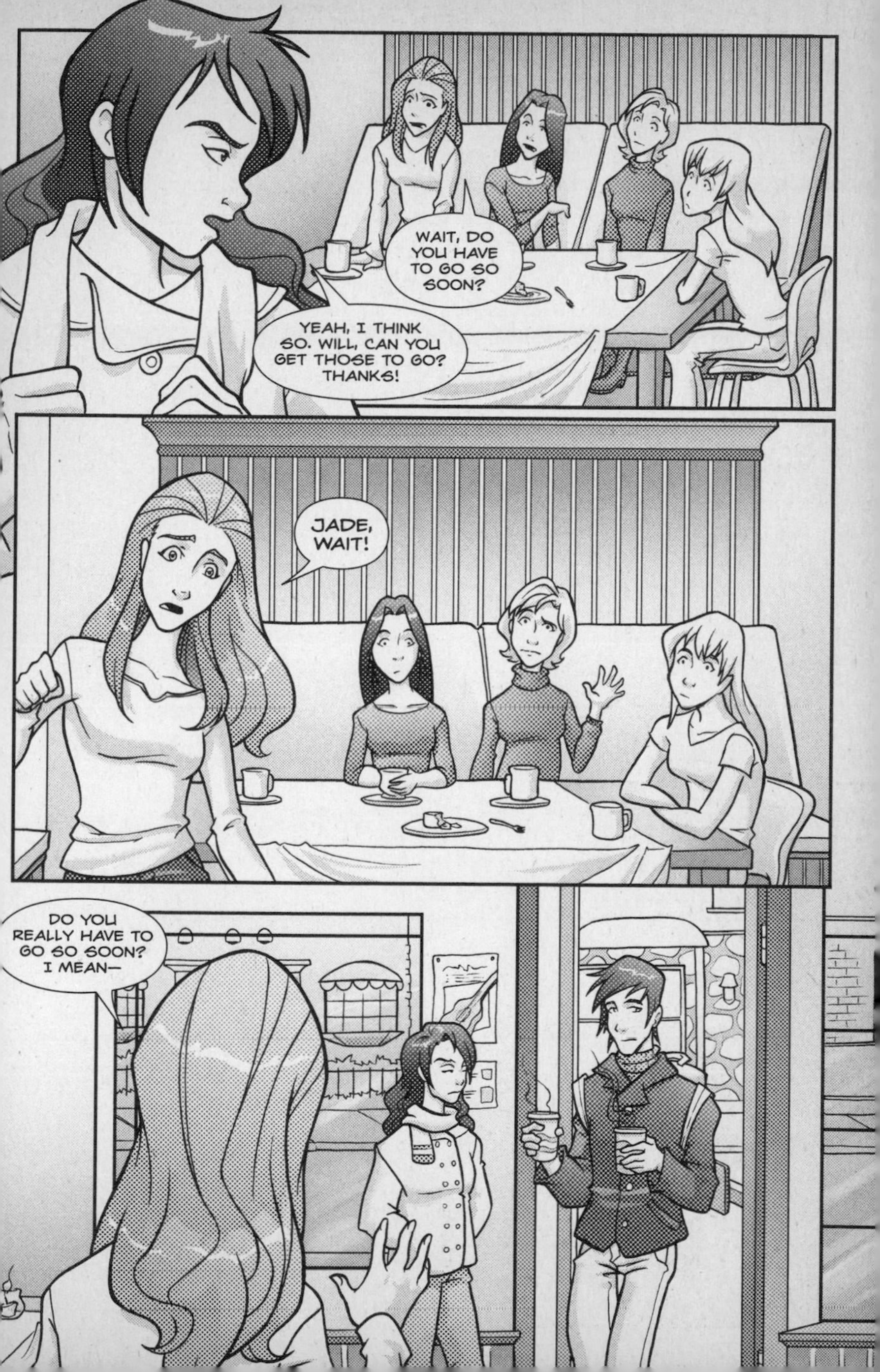
WAIT, DO YOU HAVE TO GO SO SOON?
YEAH, I THINK SO. WILL, CAN YOU GET THOSE TO GO? THANKS!
JADE, WAIT!
DO YOU REALLY HAVE TO GO SO SOON? I MEAN—

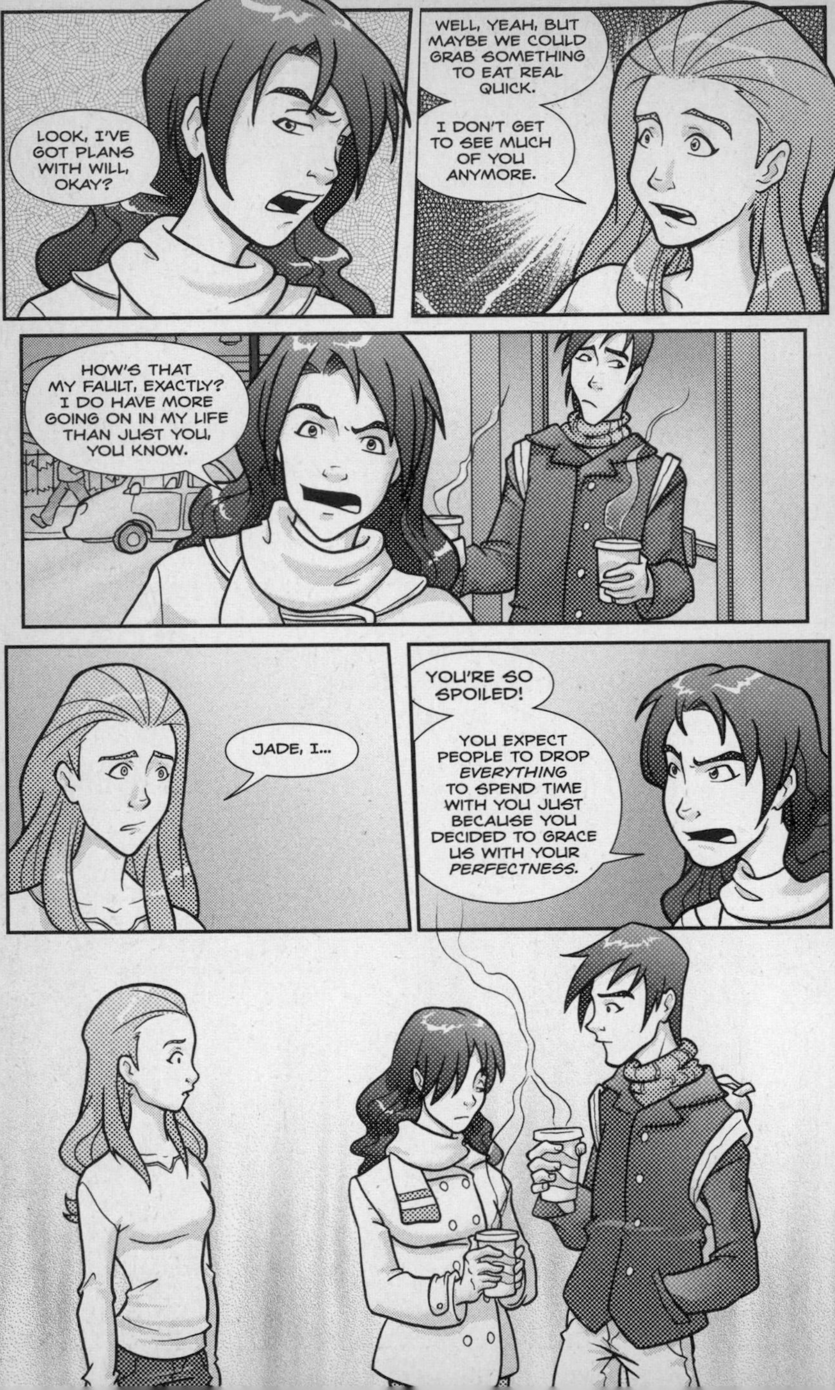
LOOK, I'VE GOT PLANS WITH WILL, OKAY?
WELL, YEAH, BUT MAYBE WE COULD GRAB SOMETHING TO EAT REAL QUICK.
I DON'T GET TO SEE MUCH OF YOU ANYMORE.
HOW'S THAT MY FAULT, EXACTLY? I DO HAVE MORE GOING ON IN MY LIFE THAN JUST YOU, YOU KNOW.
JADE, I...
YOU'RE SO SPOILED!
YOU EXPECT PEOPLE TO DROP *EVERYTHING* TO SPEND TIME WITH YOU JUST BECAUSE YOU DECIDED TO GRACE US WITH YOUR *PERFECTNESS*.

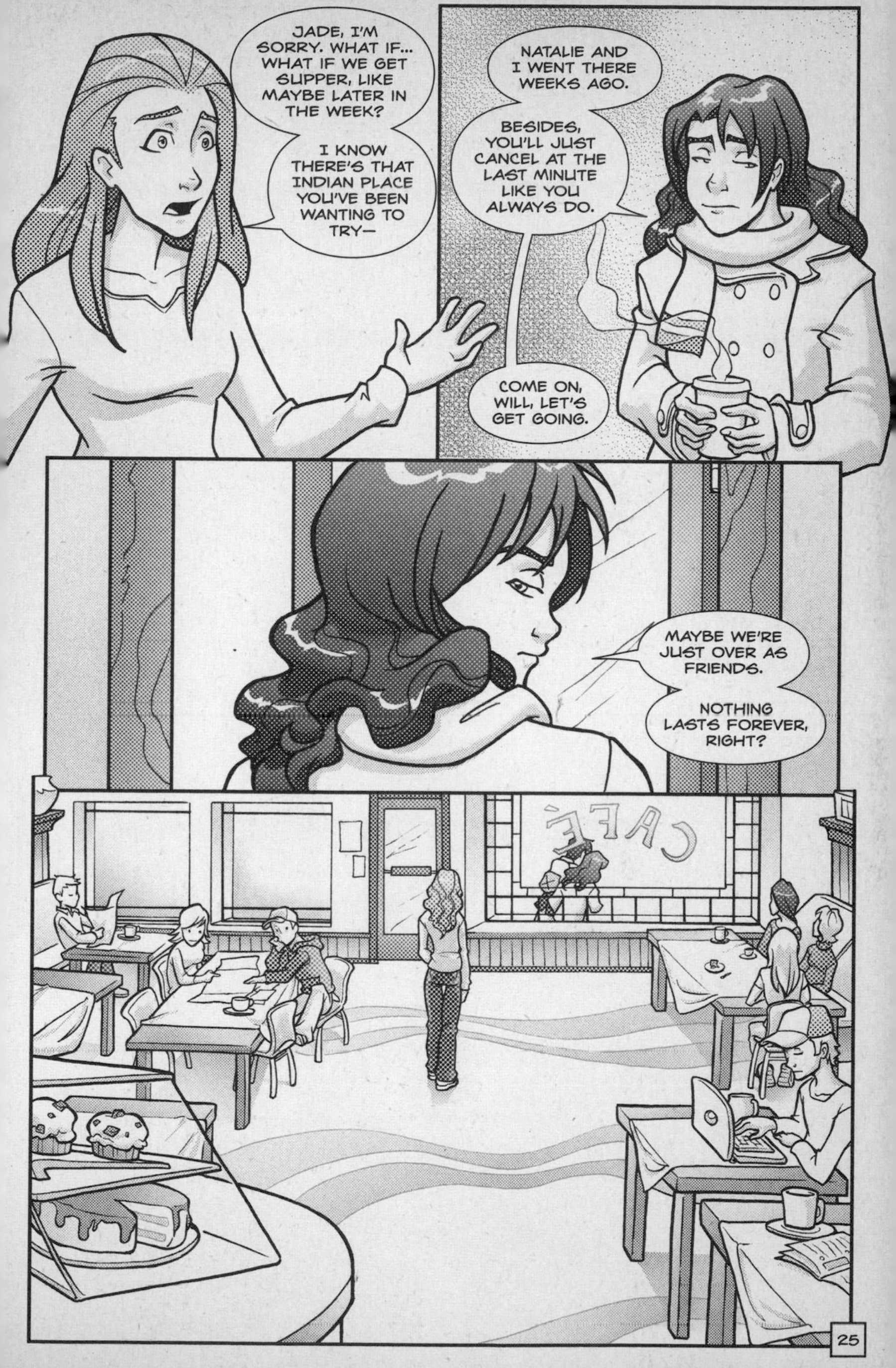
JADE, I'M SORRY. WHAT IF... WHAT IF WE GET SUPPER, LIKE MAYBE LATER IN THE WEEK?
I KNOW THERE'S THAT INDIAN PLACE YOU'VE BEEN WANTING TO TRY—
NATALIE AND I WENT THERE WEEKS AGO.
BESIDES, YOU'LL JUST CANCEL AT THE LAST MINUTE LIKE YOU ALWAYS DO.
COME ON, WILL, LET'S GET GOING.
MAYBE WE'RE JUST OVER AS FRIENDS.
NOTHING LASTS FOREVER, RIGHT?

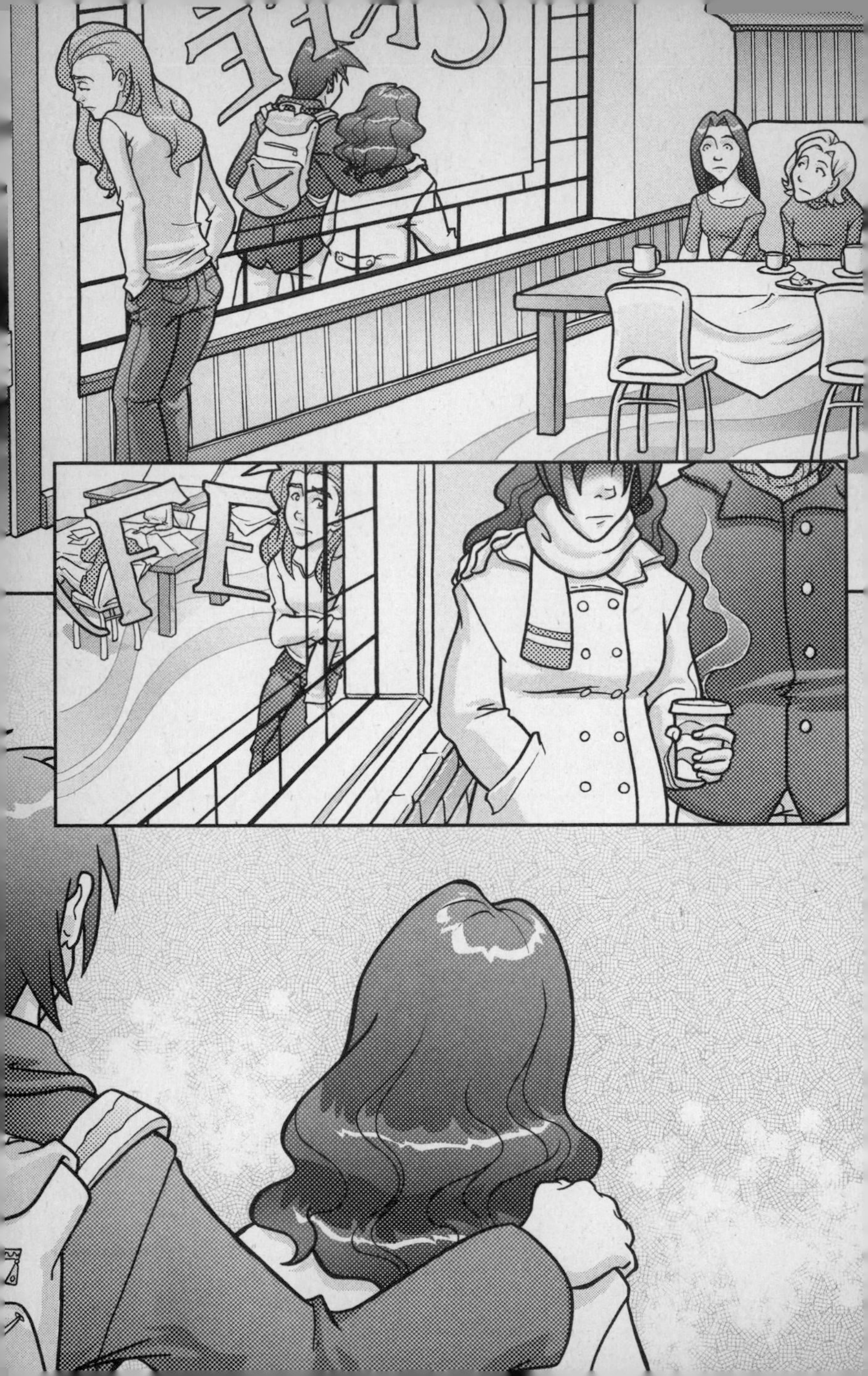
FE

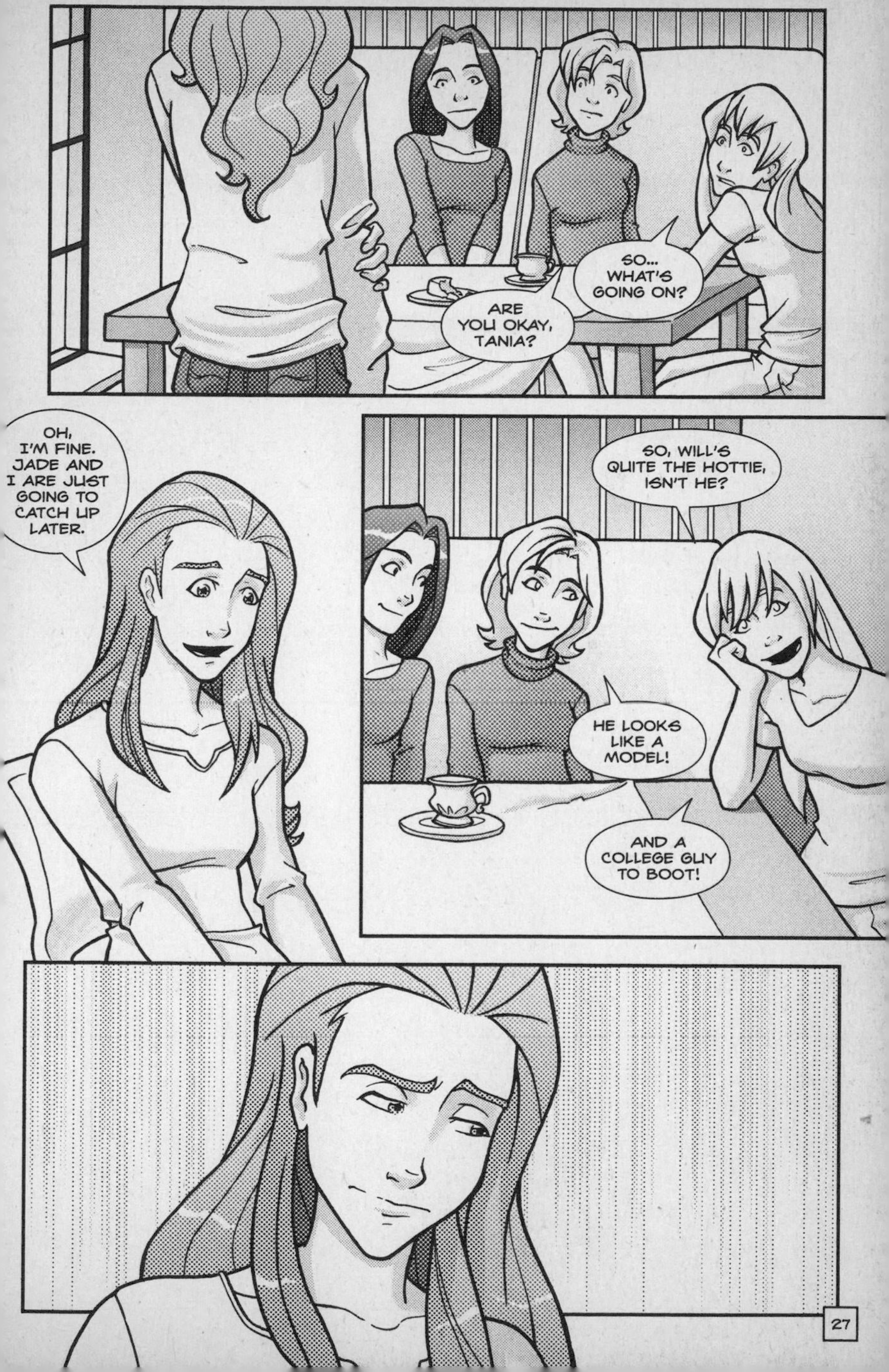
SO... WHAT'S GOING ON?
ARE YOU OKAY, TANIA?
OH, I'M FINE. JADE AND I ARE JUST GOING TO CATCH UP LATER.
SO, WILL'S QUITE THE HOTTIE, ISN'T HE?
HE LOOKS LIKE A MODEL!
AND A COLLEGE GUY TO BOOT!

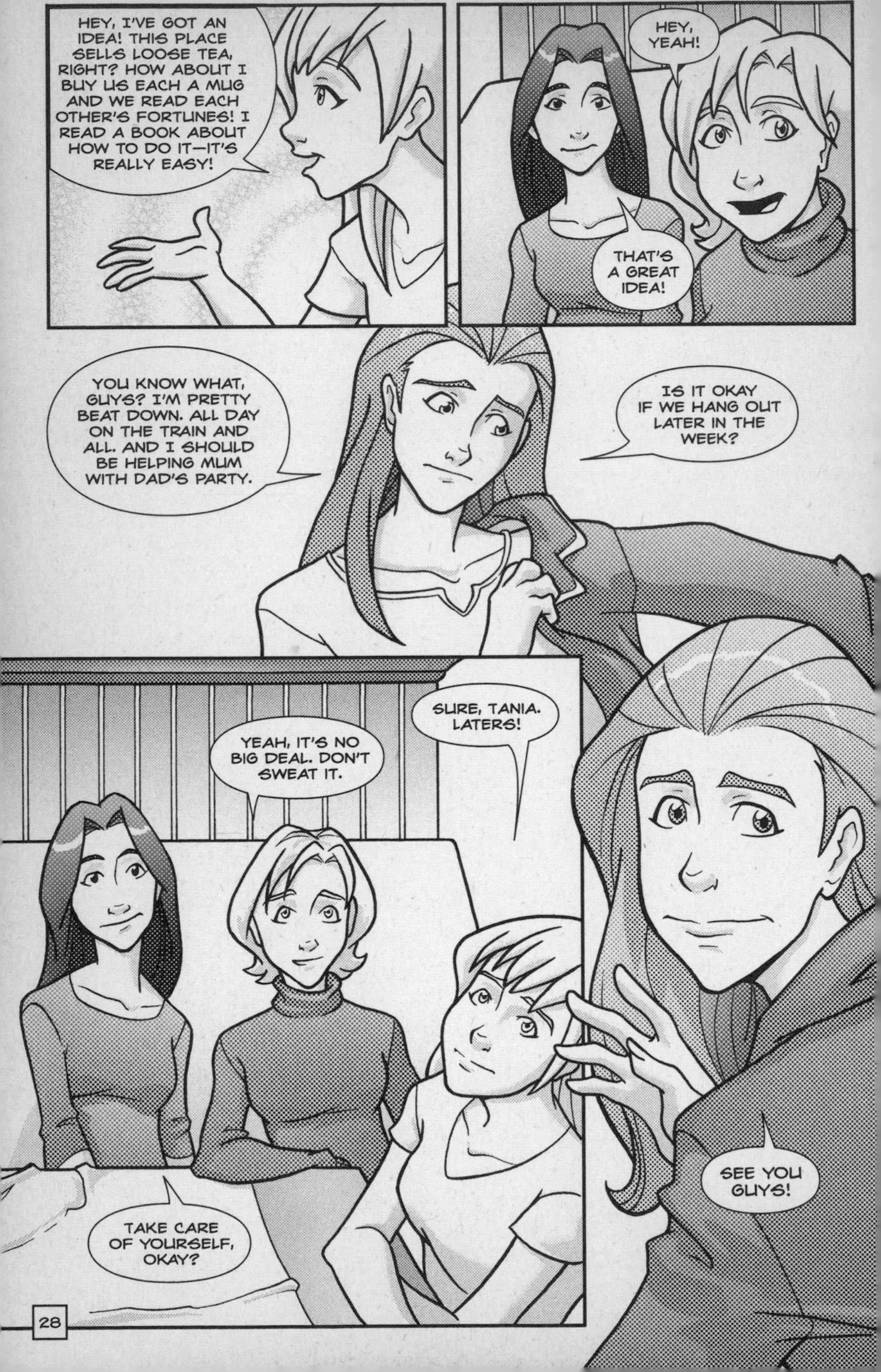
HEY, I'VE GOT AN IDEA! THIS PLACE SELLS LOOSE TEA, RIGHT? HOW ABOUT I BUY US EACH A MUG AND WE READ EACH OTHER'S FORTUNES! I READ A BOOK ABOUT HOW TO DO IT—IT'S REALLY EASY!
HEY, YEAH!
THAT'S A GREAT IDEA!
YOU KNOW WHAT, GUYS? I'M PRETTY BEAT DOWN. ALL DAY ON THE TRAIN AND ALL. AND I SHOULD BE HELPING MUM WITH DAD'S PARTY.
IS IT OKAY IF WE HANG OUT LATER IN THE WEEK?
YEAH, IT'S NO BIG DEAL. DON'T SWEAT IT.
SURE, TANIA. LATERS!
TAKE CARE OF YOURSELF, OKAY?
SEE YOU GUYS!

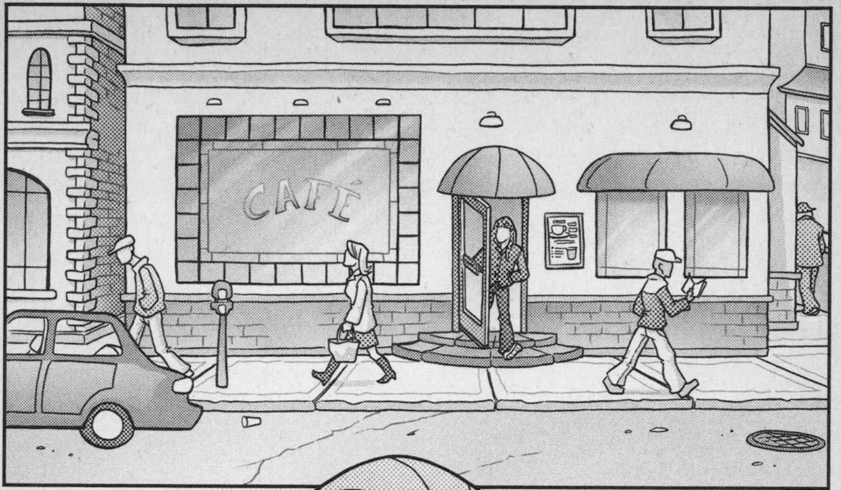
CAFÉ
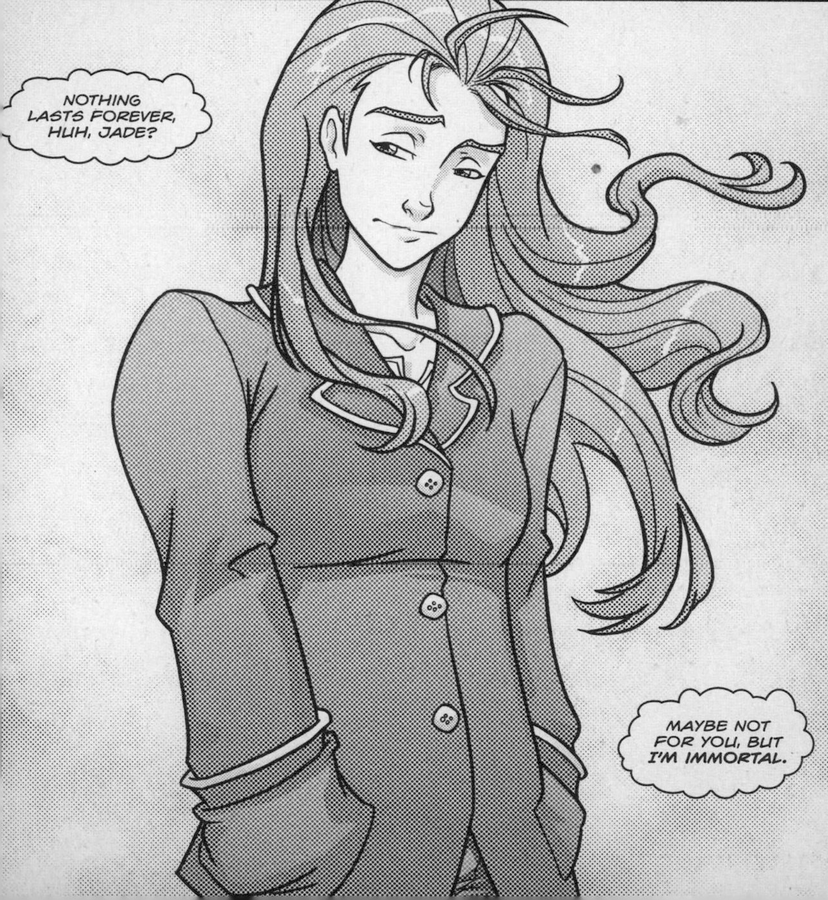
NOTHING LASTS FOREVER, HUH, JADE?
MAYBE NOT FOR YOU, BUT I'M IMMORTAL.

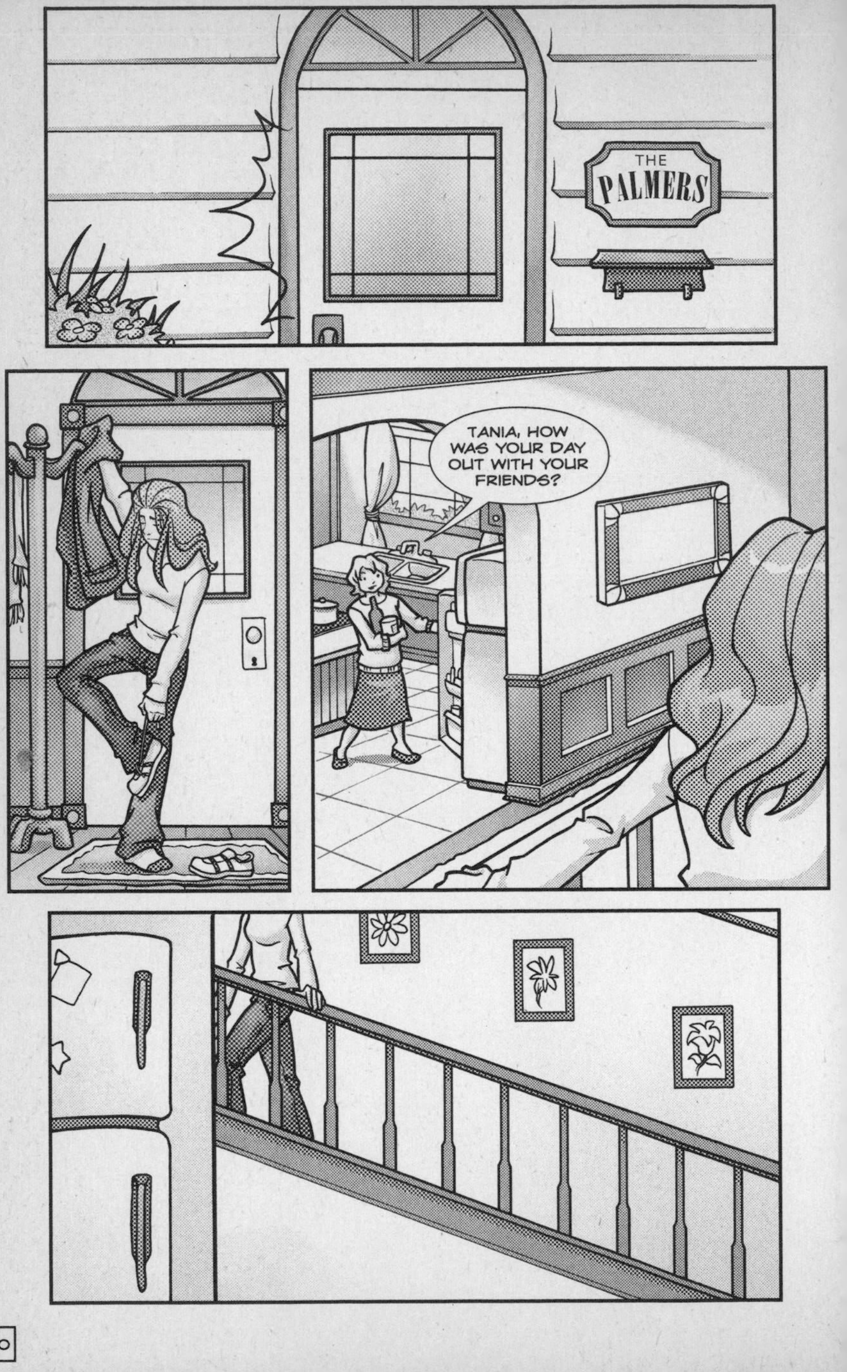
THE PALMERS
TANIA, HOW WAS YOUR DAY OUT WITH YOUR FRIENDS?

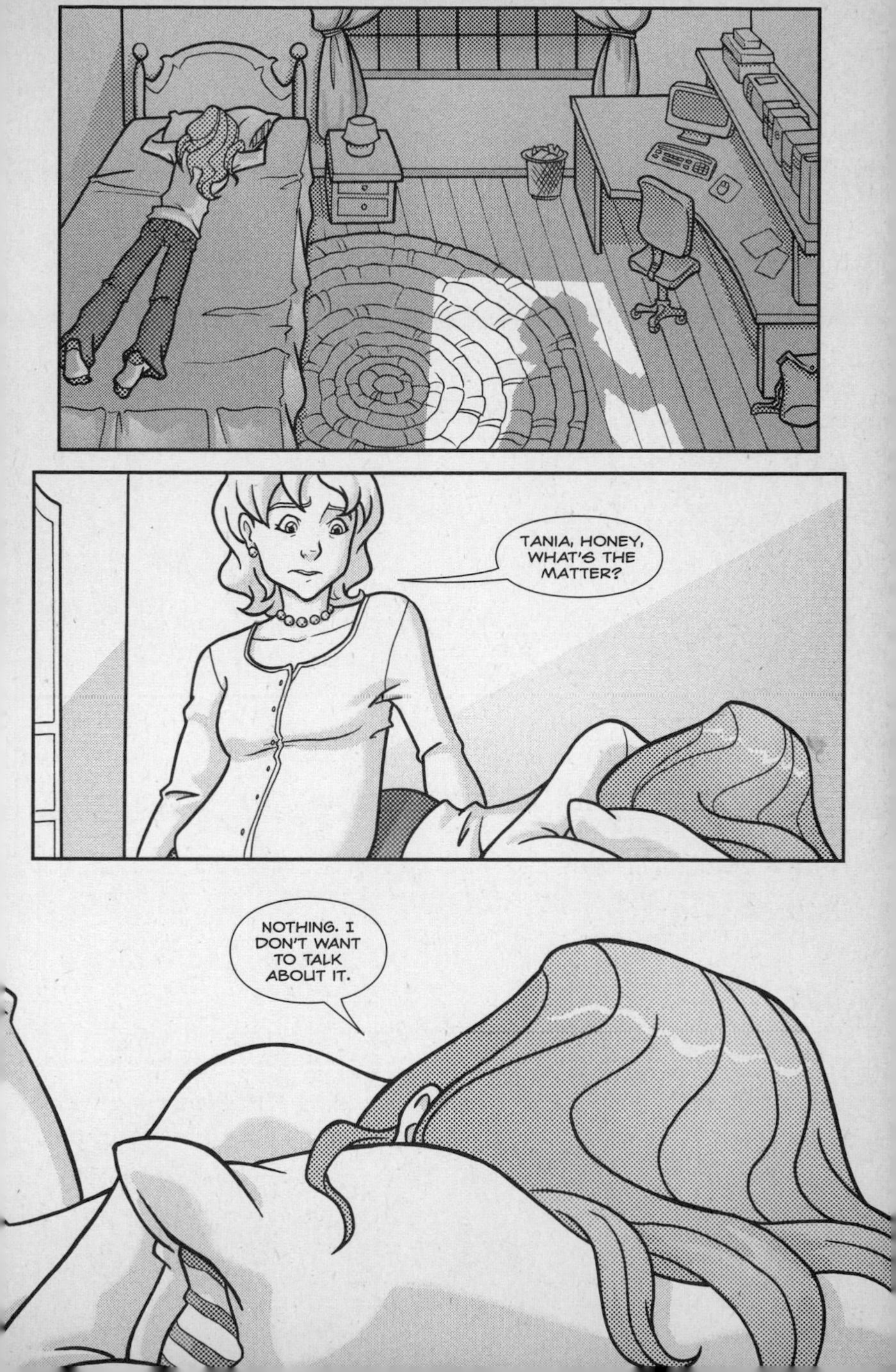
TANIA, HONEY, WHAT'S THE MATTER?
NOTHING. I DON'T WANT TO TALK ABOUT IT.

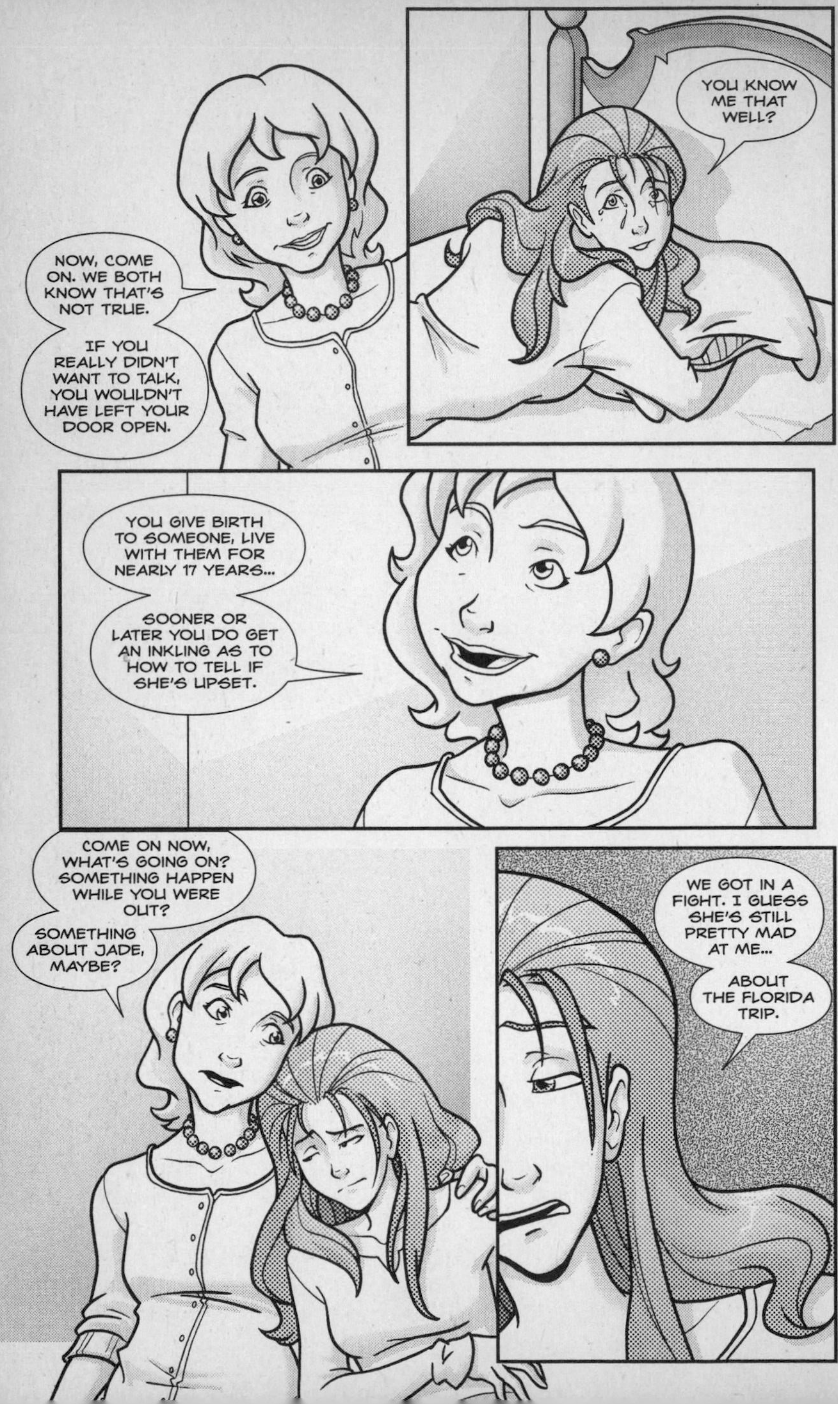
NOW, COME ON. WE BOTH KNOW THAT'S NOT TRUE.
IF YOU REALLY DIDN'T WANT TO TALK, YOU WOULDN'T HAVE LEFT YOUR DOOR OPEN.
YOU KNOW ME THAT WELL?
YOU GIVE BIRTH TO SOMEONE, LIVE WITH THEM FOR NEARLY 17 YEARS...
SOONER OR LATER YOU DO GET AN INKLING AS TO HOW TO TELL IF SHE'S UPSET.
COME ON NOW, WHAT'S GOING ON? SOMETHING HAPPEN WHILE YOU WERE OUT?
SOMETHING ABOUT JADE, MAYBE?
WE GOT IN A FIGHT. I GUESS SHE'S STILL PRETTY MAD AT ME...
ABOUT THE FLORIDA TRIP.

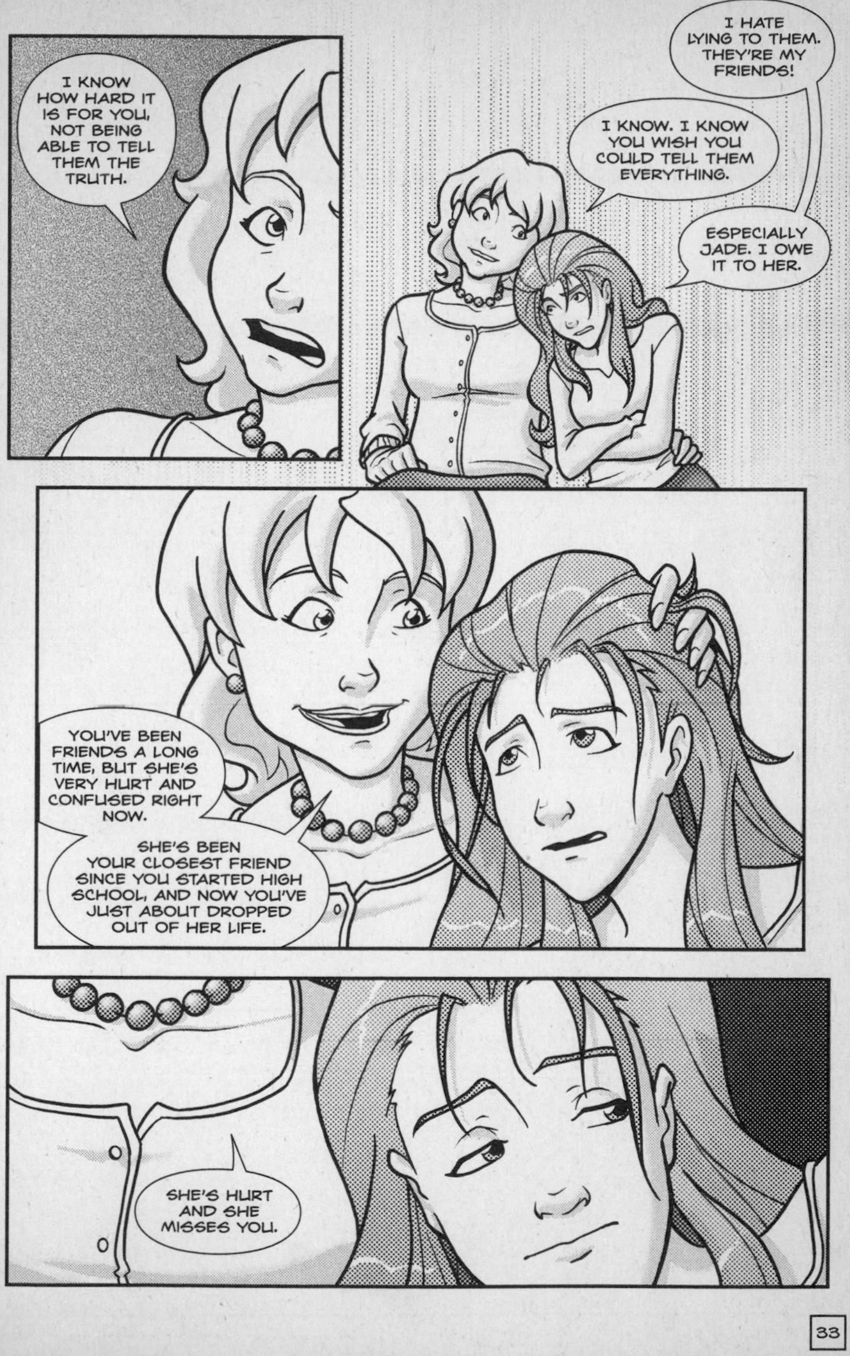
I KNOW HOW HARD IT IS FOR YOU, NOT BEING ABLE TO TELL THEM THE TRUTH.
I HATE LYING TO THEM. THEY'RE MY FRIENDS!
I KNOW. I KNOW YOU WISH YOU COULD TELL THEM EVERYTHING.
ESPECIALLY JADE. I OWE IT TO HER.
YOU'VE BEEN FRIENDS A LONG TIME, BUT SHE'S VERY HURT AND CONFUSED RIGHT NOW.
SHE'S BEEN YOUR CLOSEST FRIEND SINCE YOU STARTED HIGH SCHOOL, AND NOW YOU'VE JUST ABOUT DROPPED OUT OF HER LIFE.
SHE'S HURT AND SHE MISSES YOU.

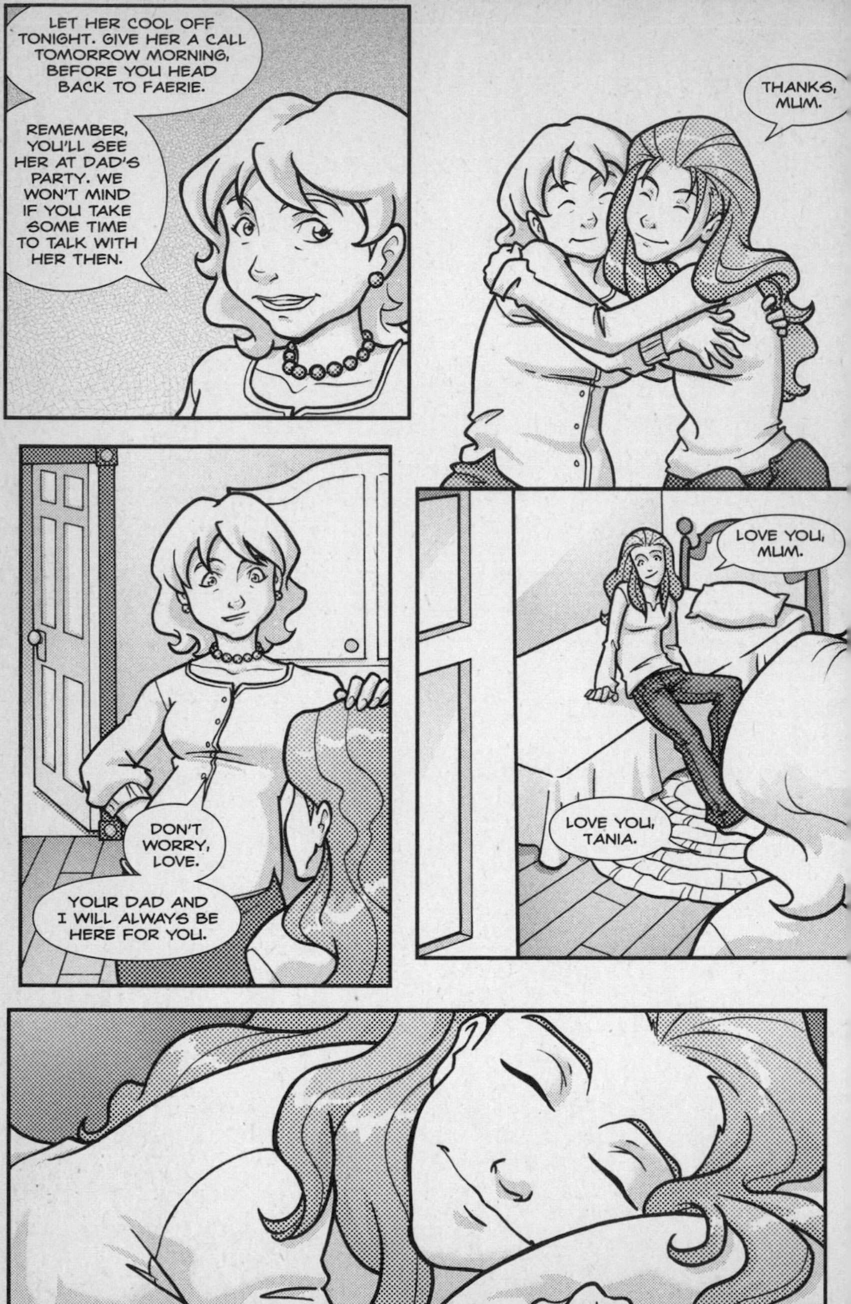
LET HER COOL OFF TONIGHT. GIVE HER A CALL TOMORROW MORNING, BEFORE YOU HEAD BACK TO FAERIE.
REMEMBER, YOU'LL SEE HER AT DAD'S PARTY. WE WON'T MIND IF YOU TAKE SOME TIME TO TALK WITH HER THEN.
THANKS, MUM.
DON'T WORRY, LOVE.
YOUR DAD AND I WILL ALWAYS BE HERE FOR YOU.
LOVE YOU, MUM.
LOVE YOU, TANIA.

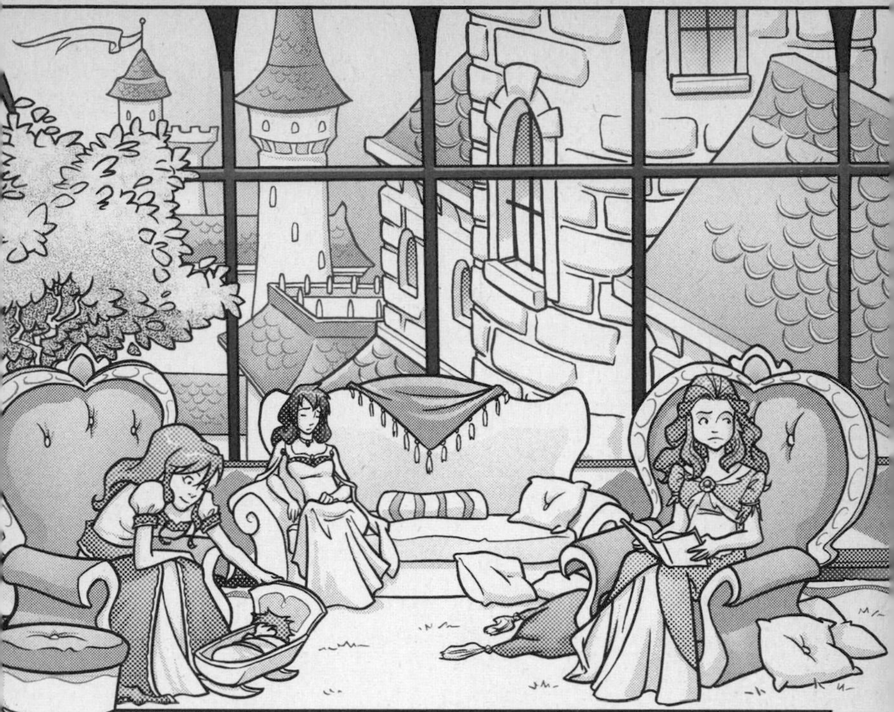

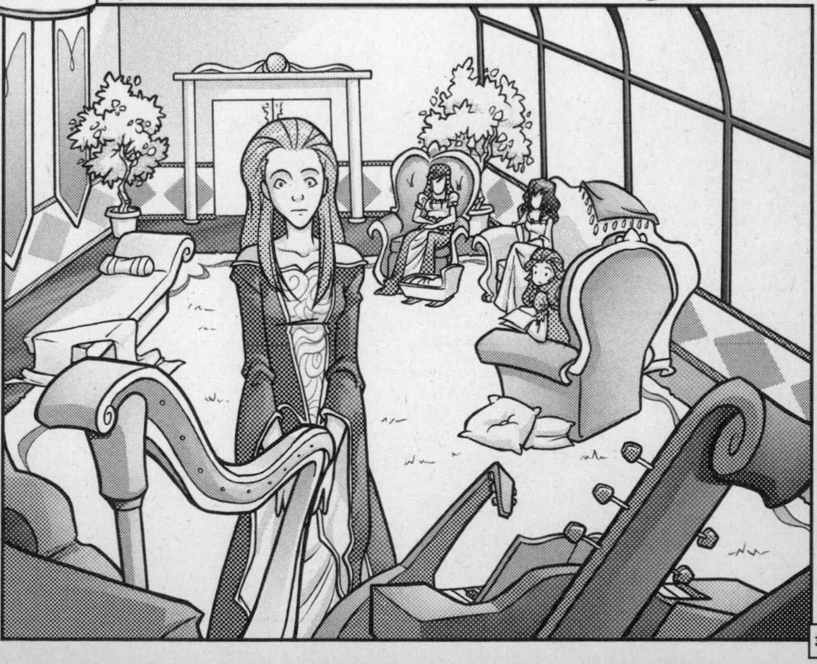

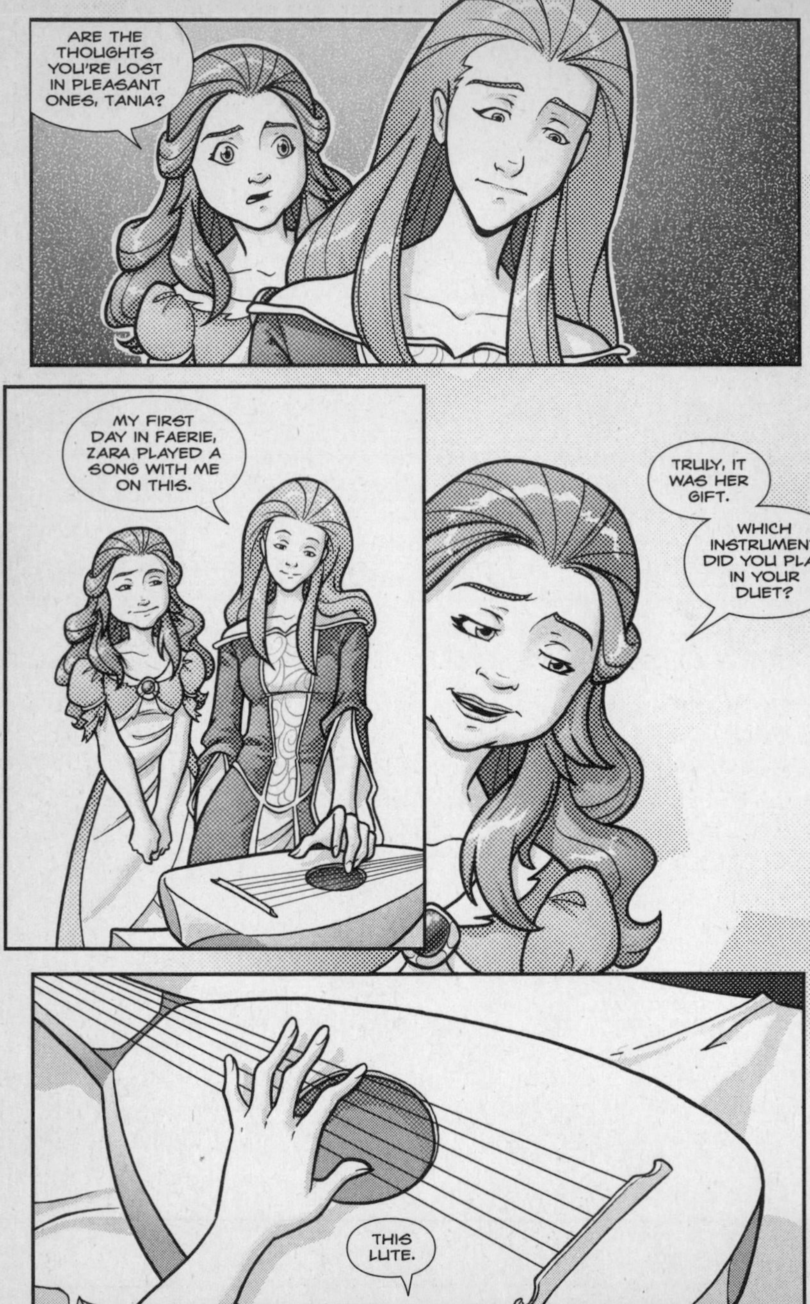
ARE THE THOUGHTS YOU'RE LOST IN PLEASANT ONES, TANIA?
MY FIRST DAY IN FAERIE, ZARA PLAYED A SONG WITH ME ON THIS.
TRULY, IT WAS HER GIFT.
WHICH INSTRUMENT DID YOU PLAY IN YOUR DUET?
THIS LUTE.

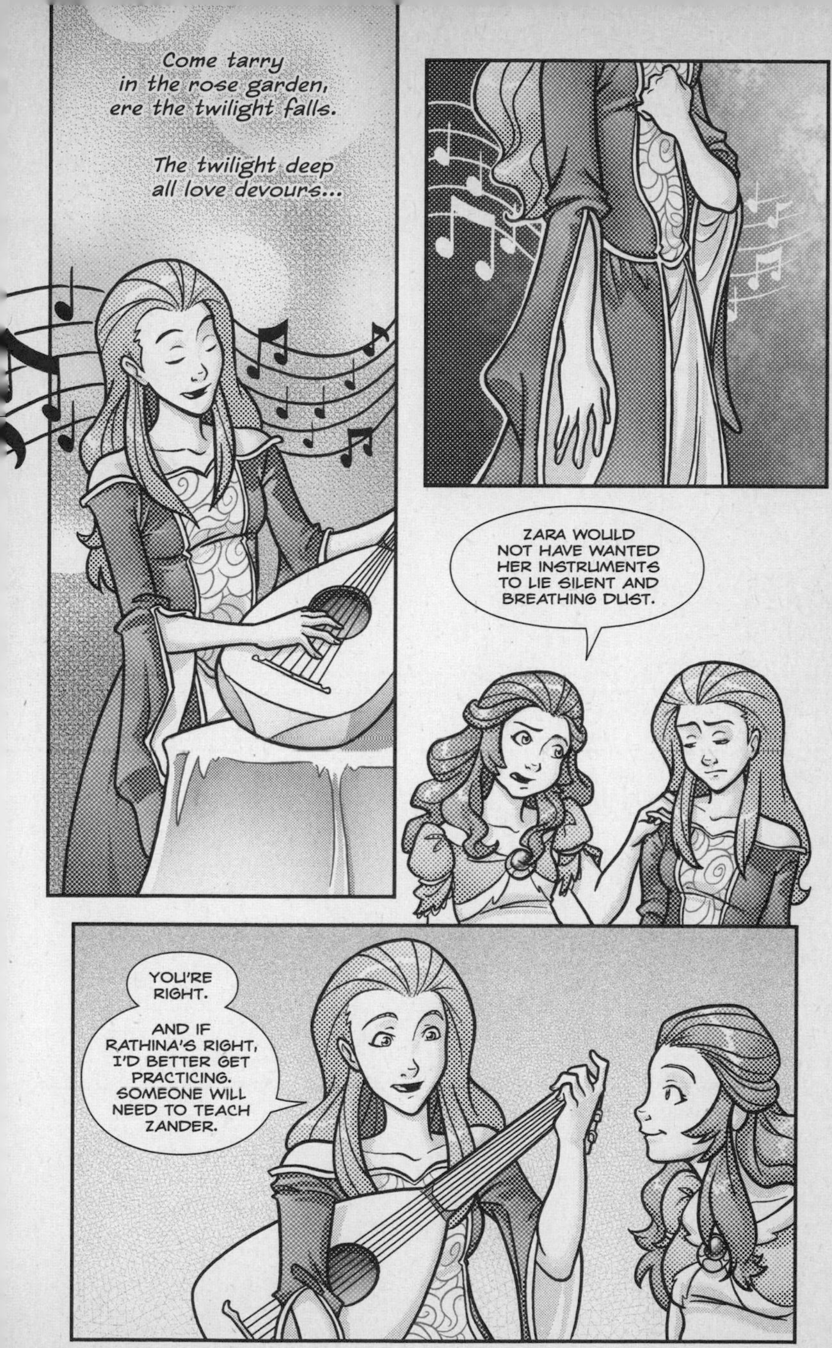
Come tarry in the rose garden, ere the twilight falls.
The twilight deep all love devours...
ZARA WOULD NOT HAVE WANTED HER INSTRUMENTS TO LIE SILENT AND BREATHING DUST.
YOU'RE RIGHT.
AND IF RATHINA'S RIGHT, I'D BETTER GET PRACTICING. SOMEONE WILL NEED TO TEACH ZANDER.

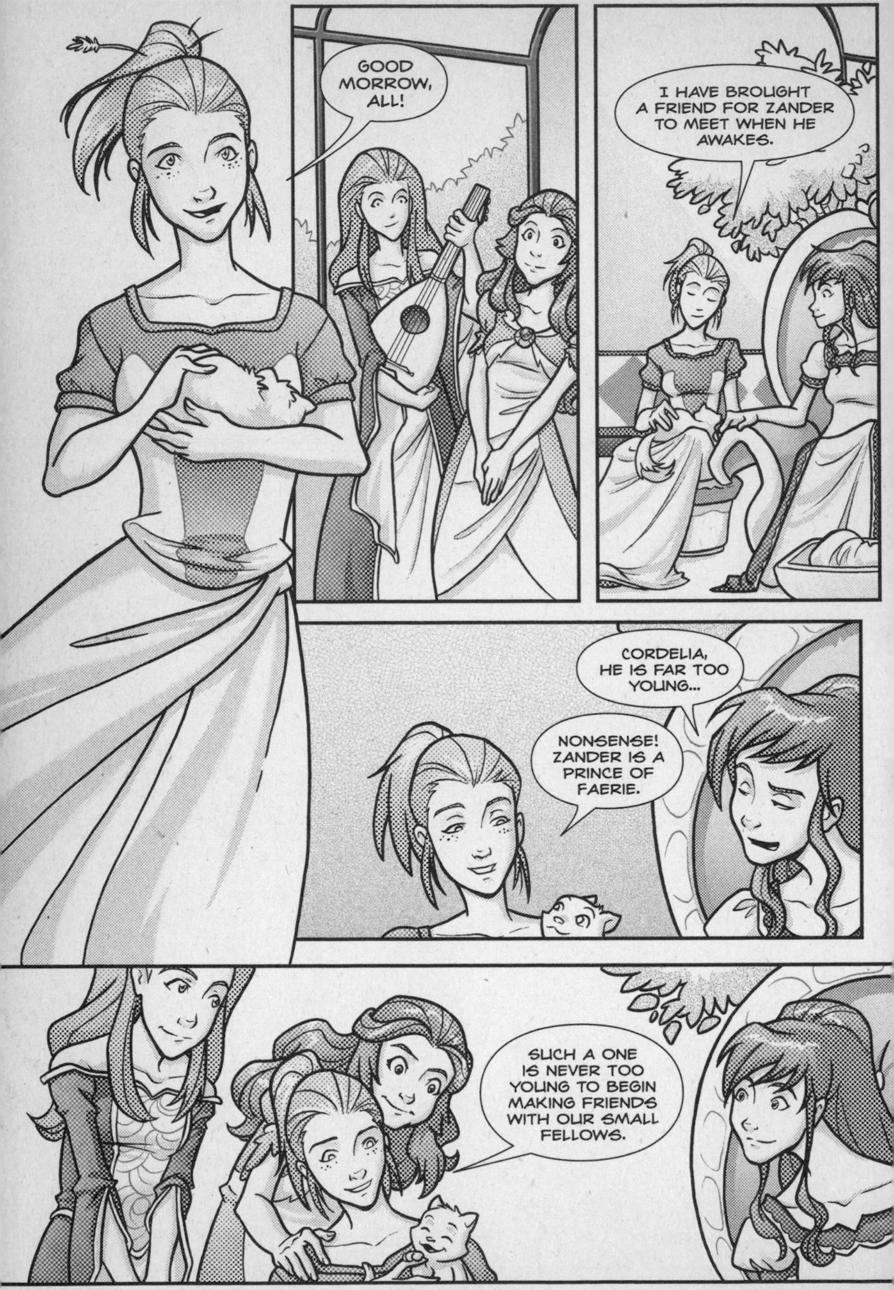
GOOD MORROW, ALL!
I HAVE BROUGHT A FRIEND FOR ZANDER TO MEET WHEN HE AWAKES.
CORDELIA, HE IS FAR TOO YOUNG...
NONSENSE! ZANDER IS A PRINCE OF FAERIE.
SUCH A ONE IS NEVER TOO YOUNG TO BEGIN MAKING FRIENDS WITH OUR SMALL FELLOWS.

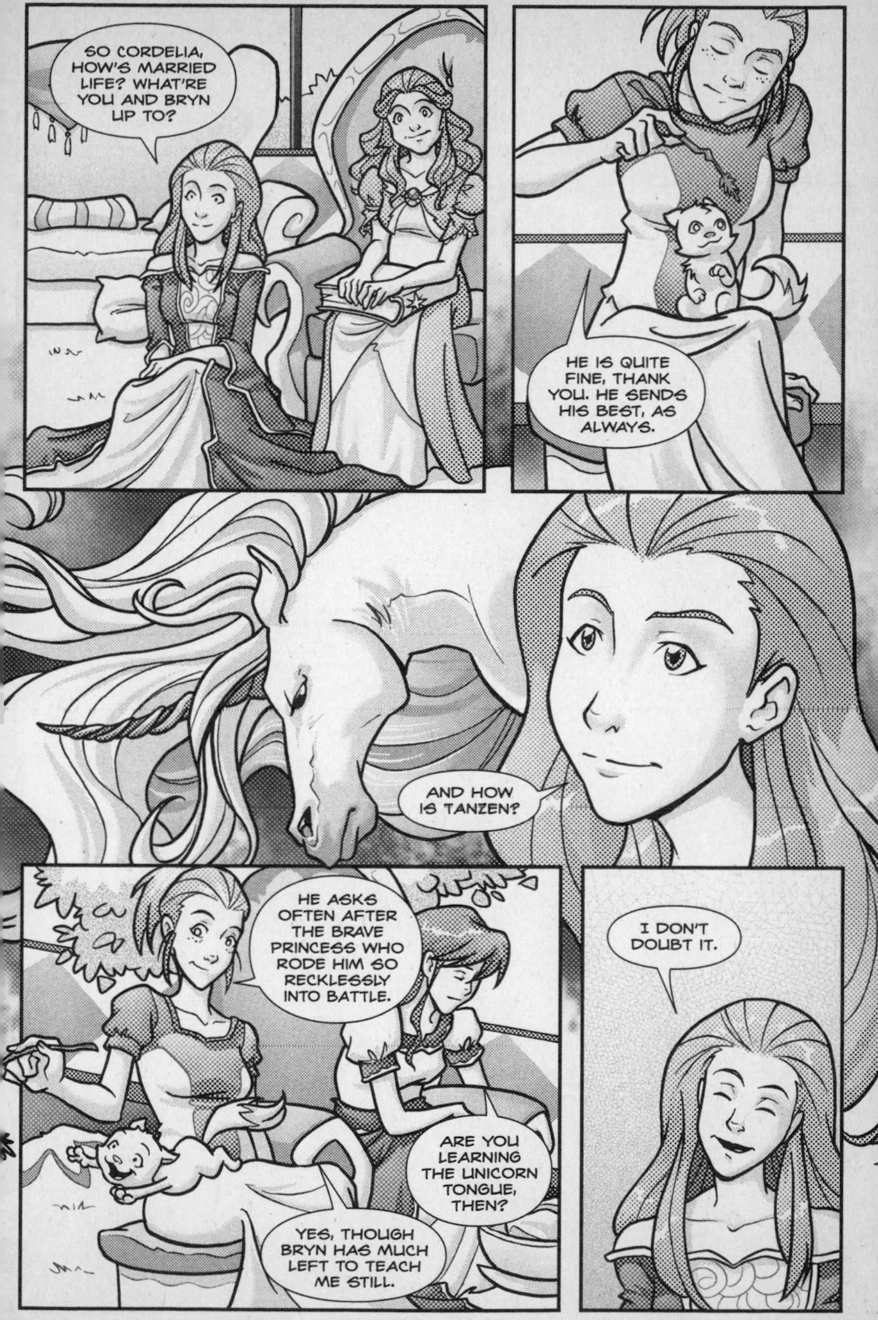
SO CORDELIA, HOW'S MARRIED LIFE? WHAT'RE YOU AND BRYN UP TO?
HE IS QUITE FINE, THANK YOU. HE SENDS HIS BEST, AS ALWAYS.
AND HOW IS TANZEN?
HE ASKS OFTEN AFTER THE BRAVE PRINCESS WHO RODE HIM SO RECKLESSLY INTO BATTLE.
ARE YOU LEARNING THE UNICORN TONGUE, THEN?
YES, THOUGH BRYN HAS MUCH LEFT TO TEACH ME STILL.
I DON'T DOUBT IT.

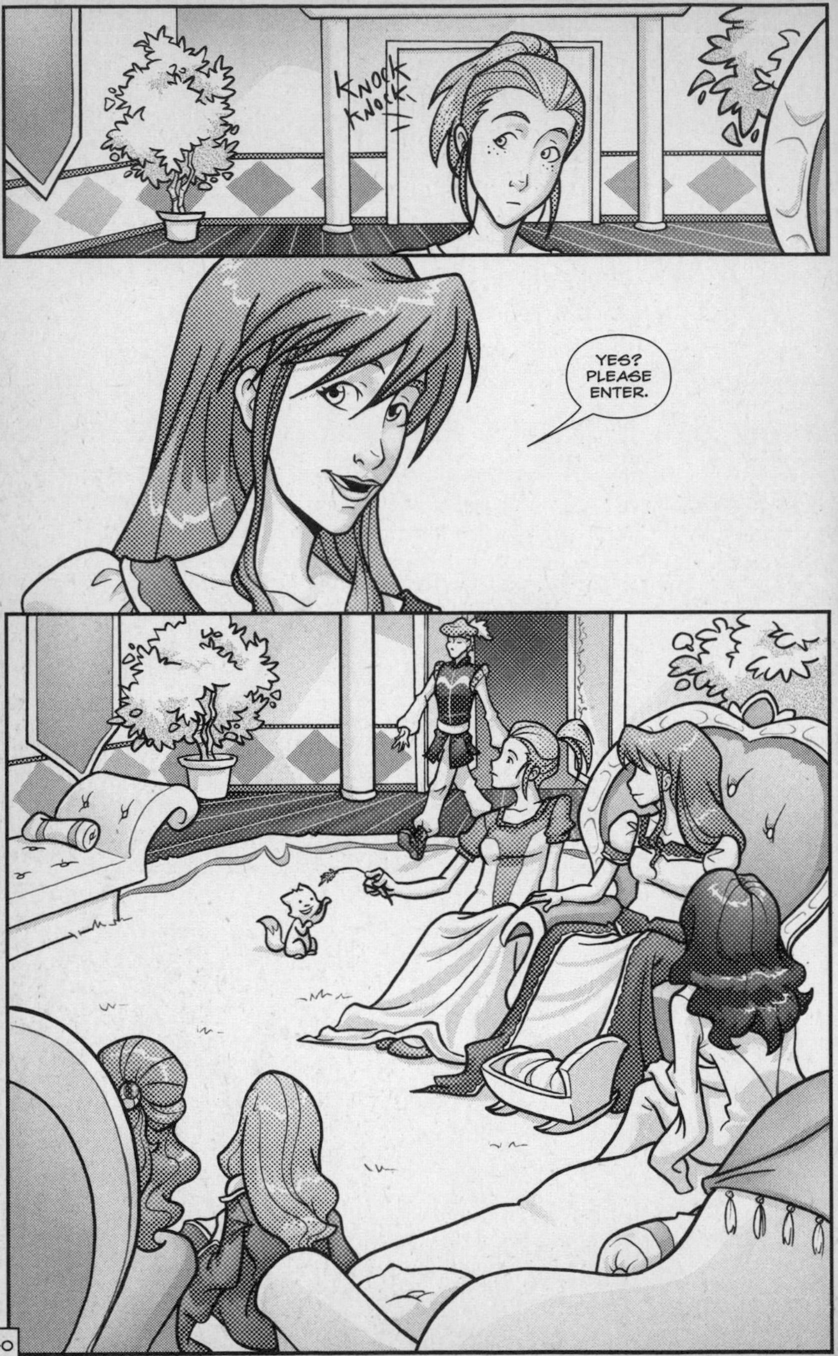
KNOCK KNOCK
YES? PLEASE ENTER.

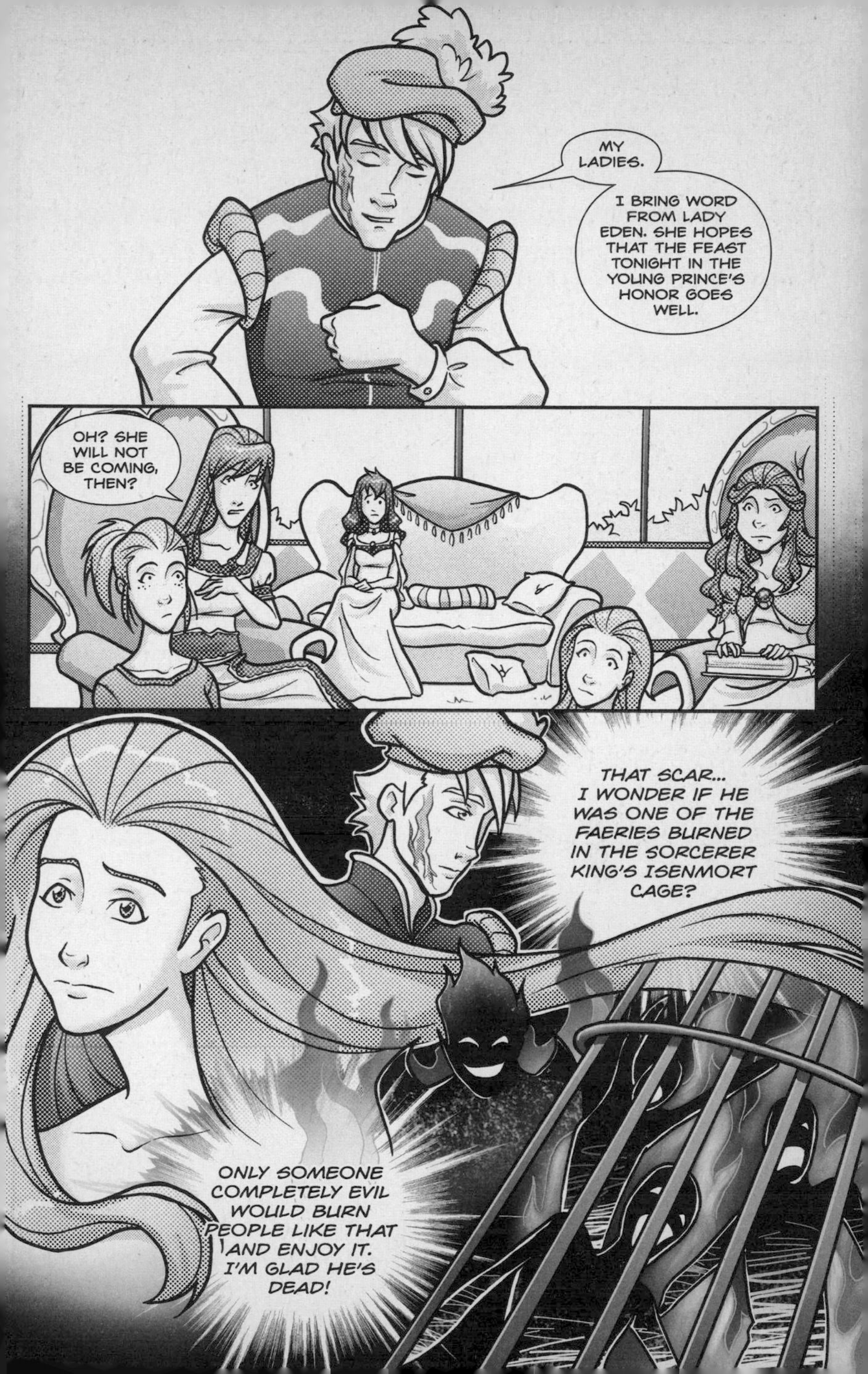
MY LADIES.
I BRING WORD FROM LADY EDEN. SHE HOPES THAT THE FEAST TONIGHT IN THE YOUNG PRINCE'S HONOR GOES WELL.
OH? SHE WILL NOT BE COMING, THEN?
THAT SCAR... I WONDER IF HE WAS ONE OF THE FAERIES BURNED IN THE SORCERER KING'S ISENMORT CAGE?
ONLY SOMEONE COMPLETELY EVIL WOULD BURN PEOPLE LIKE THAT AND ENJOY IT. I'M GLAD HE'S DEAD!

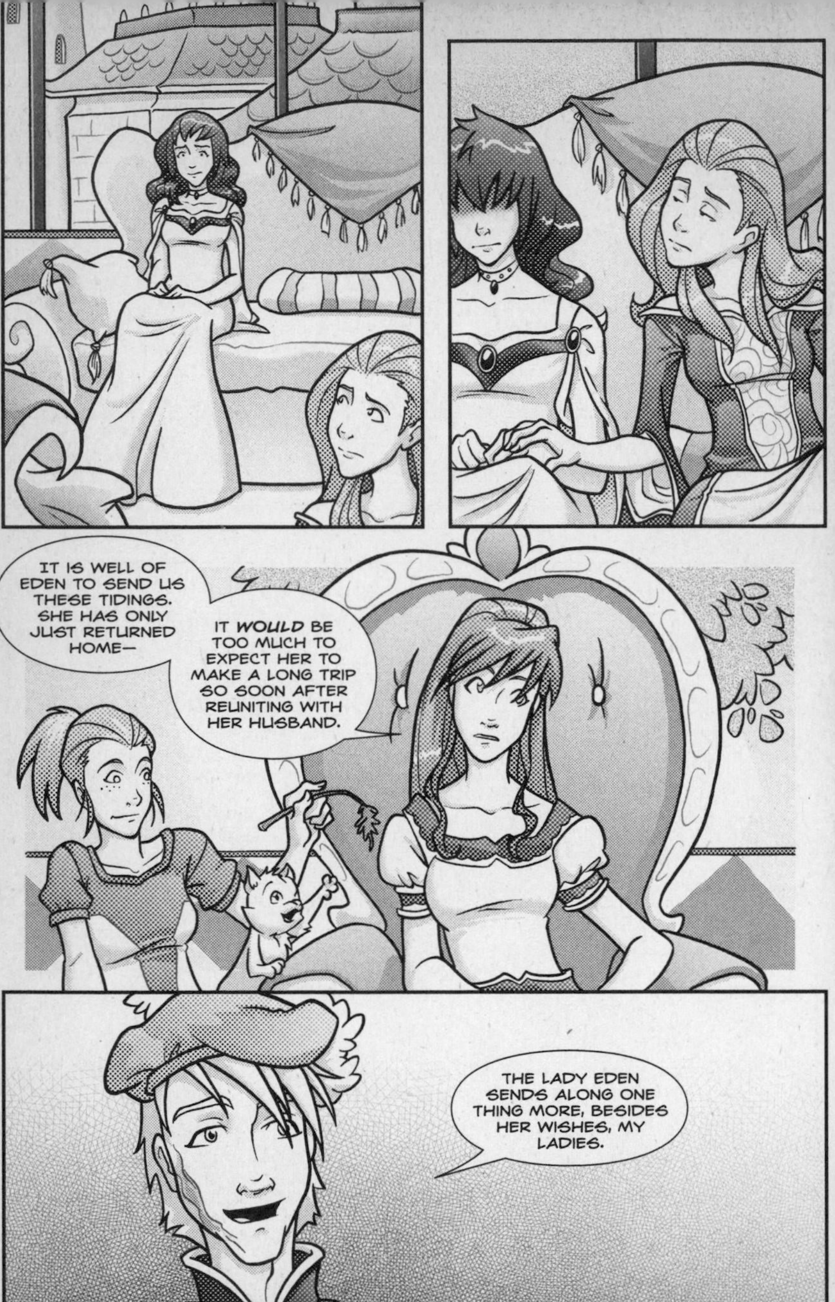
IT IS WELL OF EDEN TO SEND US THESE TIDINGS. SHE HAS ONLY JUST RETURNED HOME—
IT ***WOULD*** BE TOO MUCH TO EXPECT HER TO MAKE A LONG TRIP SO SOON AFTER REUNITING WITH HER HUSBAND.
THE LADY EDEN SENDS ALONG ONE THING MORE, BESIDES HER WISHES, MY LADIES.

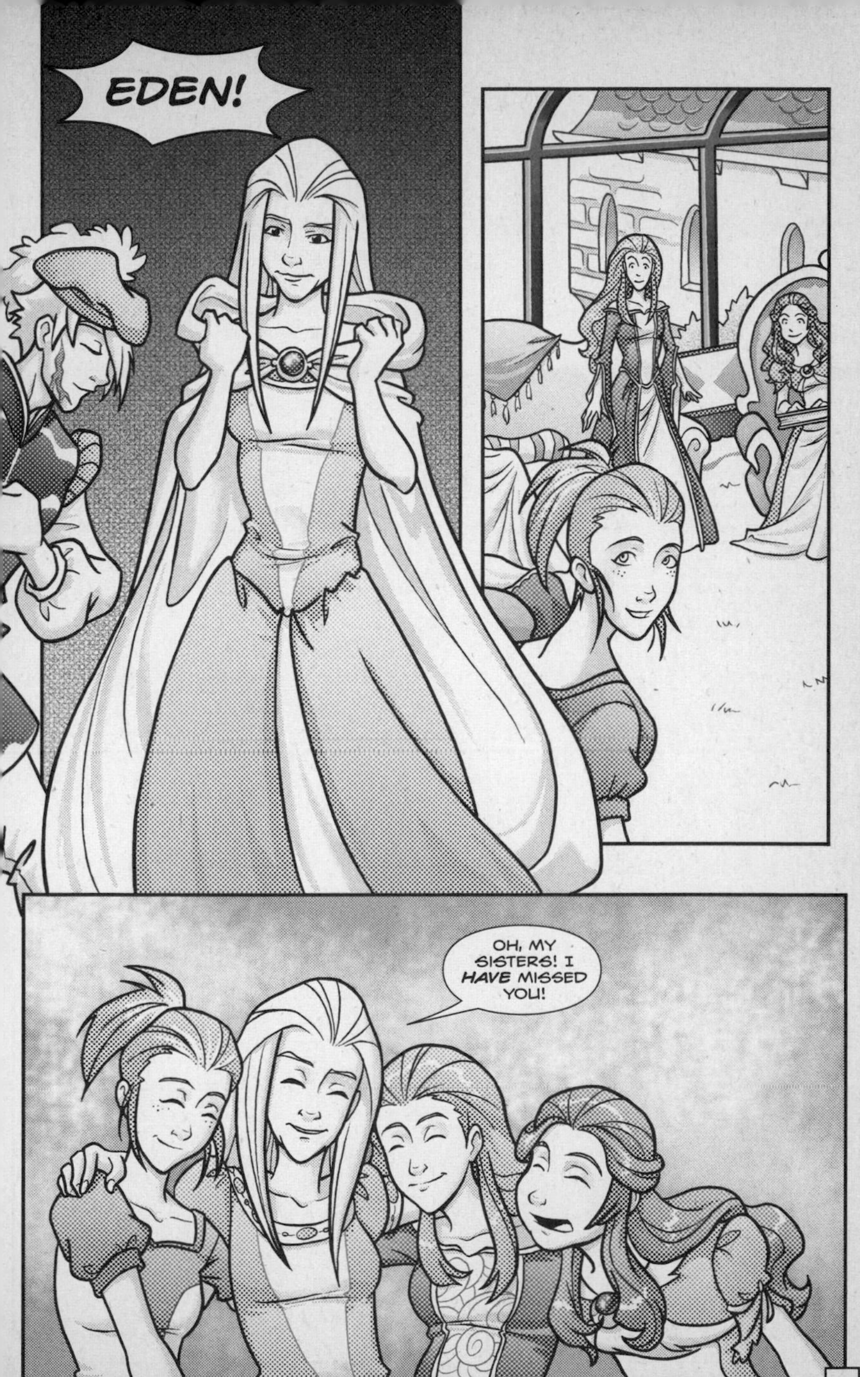
EDEN!
OH, MY SISTERS! I *HAVE* MISSED YOU!

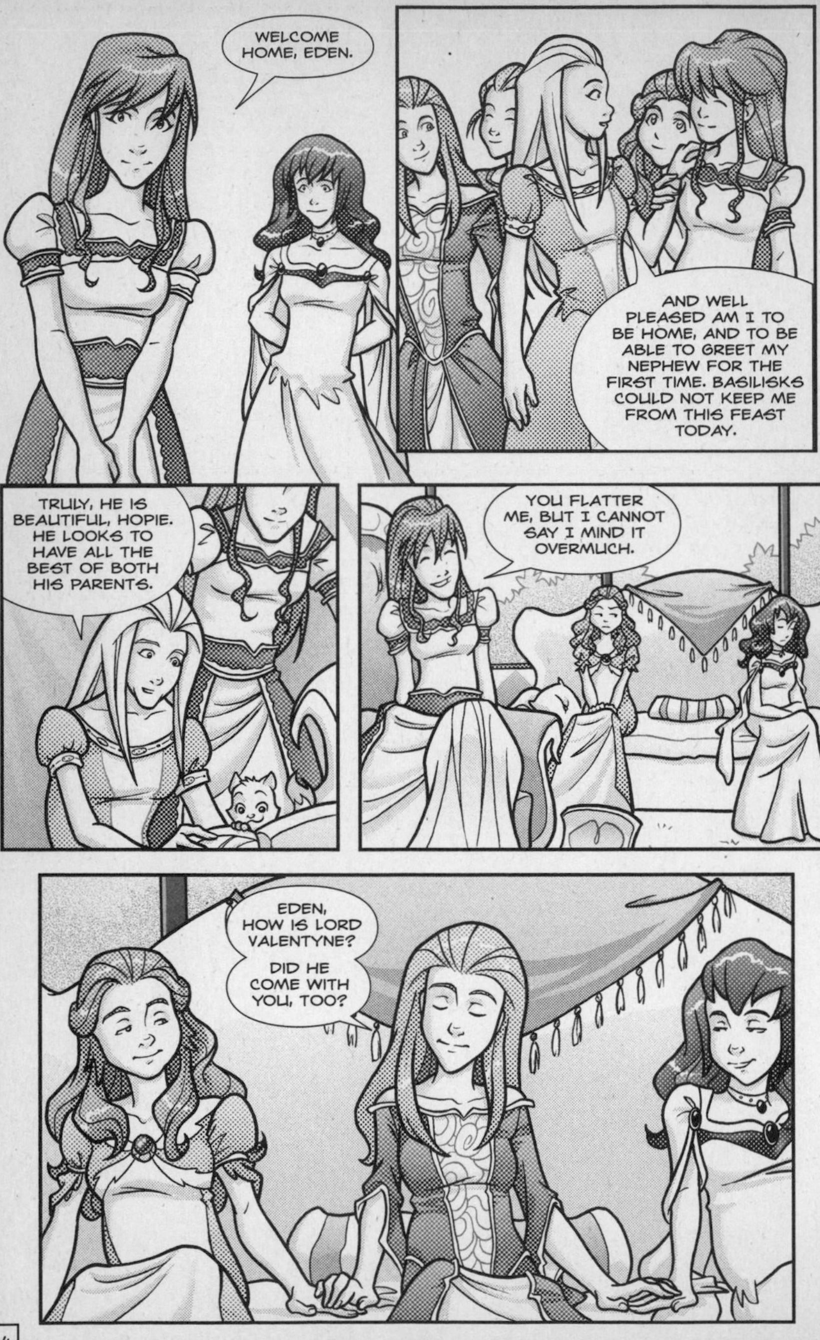
WELCOME HOME, EDEN.
AND WELL PLEASED AM I TO BE HOME, AND TO BE ABLE TO GREET MY NEPHEW FOR THE FIRST TIME. BASILISKS COULD NOT KEEP ME FROM THIS FEAST TODAY.
TRULY, HE IS BEAUTIFUL, HOPIE. HE LOOKS TO HAVE ALL THE BEST OF BOTH HIS PARENTS.
YOU FLATTER ME, BUT I CANNOT SAY I MIND IT OVERMUCH.
EDEN, HOW IS LORD VALENTYNE?
DID HE COME WITH YOU, TOO?

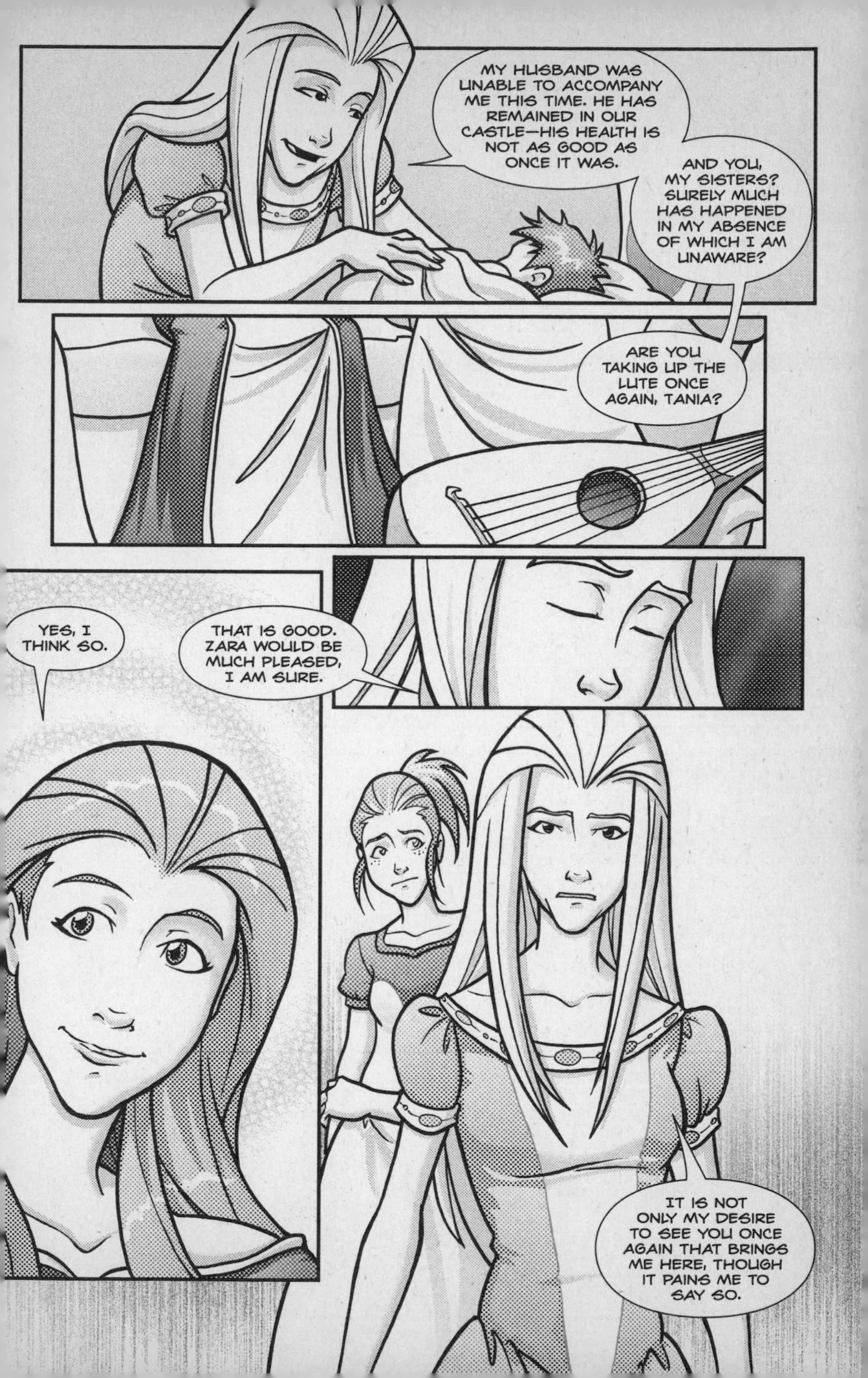
MY HUSBAND WAS UNABLE TO ACCOMPANY ME THIS TIME. HE HAS REMAINED IN OUR CASTLE—HIS HEALTH IS NOT AS GOOD AS ONCE IT WAS.
AND YOU, MY SISTERS? SURELY MUCH HAS HAPPENED IN MY ABSENCE OF WHICH I AM UNAWARE?
ARE YOU TAKING UP THE LUTE ONCE AGAIN, TANIA?
YES, I THINK SO.
THAT IS GOOD. ZARA WOULD BE MUCH PLEASED, I AM SURE.
IT IS NOT ONLY MY DESIRE TO SEE YOU ONCE AGAIN THAT BRINGS ME HERE, THOUGH IT PAINS ME TO SAY SO.

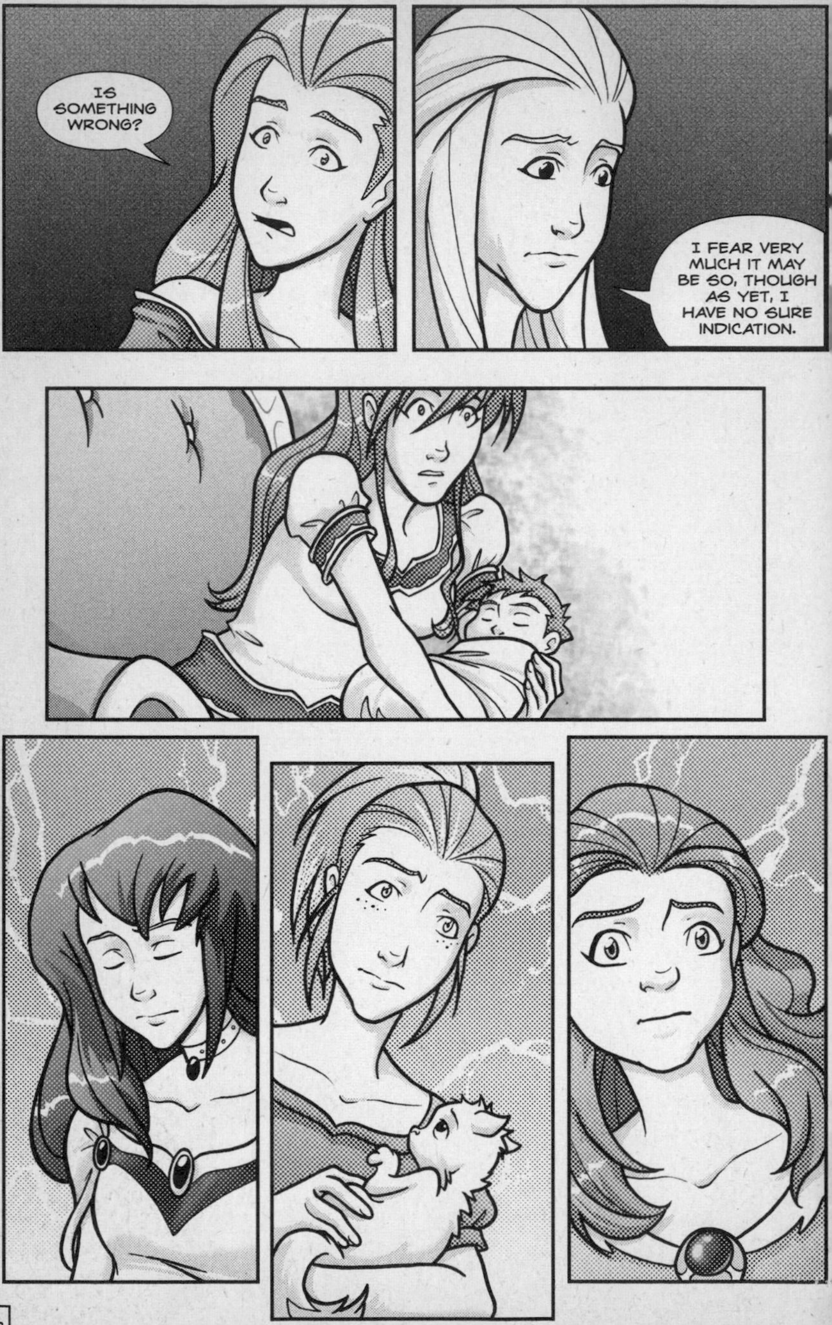
IS SOMETHING WRONG?
I FEAR VERY MUCH IT MAY BE SO, THOUGH AS YET, I HAVE NO SURE INDICATION.

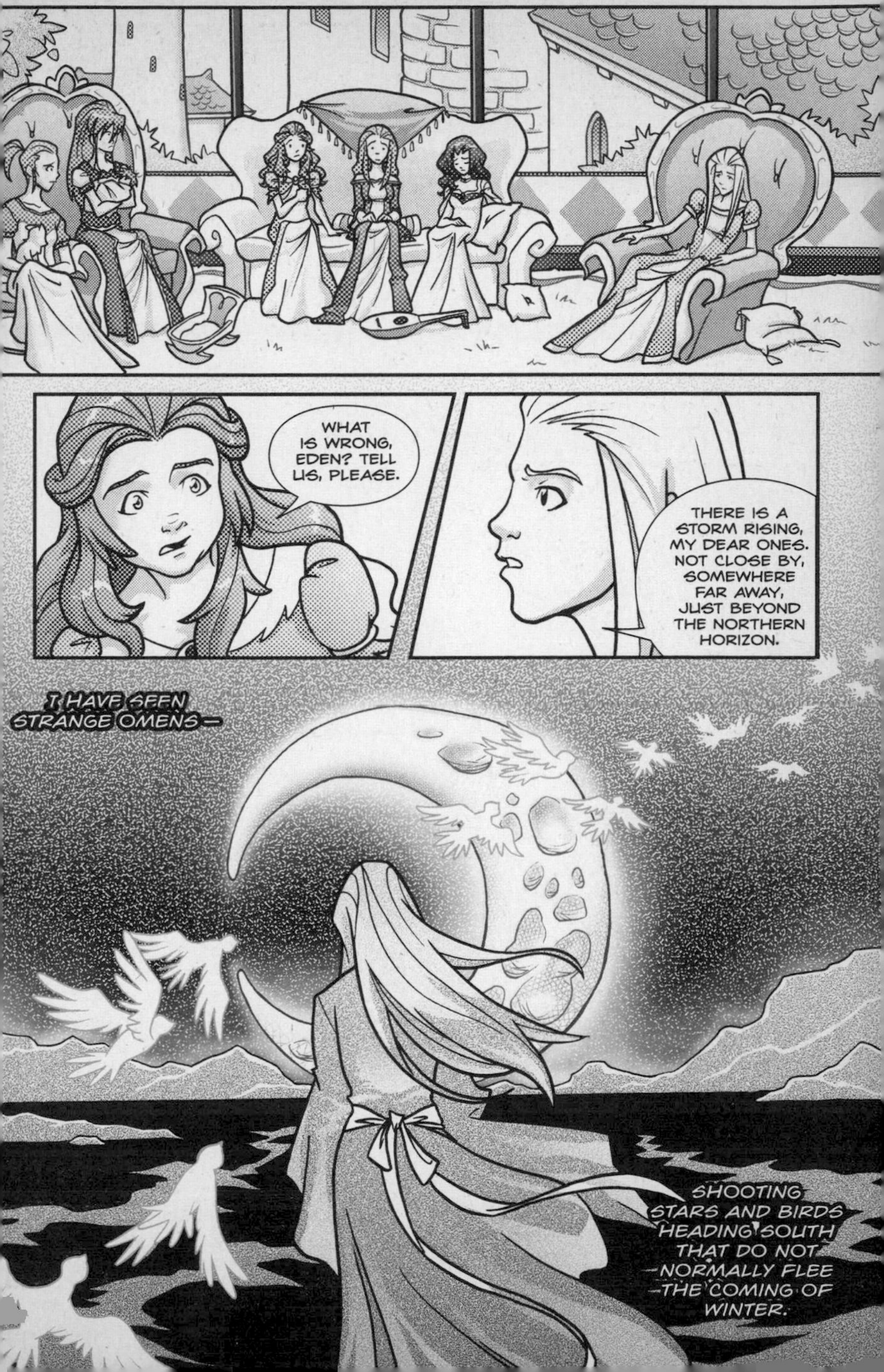
WHAT IS WRONG, EDEN? TELL US, PLEASE.
THERE IS A STORM RISING, MY DEAR ONES. NOT CLOSE BY, SOMEWHERE FAR AWAY, JUST BEYOND THE NORTHERN HORIZON.
I HAVE SEEN STRANGE OMENS—
SHOOTING STARS AND BIRDS HEADING SOUTH THAT DO NOT NORMALLY FLEE THE COMING OF WINTER.

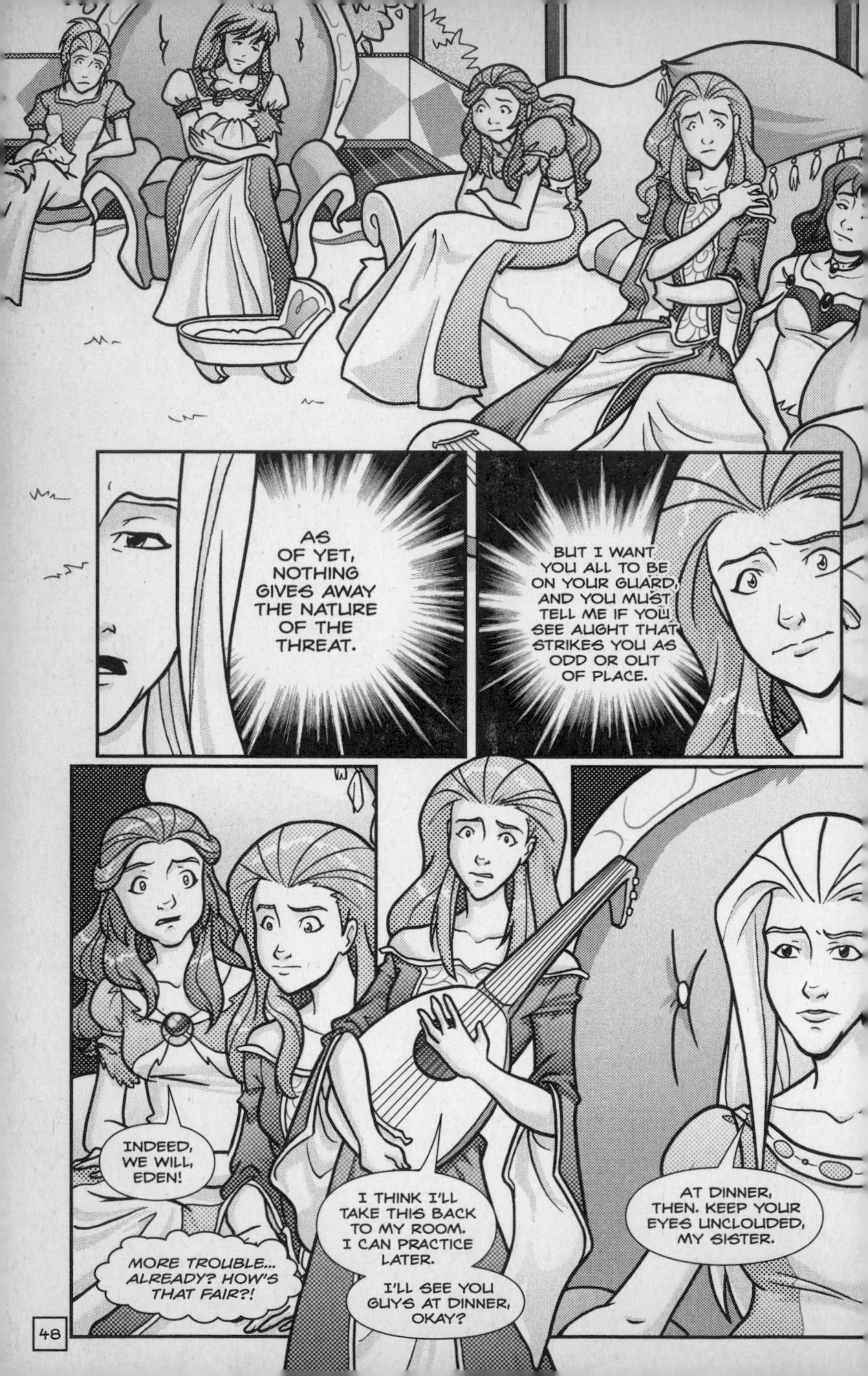
AS OF YET, NOTHING GIVES AWAY THE NATURE OF THE THREAT.
BUT I WANT YOU ALL TO BE ON YOUR GUARD, AND YOU MUST TELL ME IF YOU SEE AUGHT THAT STRIKES YOU AS ODD OR OUT OF PLACE.
INDEED, WE WILL, EDEN!
MORE TROUBLE... ALREADY? HOW'S THAT FAIR?!
I THINK I'LL TAKE THIS BACK TO MY ROOM. I CAN PRACTICE LATER.
I'LL SEE YOU GUYS AT DINNER, OKAY?
AT DINNER, THEN. KEEP YOUR EYES UNCLOUDED, MY SISTER.

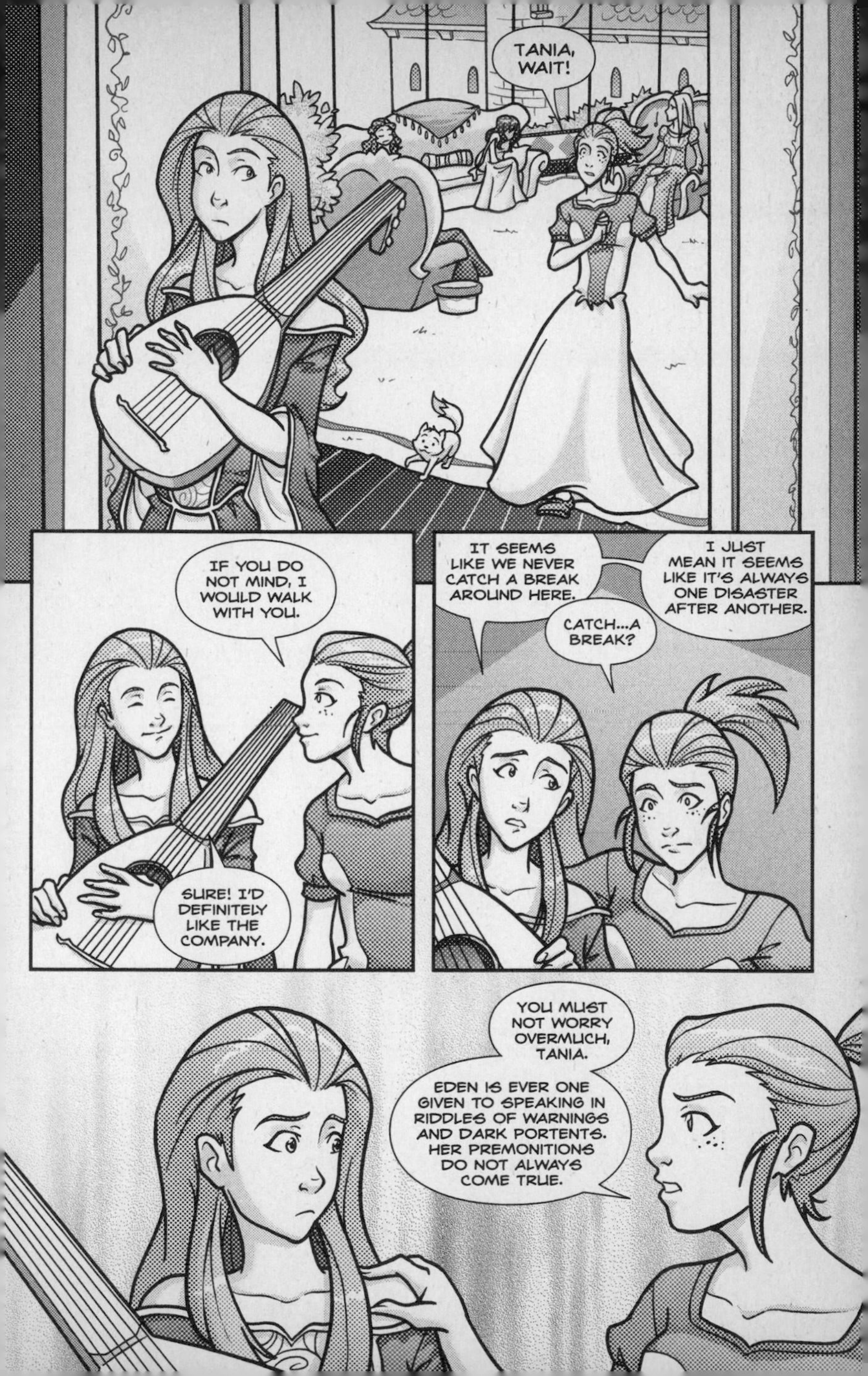
TANIA, WAIT!
IF YOU DO NOT MIND, I WOULD WALK WITH YOU.
SURE! I'D DEFINITELY LIKE THE COMPANY.
IT SEEMS LIKE WE NEVER CATCH A BREAK AROUND HERE.
CATCH...A BREAK?
I JUST MEAN IT SEEMS LIKE IT'S ALWAYS ONE DISASTER AFTER ANOTHER.
YOU MUST NOT WORRY OVERMUCH, TANIA.
EDEN IS EVER ONE GIVEN TO SPEAKING IN RIDDLES OF WARNINGS AND DARK PORTENTS. HER PREMONITIONS DO NOT ALWAYS COME TRUE.

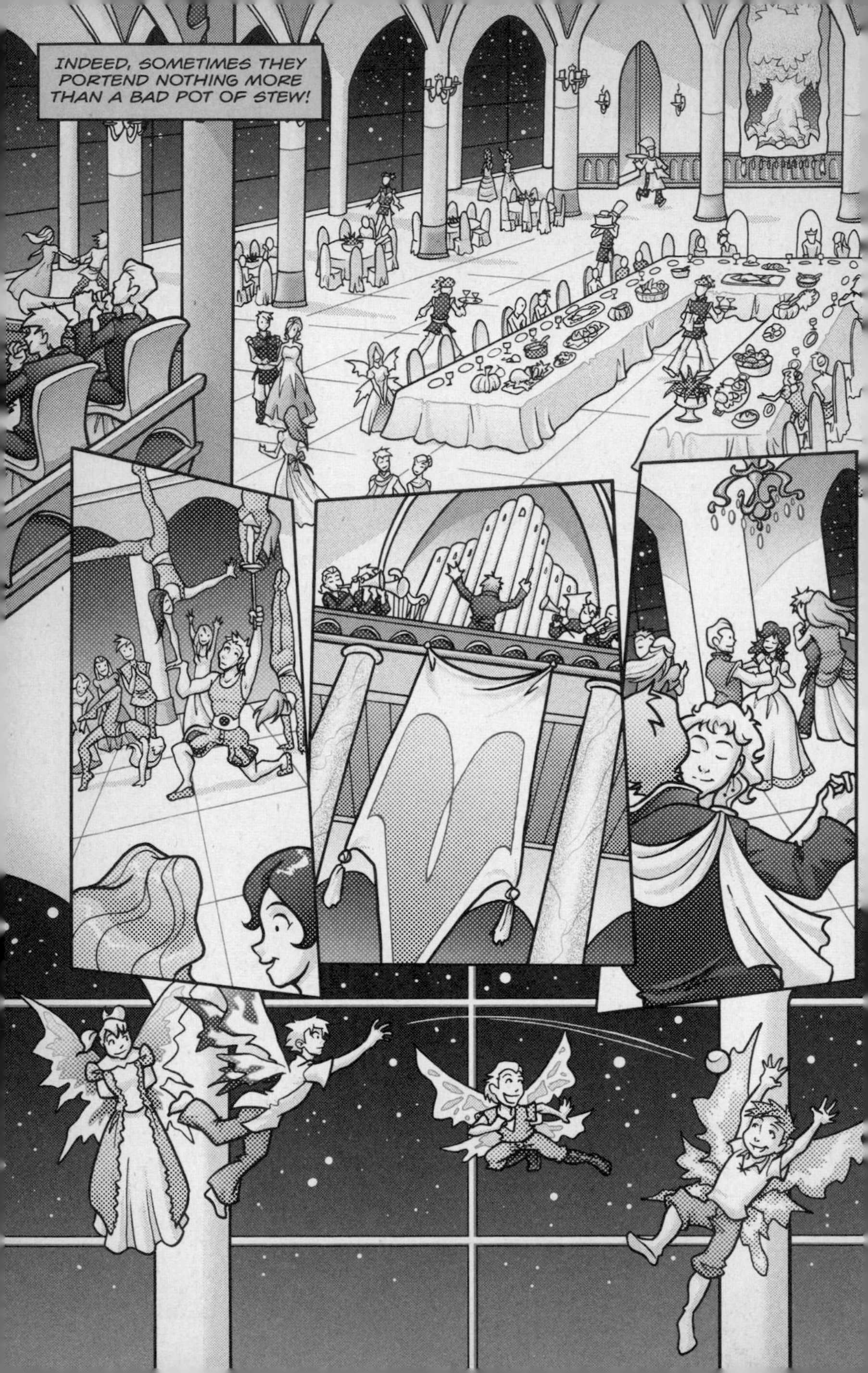
INDEED, SOMETIMES THEY PORTEND NOTHING MORE THAN A BAD POT OF STEW!

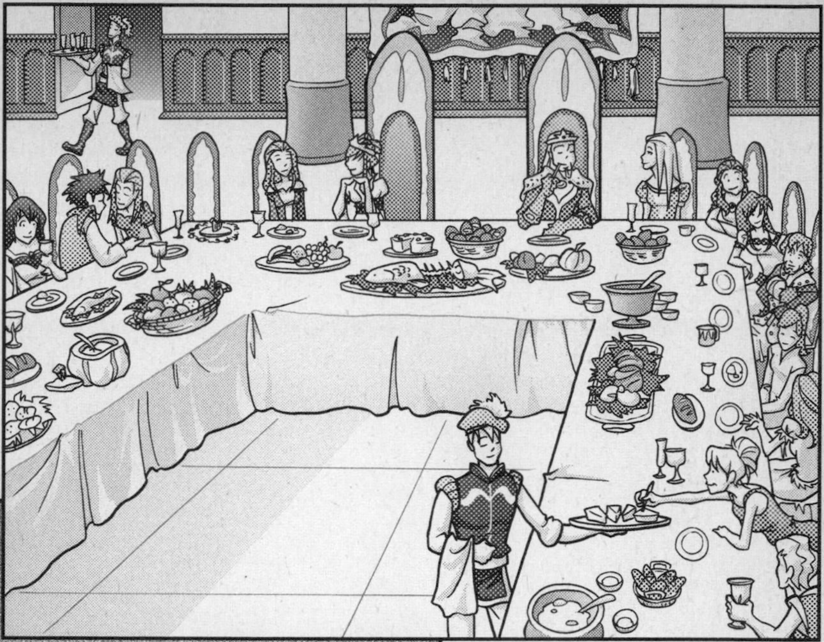
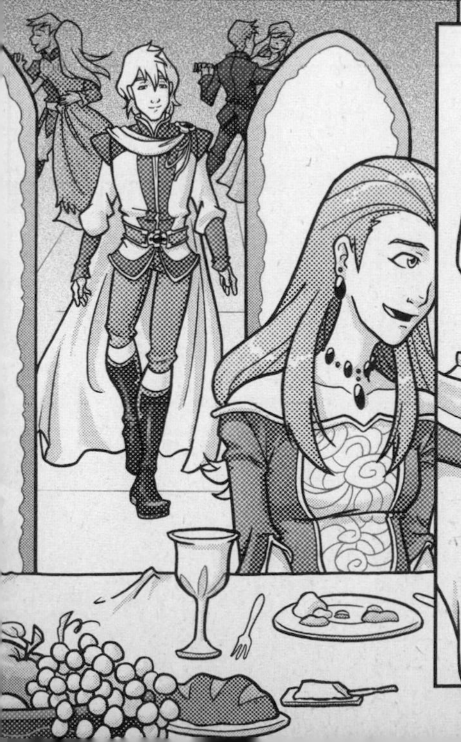
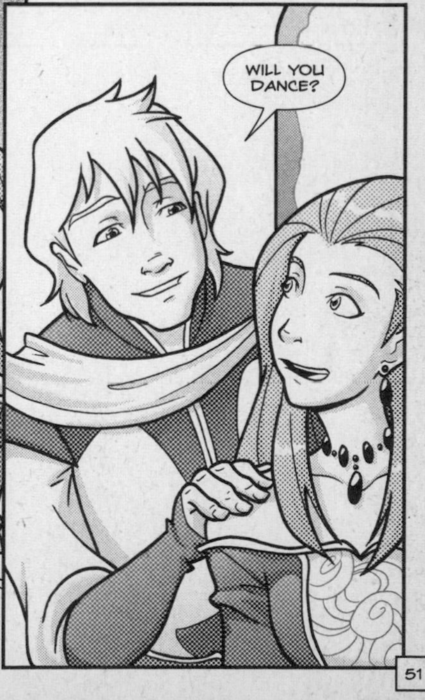
WILL YOU DANCE?

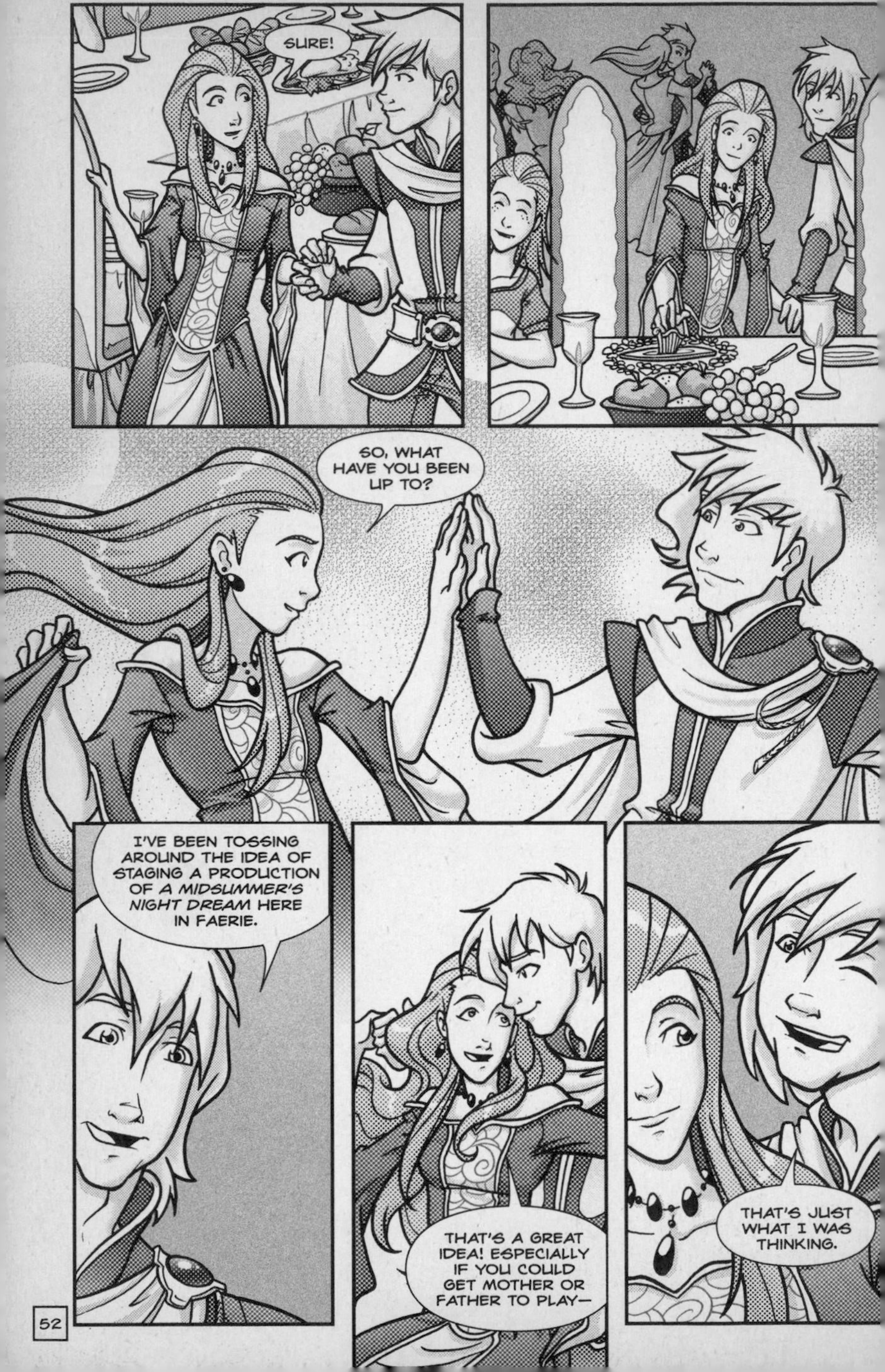
SURE!
SO, WHAT HAVE YOU BEEN UP TO?
I'VE BEEN TOSSING AROUND THE IDEA OF STAGING A PRODUCTION OF A *MIDSUMMER'S NIGHT DREAM* HERE IN FAERIE.
THAT'S A GREAT IDEA! ESPECIALLY IF YOU COULD GET MOTHER OR FATHER TO PLAY—
THAT'S JUST WHAT I WAS THINKING.

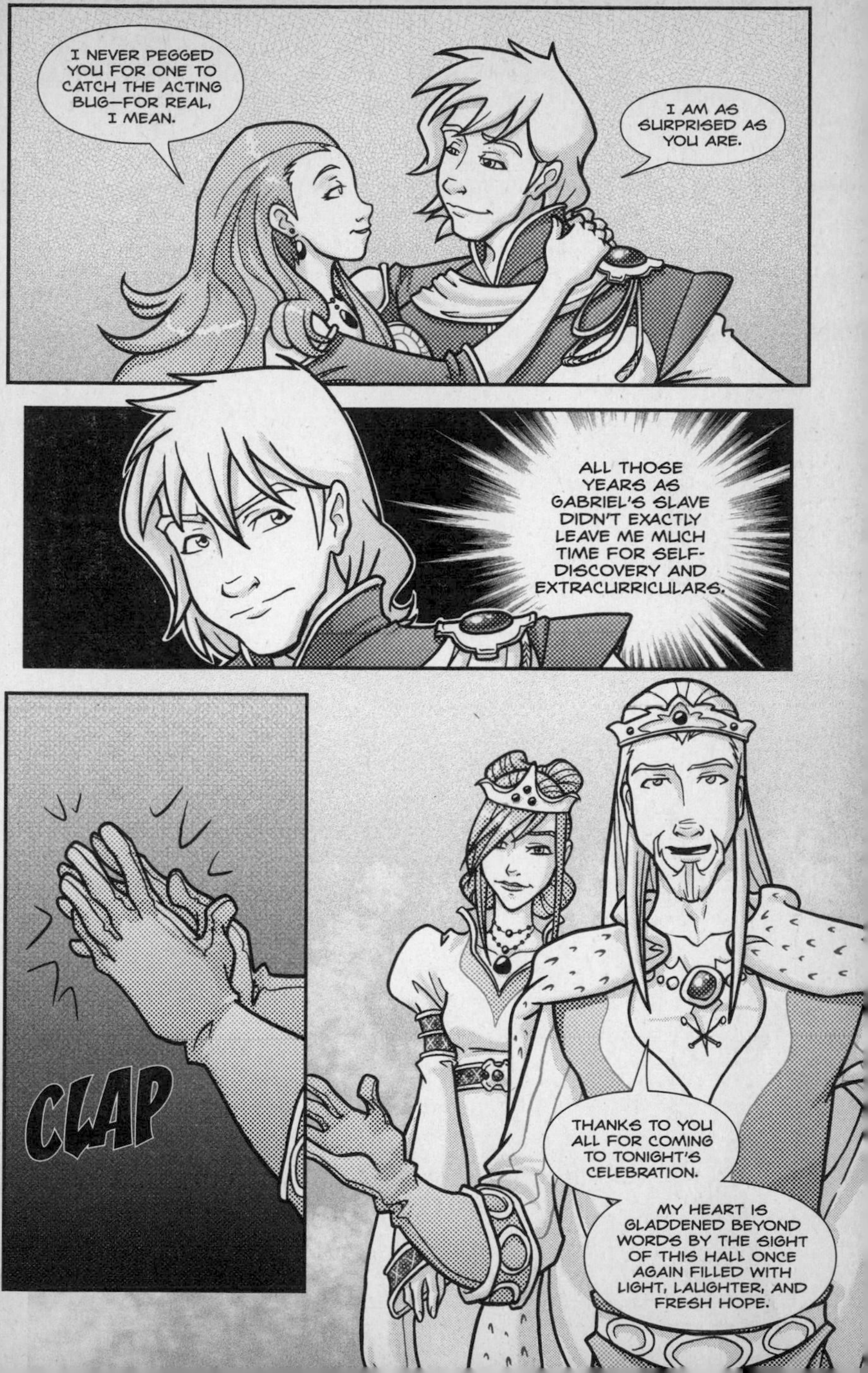
I NEVER PEGGED YOU FOR ONE TO CATCH THE ACTING BUG—FOR REAL, I MEAN.
I AM AS SURPRISED AS YOU ARE.
ALL THOSE YEARS AS GABRIEL'S SLAVE DIDN'T EXACTLY LEAVE ME MUCH TIME FOR SELF-DISCOVERY AND EXTRACURRICULARS.
CLAP
THANKS TO YOU ALL FOR COMING TO TONIGHT'S CELEBRATION.
MY HEART IS GLADDENED BEYOND WORDS BY THE SIGHT OF THIS HALL ONCE AGAIN FILLED WITH LIGHT, LAUGHTER, AND FRESH HOPE.

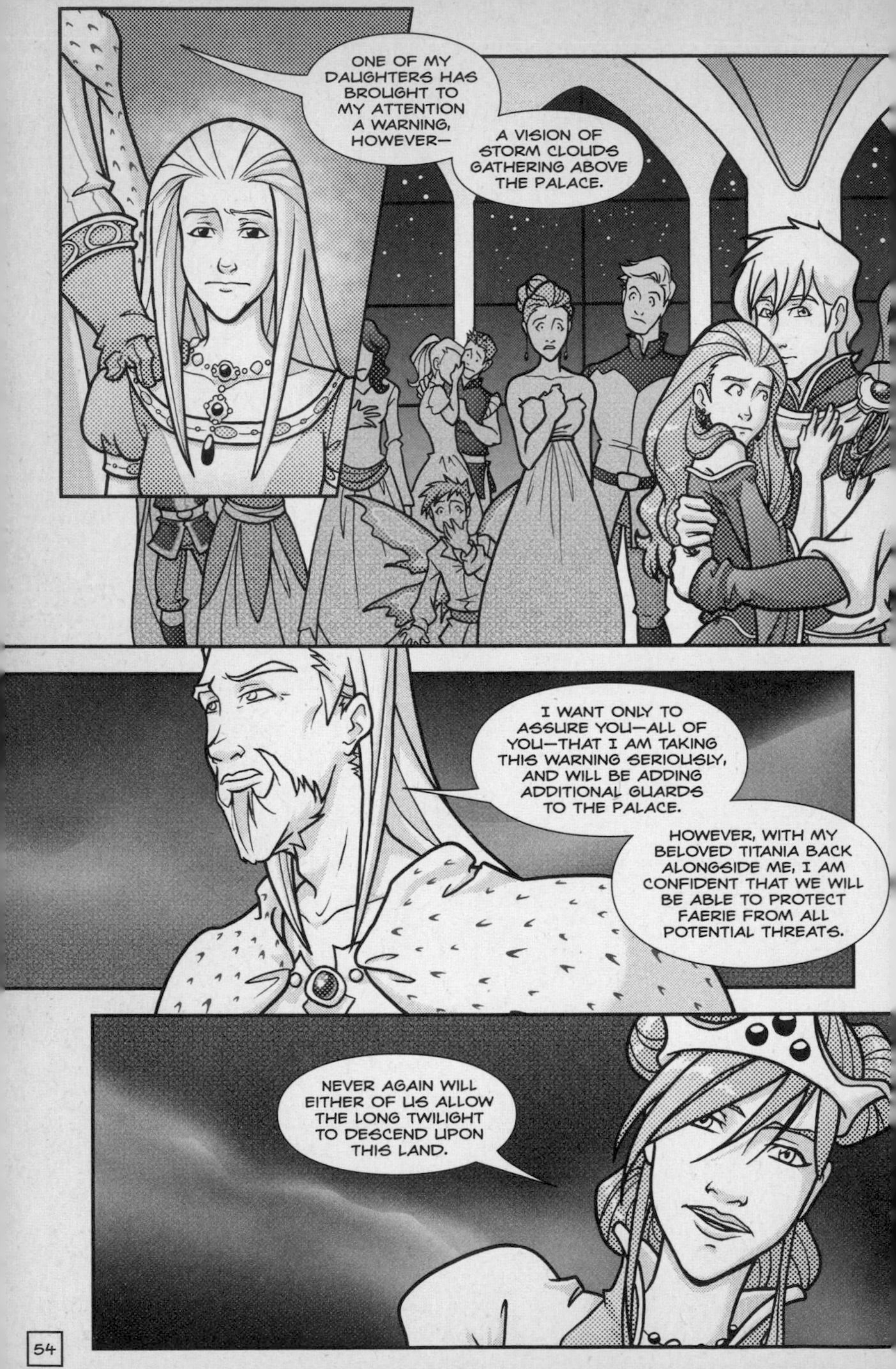
ONE OF MY DAUGHTERS HAS BROUGHT TO MY ATTENTION A WARNING, HOWEVER—
A VISION OF STORM CLOUDS GATHERING ABOVE THE PALACE.
I WANT ONLY TO ASSURE YOU—ALL OF YOU—THAT I AM TAKING THIS WARNING SERIOUSLY, AND WILL BE ADDING ADDITIONAL GUARDS TO THE PALACE.
HOWEVER, WITH MY BELOVED TITANIA BACK ALONGSIDE ME, I AM CONFIDENT THAT WE WILL BE ABLE TO PROTECT FAERIE FROM ALL POTENTIAL THREATS.
NEVER AGAIN WILL EITHER OF US ALLOW THE LONG TWILIGHT TO DESCEND UPON THIS LAND.

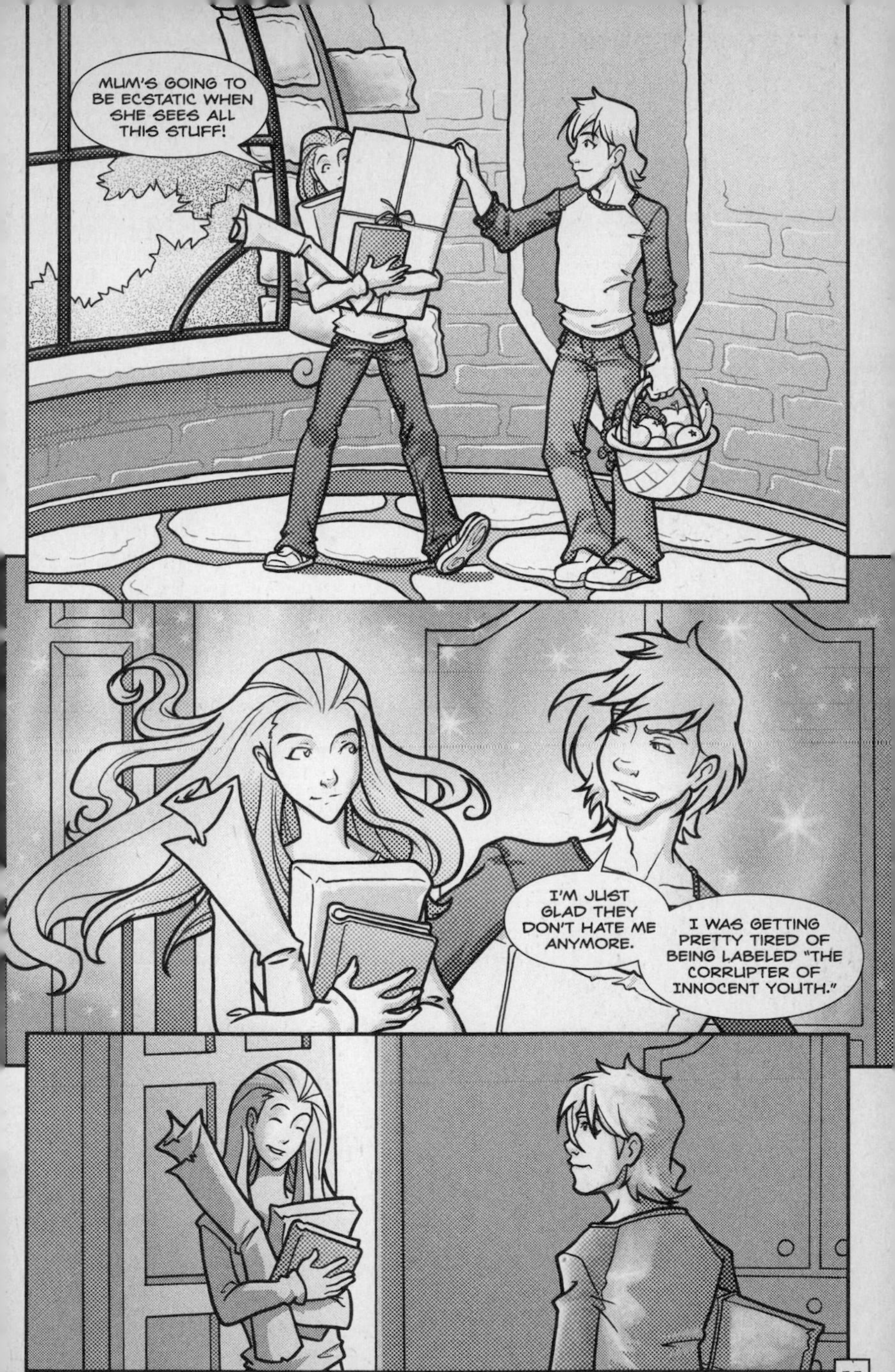
MUM'S GOING TO BE ECSTATIC WHEN SHE SEES ALL THIS STUFF!
I'M JUST GLAD THEY DON'T HATE ME ANYMORE.
I WAS GETTING PRETTY TIRED OF BEING LABELED "THE CORRUPTER OF INNOCENT YOUTH."

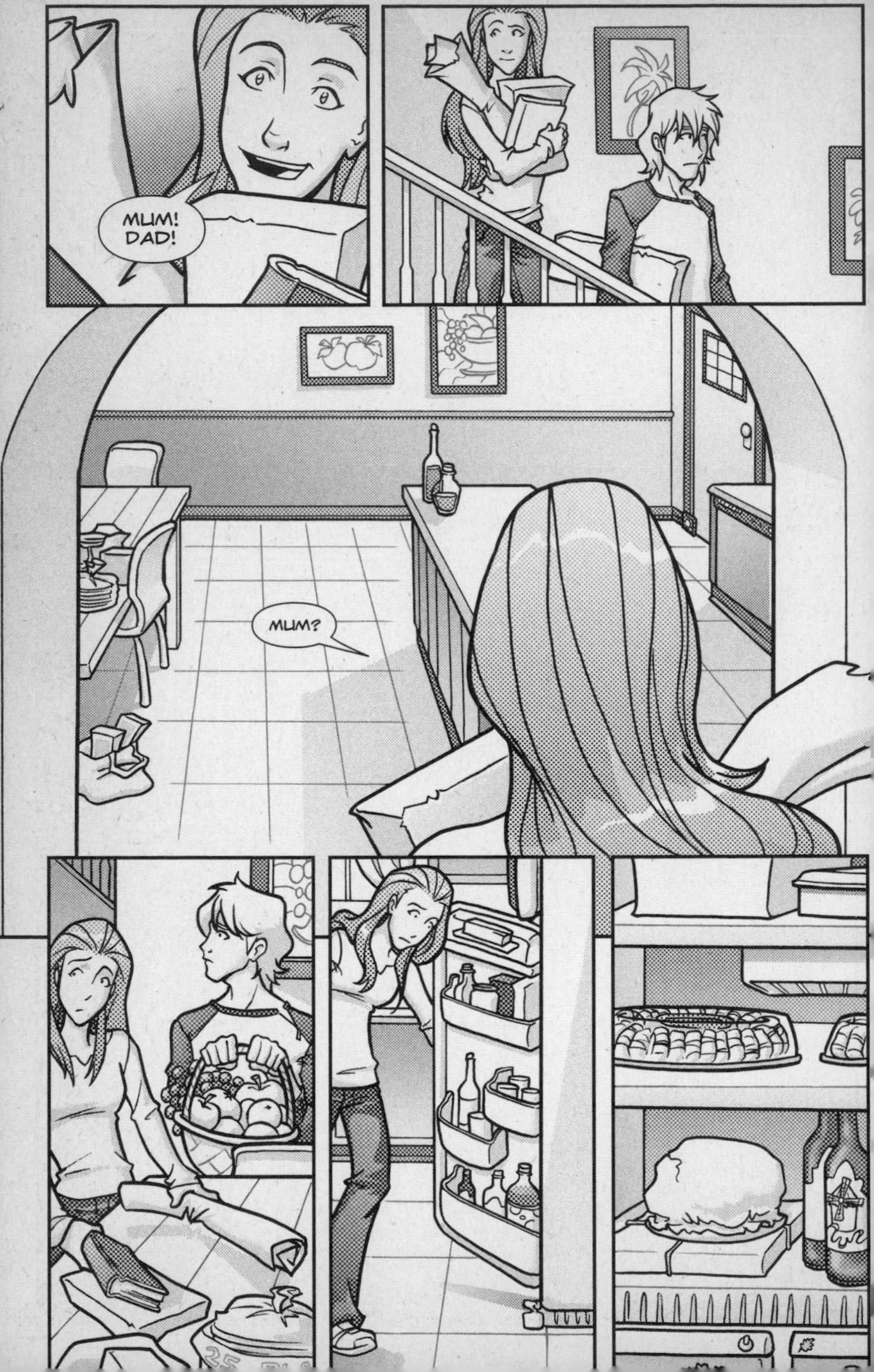
MUM! DAD!
MUM?

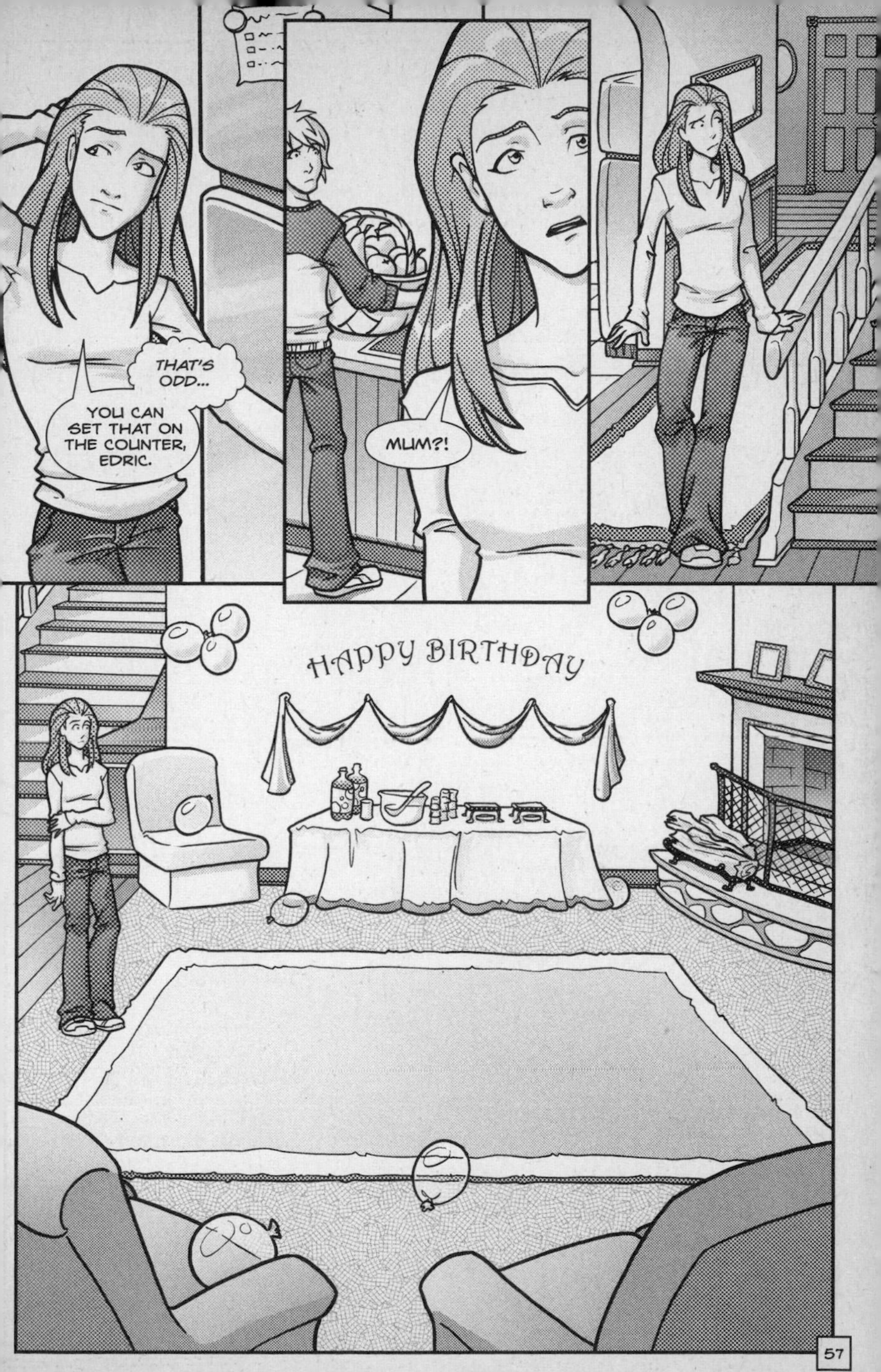
THAT'S ODD...
YOU CAN SET THAT ON THE COUNTER, EDRIC.
MUM?!
HAPPY BIRTHDAY

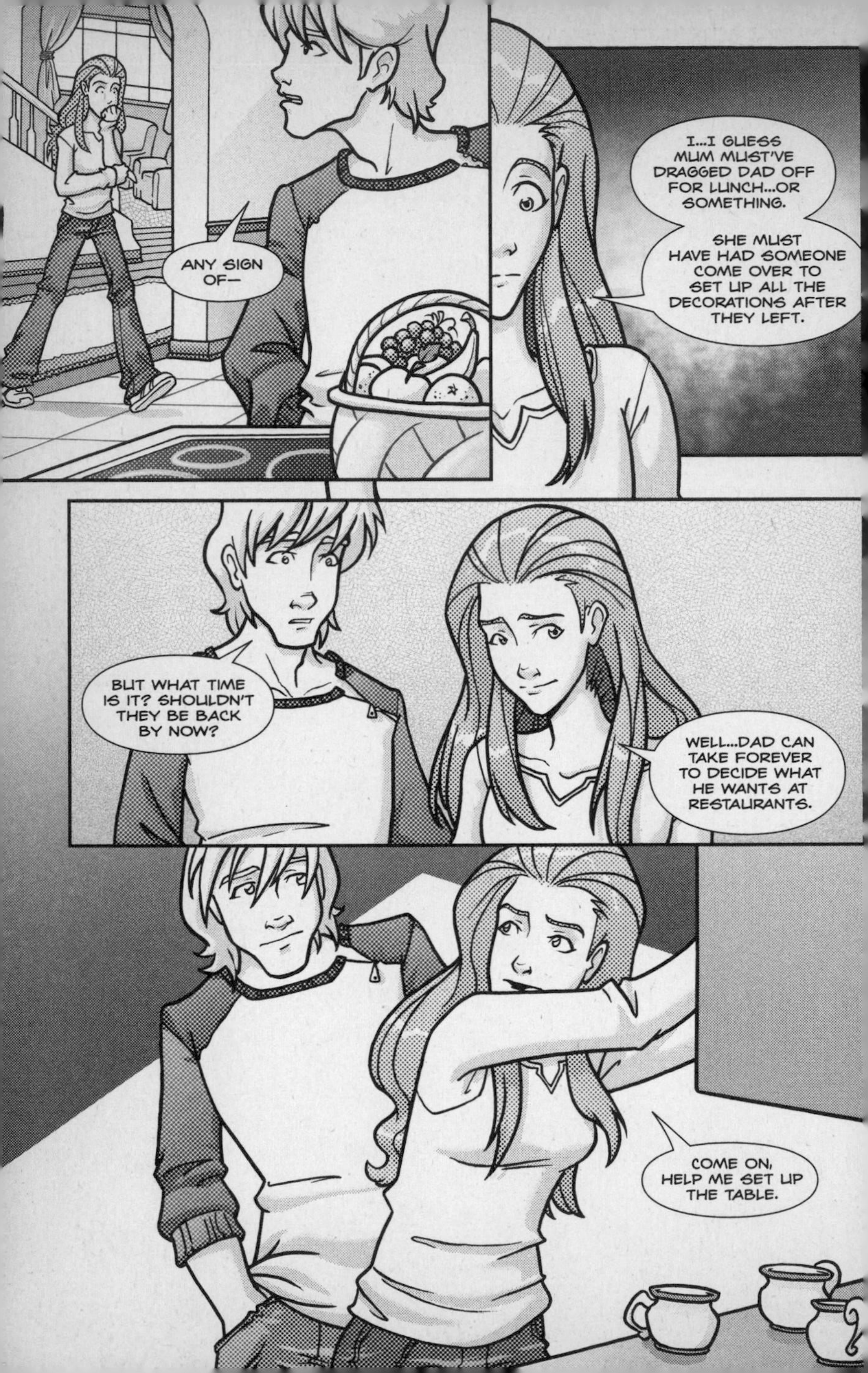
ANY SIGN OF—
I...I GUESS MUM MUST'VE DRAGGED DAD OFF FOR LUNCH...OR SOMETHING.
SHE MUST HAVE HAD SOMEONE COME OVER TO SET UP ALL THE DECORATIONS AFTER THEY LEFT.
BUT WHAT TIME IS IT? SHOULDN'T THEY BE BACK BY NOW?
WELL...DAD CAN TAKE FOREVER TO DECIDE WHAT HE WANTS AT RESTAURANTS.
COME ON, HELP ME SET UP THE TABLE.

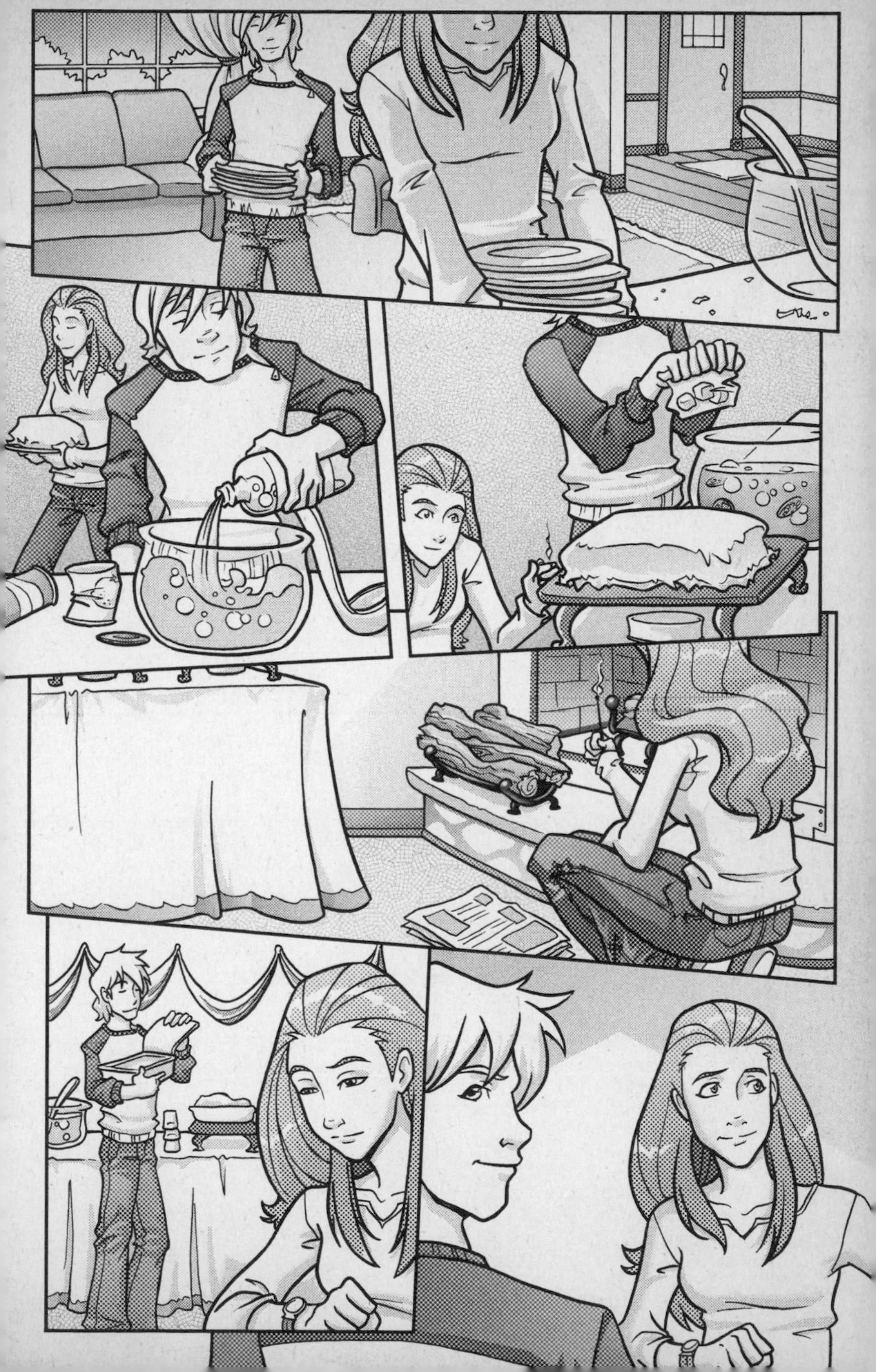

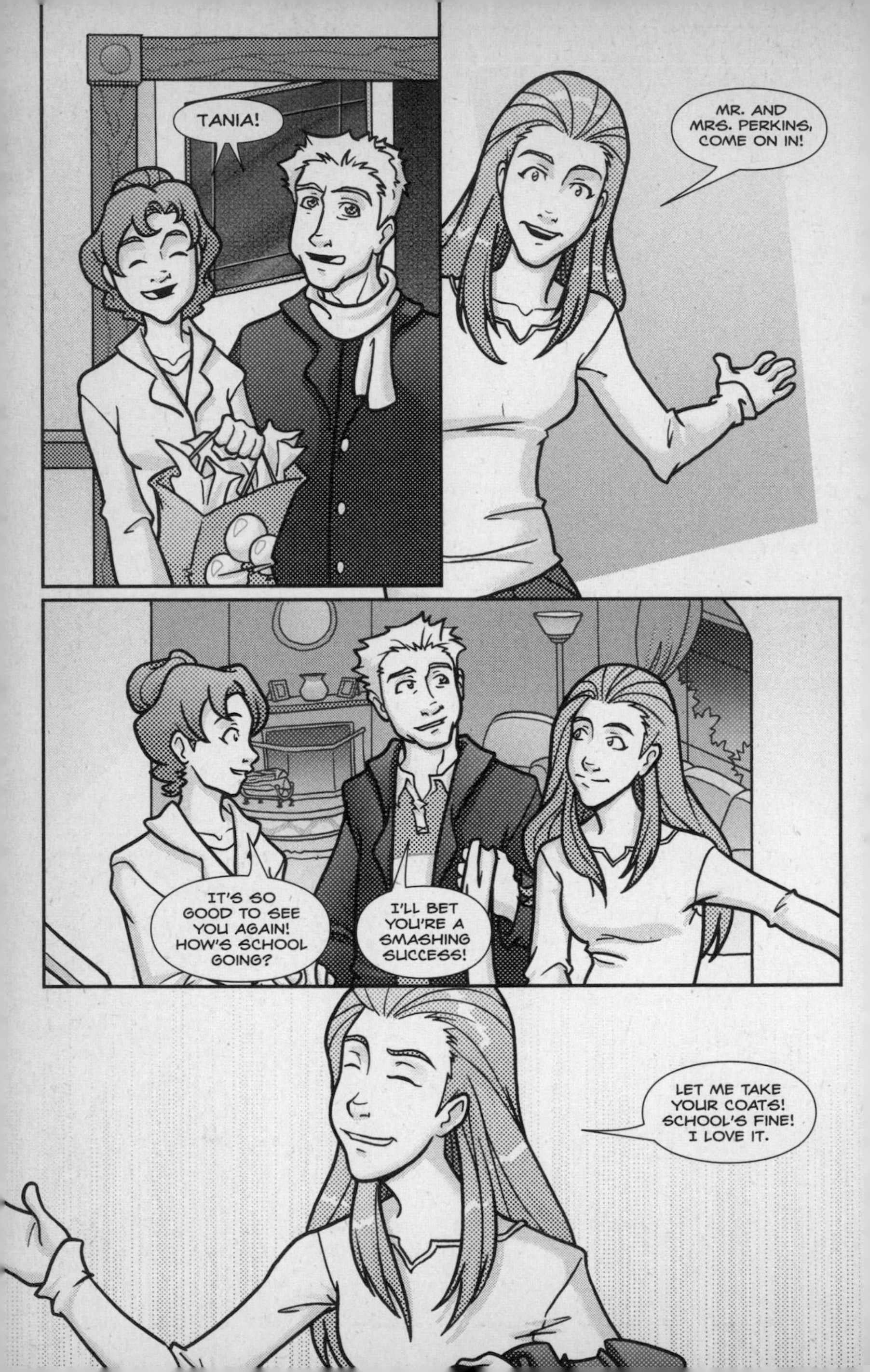
TANIA!
MR. AND MRS. PERKINS, COME ON IN!
IT'S SO GOOD TO SEE YOU AGAIN! HOW'S SCHOOL GOING?
I'LL BET YOU'RE A SMASHING SUCCESS!
LET ME TAKE YOUR COATS! SCHOOL'S FINE! I LOVE IT.

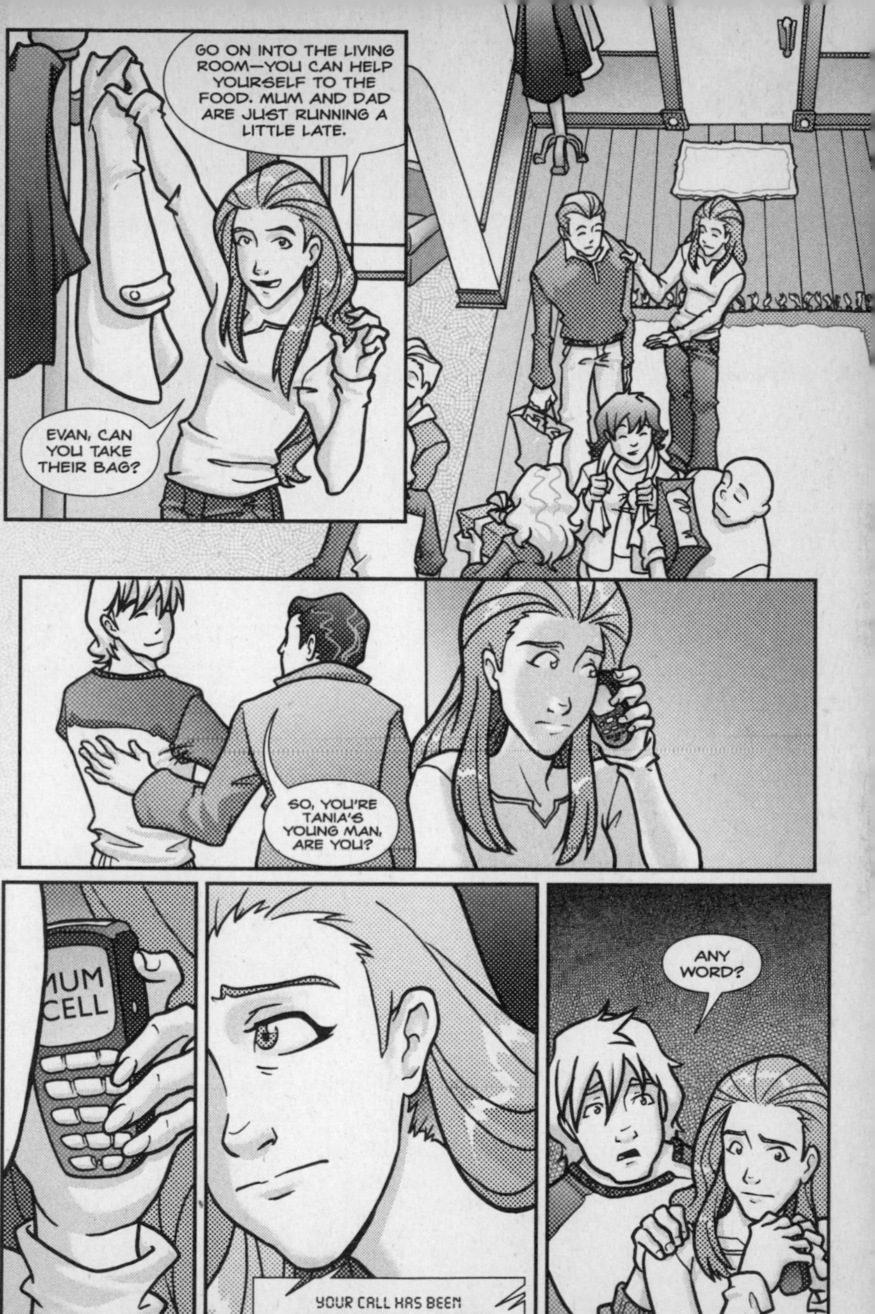
GO ON INTO THE LIVING ROOM—YOU CAN HELP YOURSELF TO THE FOOD. MUM AND DAD ARE JUST RUNNING A LITTLE LATE.
EVAN, CAN YOU TAKE THEIR BAG?
SO, YOU'RE TANIA'S YOUNG MAN, ARE YOU?
MUM CELL
YOUR CALL HAS BEEN FORWARDED TO AN AUTOMATIC VOICE MESSAGING SYSTEM.
ANY WORD?

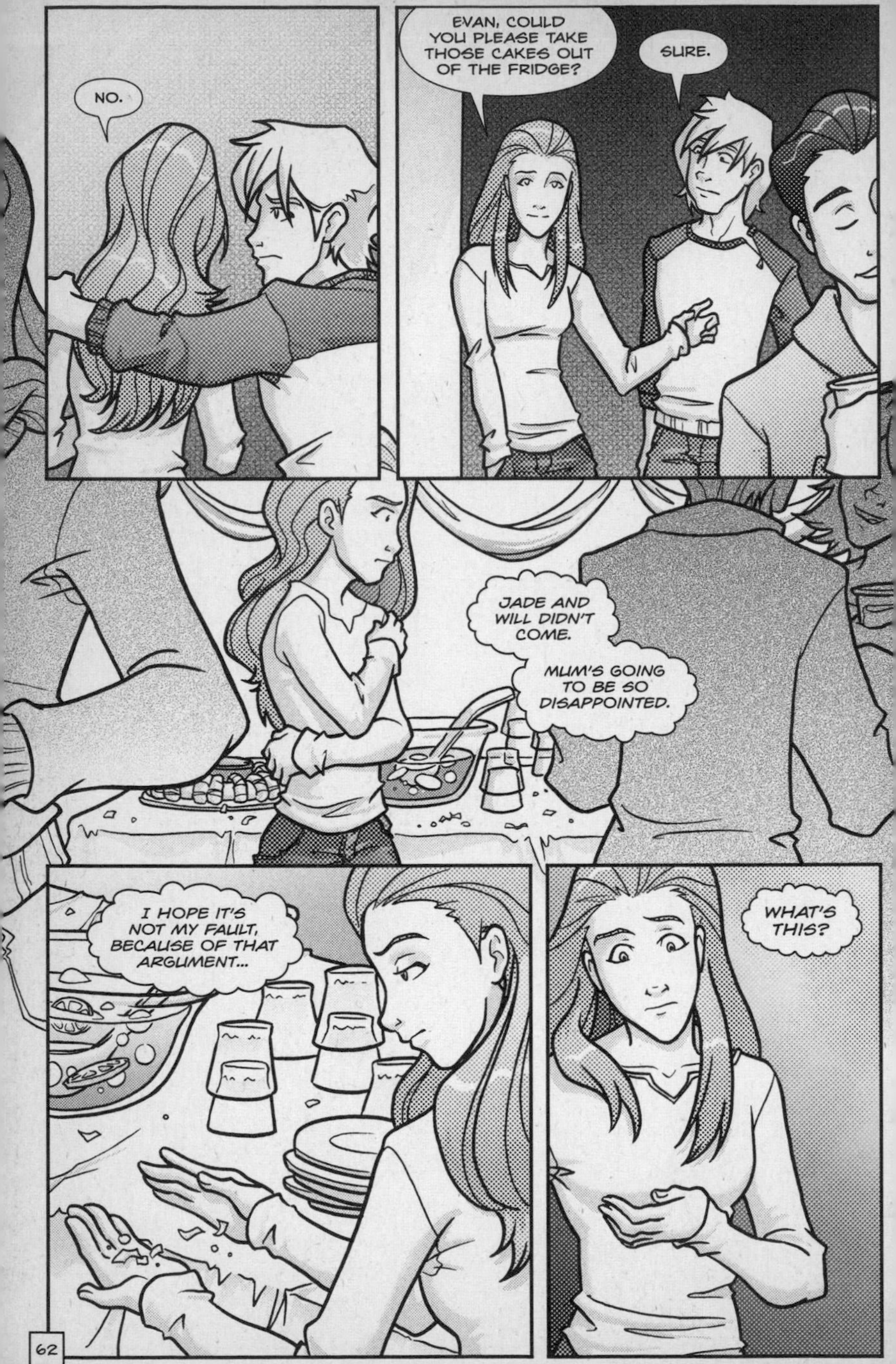
NO.
EVAN, COULD YOU PLEASE TAKE THOSE CAKES OUT OF THE FRIDGE?
SURE.
JADE AND WILL DIDN'T COME.
MUM'S GOING TO BE SO DISAPPOINTED.
I HOPE IT'S NOT MY FAULT, BECAUSE OF THAT ARGUMENT...
WHAT'S THIS?

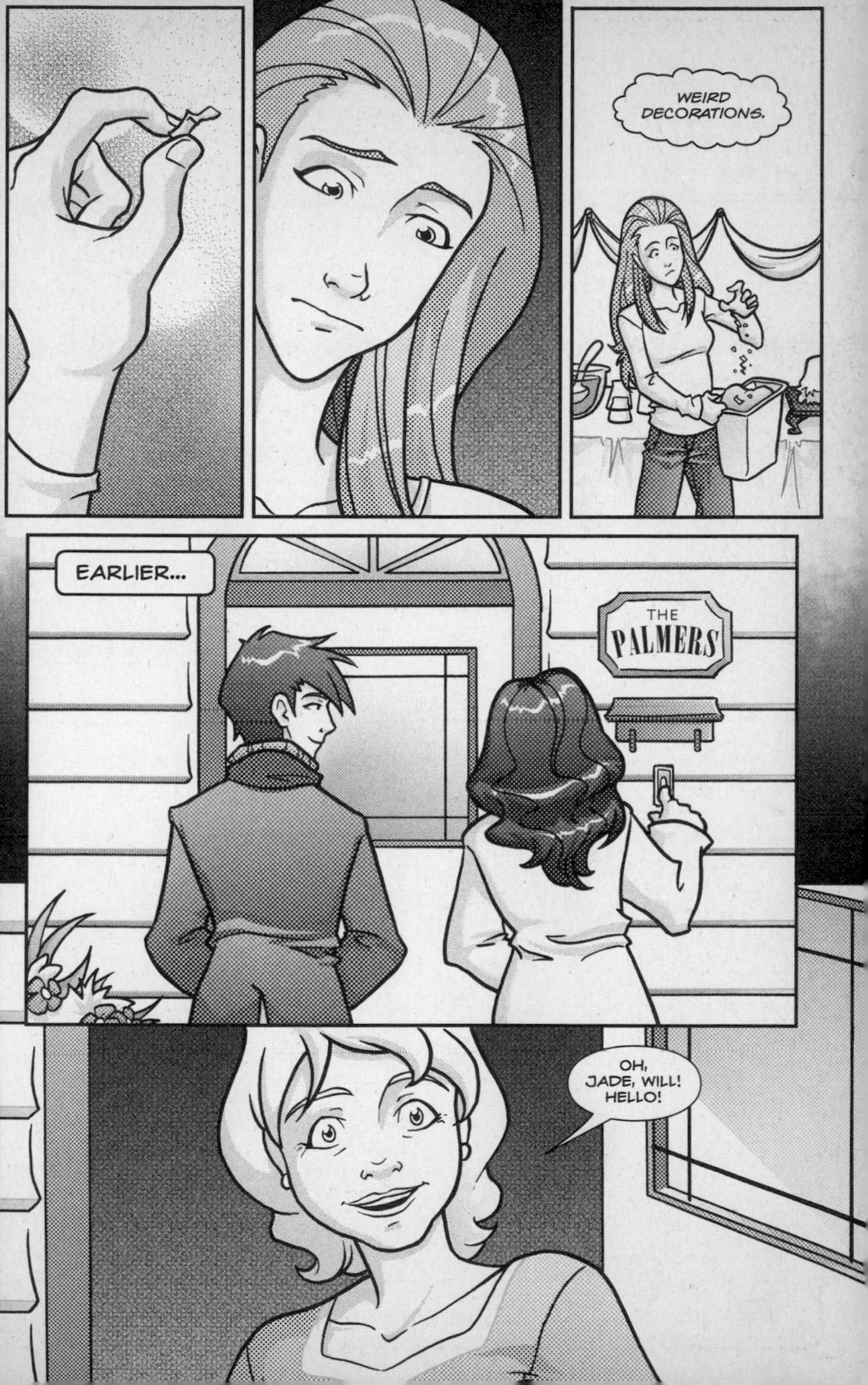
WEIRD DECORATIONS.
EARLIER...
THE PALMERS
OH, JADE, WILL! HELLO!

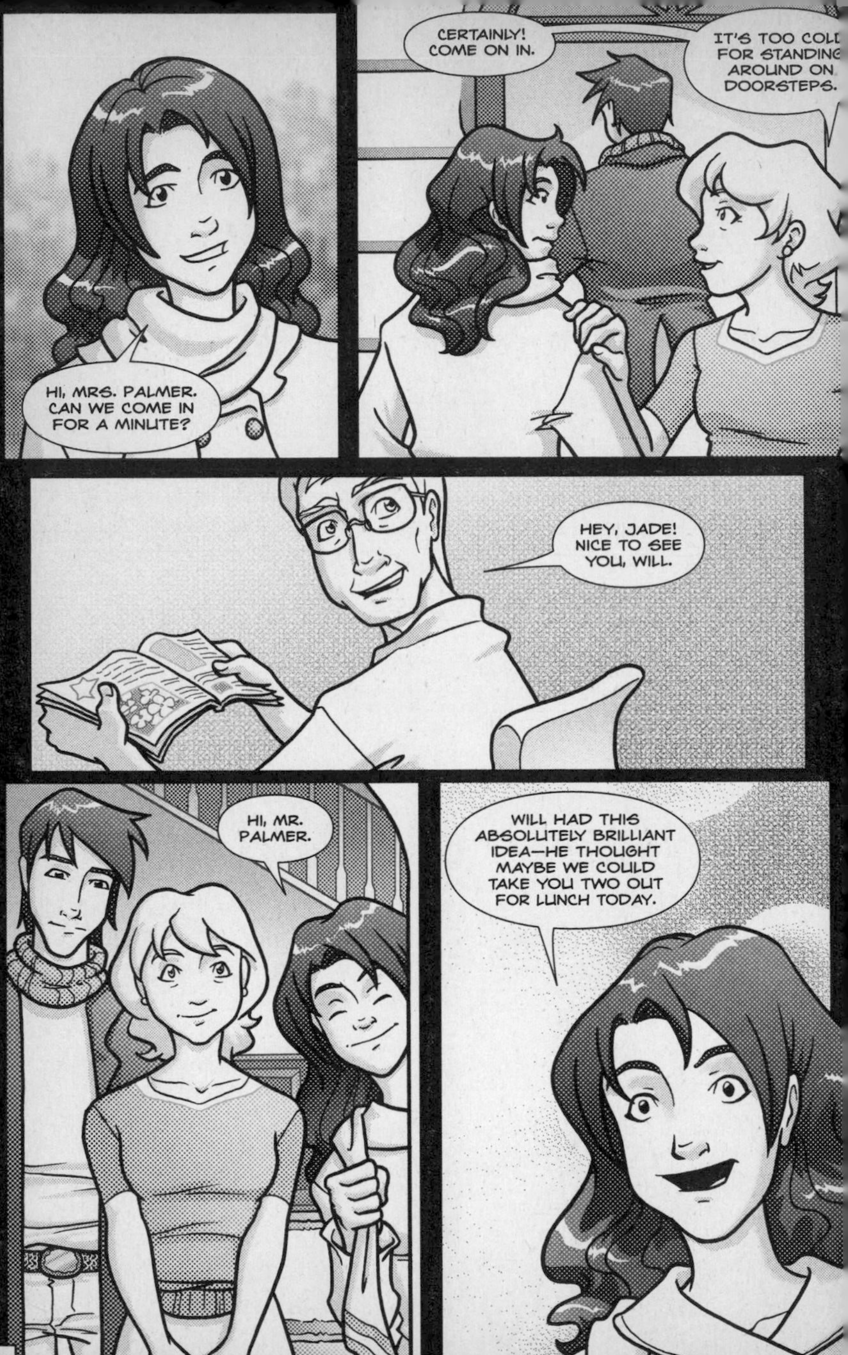
HI, MRS. PALMER. CAN WE COME IN FOR A MINUTE?
CERTAINLY! COME ON IN.
IT'S TOO COL FOR STANDING AROUND ON DOORSTEPS.
HEY, JADE! NICE TO SEE YOU, WILL.
HI, MR. PALMER.
WILL HAD THIS ABSOLUTELY BRILLIANT IDEA—HE THOUGHT MAYBE WE COULD TAKE YOU TWO OUT FOR LUNCH TODAY.

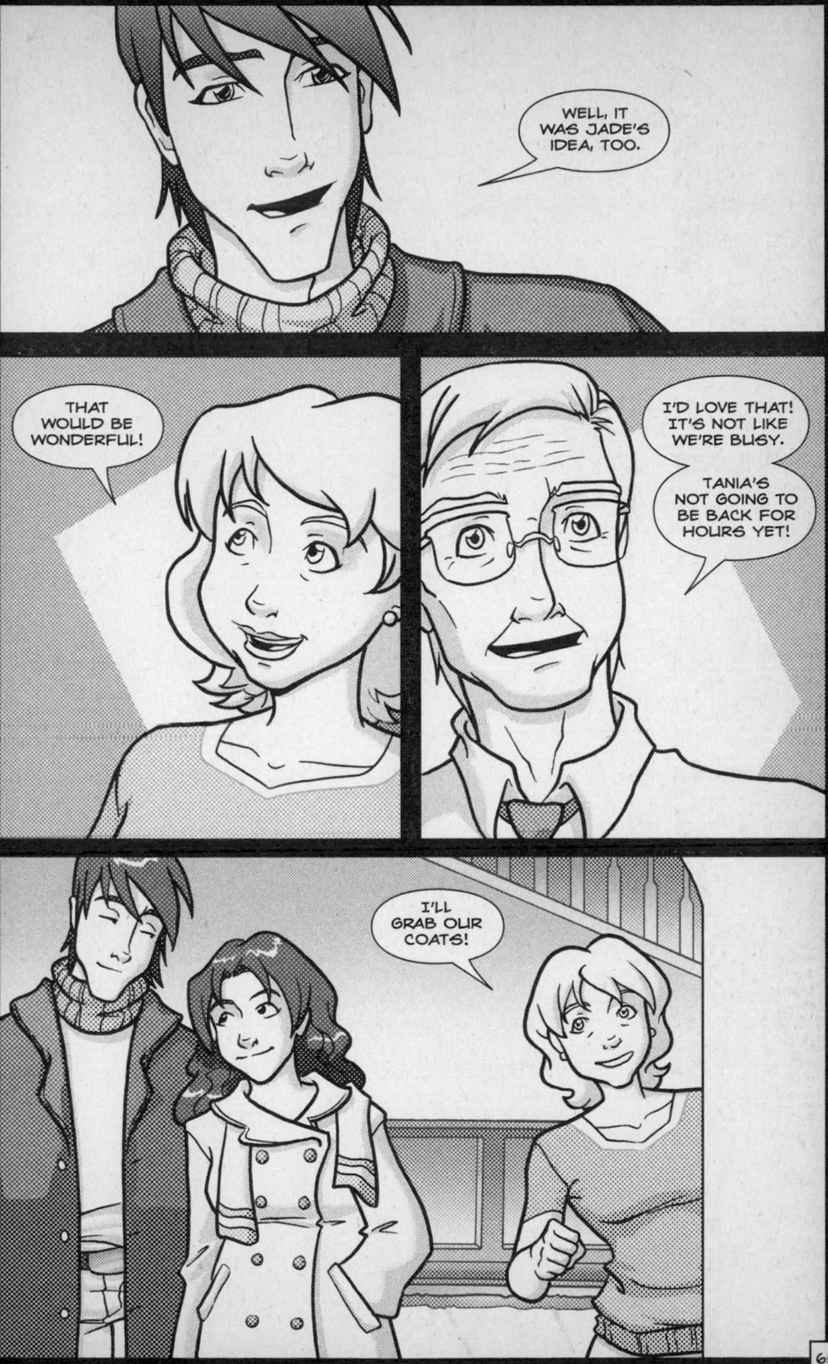
WELL, IT WAS JADE'S IDEA, TOO.
I'D LOVE THAT! IT'S NOT LIKE WE'RE BUSY.
TANIA'S NOT GOING TO BE BACK FOR HOURS YET!
THAT WOULD BE WONDERFUL!
I'LL GRAB OUR COATS!

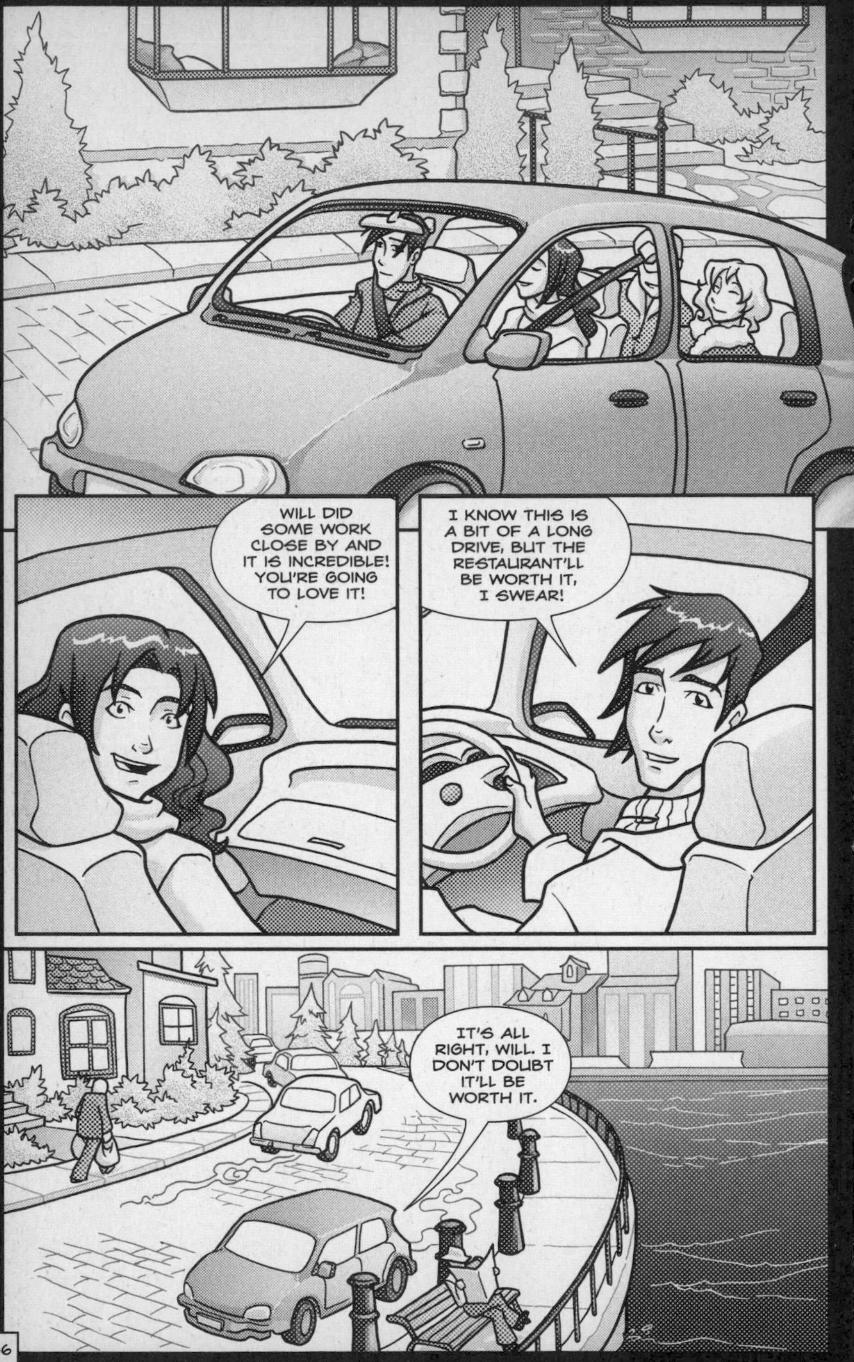
WILL DID SOME WORK CLOSE BY AND IT IS INCREDIBLE! YOU'RE GOING TO LOVE IT!
I KNOW THIS IS A BIT OF A LONG DRIVE, BUT THE RESTAURANT'LL BE WORTH IT, I SWEAR!
IT'S ALL RIGHT, WILL. I DON'T DOUBT IT'LL BE WORTH IT.

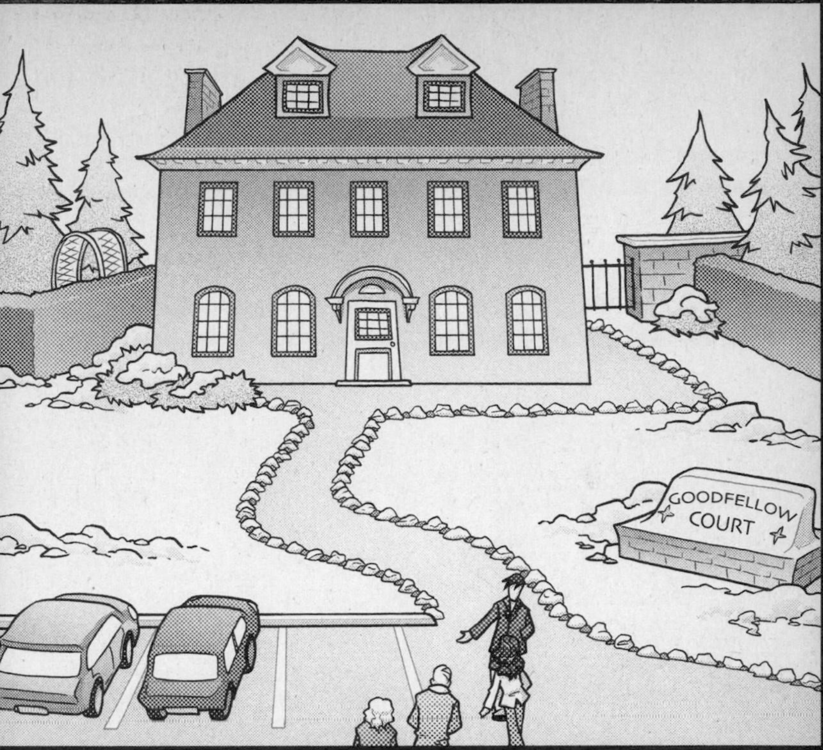
GOODFELLOW
COURT

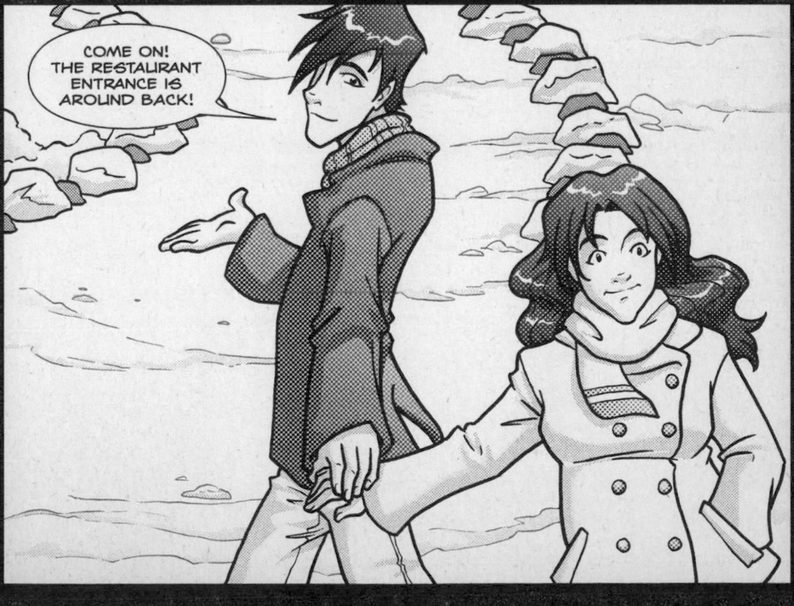
COME ON! THE RESTAURANT ENTRANCE IS AROUND BACK!

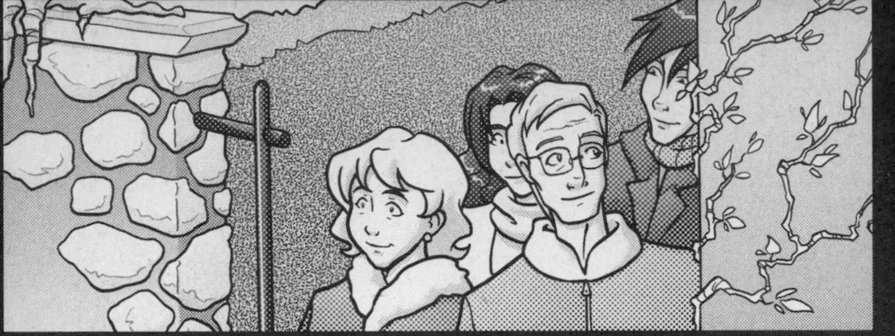

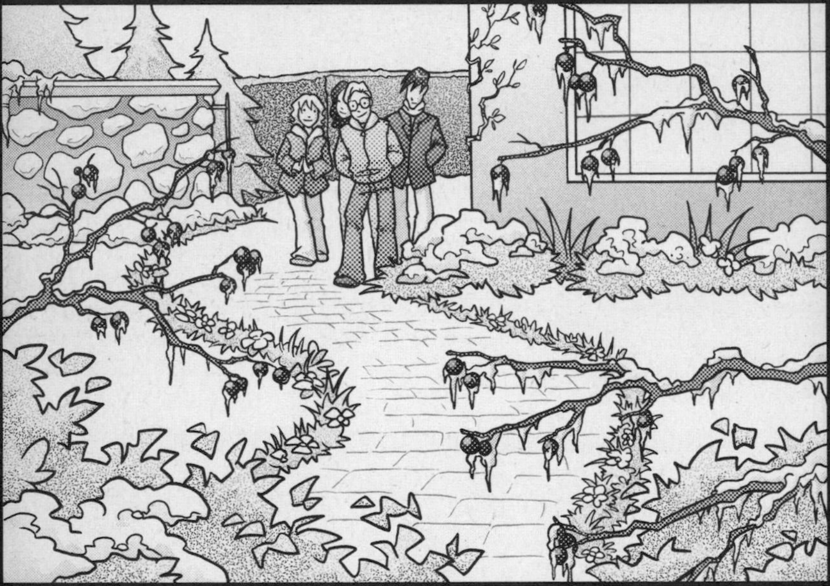

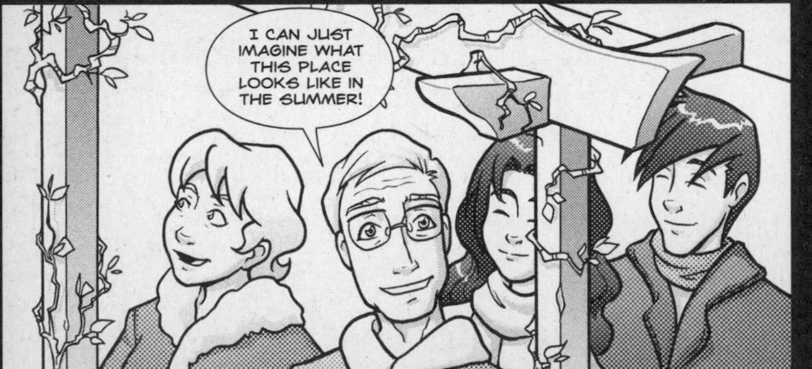
I CAN JUST IMAGINE WHAT THIS PLACE LOOKS LIKE IN THE SUMMER!

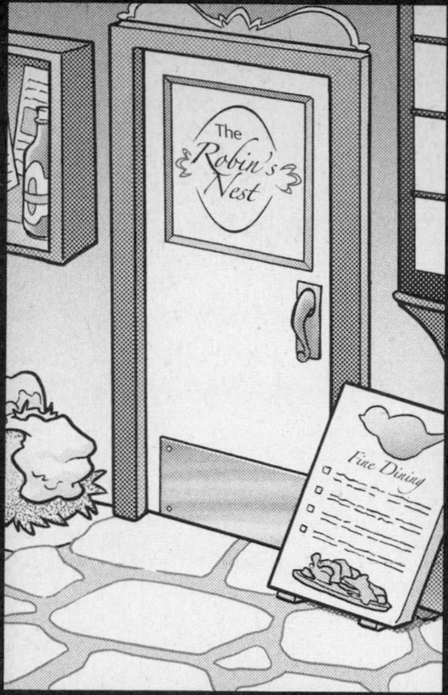
The Robin's Nest
Fine Dining

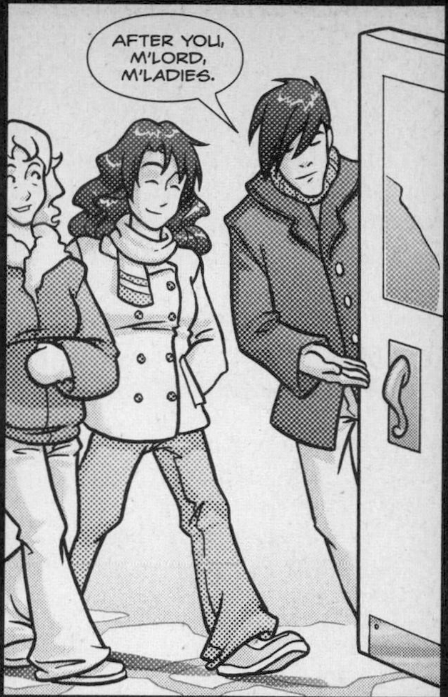
AFTER YOU, M'LORD, M'LADIES.

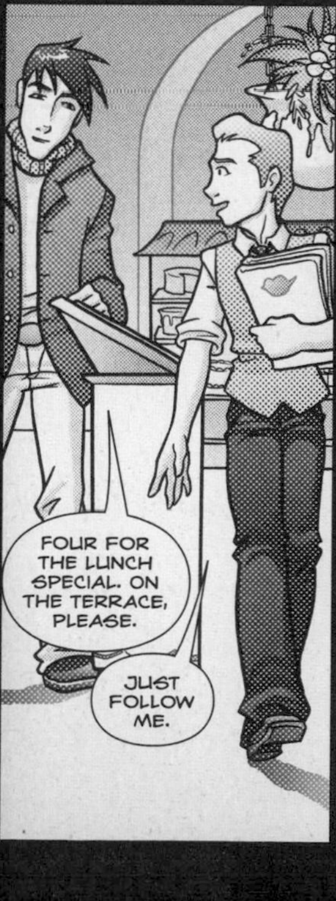
FOUR FOR THE LUNCH SPECIAL. ON THE TERRACE, PLEASE.
JUST FOLLOW ME.

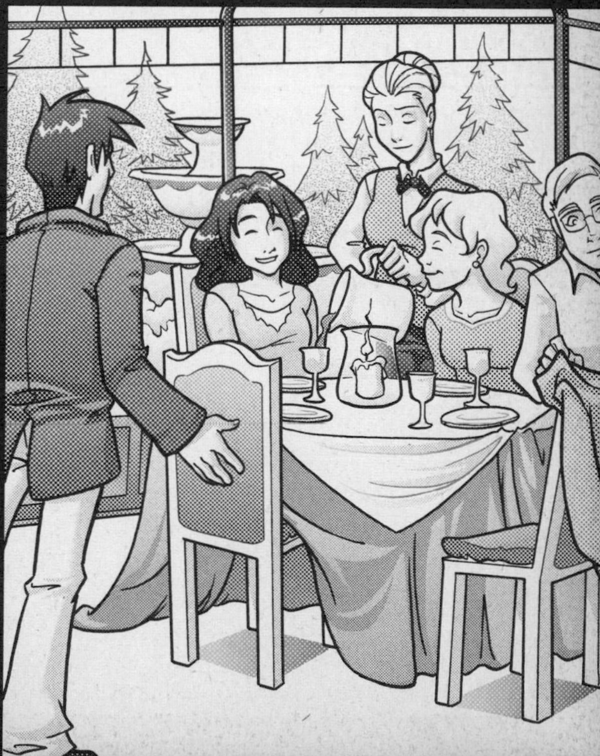

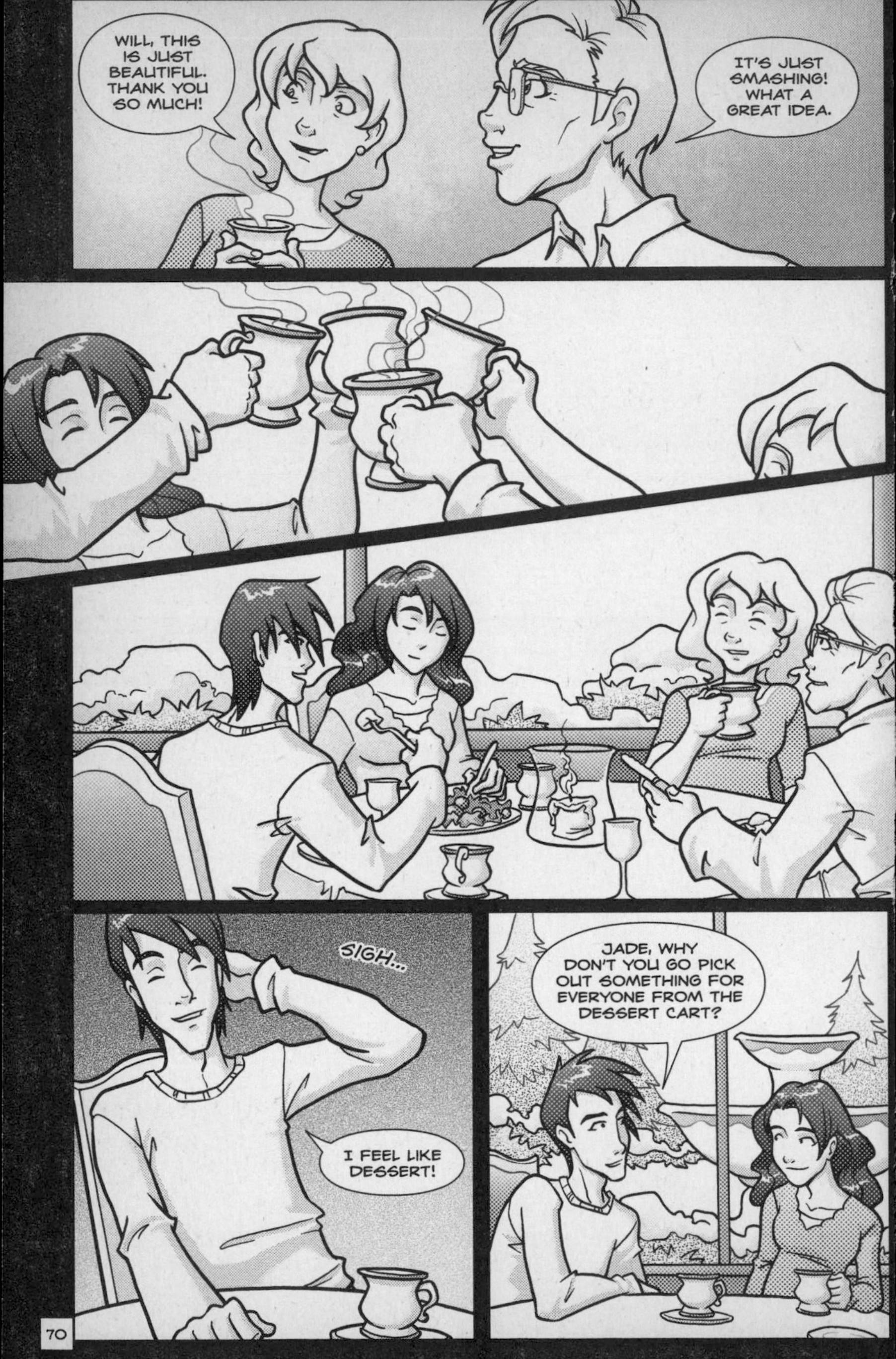
WILL, THIS IS JUST BEAUTIFUL. THANK YOU SO MUCH!
IT'S JUST SMASHING! WHAT A GREAT IDEA.
SIGH...
I FEEL LIKE DESSERT!
JADE, WHY DON'T YOU GO PICK OUT SOMETHING FOR EVERYONE FROM THE DESSERT CART?

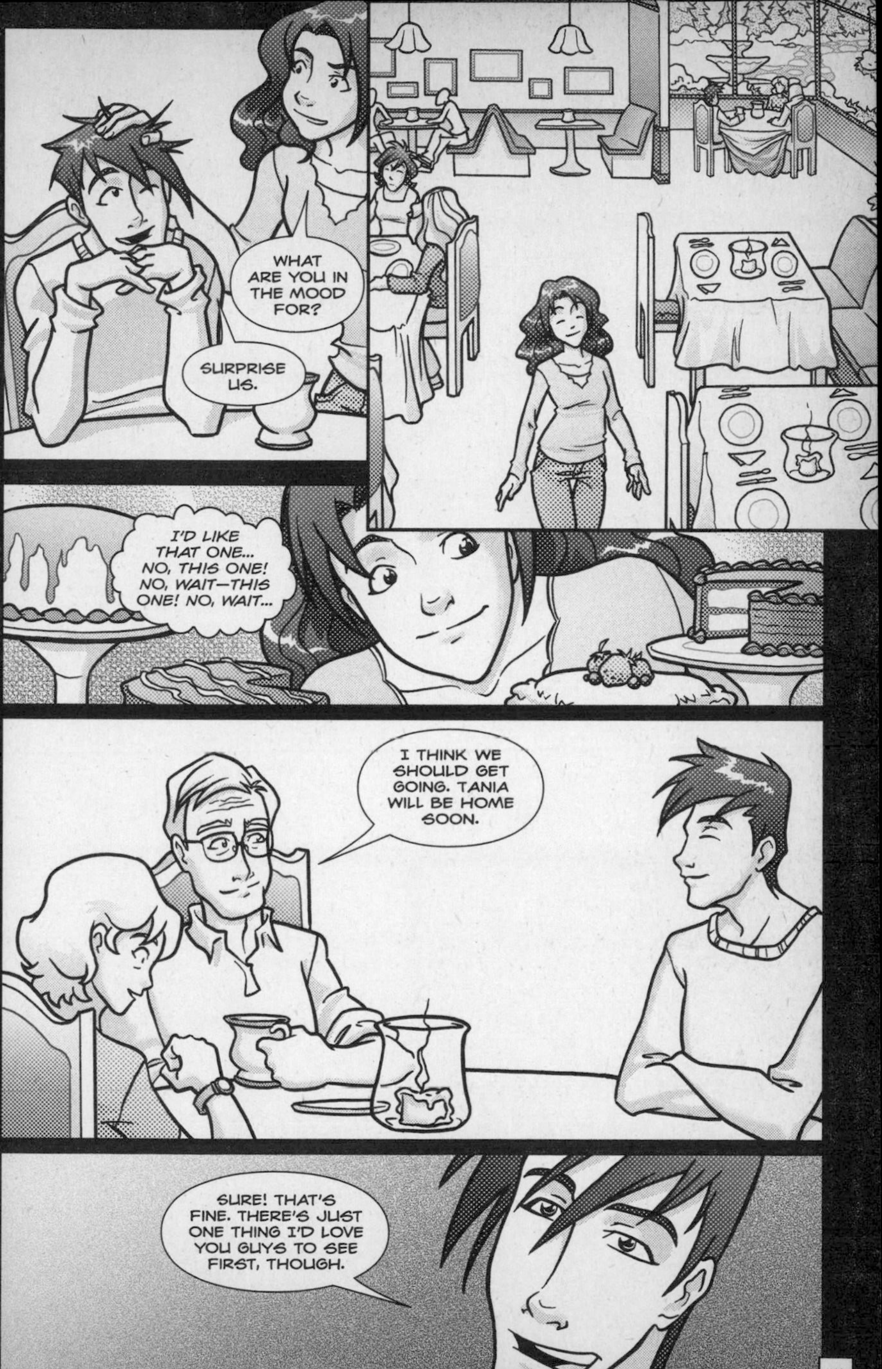
WHAT ARE YOU IN THE MOOD FOR?
SURPRISE US.
I'D LIKE THAT ONE... NO, THIS ONE! NO, WAIT—THIS ONE! NO, WAIT...
I THINK WE SHOULD GET GOING. TANIA WILL BE HOME SOON.
SURE! THAT'S FINE. THERE'S JUST ONE THING I'D LOVE YOU GUYS TO SEE FIRST, THOUGH.

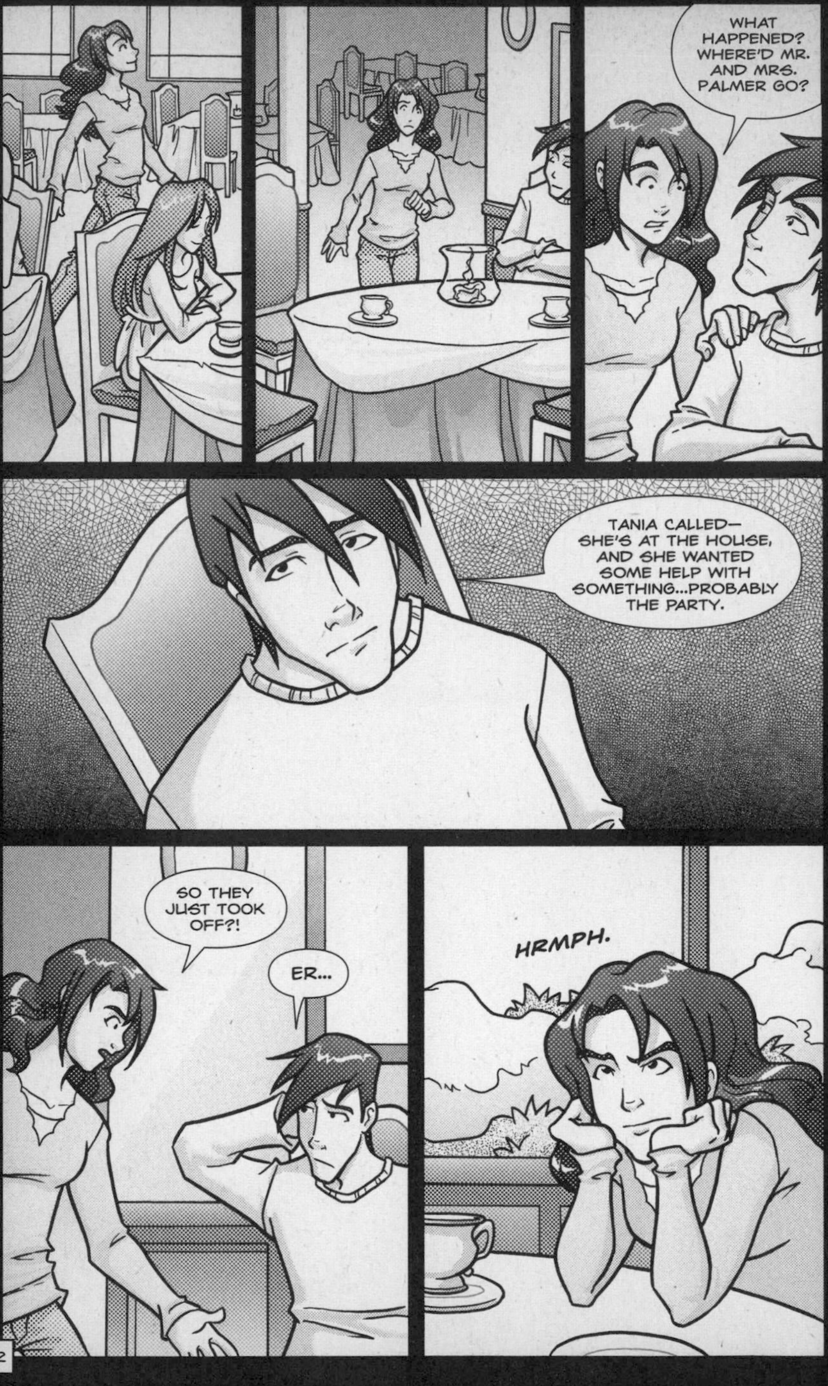
WHAT HAPPENED? WHERE'D MR. AND MRS. PALMER GO?
TANIA CALLED— SHE'S AT THE HOUSE, AND SHE WANTED SOME HELP WITH SOMETHING...PROBABLY THE PARTY.
SO THEY JUST TOOK OFF?!
ER...
HRMPH.

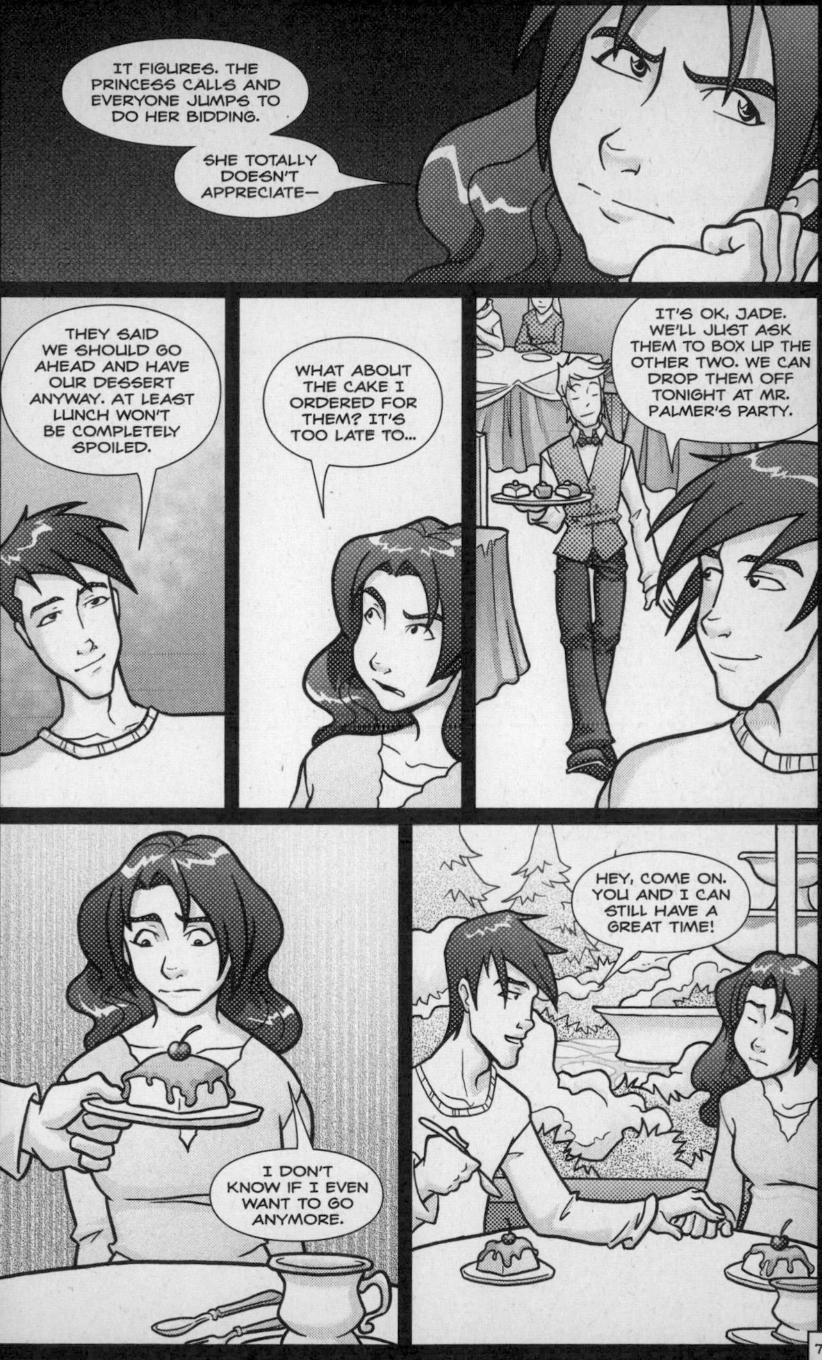
IT FIGURES. THE PRINCESS CALLS AND EVERYONE JUMPS TO DO HER BIDDING.
SHE TOTALLY DOESN'T APPRECIATE—
THEY SAID WE SHOULD GO AHEAD AND HAVE OUR DESSERT ANYWAY. AT LEAST LUNCH WON'T BE COMPLETELY SPOILED.
WHAT ABOUT THE CAKE I ORDERED FOR THEM? IT'S TOO LATE TO...
IT'S OK, JADE. WE'LL JUST ASK THEM TO BOX UP THE OTHER TWO. WE CAN DROP THEM OFF TONIGHT AT MR. PALMER'S PARTY.
I DON'T KNOW IF I EVEN WANT TO GO ANYMORE.
HEY, COME ON. YOU AND I CAN STILL HAVE A GREAT TIME!

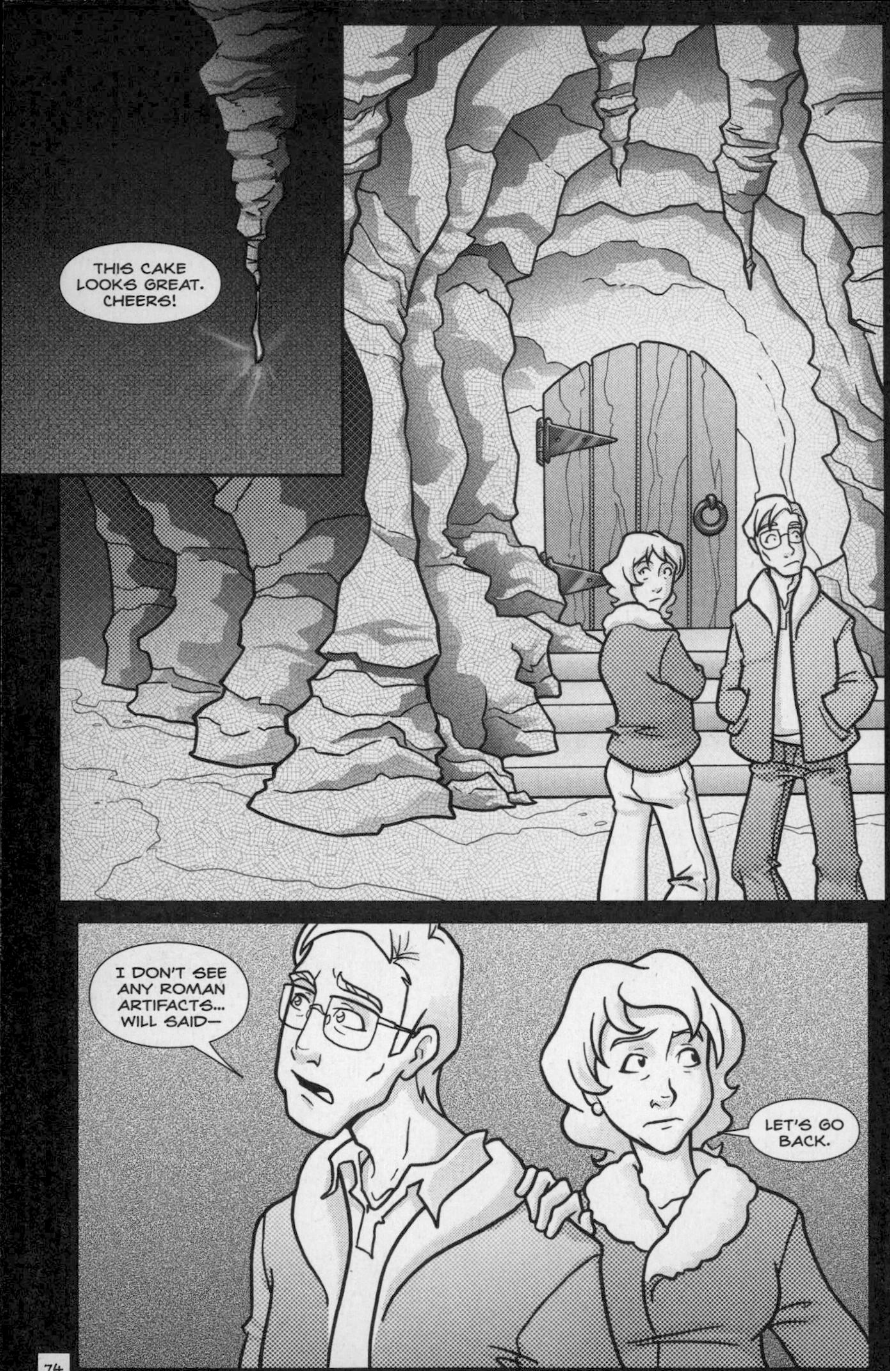
THIS CAKE LOOKS GREAT. CHEERS!
I DON'T SEE ANY ROMAN ARTIFACTS... WILL SAID—
LET'S GO BACK.

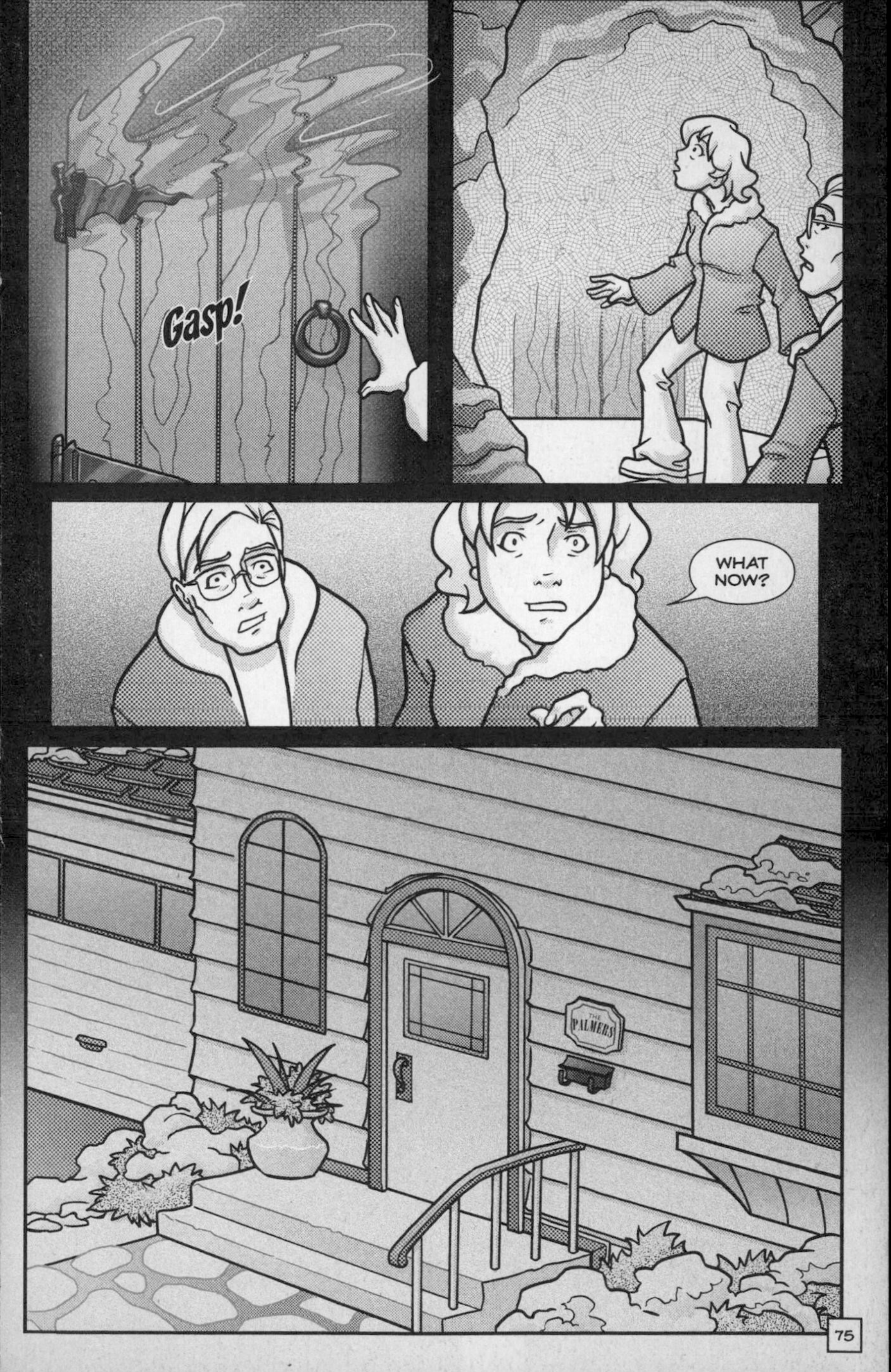
Gasp!
WHAT NOW?
THE PALMERS

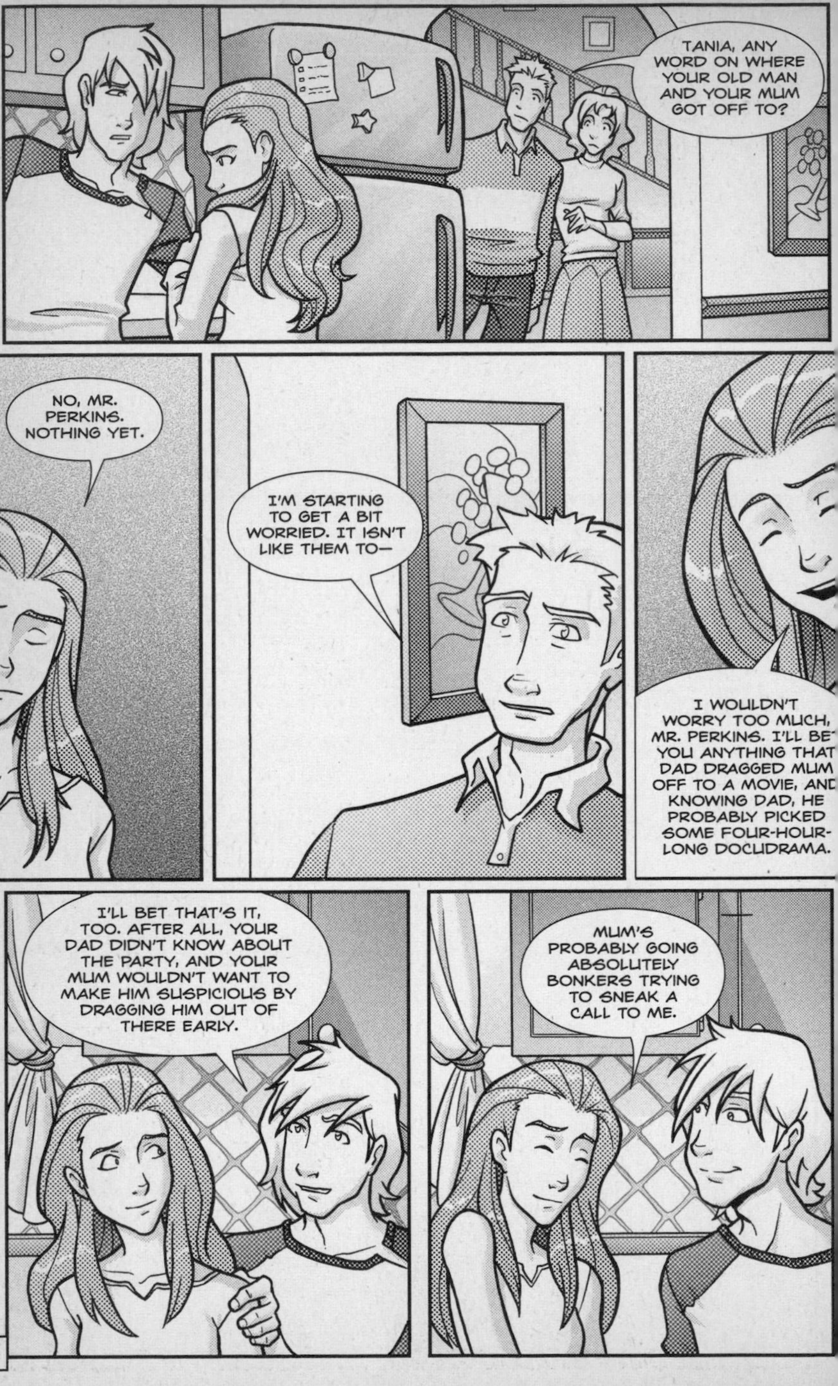
TANIA, ANY WORD ON WHERE YOUR OLD MAN AND YOUR MUM GOT OFF TO?
NO, MR. PERKINS. NOTHING YET.
I'M STARTING TO GET A BIT WORRIED. IT ISN'T LIKE THEM TO—
I WOULDN'T WORRY TOO MUCH, MR. PERKINS. I'LL BET YOU ANYTHING THAT DAD DRAGGED MUM OFF TO A MOVIE, AND KNOWING DAD, HE PROBABLY PICKED SOME FOUR-HOUR-LONG DOCUDRAMA.
I'LL BET THAT'S IT, TOO. AFTER ALL, YOUR DAD DIDN'T KNOW ABOUT THE PARTY, AND YOUR MUM WOULDN'T WANT TO MAKE HIM SUSPICIOUS BY DRAGGING HIM OUT OF THERE EARLY.
MUM'S PROBABLY GOING ABSOLUTELY BONKERS TRYING TO SNEAK A CALL TO ME.

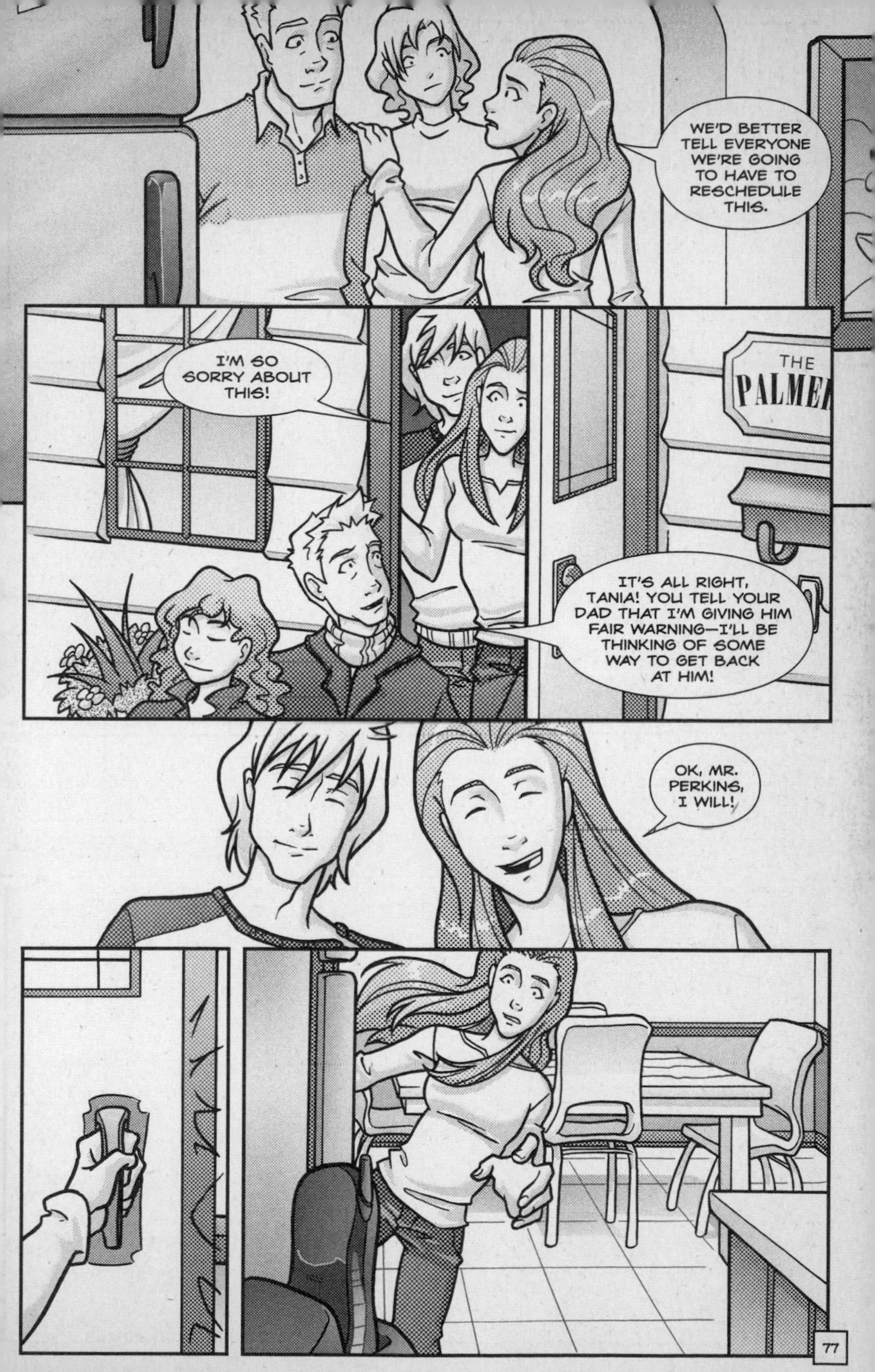
WE'D BETTER TELL EVERYONE WE'RE GOING TO HAVE TO RESCHEDULE THIS.
I'M SO SORRY ABOUT THIS!
THE PALMER
IT'S ALL RIGHT, TANIA! YOU TELL YOUR DAD THAT I'M GIVING HIM FAIR WARNING—I'LL BE THINKING OF SOME WAY TO GET BACK AT HIM!
OK, MR. PERKINS, I WILL!

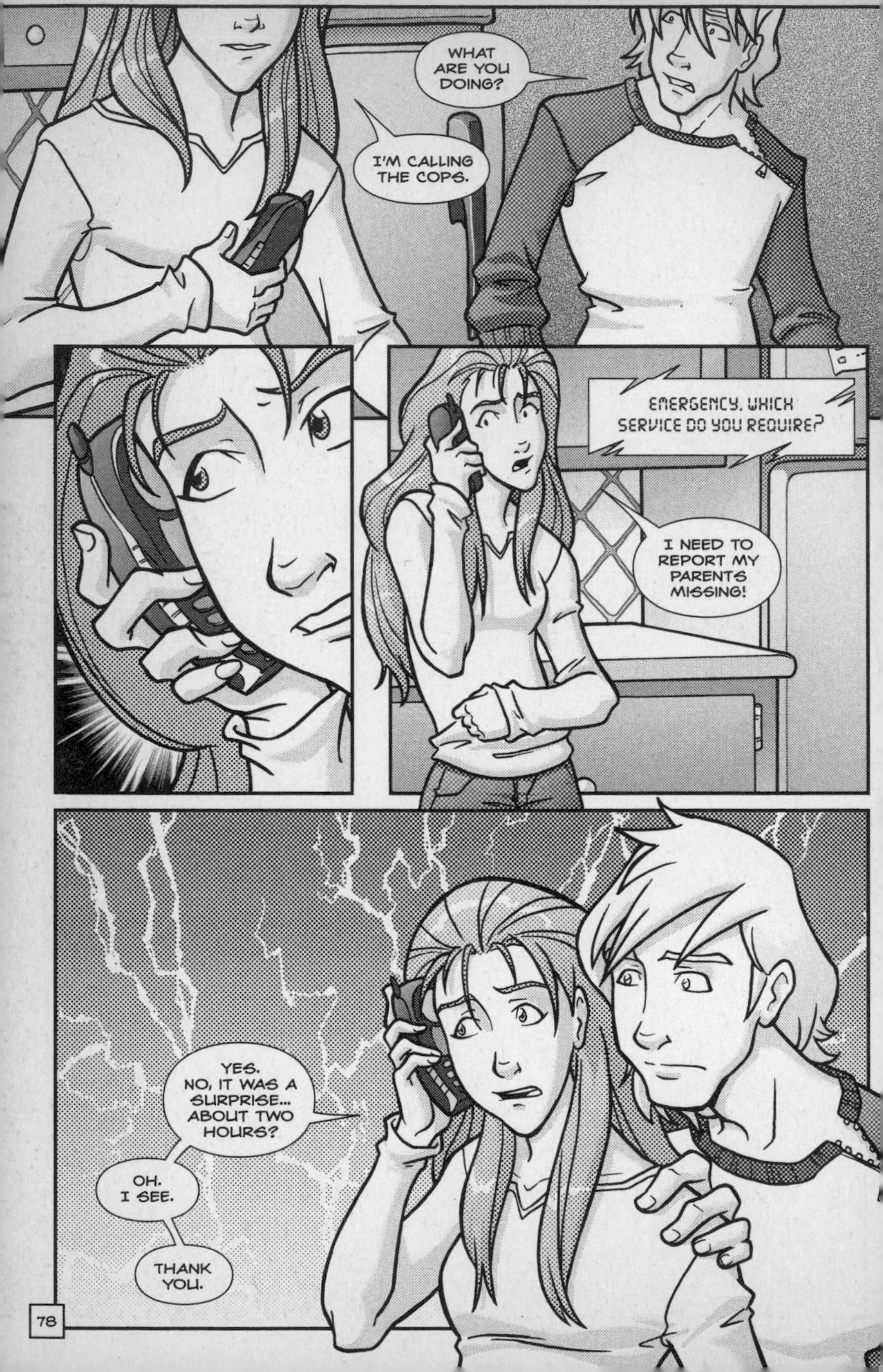
WHAT ARE YOU DOING?
I'M CALLING THE COPS.
EMERGENCY, WHICH SERVICE DO YOU REQUIRE?
I NEED TO REPORT MY PARENTS MISSING!
YES. NO, IT WAS A SURPRISE... ABOUT TWO HOURS?
OH. I SEE.
THANK YOU.

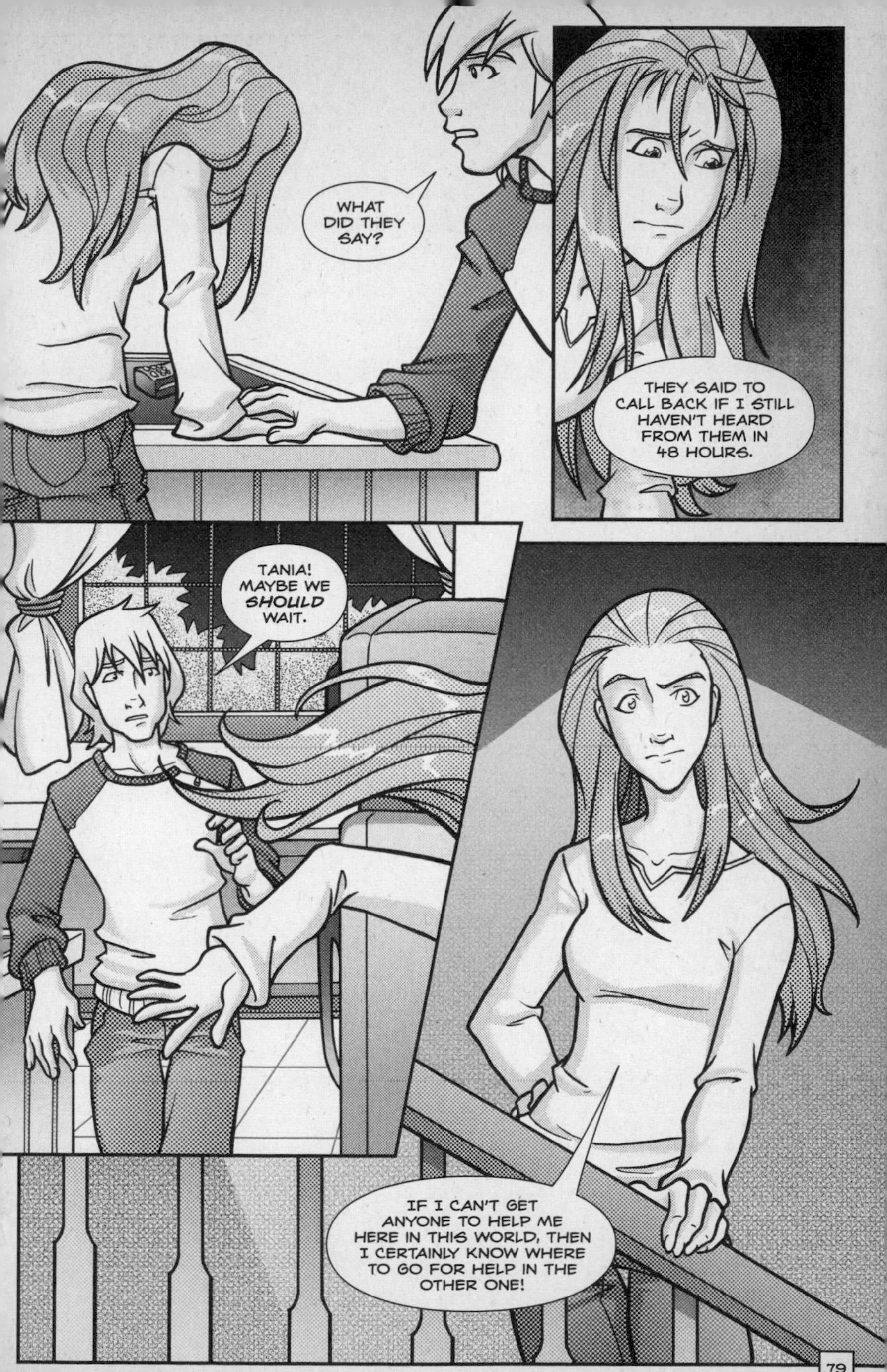
WHAT DID THEY SAY?
THEY SAID TO CALL BACK IF I STILL HAVEN'T HEARD FROM THEM IN 48 HOURS.
TANIA! MAYBE WE *SHOULD* WAIT.
IF I CAN'T GET ANYONE TO HELP ME HERE IN THIS WORLD, THEN I CERTAINLY KNOW WHERE TO GO FOR HELP IN THE OTHER ONE!

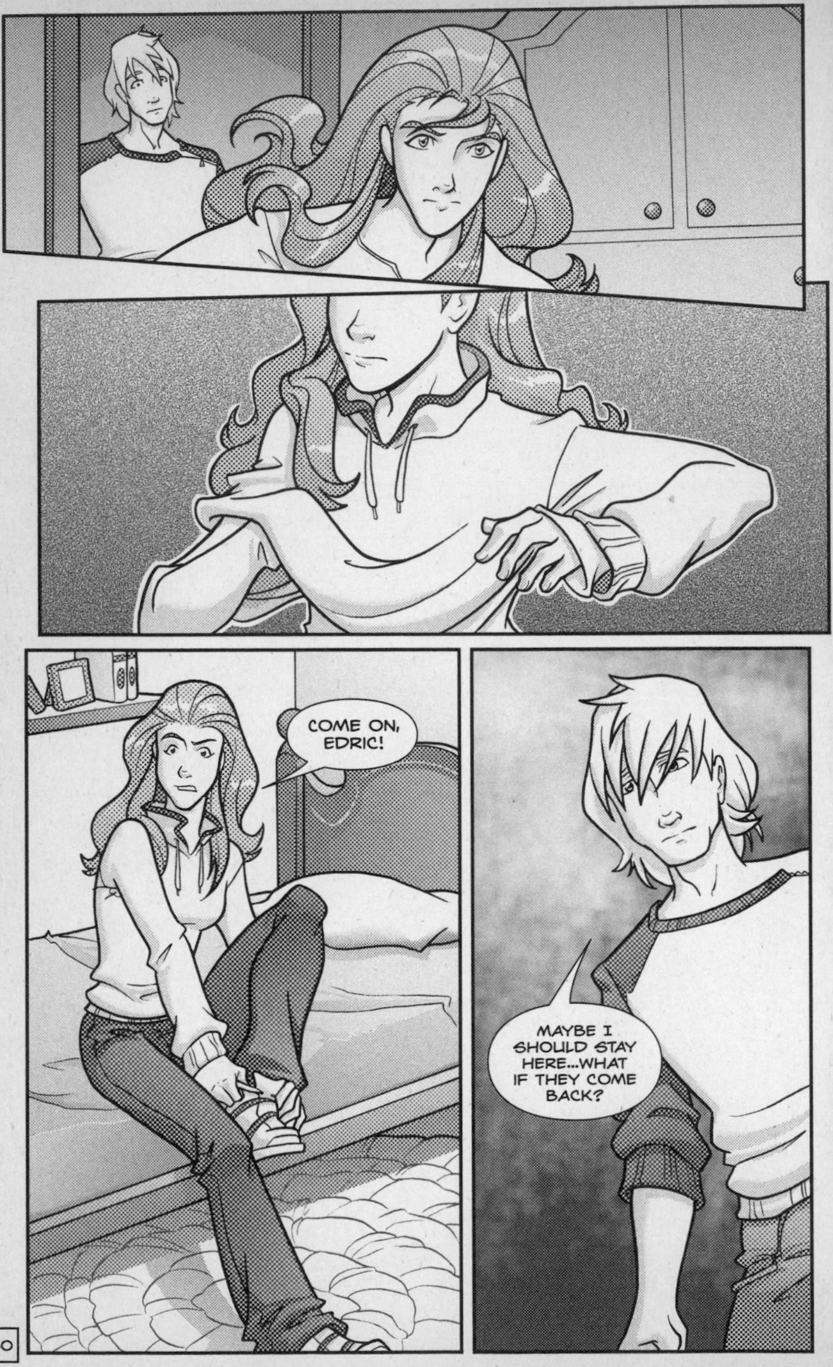
COME ON, EDRIC!
MAYBE I SHOULD STAY HERE...WHAT IF THEY COME BACK?

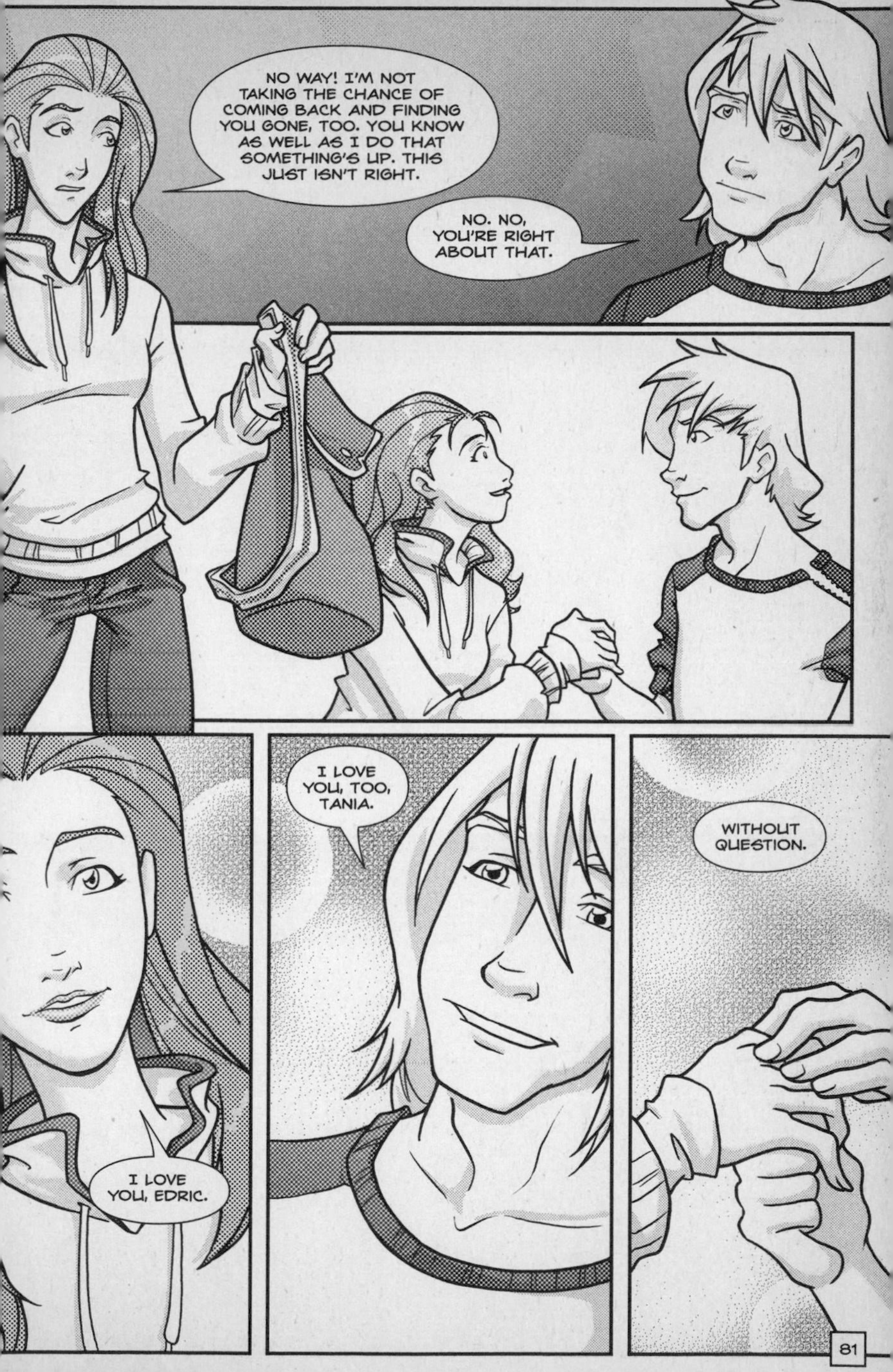
NO WAY! I'M NOT TAKING THE CHANCE OF COMING BACK AND FINDING YOU GONE, TOO. YOU KNOW AS WELL AS I DO THAT SOMETHING'S UP. THIS JUST ISN'T RIGHT.
NO. NO, YOU'RE RIGHT ABOUT THAT.
I LOVE YOU, EDRIC.
I LOVE YOU, TOO, TANIA.
WITHOUT QUESTION.

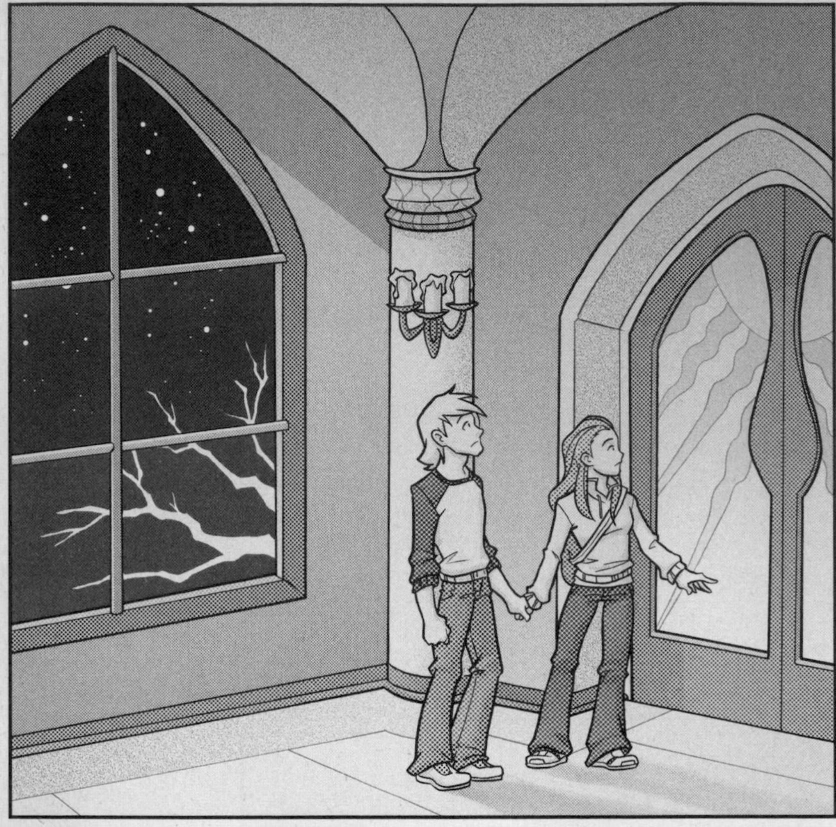
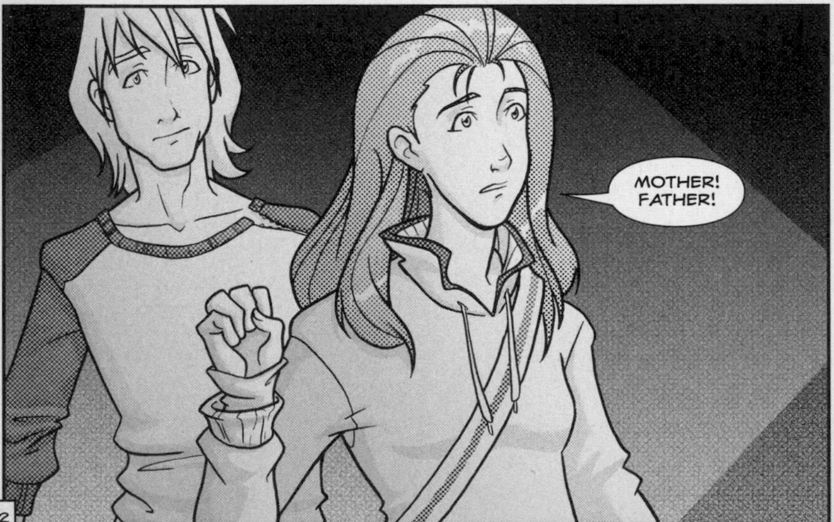
MOTHER! FATHER!

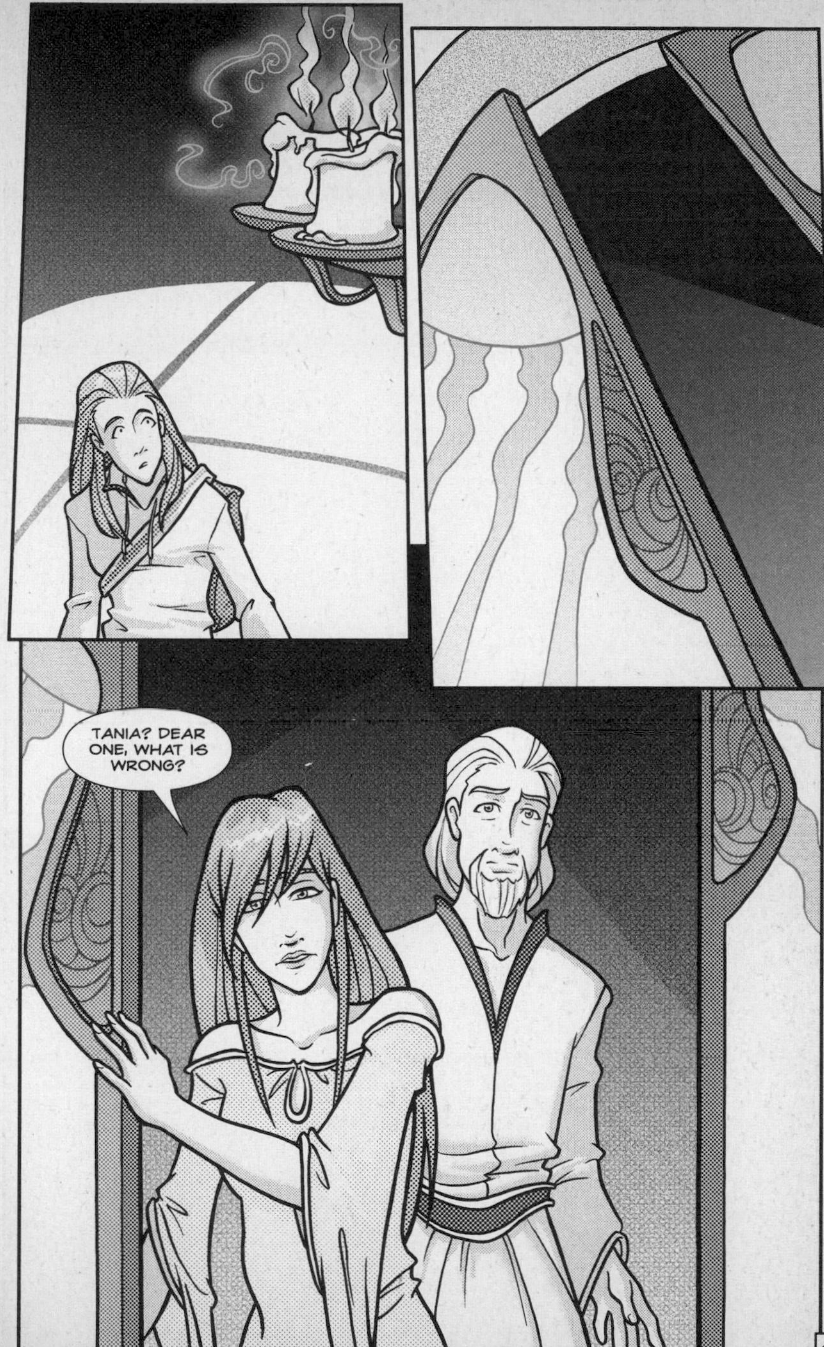
TANIA? DEAR ONE, WHAT IS WRONG?

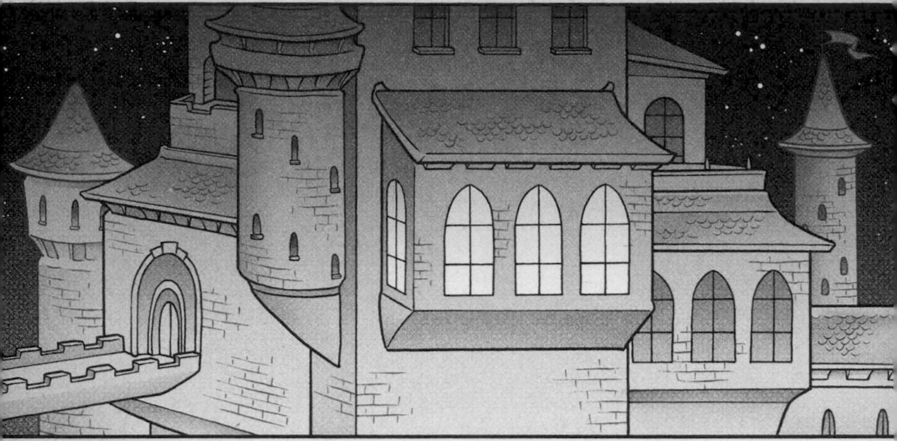
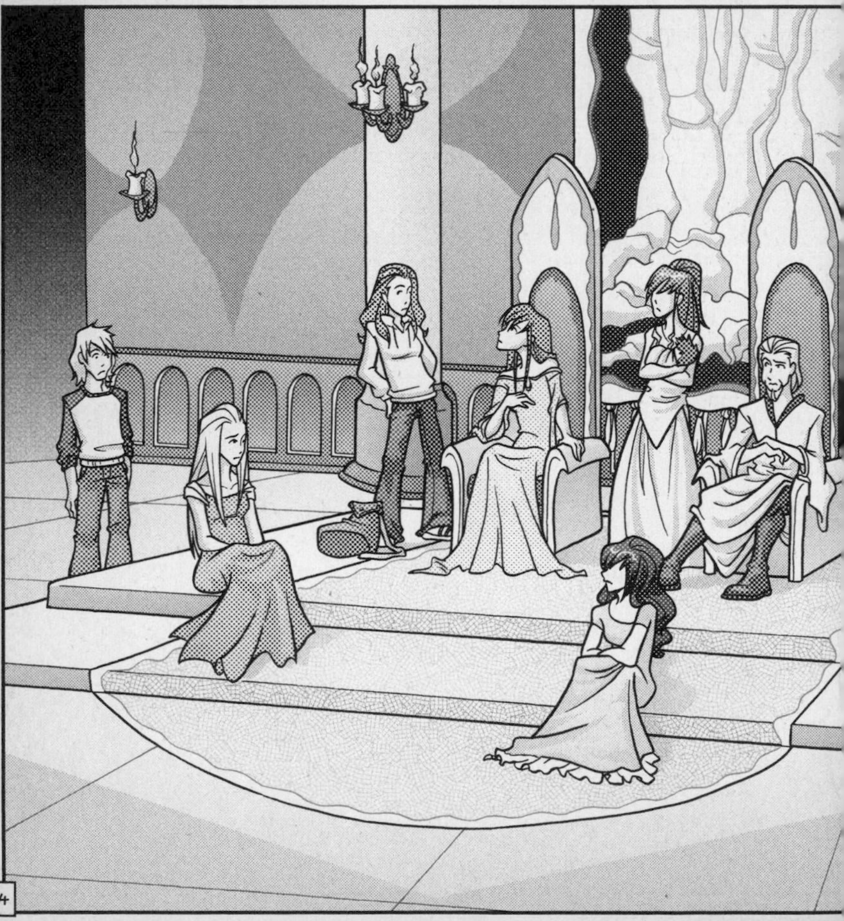

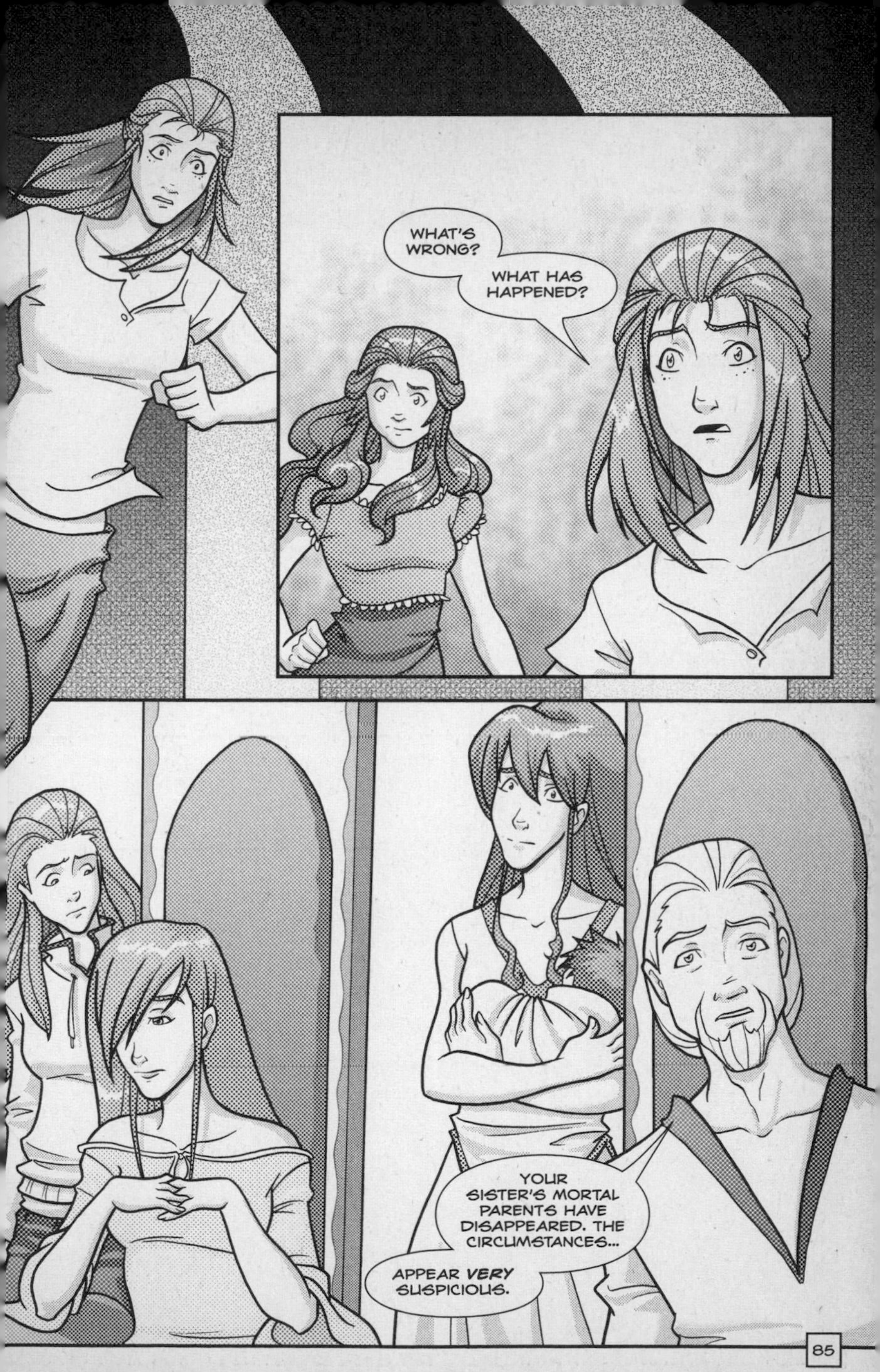
WHAT'S WRONG?
WHAT HAS HAPPENED?
YOUR SISTER'S MORTAL PARENTS HAVE DISAPPEARED. THE CIRCUMSTANCES...
APPEAR *VERY* SUSPICIOUS.

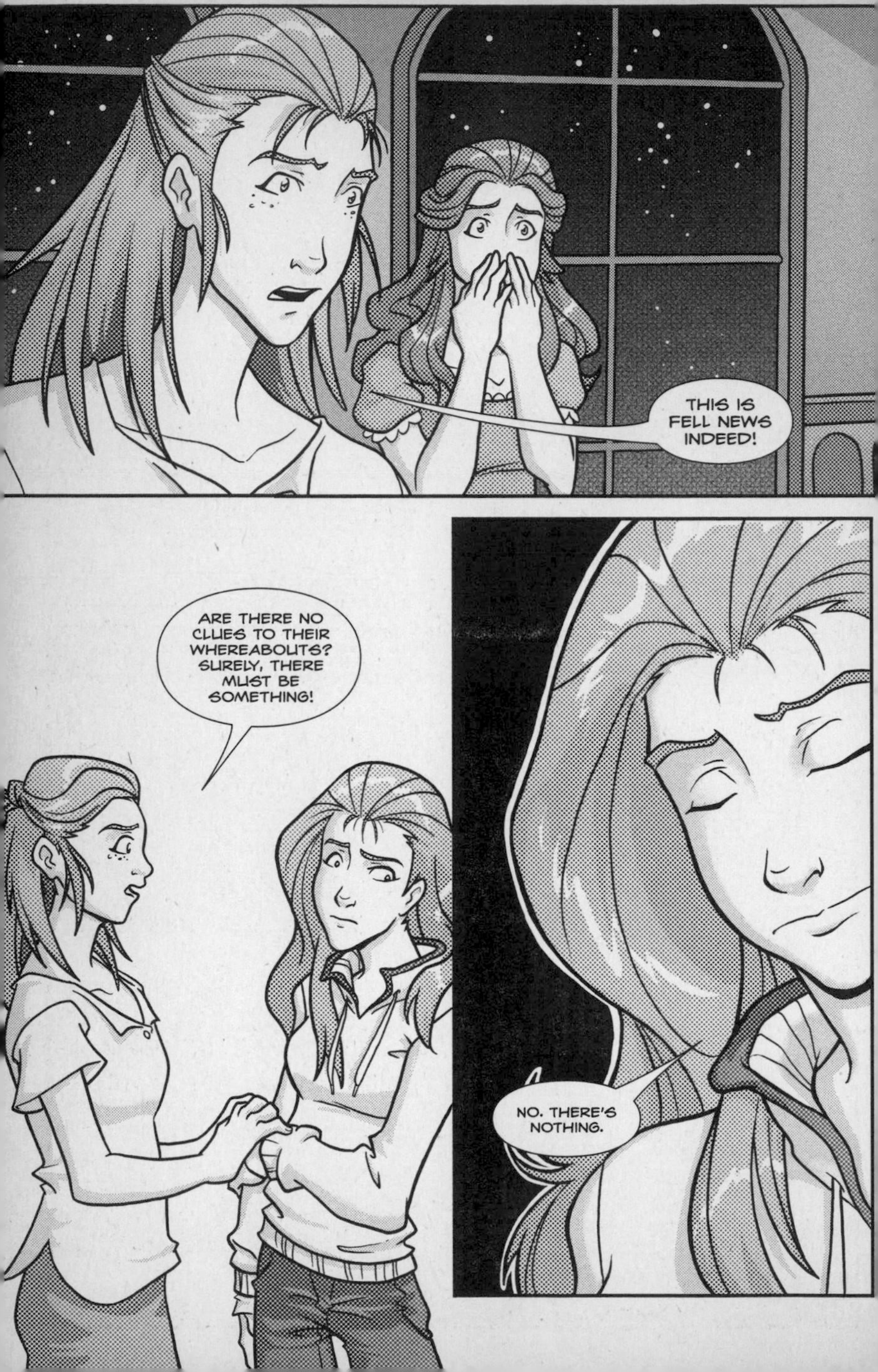
THIS IS FELL NEWS INDEED!
ARE THERE NO CLUES TO THEIR WHEREABOUTS? SURELY, THERE MUST BE SOMETHING!
NO. THERE'S NOTHING.

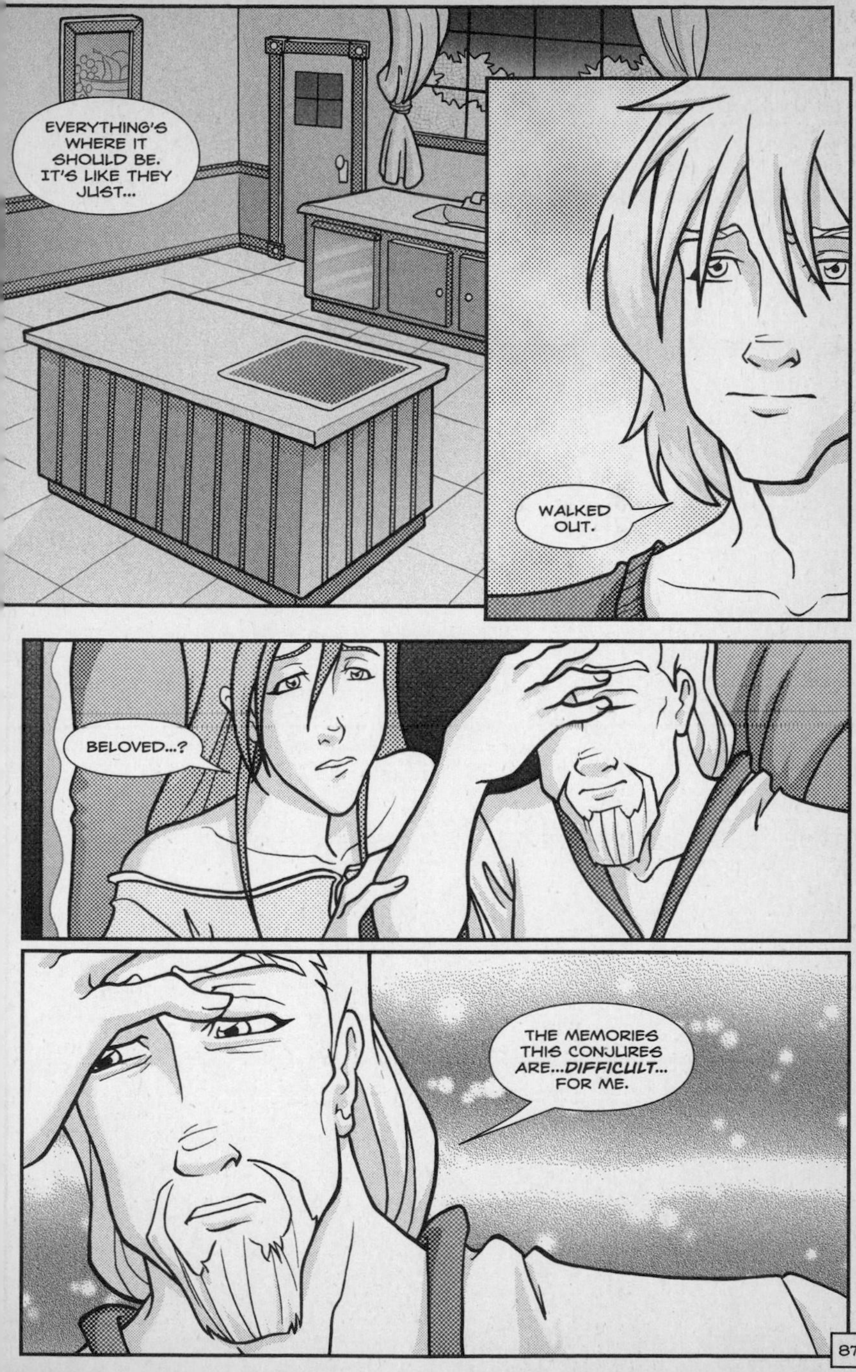
EVERYTHING'S WHERE IT SHOULD BE. IT'S LIKE THEY JUST...
WALKED OUT.
BELOVED...?
THE MEMORIES THIS CONJURES ARE...*DIFFICULT*... FOR ME.

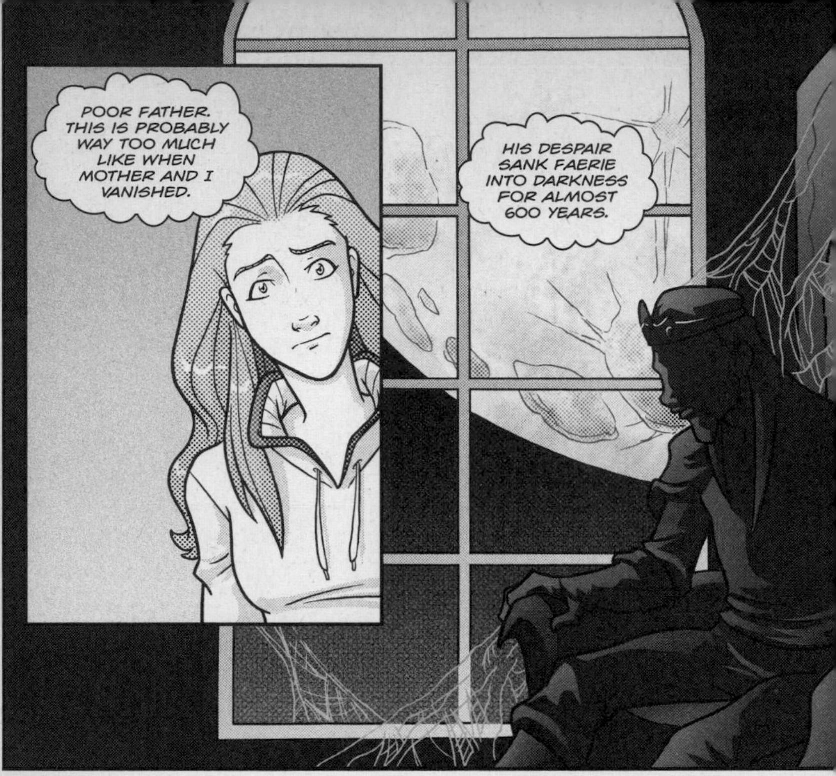
POOR FATHER. THIS IS PROBABLY WAY TOO MUCH LIKE WHEN MOTHER AND I VANISHED.
HIS DESPAIR SANK FAERIE INTO DARKNESS FOR ALMOST 600 YEARS.

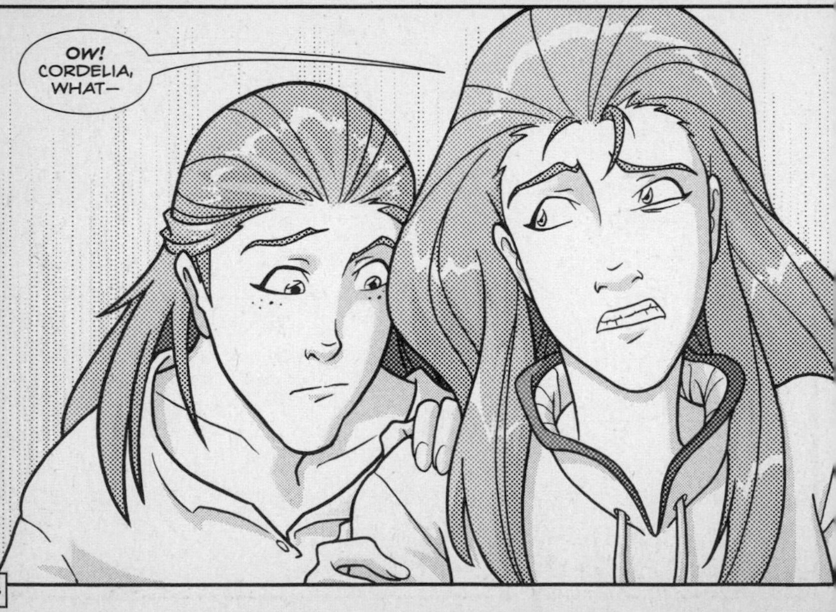
OW! CORDELIA, WHAT—

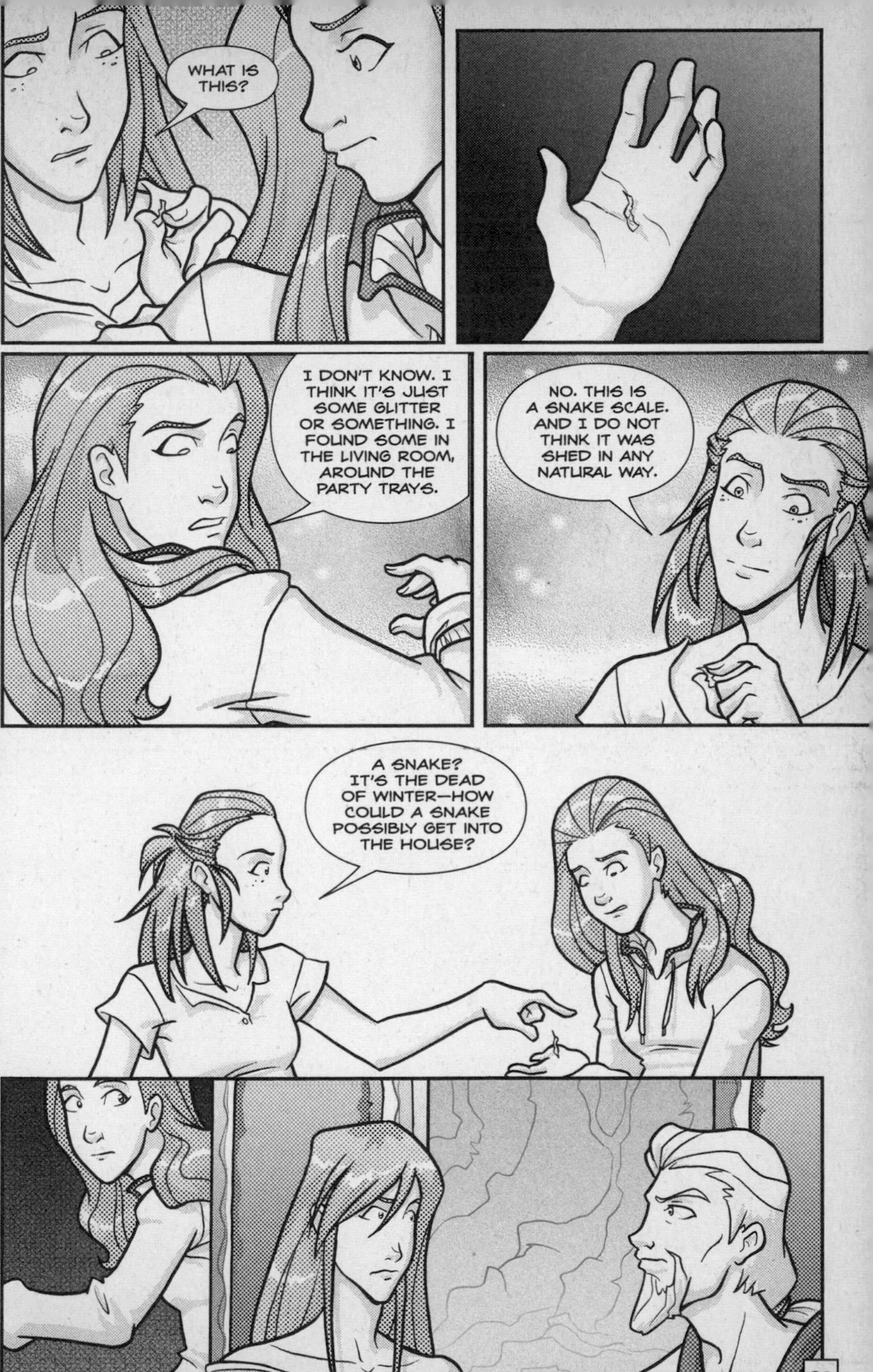
WHAT IS THIS?
I DON'T KNOW. I THINK IT'S JUST SOME GLITTER OR SOMETHING. I FOUND SOME IN THE LIVING ROOM, AROUND THE PARTY TRAYS.
NO. THIS IS A SNAKE SCALE. AND I DO NOT THINK IT WAS SHED IN ANY NATURAL WAY.
A SNAKE? IT'S THE DEAD OF WINTER—HOW COULD A SNAKE POSSIBLY GET INTO THE HOUSE?

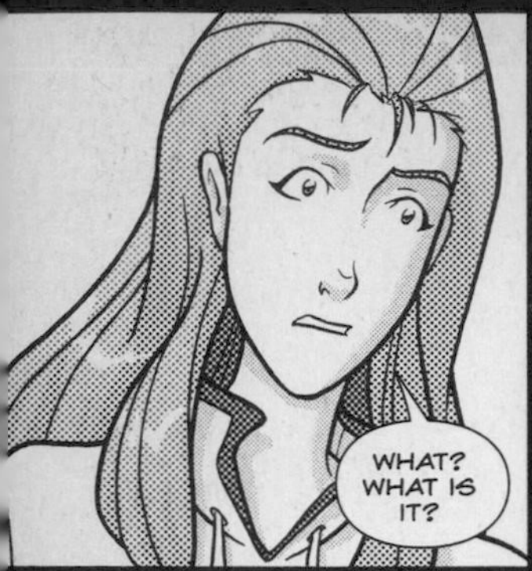
WHAT? WHAT IS IT?

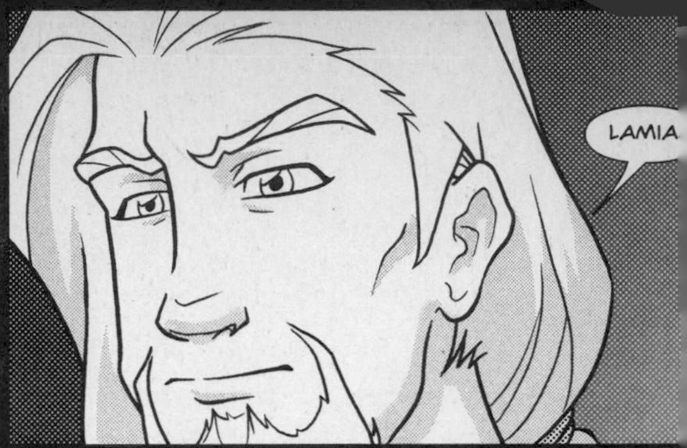
LAMIA.

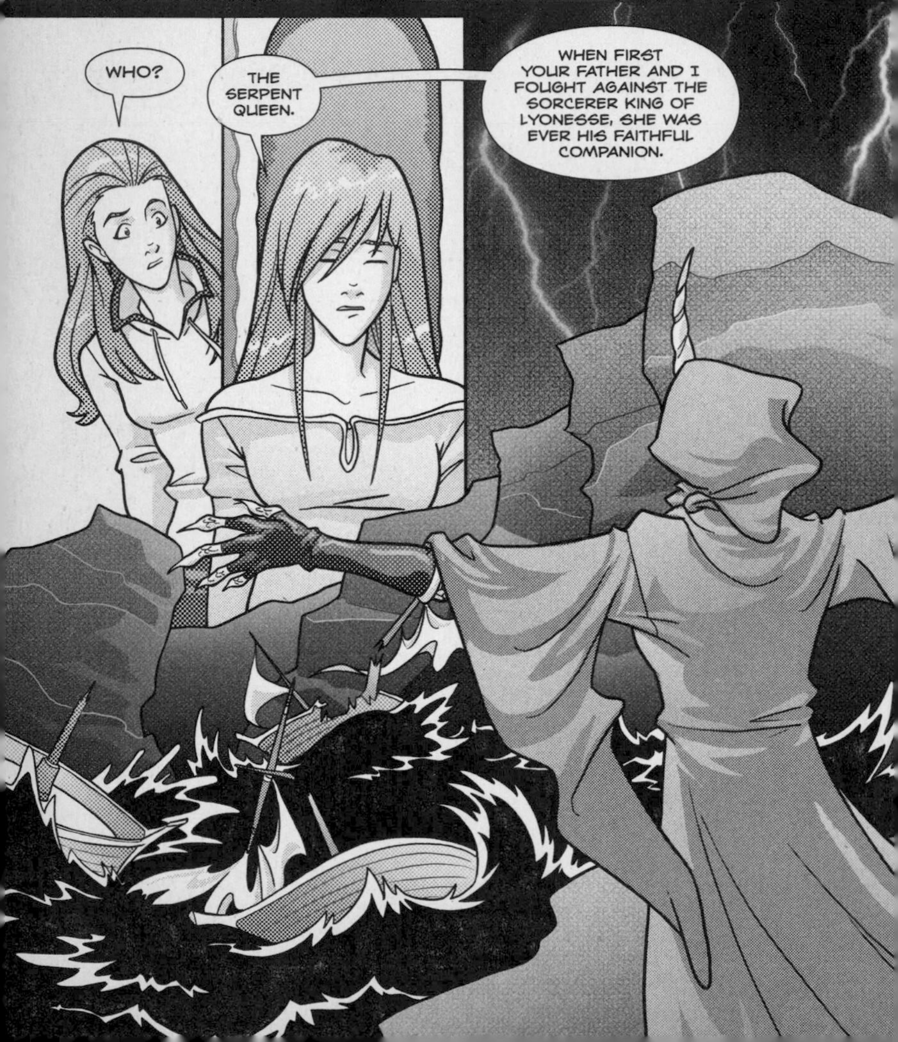
WHO?
THE SERPENT QUEEN.
WHEN FIRST YOUR FATHER AND I FOUGHT AGAINST THE SORCERER KING OF LYONESSE, SHE WAS EVER HIS FAITHFUL COMPANION.

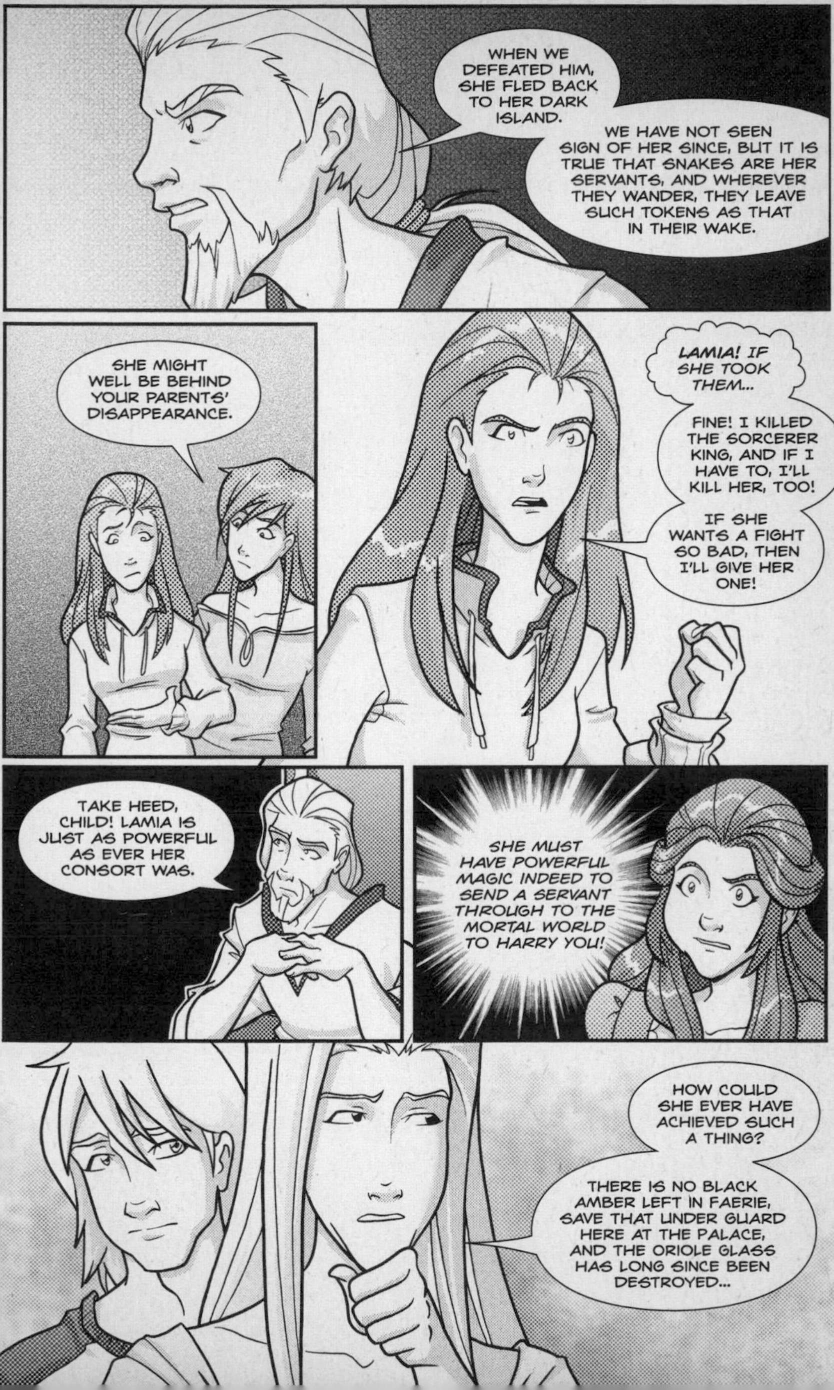
WHEN WE DEFEATED HIM, SHE FLED BACK TO HER DARK ISLAND.
WE HAVE NOT SEEN SIGN OF HER SINCE, BUT IT IS TRUE THAT SNAKES ARE HER SERVANTS, AND WHEREVER THEY WANDER, THEY LEAVE SUCH TOKENS AS THAT IN THEIR WAKE.
SHE MIGHT WELL BE BEHIND YOUR PARENTS' DISAPPEARANCE.
LAMIA! IF SHE TOOK THEM...
FINE! I KILLED THE SORCERER KING, AND IF I HAVE TO, I'LL KILL HER, TOO!
IF SHE WANTS A FIGHT SO BAD, THEN I'LL GIVE HER ONE!
TAKE HEED, CHILD! LAMIA IS JUST AS POWERFUL AS EVER HER CONSORT WAS.
SHE MUST HAVE POWERFUL MAGIC INDEED TO SEND A SERVANT THROUGH TO THE MORTAL WORLD TO HARRY YOU!
HOW COULD SHE EVER HAVE ACHIEVED SUCH A THING?
THERE IS NO BLACK AMBER LEFT IN FAERIE, SAVE THAT UNDER GUARD HERE AT THE PALACE, AND THE ORIOLE GLASS HAS LONG SINCE BEEN DESTROYED...

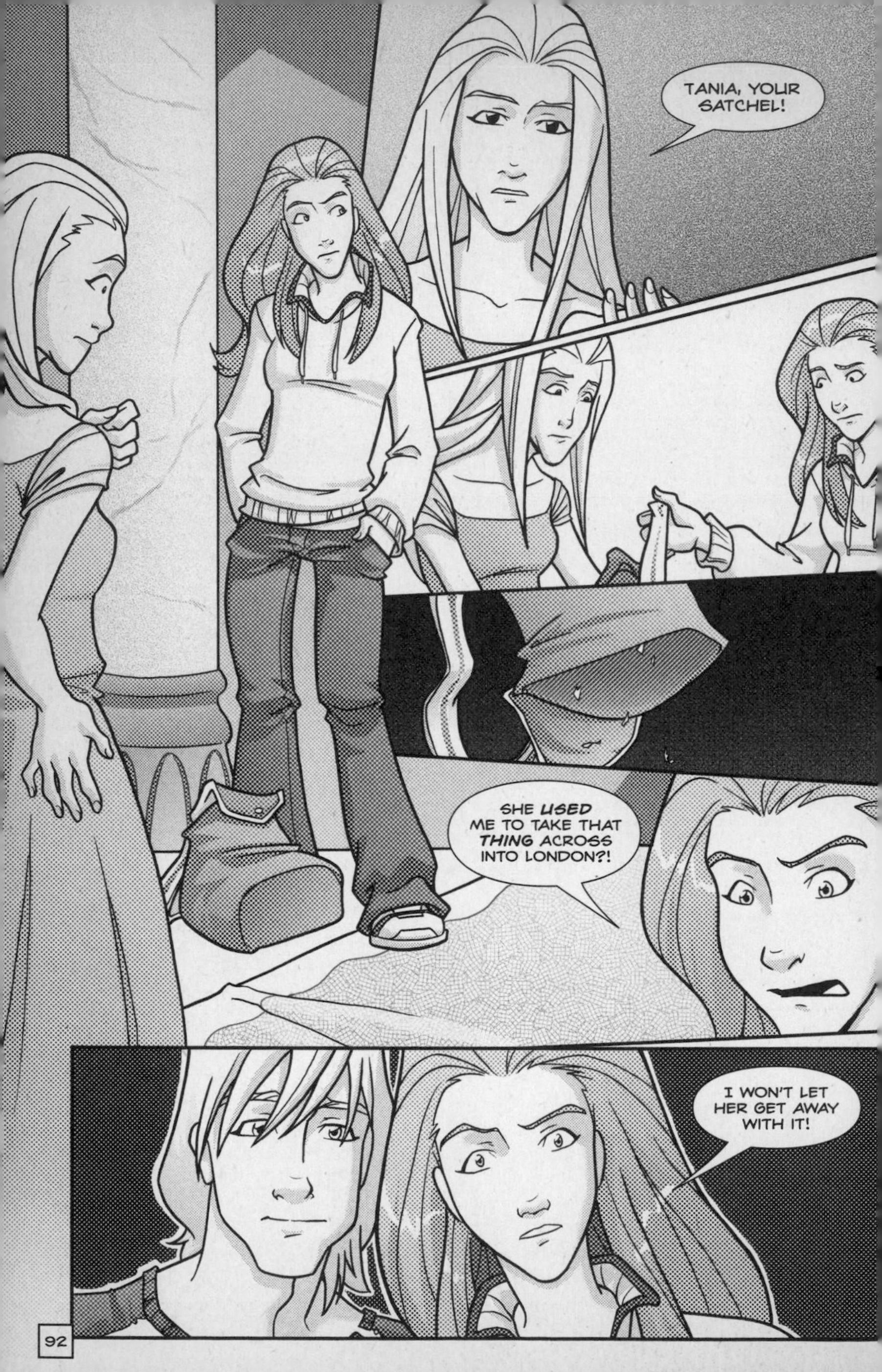
TANIA, YOUR SATCHEL!
SHE *USED* ME TO TAKE THAT *THING* ACROSS INTO LONDON?!
I WON'T LET HER GET AWAY WITH IT!

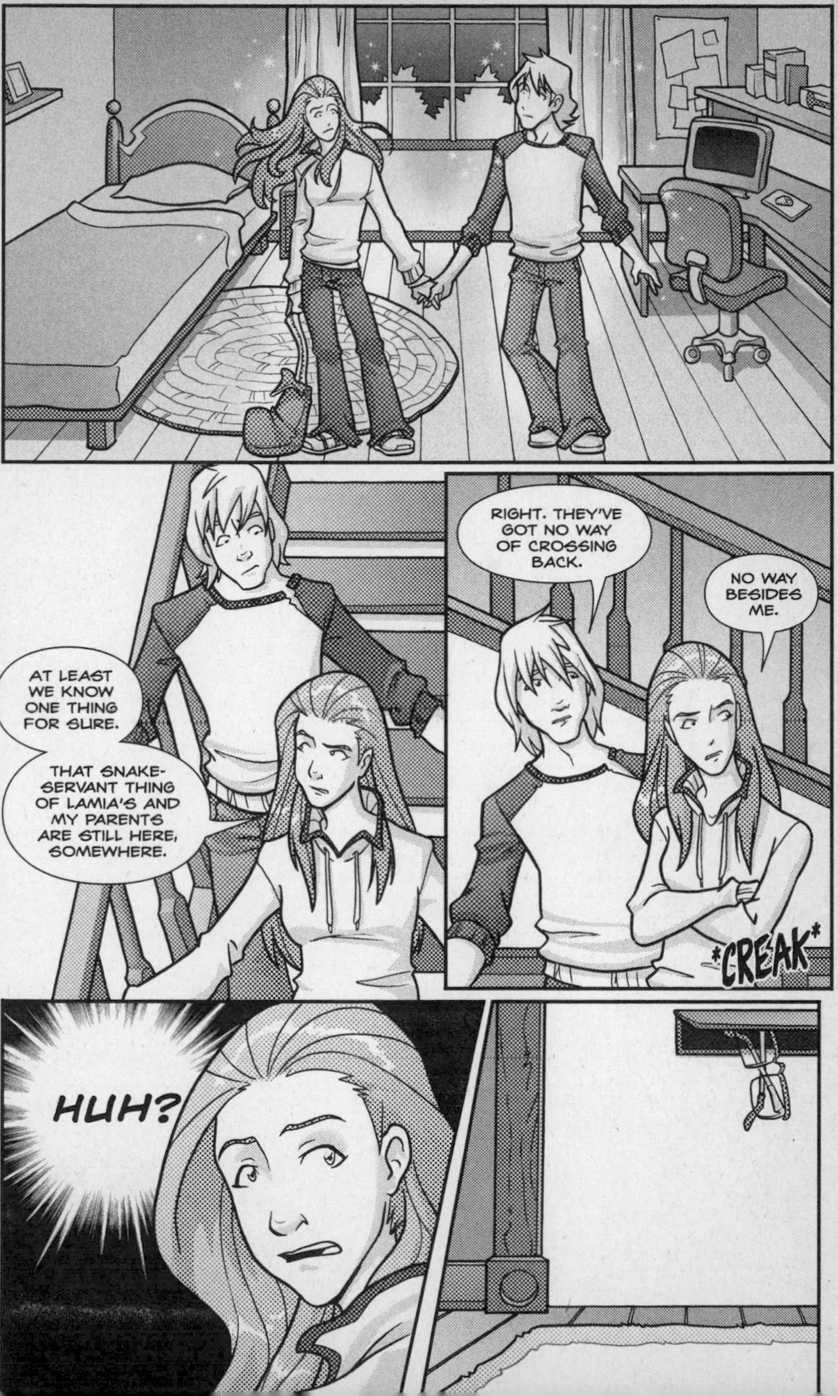
AT LEAST WE KNOW ONE THING FOR SURE.
THAT SNAKE-SERVANT THING OF LAMIA'S AND MY PARENTS ARE STILL HERE, SOMEWHERE.
RIGHT. THEY'VE GOT NO WAY OF CROSSING BACK.
NO WAY BESIDES ME.
CREAK
HUH?

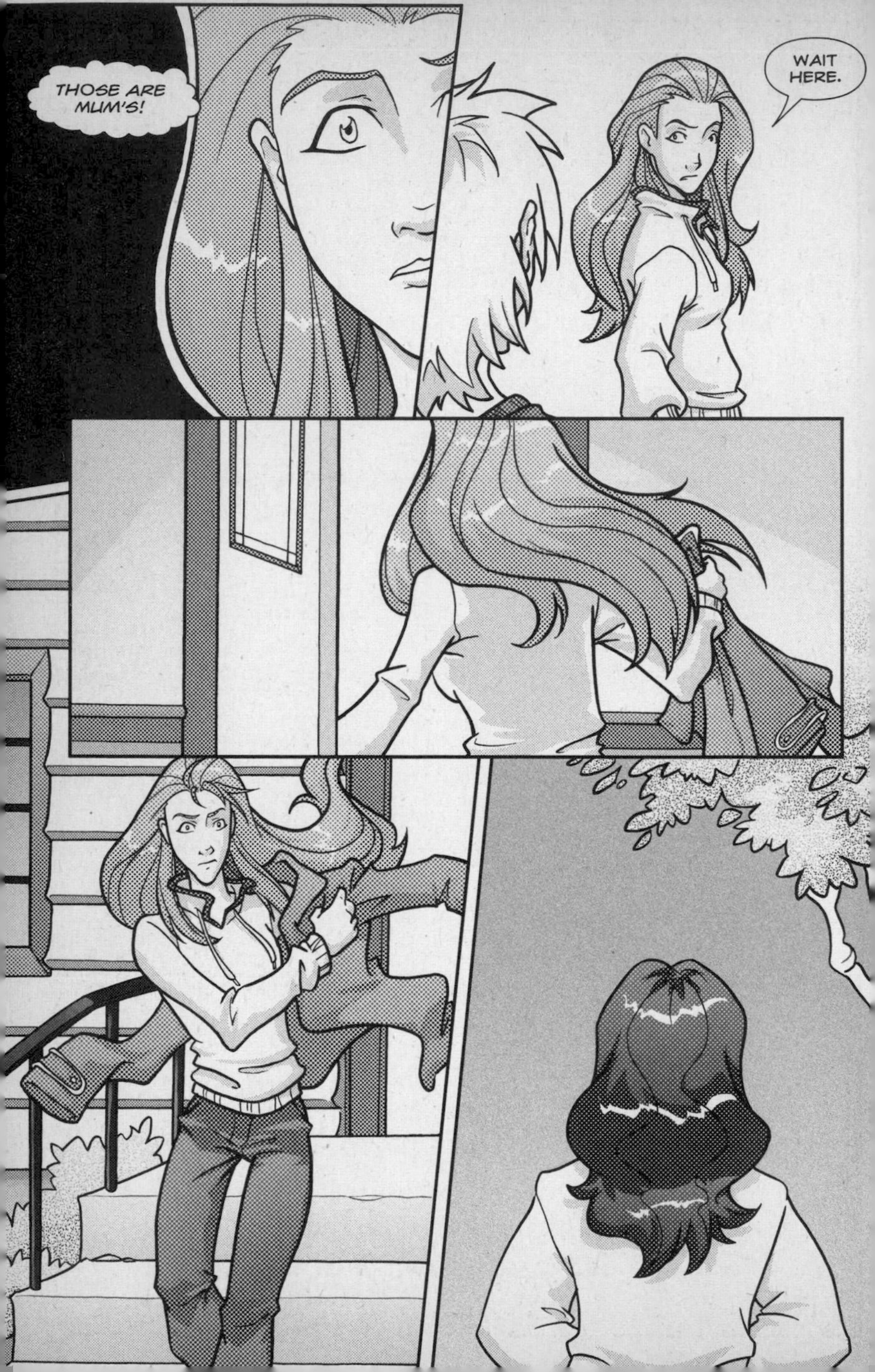
THOSE ARE MUM'S!
WAIT HERE.

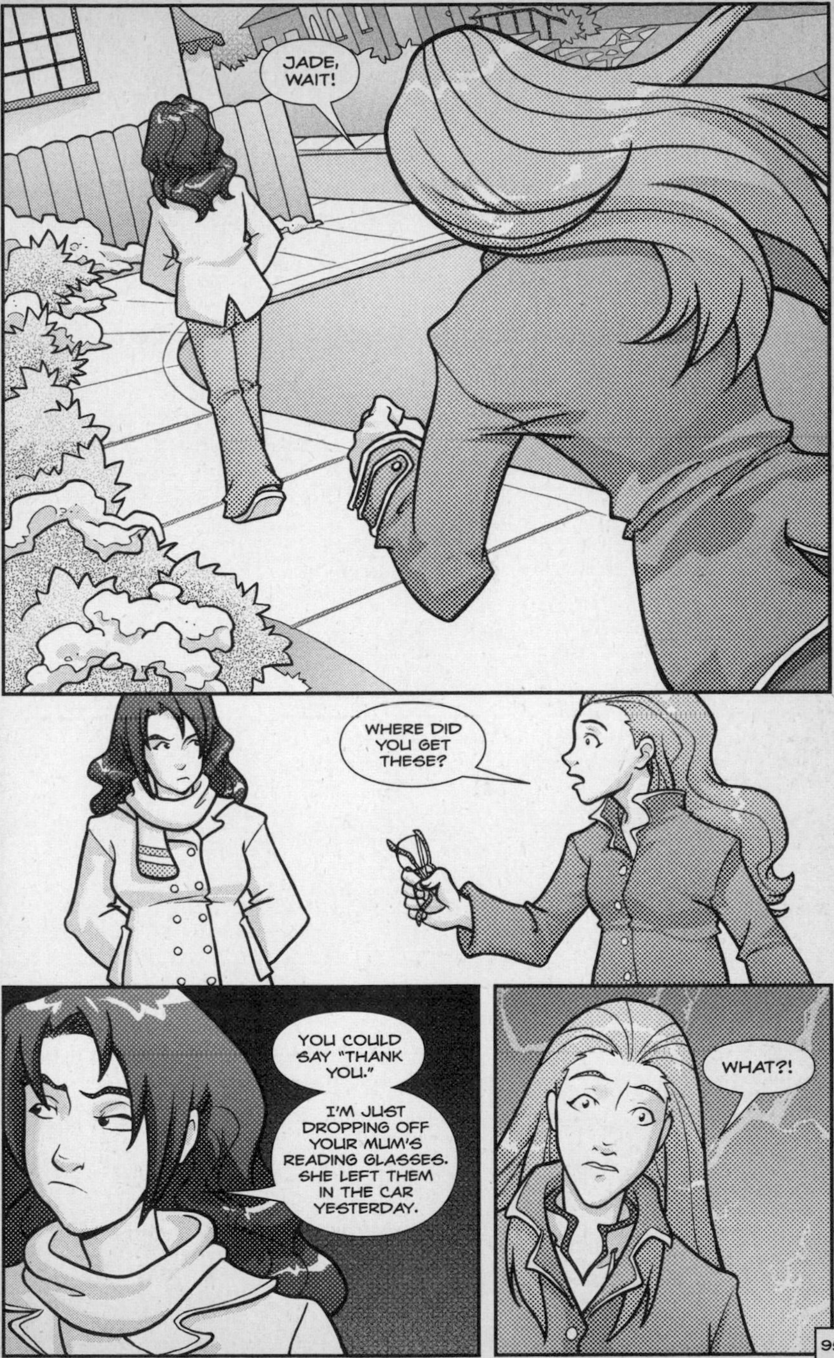
JADE, WAIT!
WHERE DID YOU GET THESE?
YOU COULD SAY "THANK YOU."
I'M JUST DROPPING OFF YOUR MUM'S READING GLASSES. SHE LEFT THEM IN THE CAR YESTERDAY.
WHAT?!

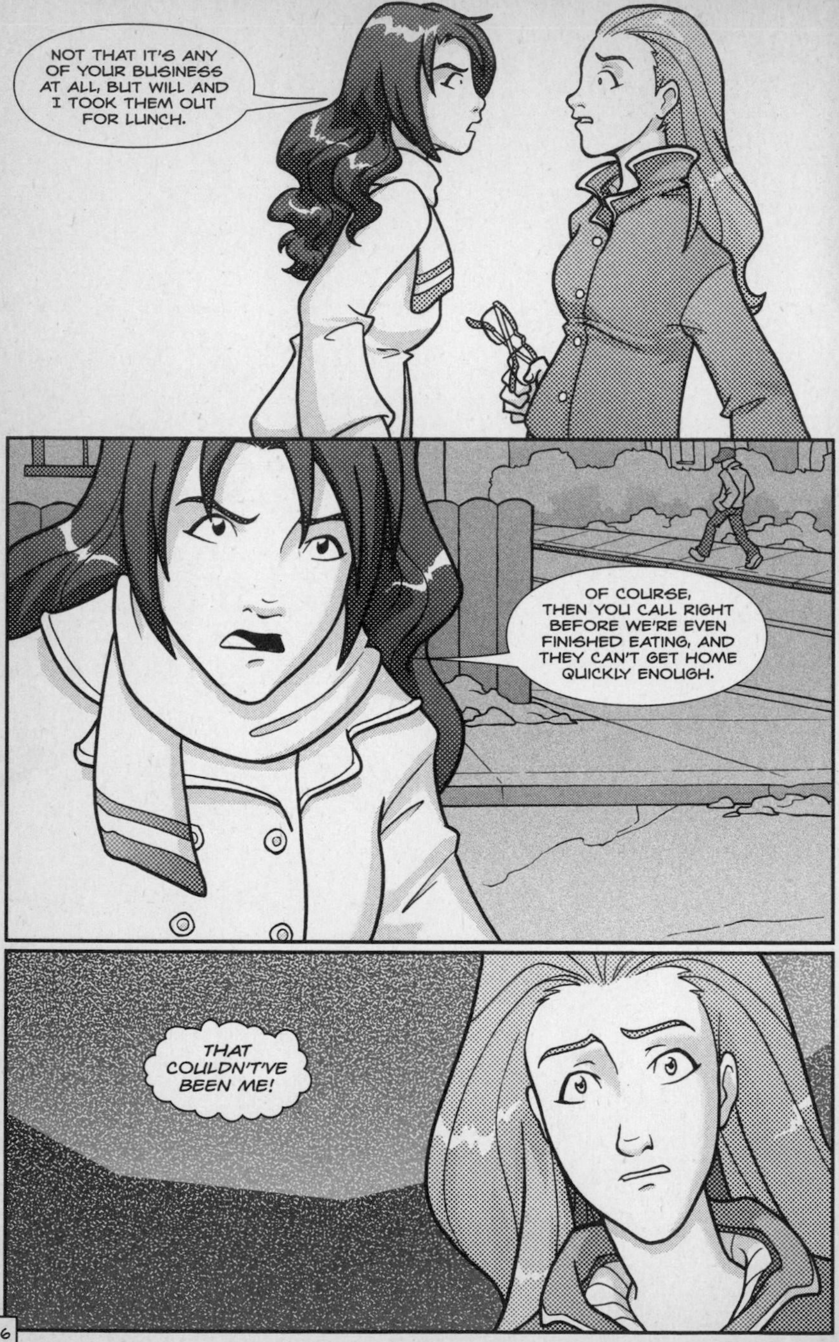
NOT THAT IT'S ANY OF YOUR BUSINESS AT ALL, BUT WILL AND I TOOK THEM OUT FOR LUNCH.
OF COURSE, THEN YOU CALL RIGHT BEFORE WE'RE EVEN FINISHED EATING, AND THEY CAN'T GET HOME QUICKLY ENOUGH.
THAT COULDN'T'VE BEEN ME!

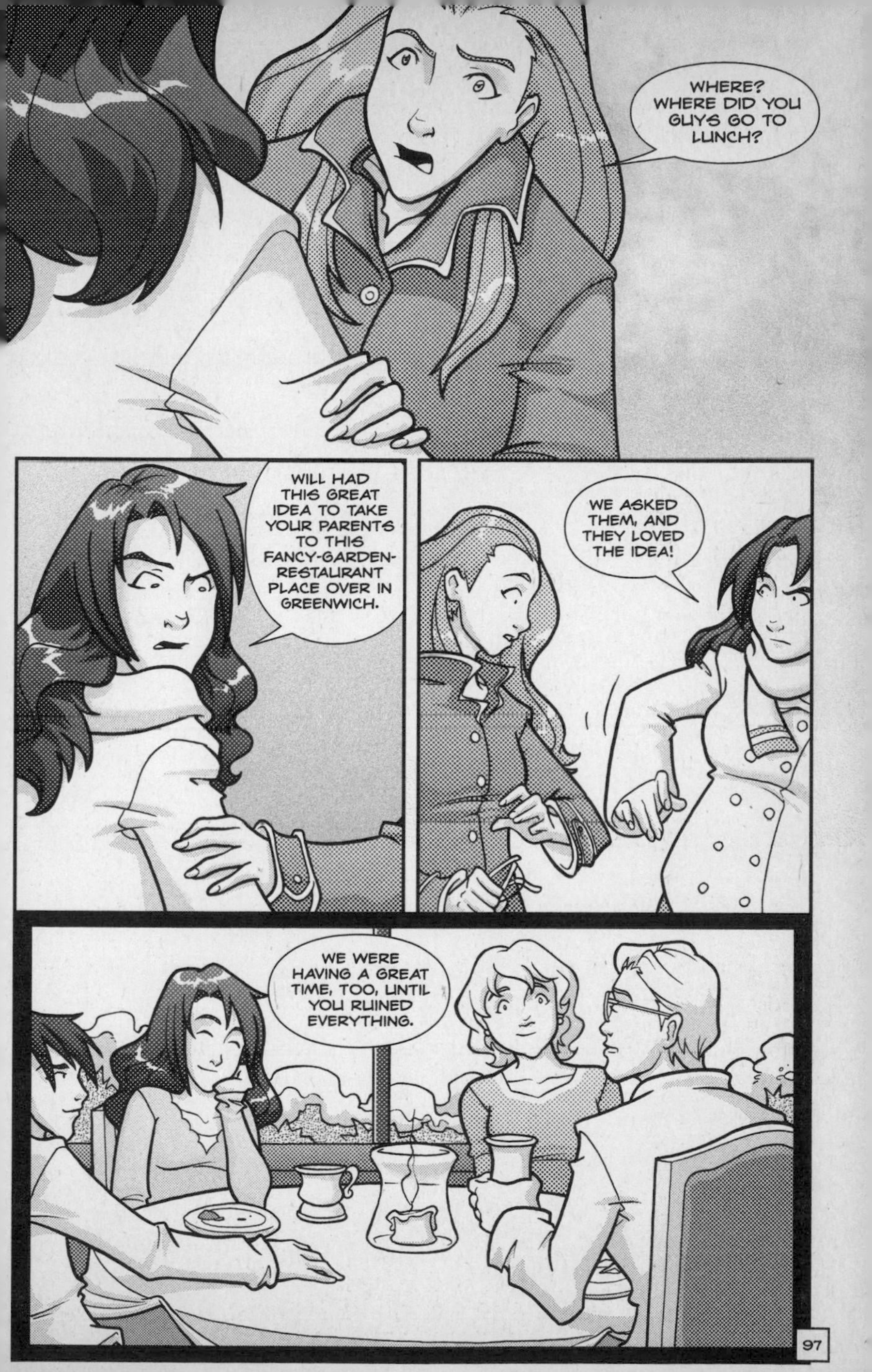
WHERE? WHERE DID YOU GUYS GO TO LUNCH?
WILL HAD THIS GREAT IDEA TO TAKE YOUR PARENTS TO THIS FANCY-GARDEN-RESTAURANT PLACE OVER IN GREENWICH.
WE ASKED THEM, AND THEY LOVED THE IDEA!
WE WERE HAVING A GREAT TIME, TOO, UNTIL YOU RUINED EVERYTHING.

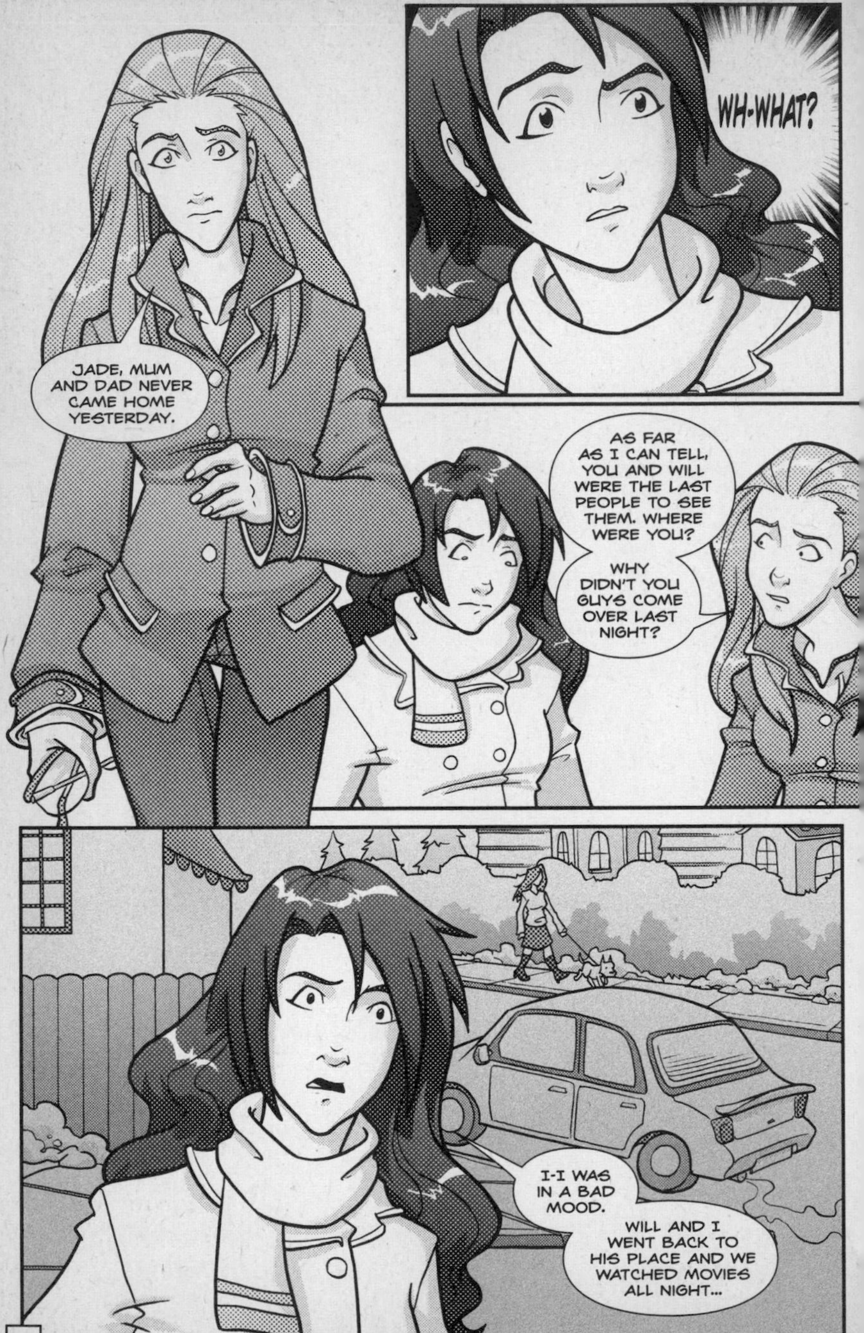
JADE, MUM AND DAD NEVER CAME HOME YESTERDAY.
WH-WHAT?
AS FAR AS I CAN TELL, YOU AND WILL WERE THE LAST PEOPLE TO SEE THEM. WHERE WERE YOU?
WHY DIDN'T YOU GUYS COME OVER LAST NIGHT?
I-I WAS IN A BAD MOOD.
WILL AND I WENT BACK TO HIS PLACE AND WE WATCHED MOVIES ALL NIGHT...

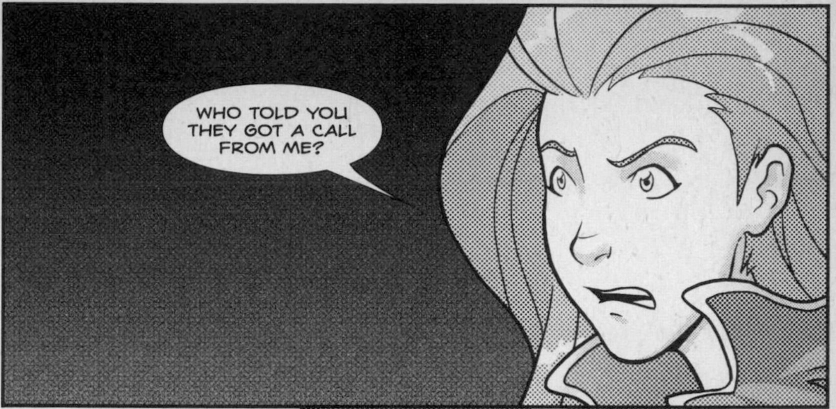
WHO TOLD YOU THEY GOT A CALL FROM ME?
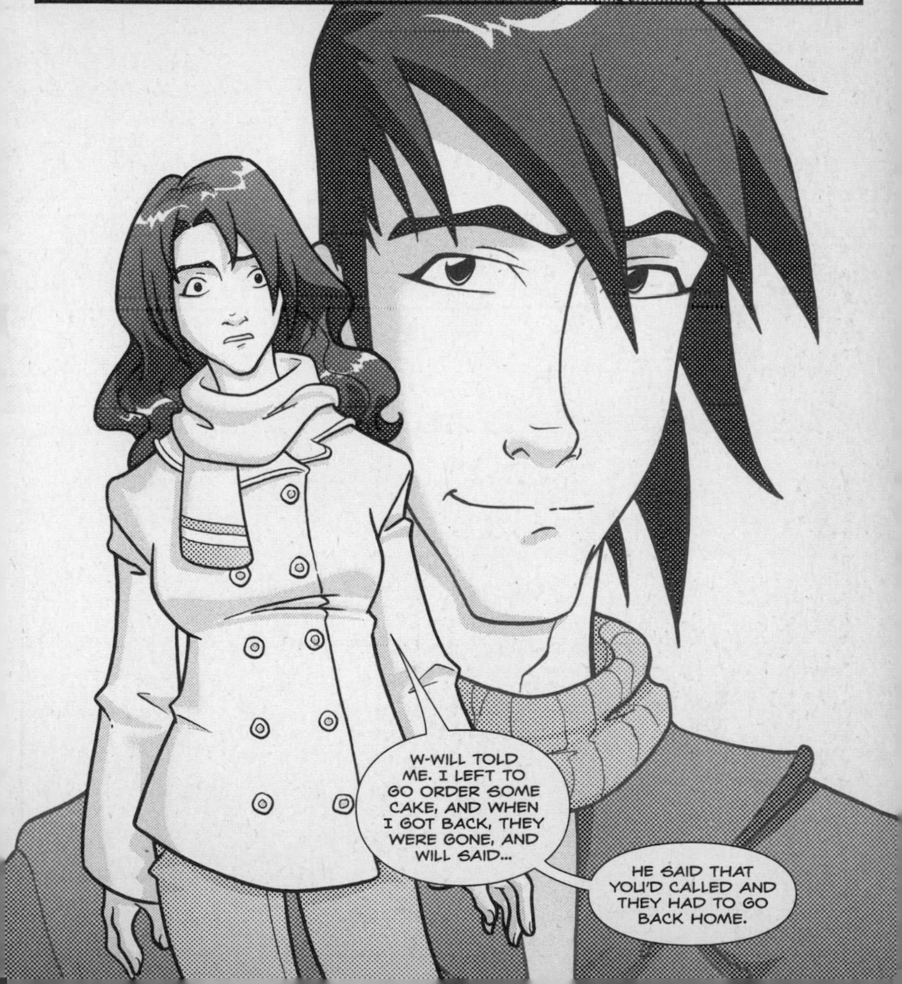
W-WILL TOLD ME. I LEFT TO GO ORDER SOME CAKE, AND WHEN I GOT BACK, THEY WERE GONE, AND WILL SAID...
HE SAID THAT YOU'D CALLED AND THEY HAD TO GO BACK HOME.

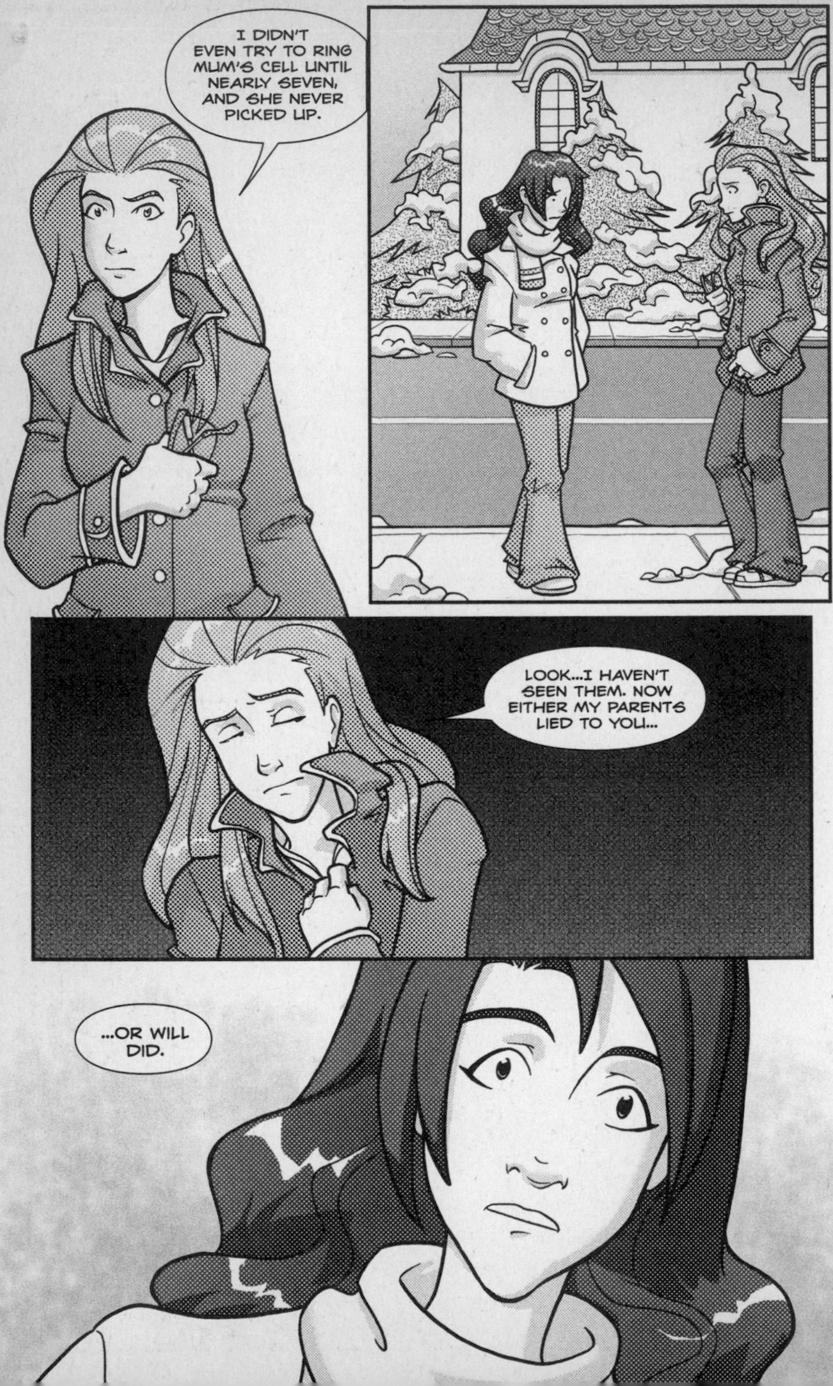
I DIDN'T EVEN TRY TO RING MUM'S CELL UNTIL NEARLY SEVEN, AND SHE NEVER PICKED UP.
LOOK...I HAVEN'T SEEN THEM. NOW EITHER MY PARENTS LIED TO YOU...
...OR WILL DID.

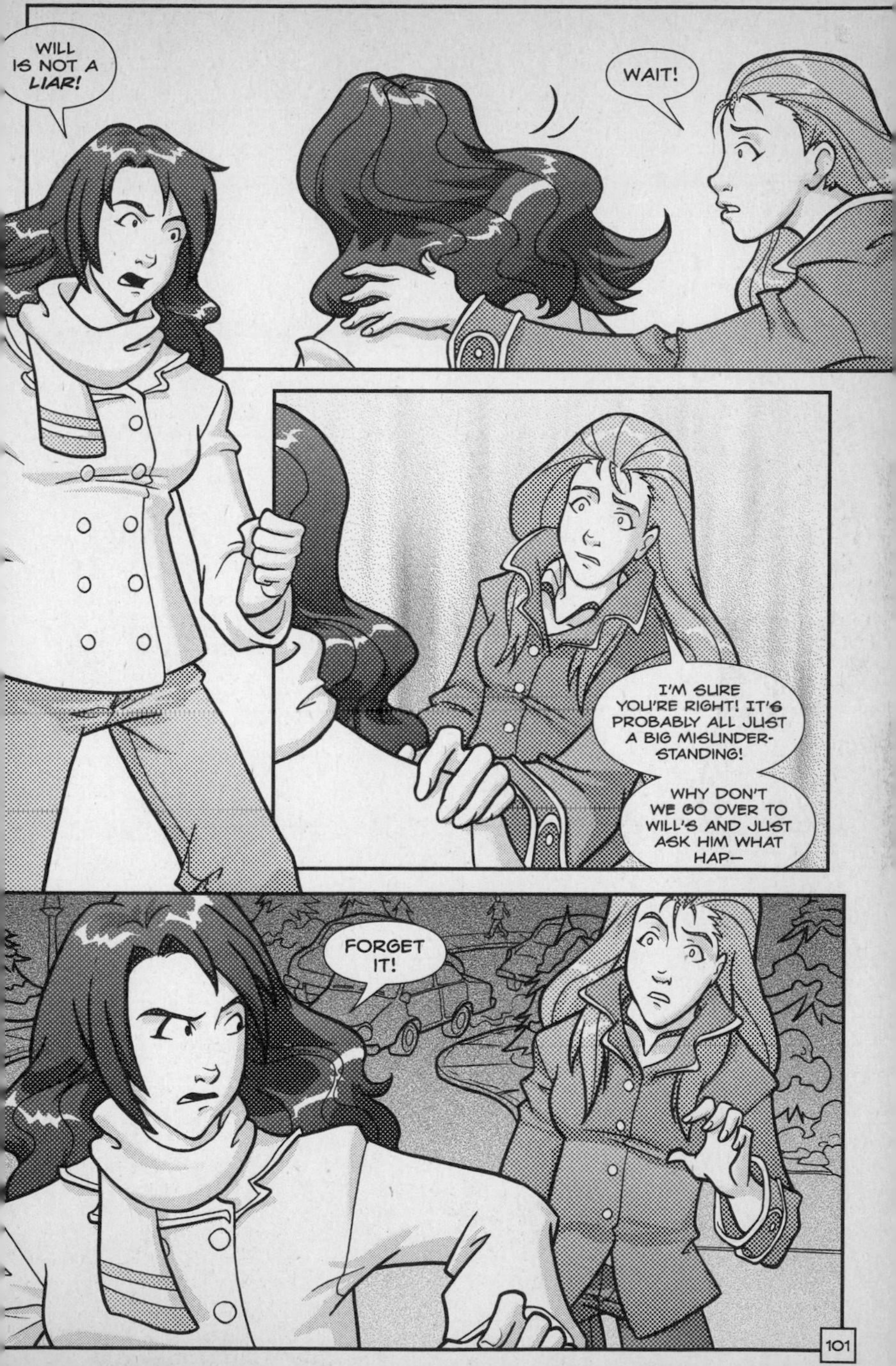
WILL IS NOT A *LIAR!*
WAIT!
I'M SURE YOU'RE RIGHT! IT'S PROBABLY ALL JUST A BIG MISUNDER-STANDING!
WHY DON'T WE GO OVER TO WILL'S AND JUST ASK HIM WHAT HAP—
FORGET IT!

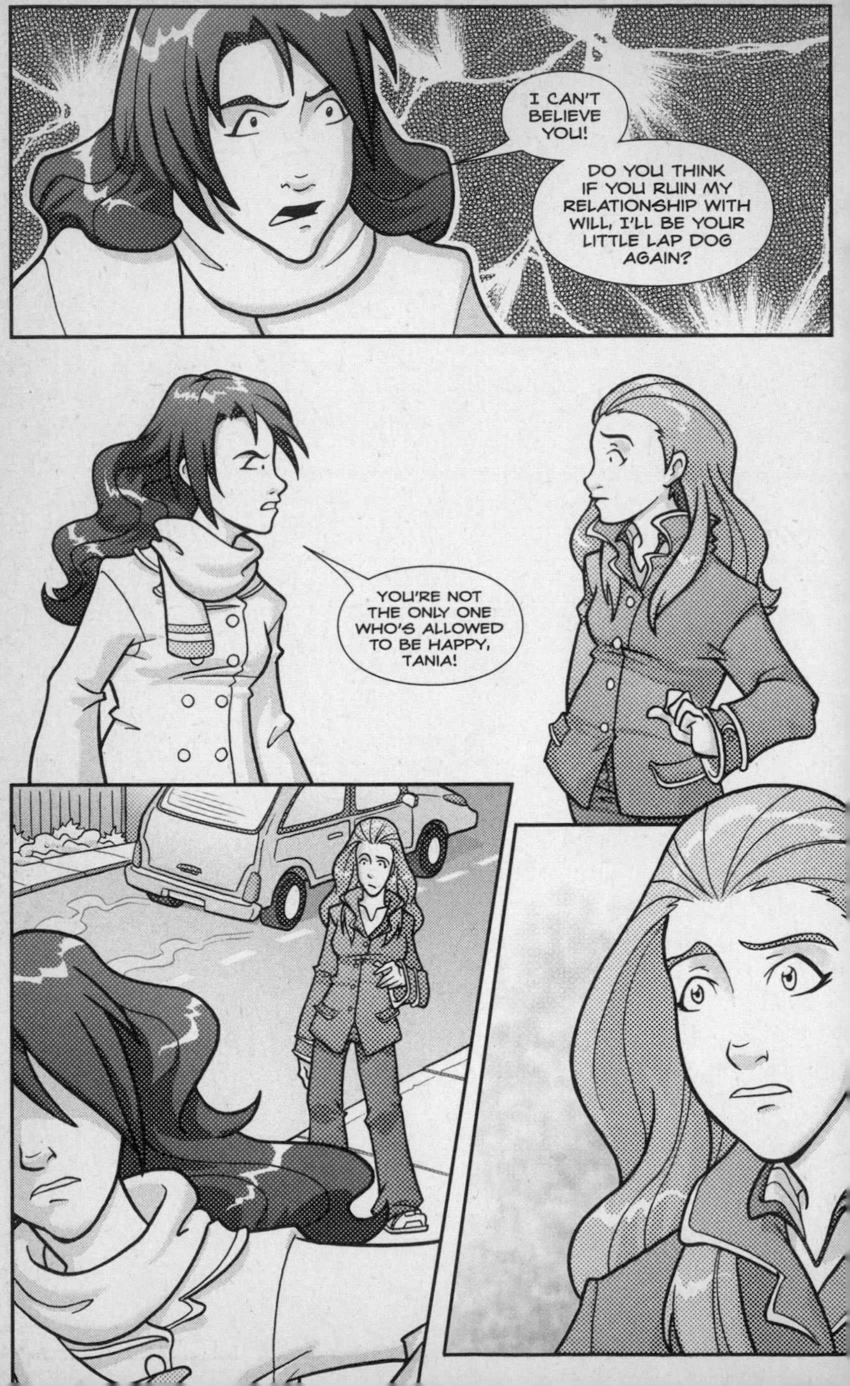
I CAN'T BELIEVE YOU!
DO YOU THINK IF YOU RUIN MY RELATIONSHIP WITH WILL, I'LL BE YOUR LITTLE LAP DOG AGAIN?
YOU'RE NOT THE ONLY ONE WHO'S ALLOWED TO BE HAPPY, TANIA!

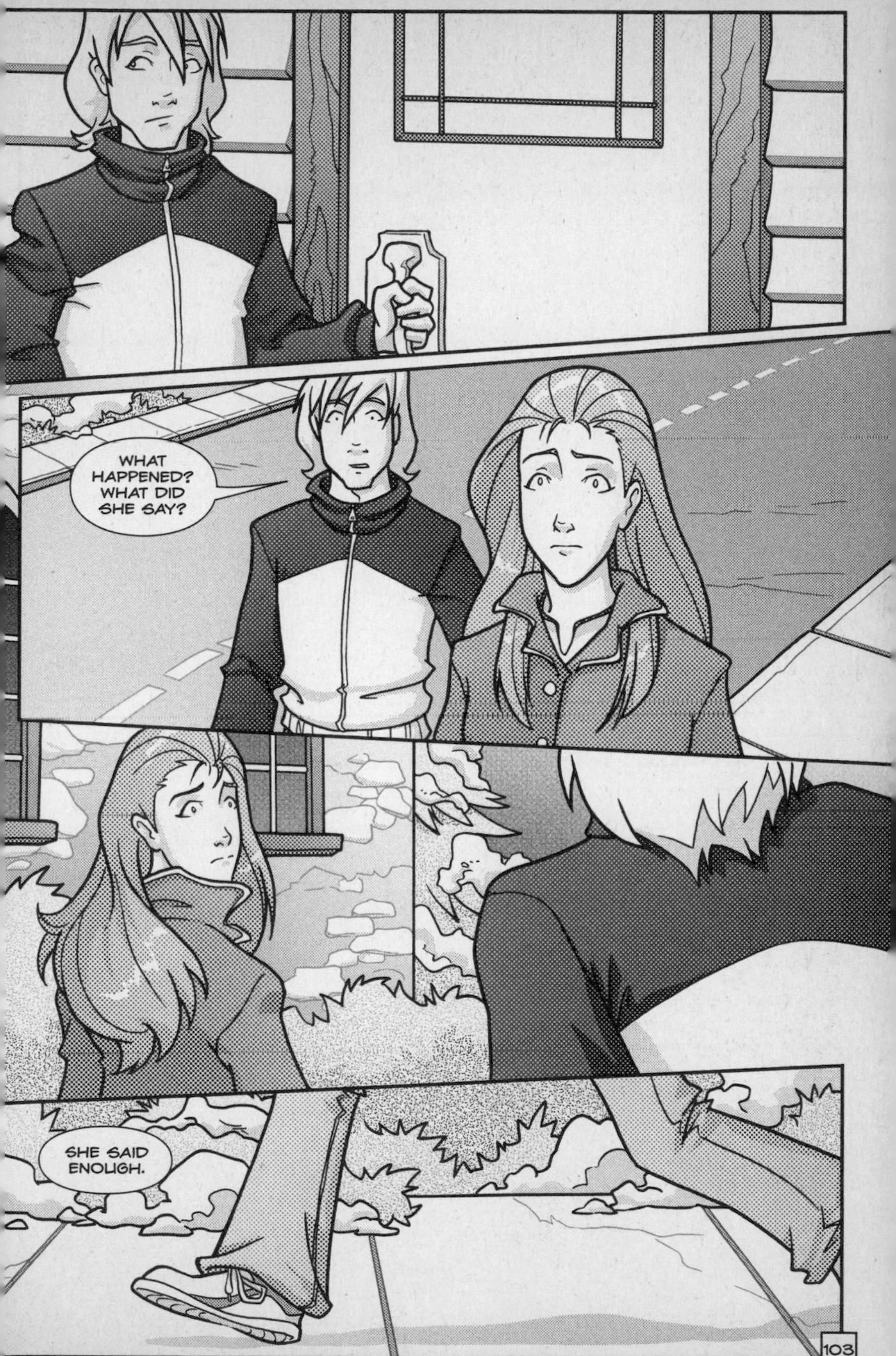
WHAT HAPPENED? WHAT DID SHE SAY?
SHE SAID ENOUGH.

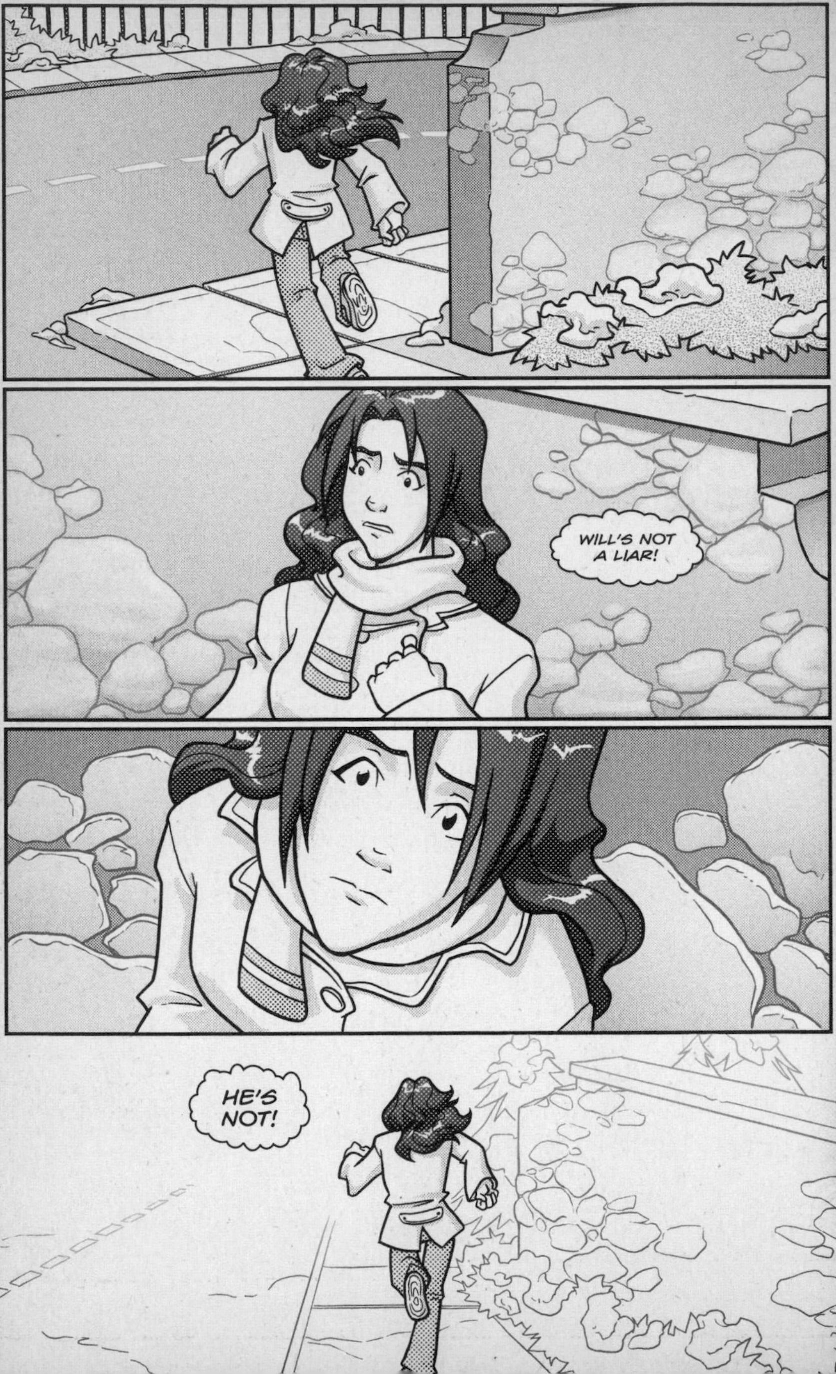
WILL'S NOT A LIAR!
HE'S NOT!

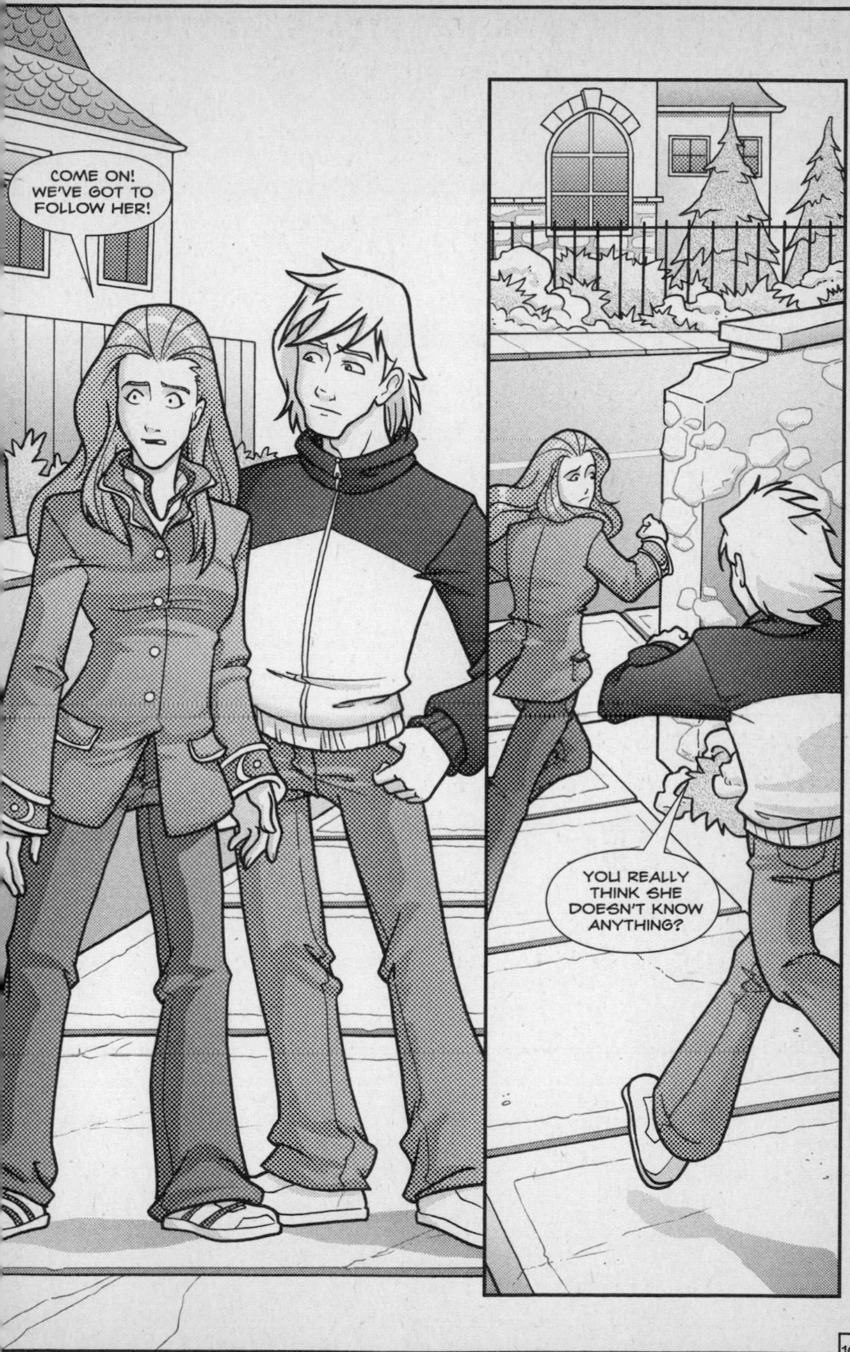
COME ON! WE'VE GOT TO FOLLOW HER!
YOU REALLY THINK SHE DOESN'T KNOW ANYTHING?

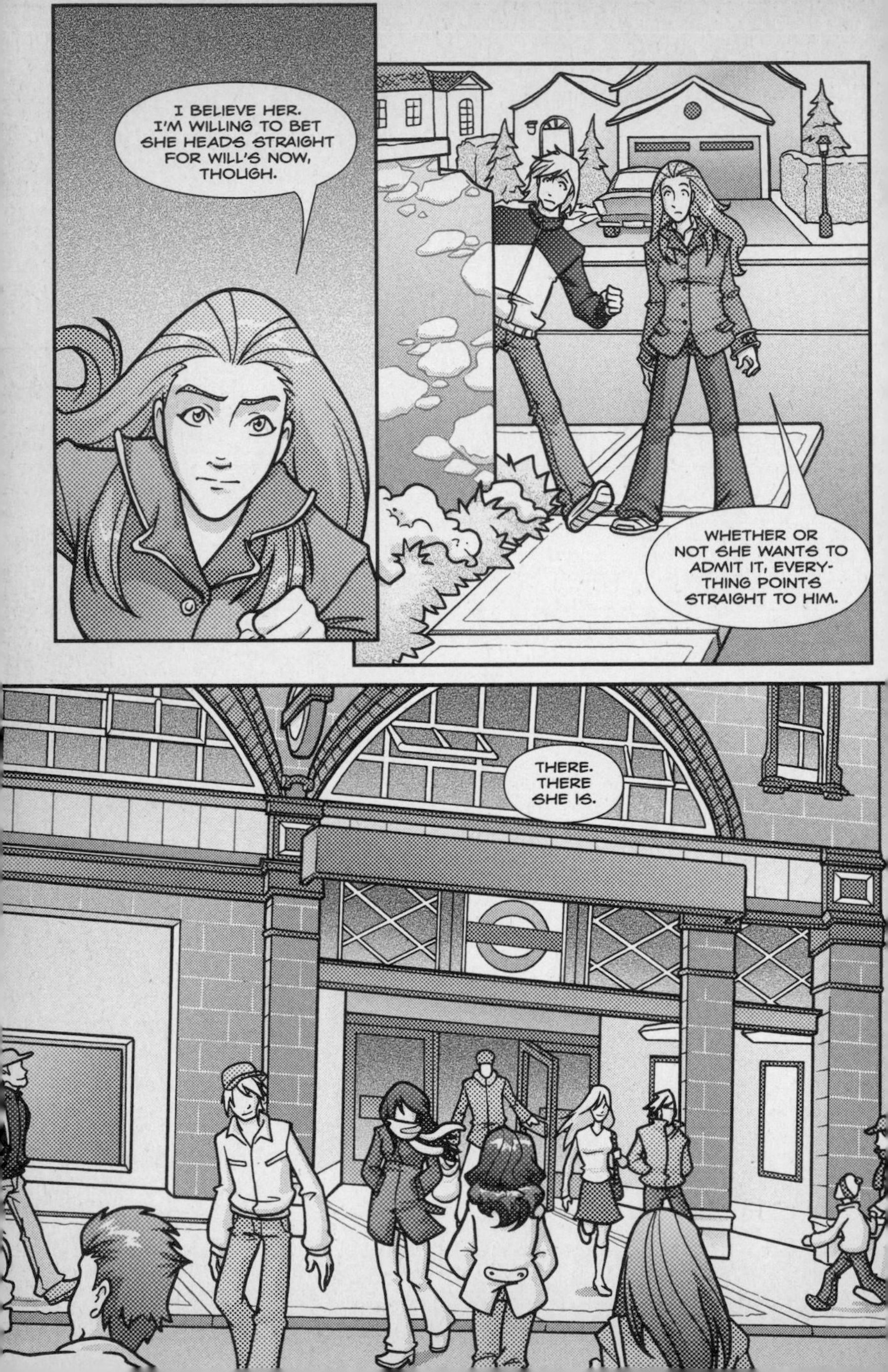
I BELIEVE HER. I'M WILLING TO BET SHE HEADS STRAIGHT FOR WILL'S NOW, THOUGH.
WHETHER OR NOT SHE WANTS TO ADMIT IT, EVERY-THING POINTS STRAIGHT TO HIM.
THERE. THERE SHE IS.

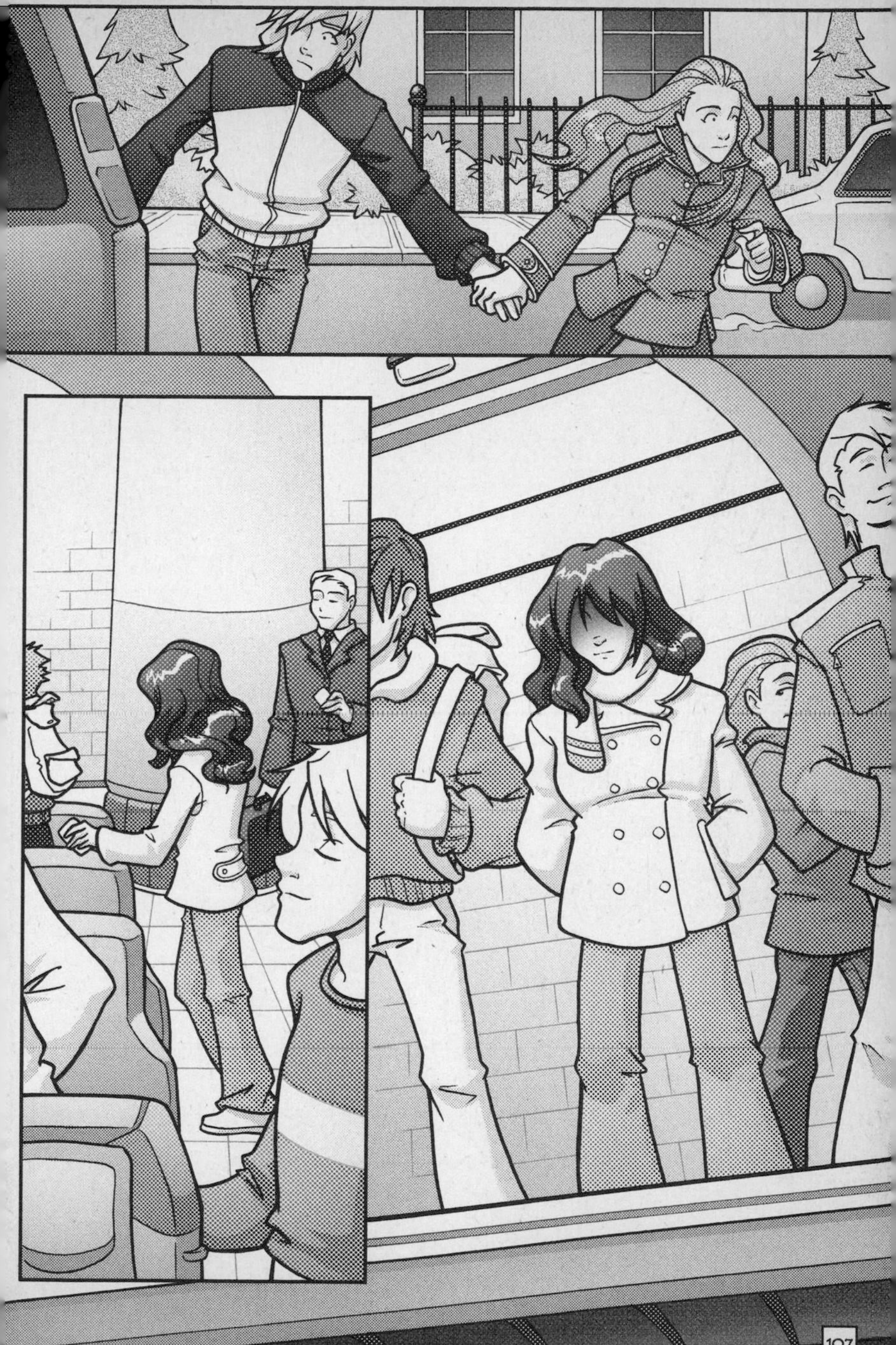

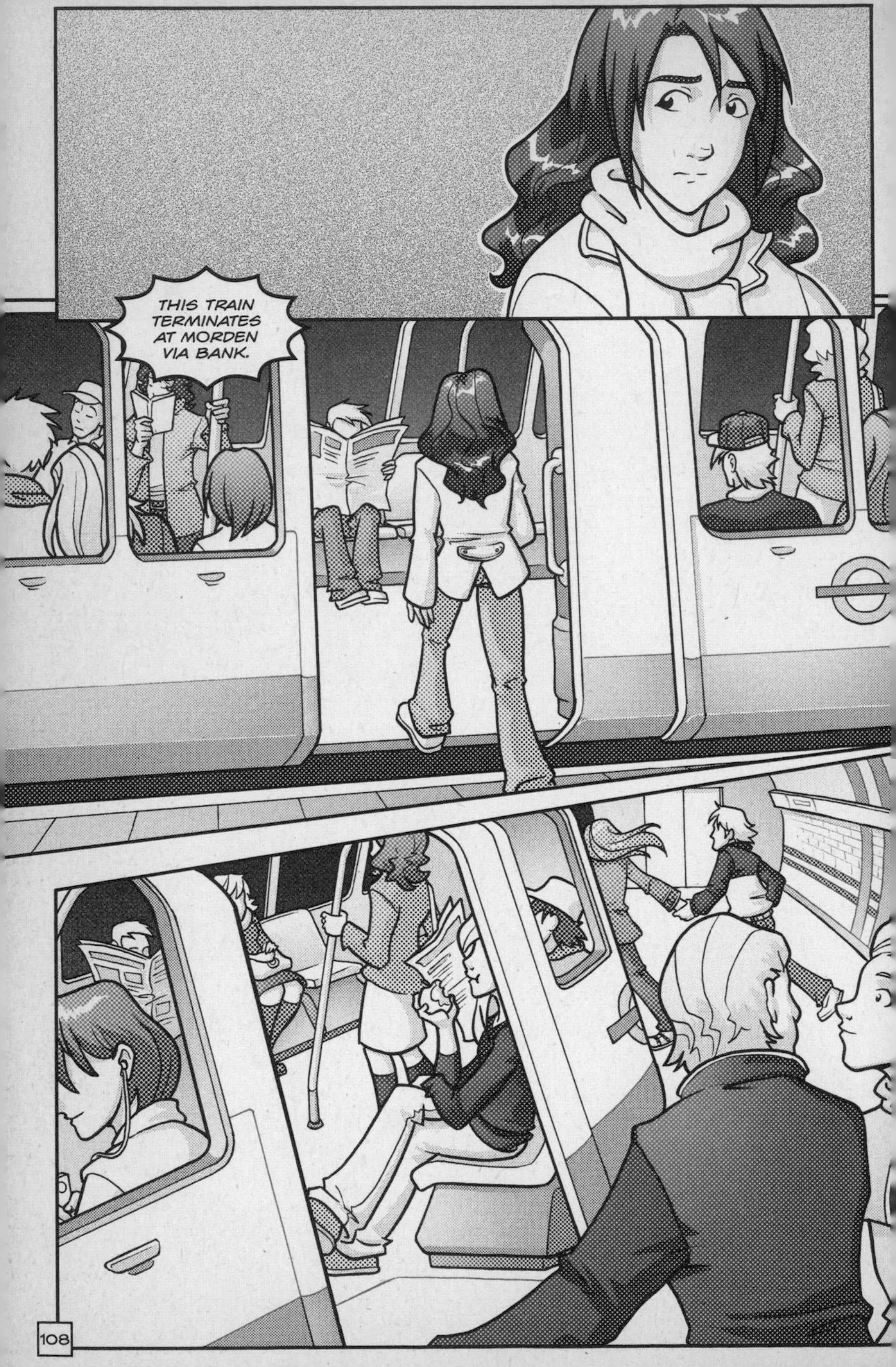
THIS TRAIN TERMINATES AT MORDEN VIA BANK.

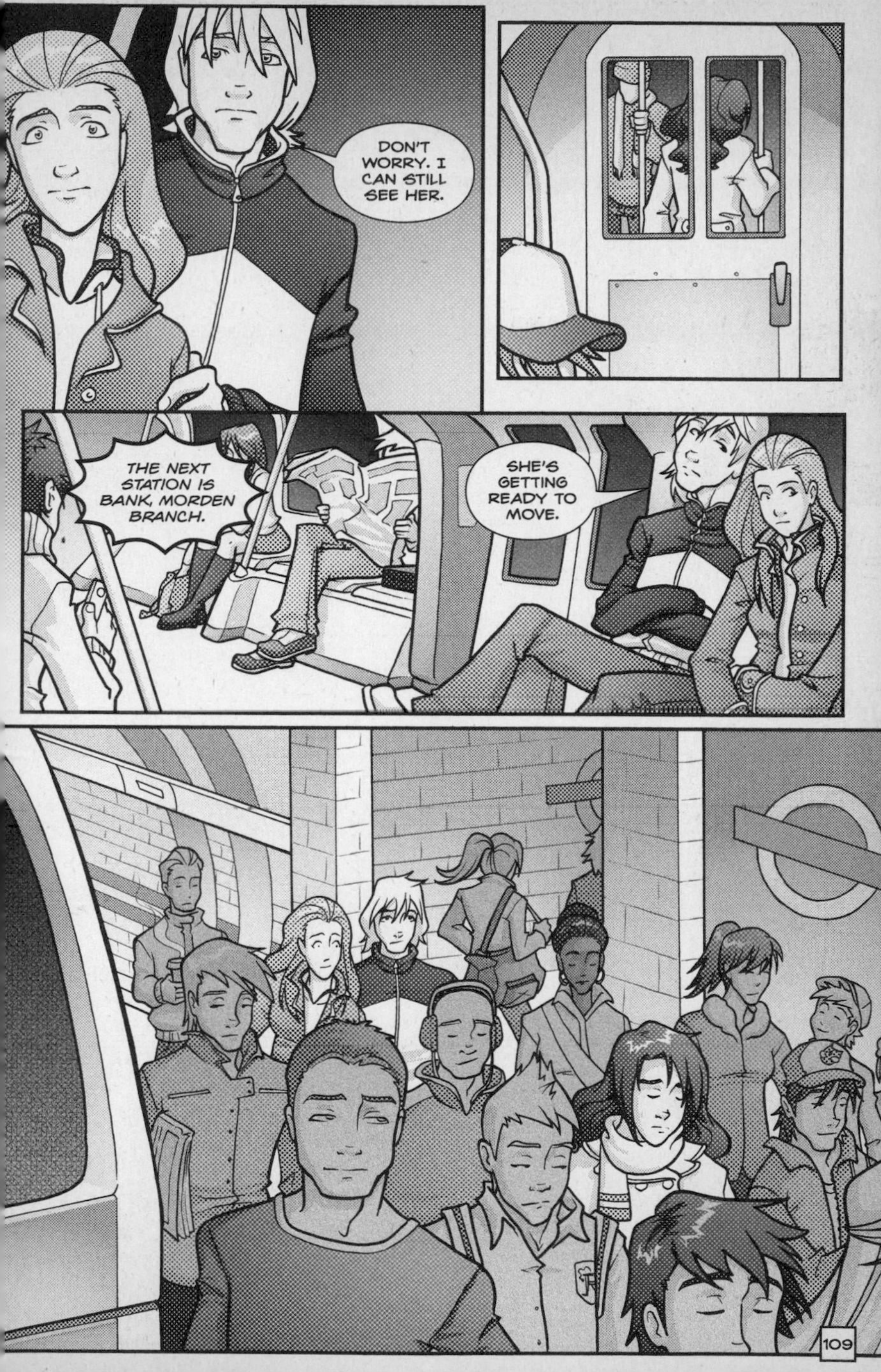
DON'T WORRY. I CAN STILL SEE HER.
THE NEXT STATION IS BANK, MORDEN BRANCH.
SHE'S GETTING READY TO MOVE.

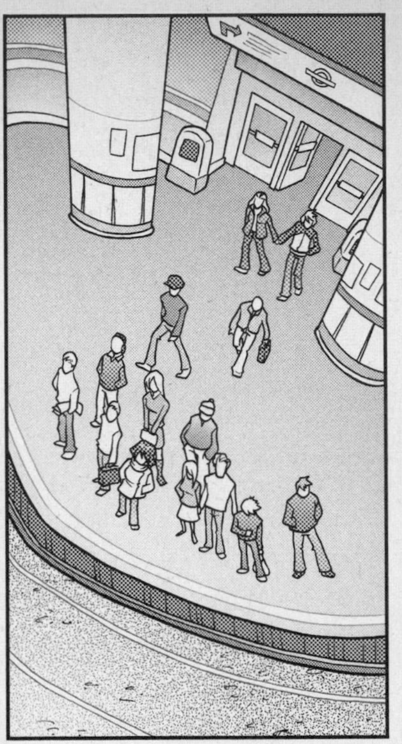
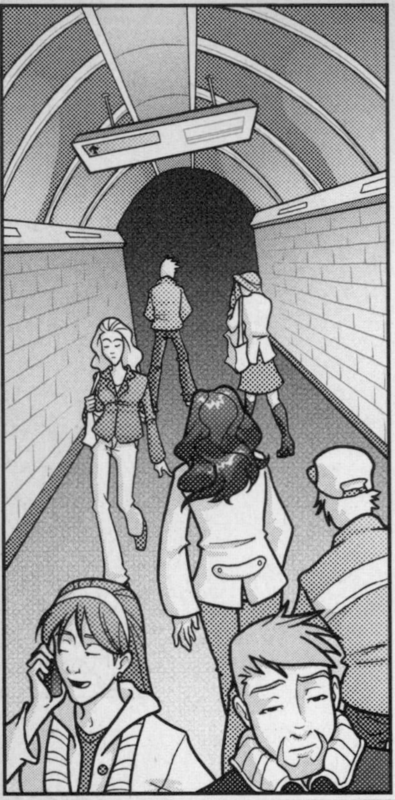
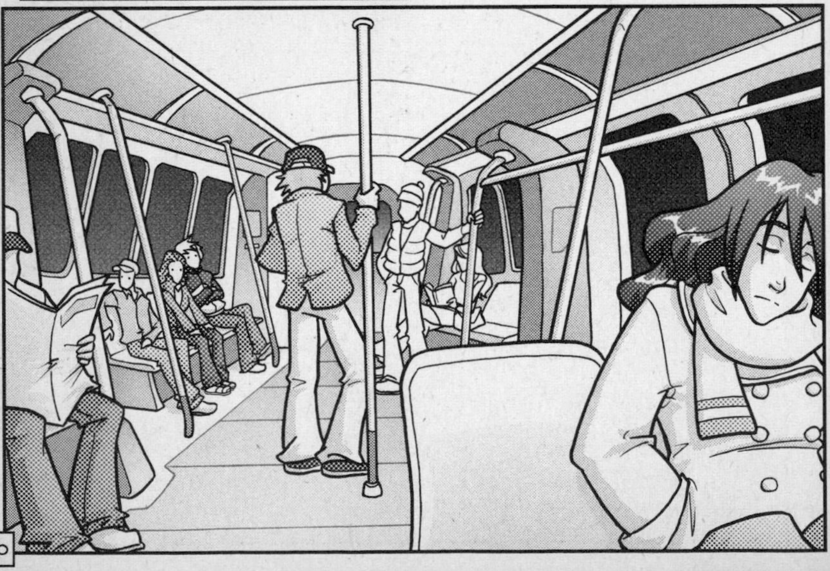

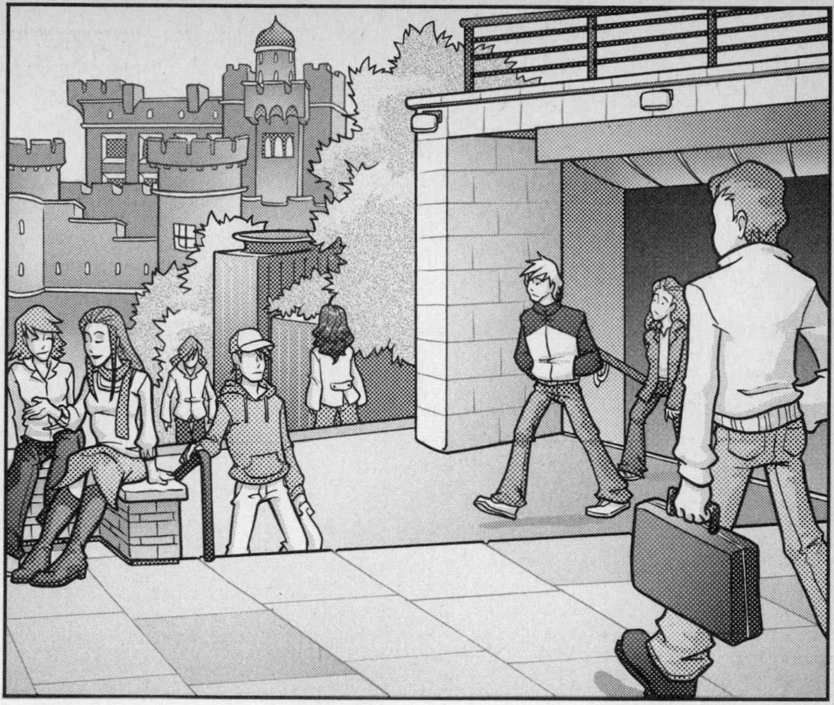

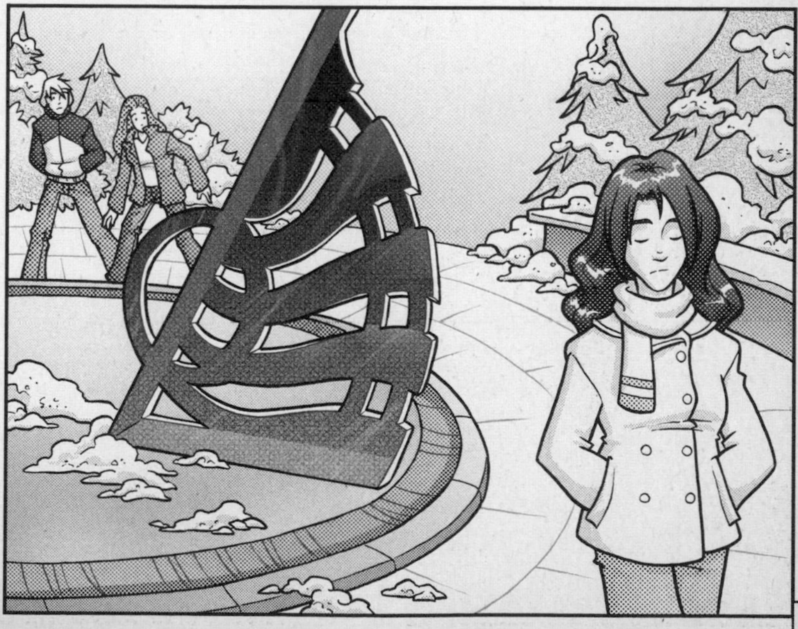

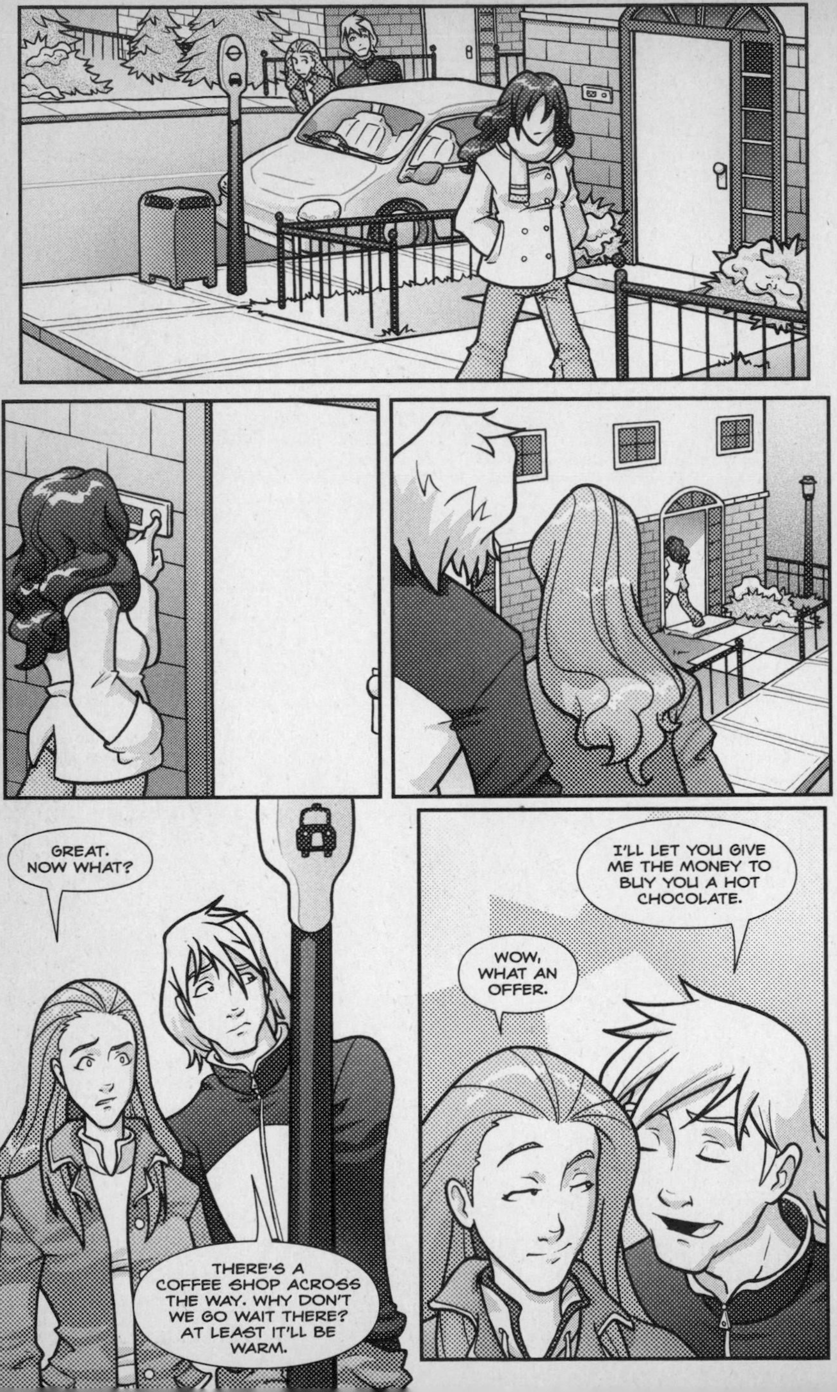
GREAT. NOW WHAT?
THERE'S A COFFEE SHOP ACROSS THE WAY. WHY DON'T WE GO WAIT THERE? AT LEAST IT'LL BE WARM.
I'LL LET YOU GIVE ME THE MONEY TO BUY YOU A HOT CHOCOLATE.
WOW, WHAT AN OFFER.

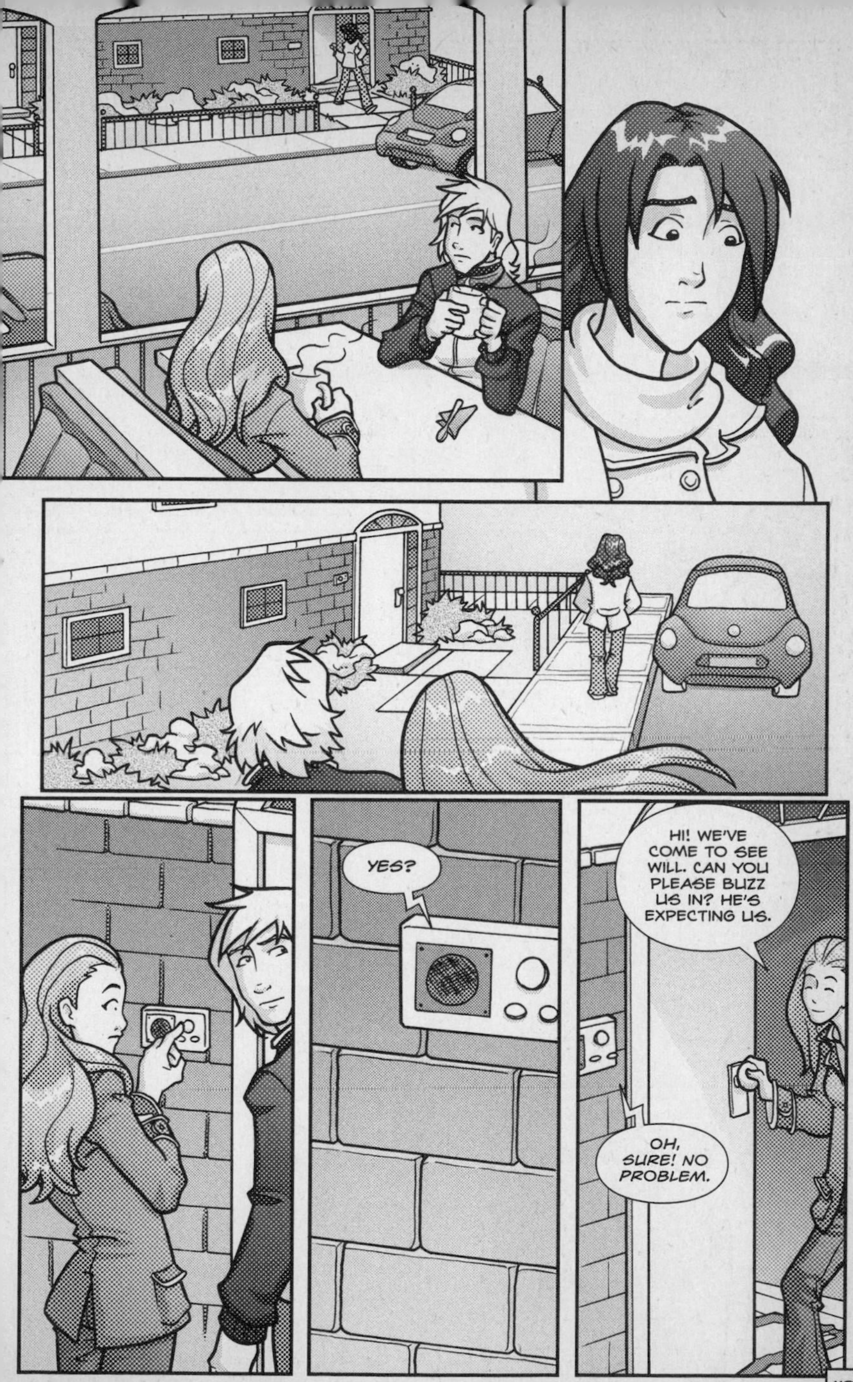
YES?
HI! WE'VE COME TO SEE WILL. CAN YOU PLEASE BUZZ US IN? HE'S EXPECTING US.
OH, SURE! NO PROBLEM.

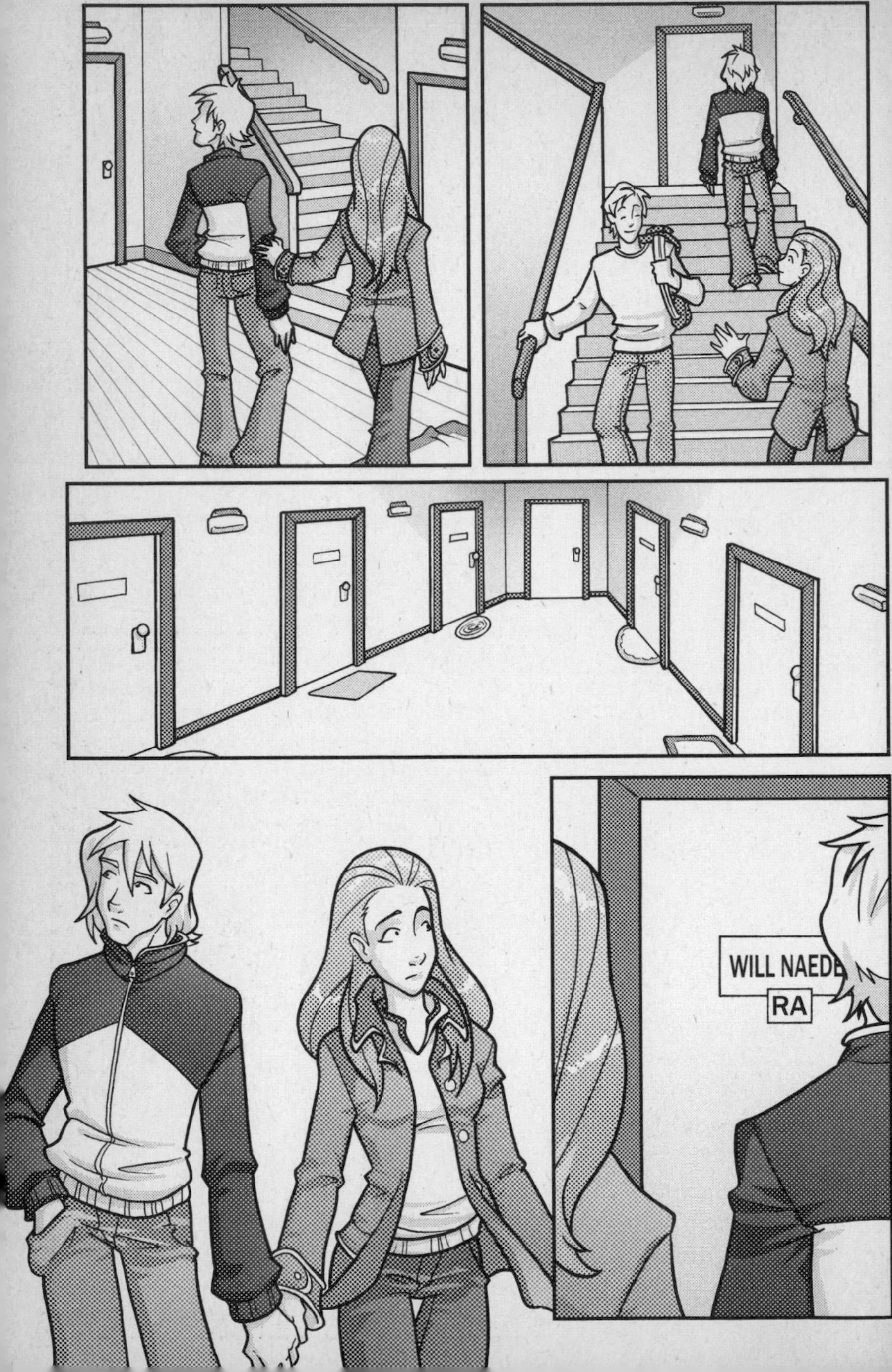
WILL NAEDE
RA

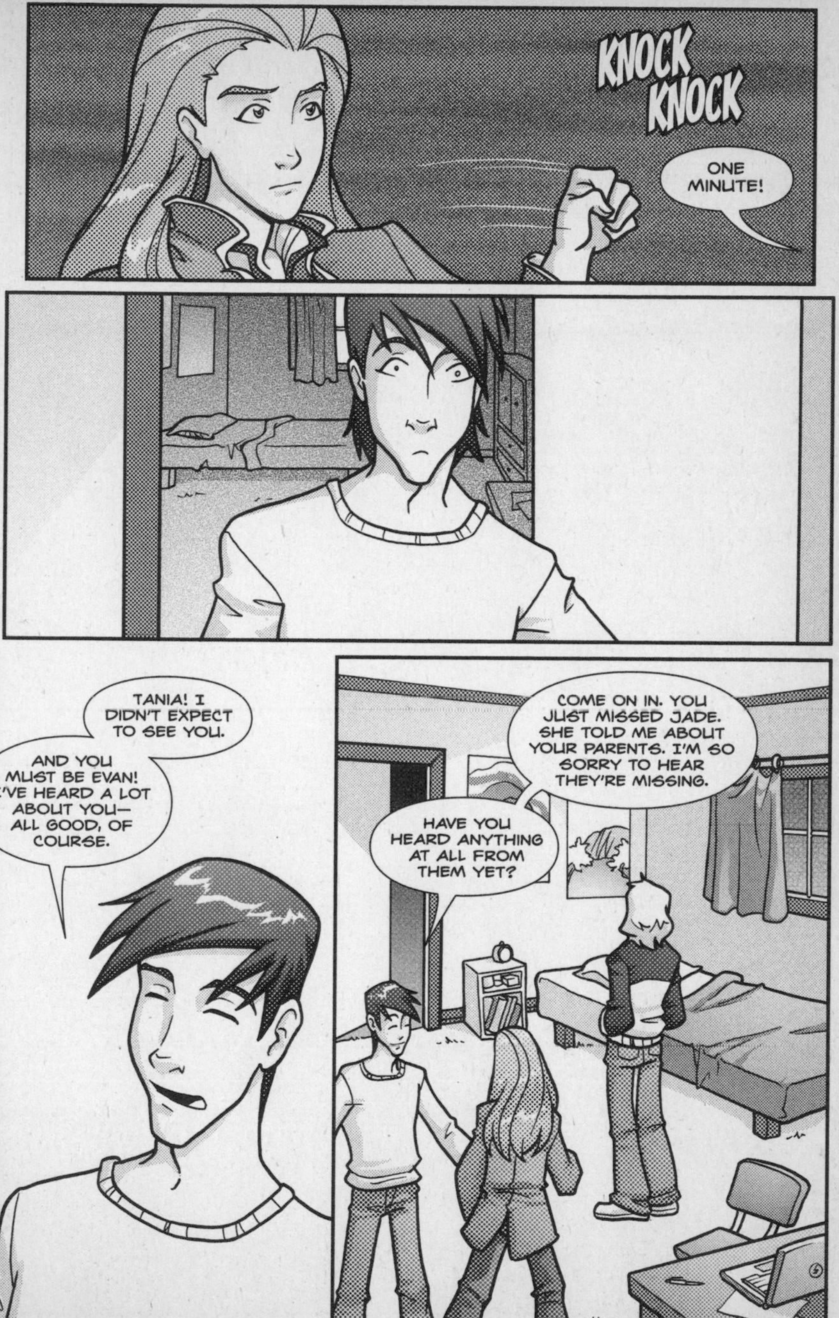
KNOCK KNOCK
ONE MINUTE!
TANIA! I DIDN'T EXPECT TO SEE YOU.
AND YOU MUST BE EVAN! I'VE HEARD A LOT ABOUT YOU— ALL GOOD, OF COURSE.
COME ON IN. YOU JUST MISSED JADE. SHE TOLD ME ABOUT YOUR PARENTS. I'M SO SORRY TO HEAR THEY'RE MISSING.
HAVE YOU HEARD ANYTHING AT ALL FROM THEM YET?

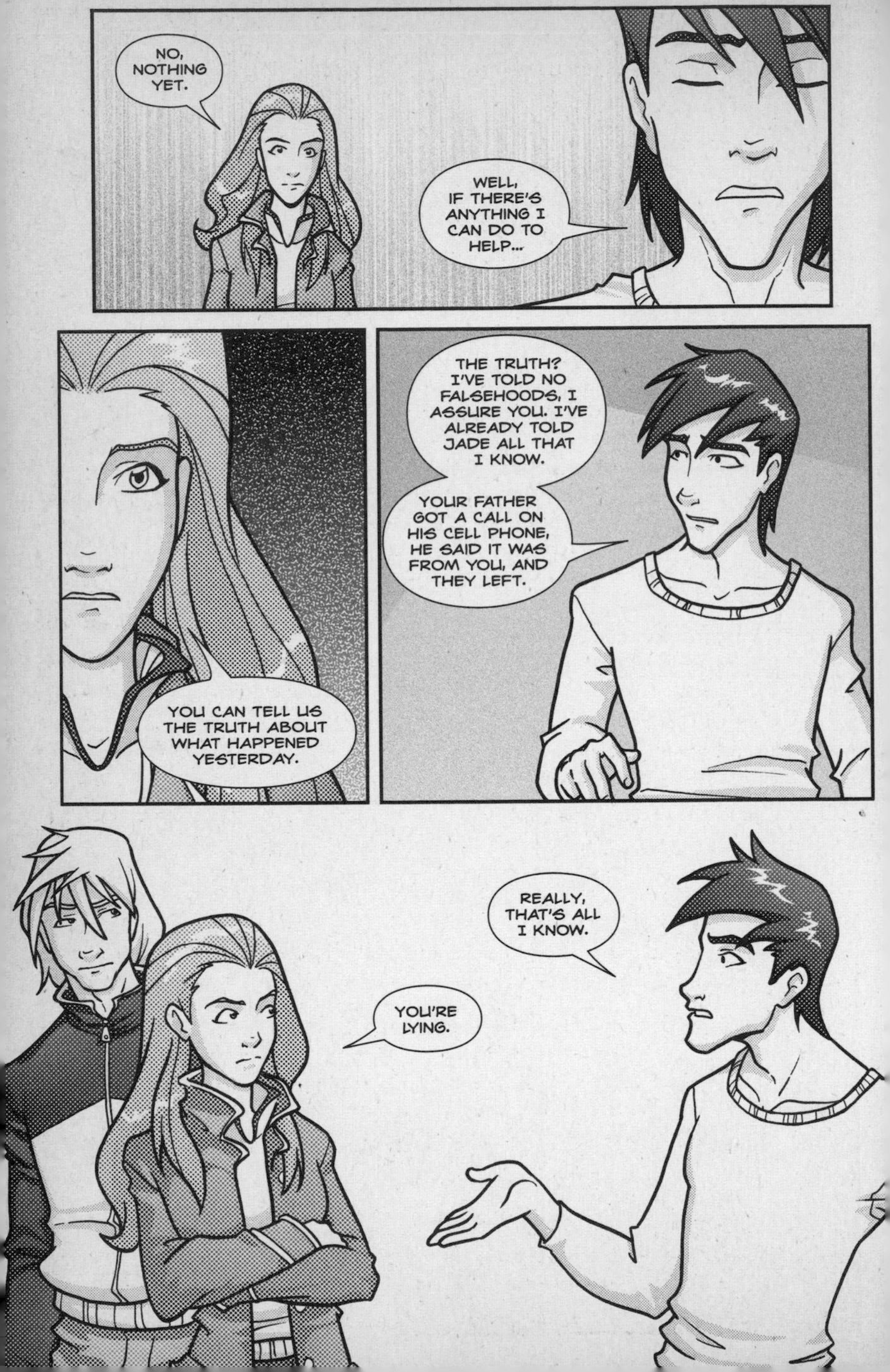
NO, NOTHING YET.
WELL, IF THERE'S ANYTHING I CAN DO TO HELP...
YOU CAN TELL US THE TRUTH ABOUT WHAT HAPPENED YESTERDAY.
THE TRUTH? I'VE TOLD NO FALSEHOODS, I ASSURE YOU. I'VE ALREADY TOLD JADE ALL THAT I KNOW.
YOUR FATHER GOT A CALL ON HIS CELL PHONE, HE SAID IT WAS FROM YOU, AND THEY LEFT.
REALLY, THAT'S ALL I KNOW.
YOU'RE LYING.

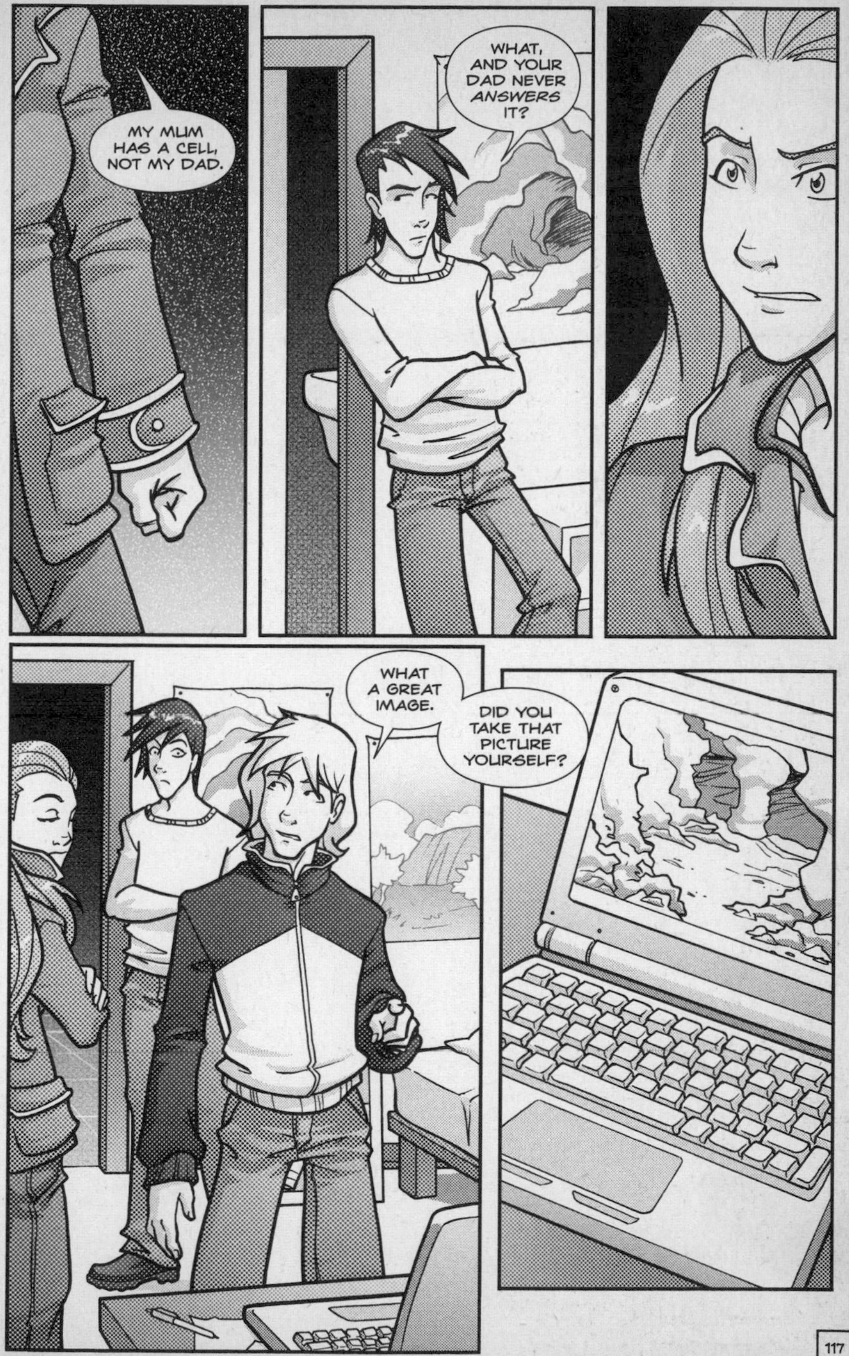
MY MUM HAS A CELL, NOT MY DAD.
WHAT, AND YOUR DAD NEVER *ANSWERS* IT?
WHAT A GREAT IMAGE.
DID YOU TAKE THAT PICTURE YOURSELF?

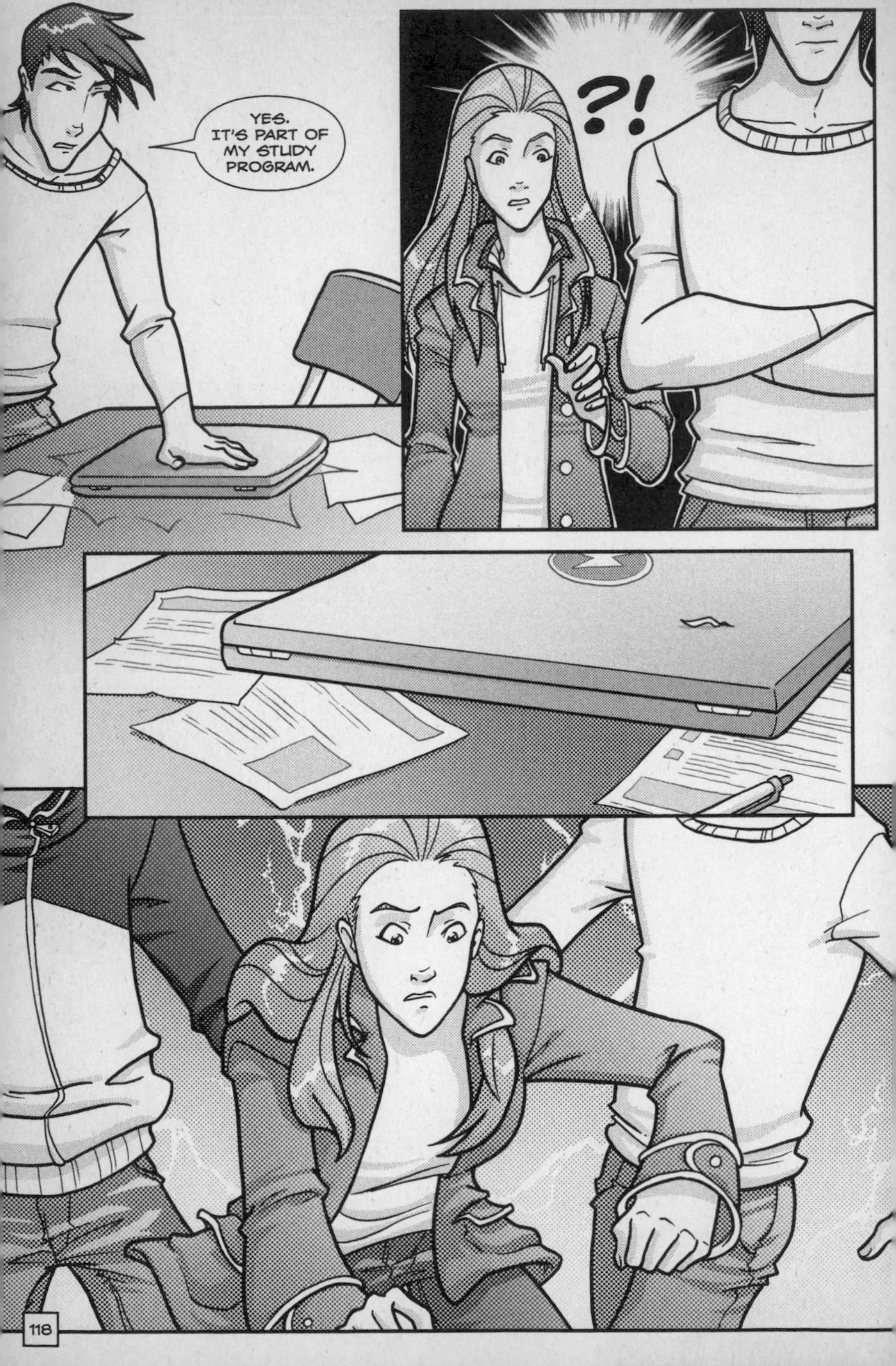
YES. IT'S PART OF MY STUDY PROGRAM.
?!

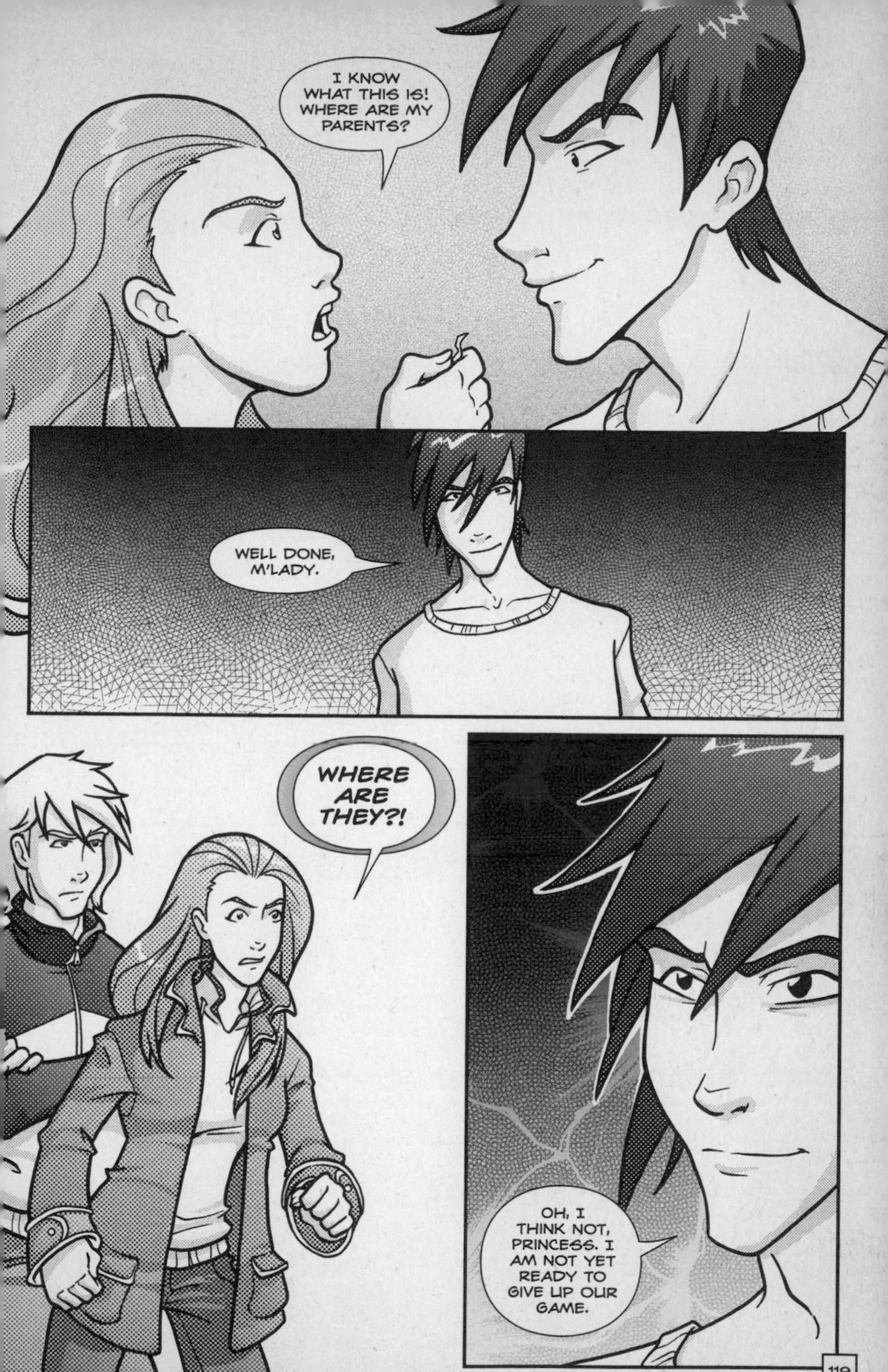
I KNOW WHAT THIS IS! WHERE ARE MY PARENTS?
WELL DONE, M'LADY.
WHERE ARE THEY?!
OH, I THINK NOT, PRINCESS. I AM NOT YET READY TO GIVE UP OUR GAME.

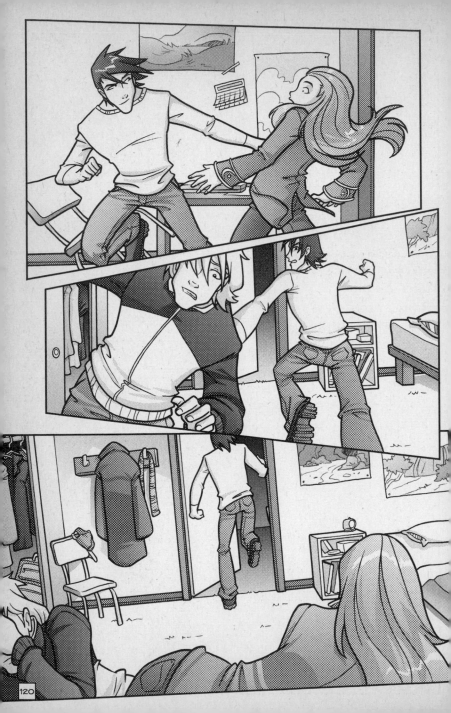

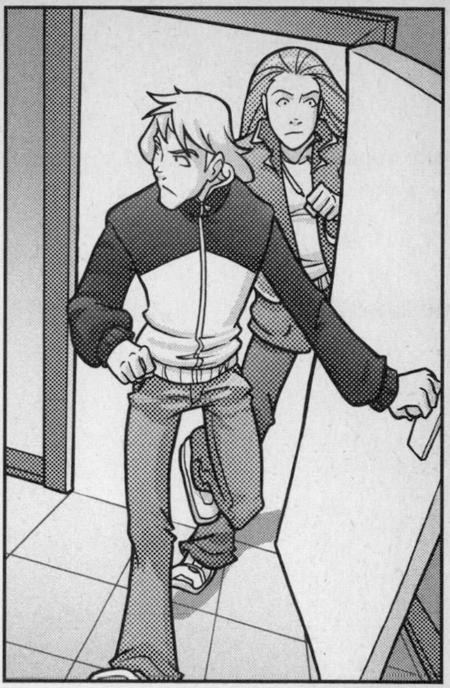
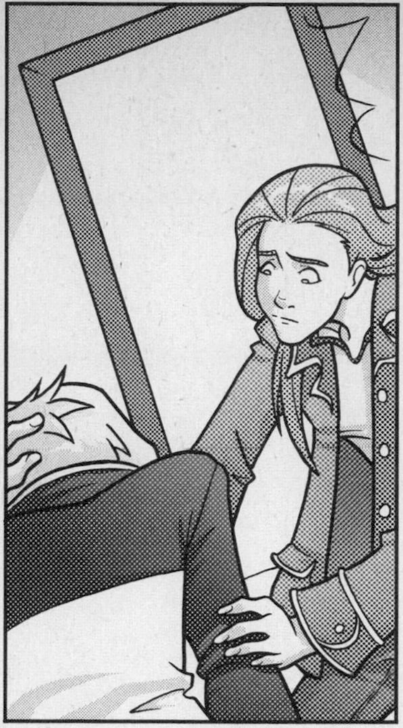
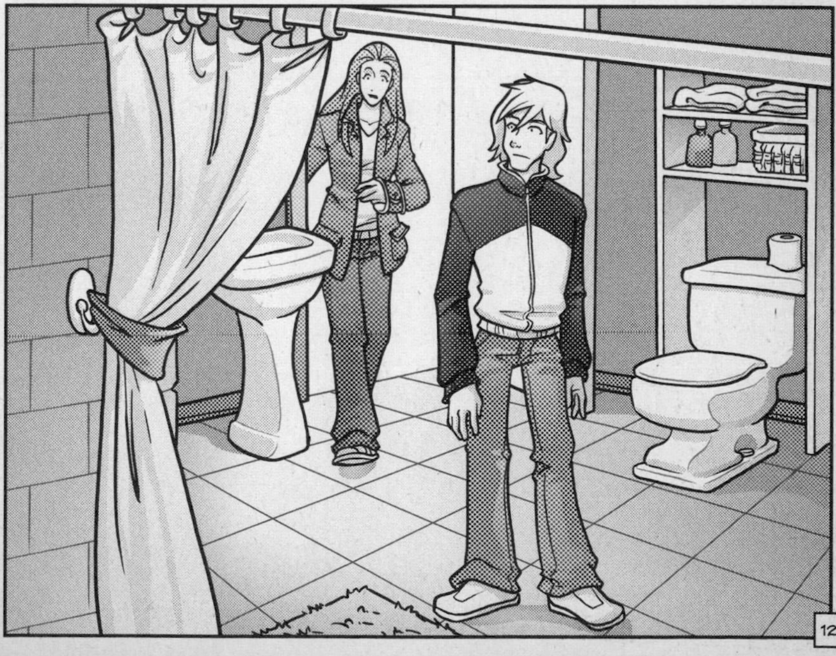

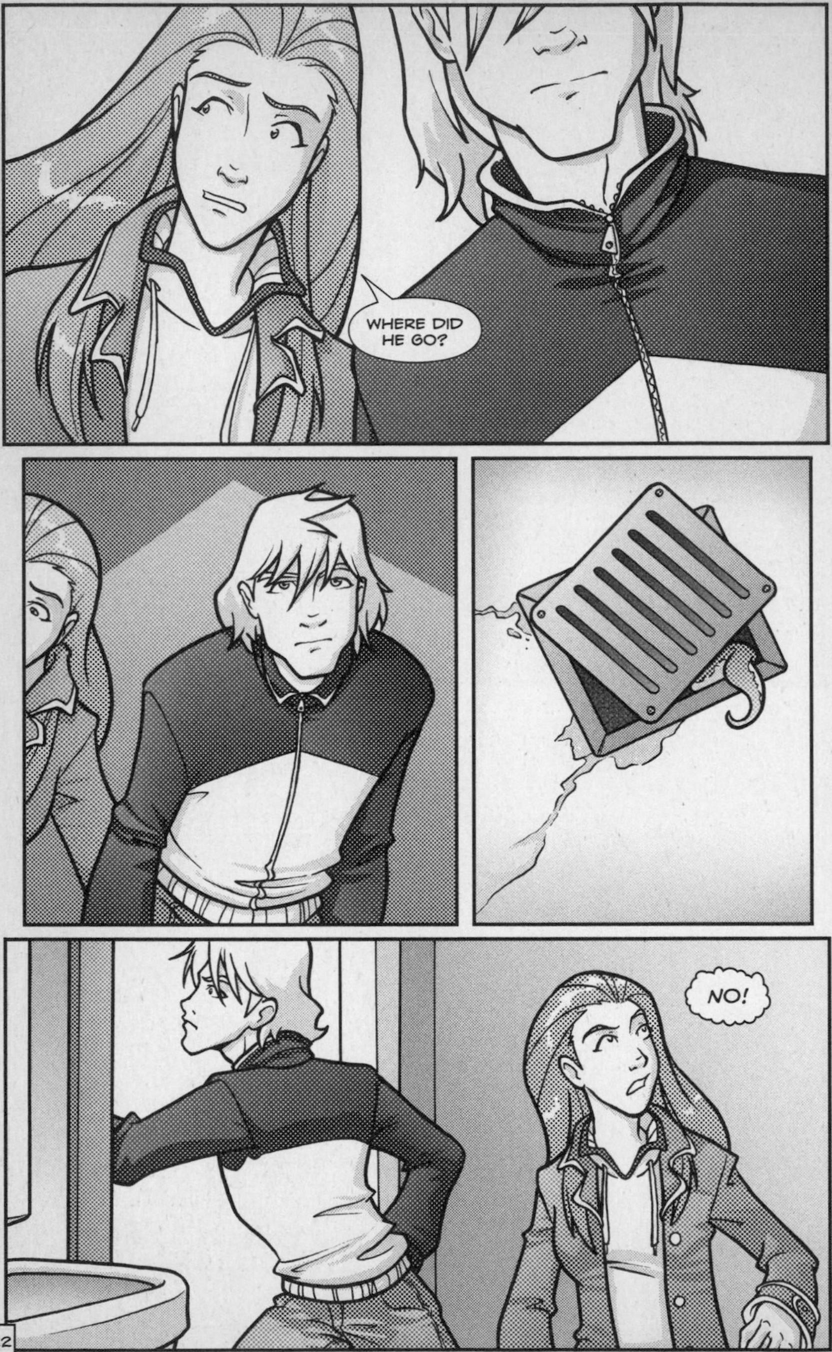
WHERE DID HE GO?
NO!

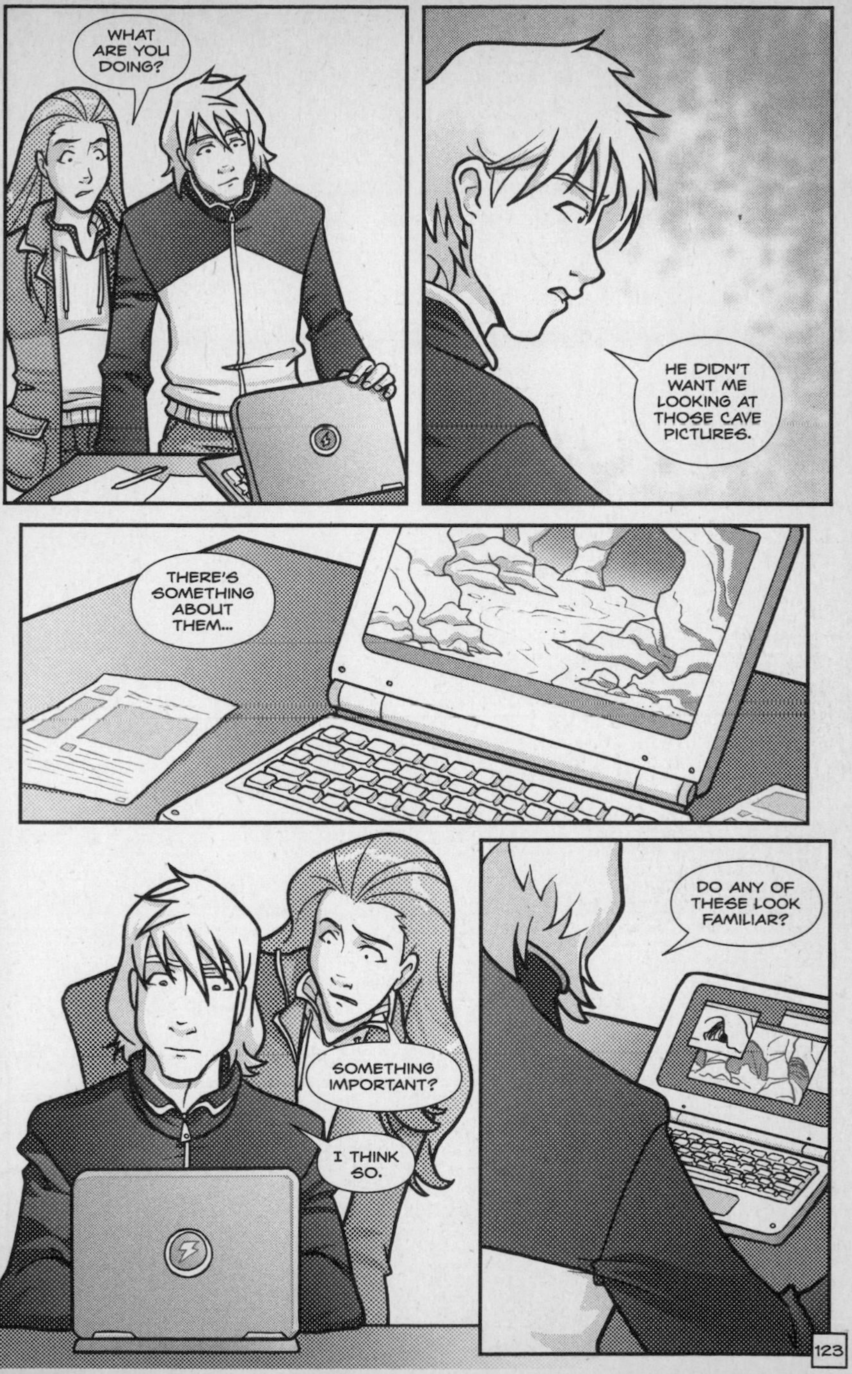
WHAT ARE YOU DOING?
HE DIDN'T WANT ME LOOKING AT THOSE CAVE PICTURES.
THERE'S SOMETHING ABOUT THEM...
SOMETHING IMPORTANT?
I THINK SO.
DO ANY OF THESE LOOK FAMILIAR?

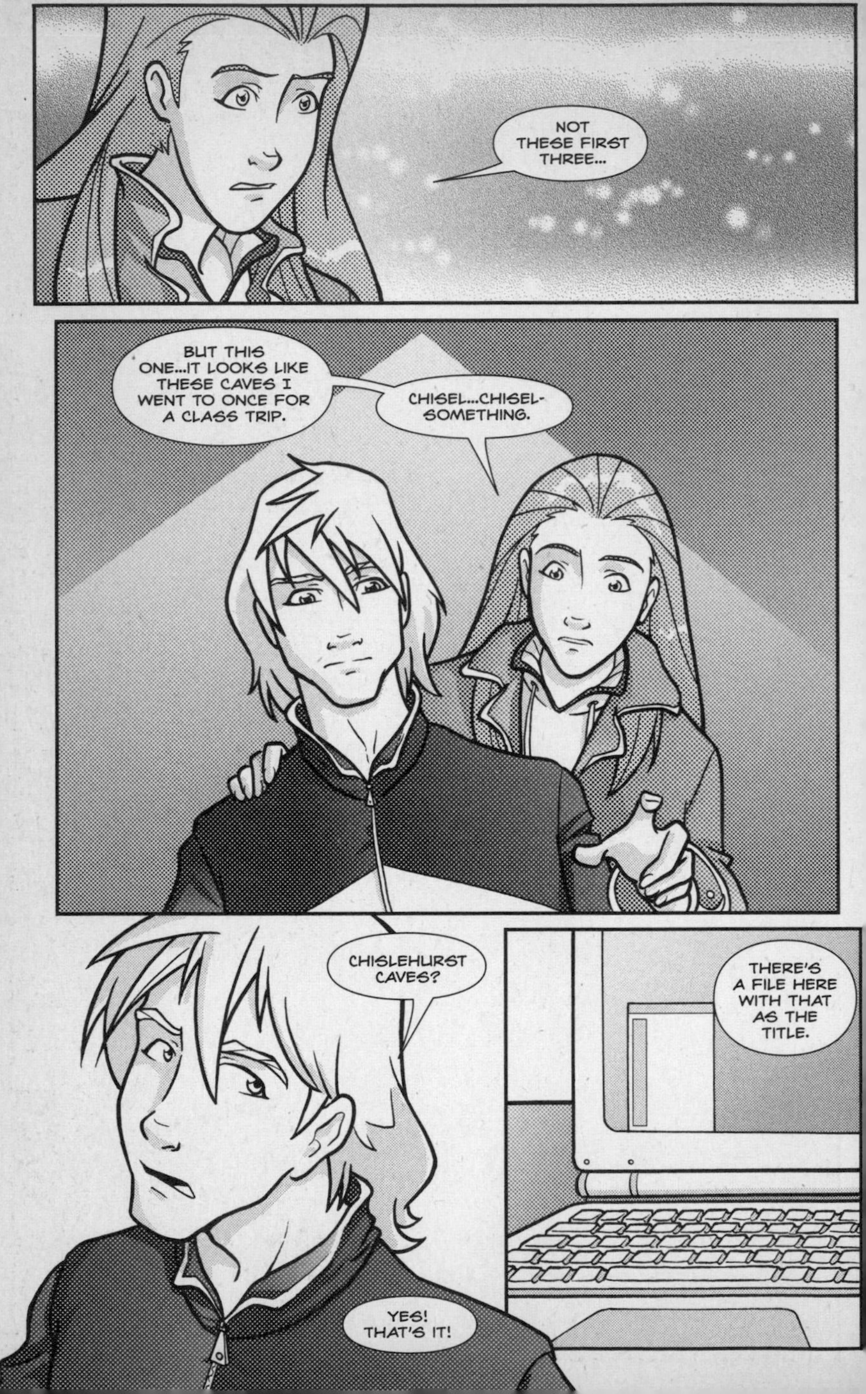
NOT THESE FIRST THREE...
BUT THIS ONE...IT LOOKS LIKE THESE CAVES I WENT TO ONCE FOR A CLASS TRIP.
CHISEL...CHISEL-SOMETHING.
CHISLEHURST CAVES?
THERE'S A FILE HERE WITH THAT AS THE TITLE.
YES! THAT'S IT!

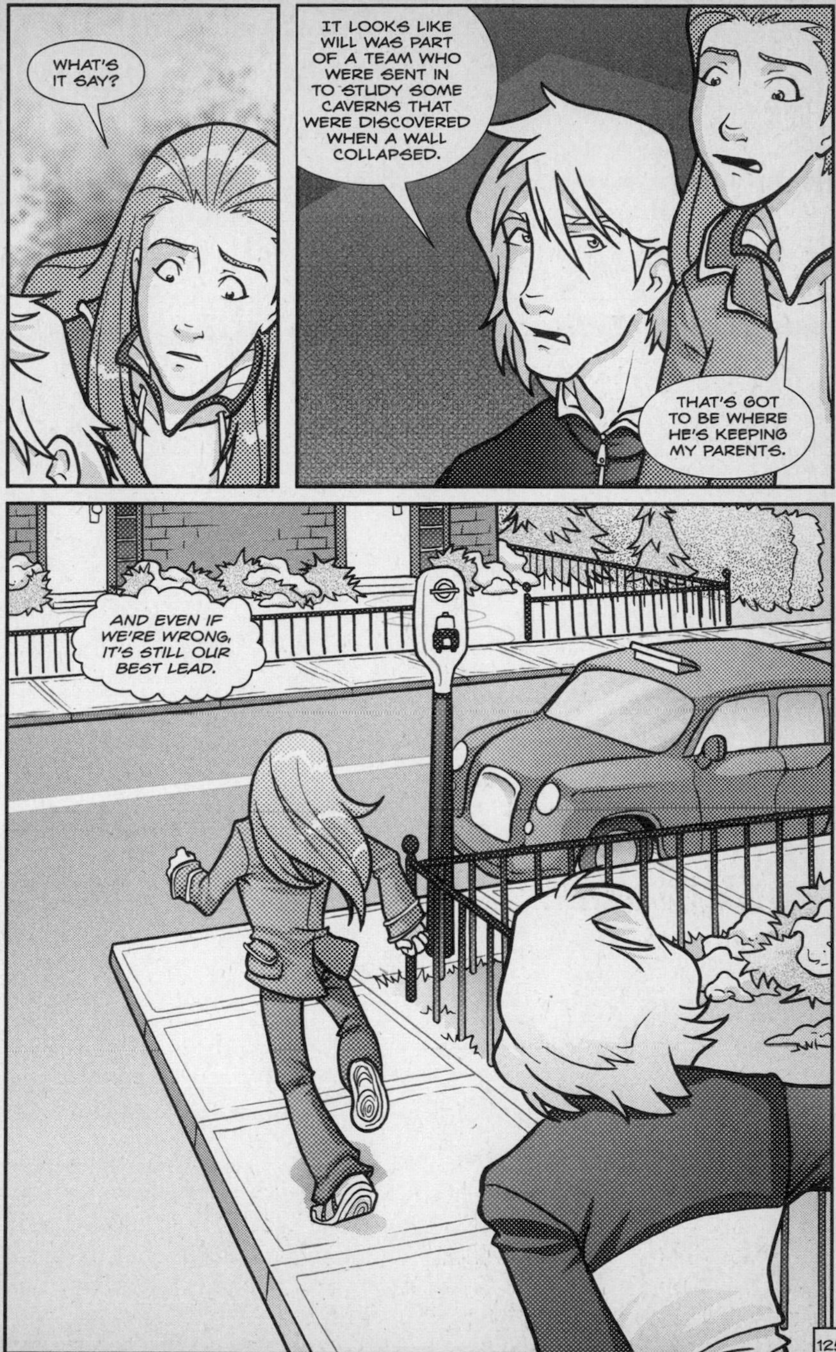
WHAT'S IT SAY?
IT LOOKS LIKE WILL WAS PART OF A TEAM WHO WERE SENT IN TO STUDY SOME CAVERNS THAT WERE DISCOVERED WHEN A WALL COLLAPSED.
THAT'S GOT TO BE WHERE HE'S KEEPING MY PARENTS.
AND EVEN IF WE'RE WRONG, IT'S STILL OUR BEST LEAD.

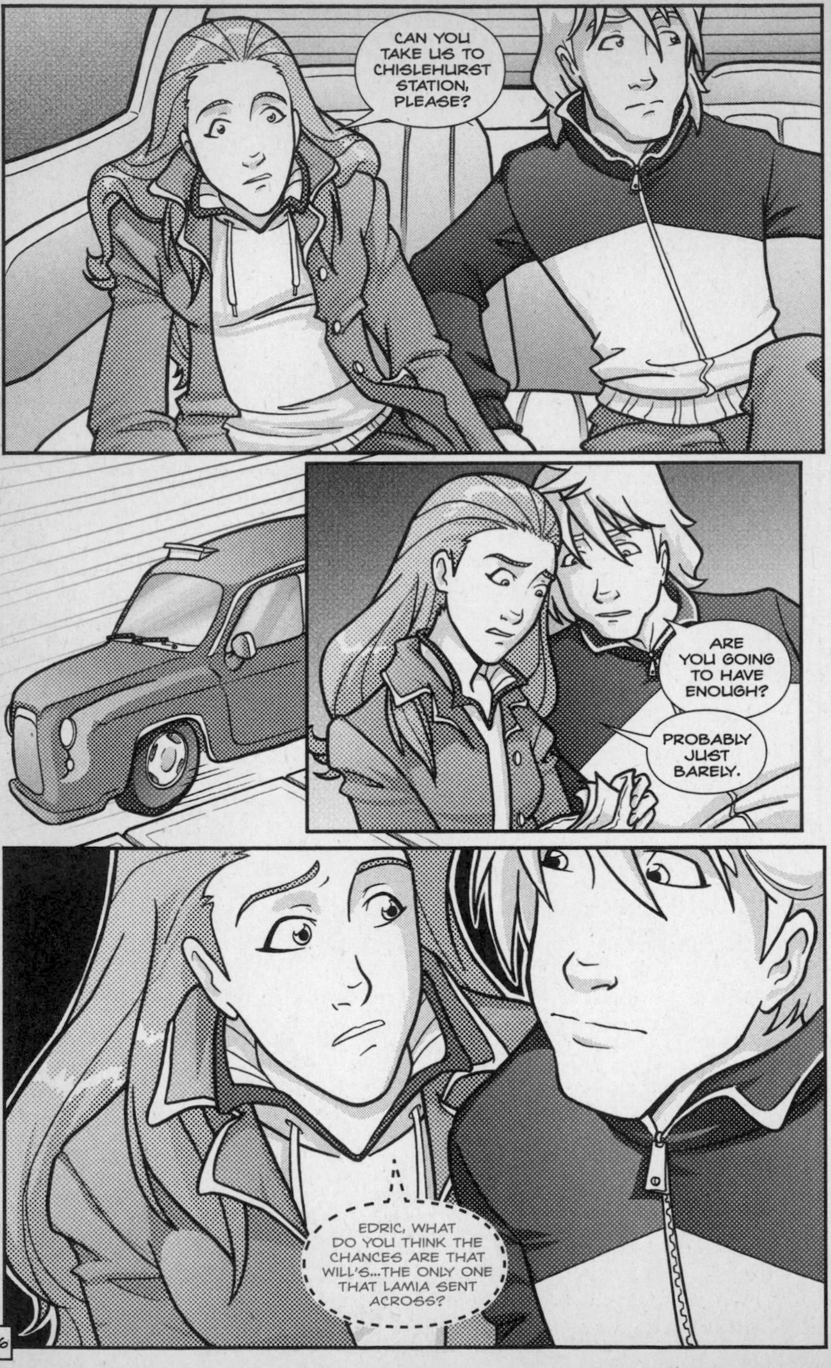
CAN YOU TAKE US TO CHISLEHURST STATION, PLEASE?
ARE YOU GOING TO HAVE ENOUGH?
PROBABLY JUST BARELY.
EDRIC, WHAT DO YOU THINK THE CHANCES ARE THAT WILL'S...THE ONLY ONE THAT LAMIA SENT ACROSS?

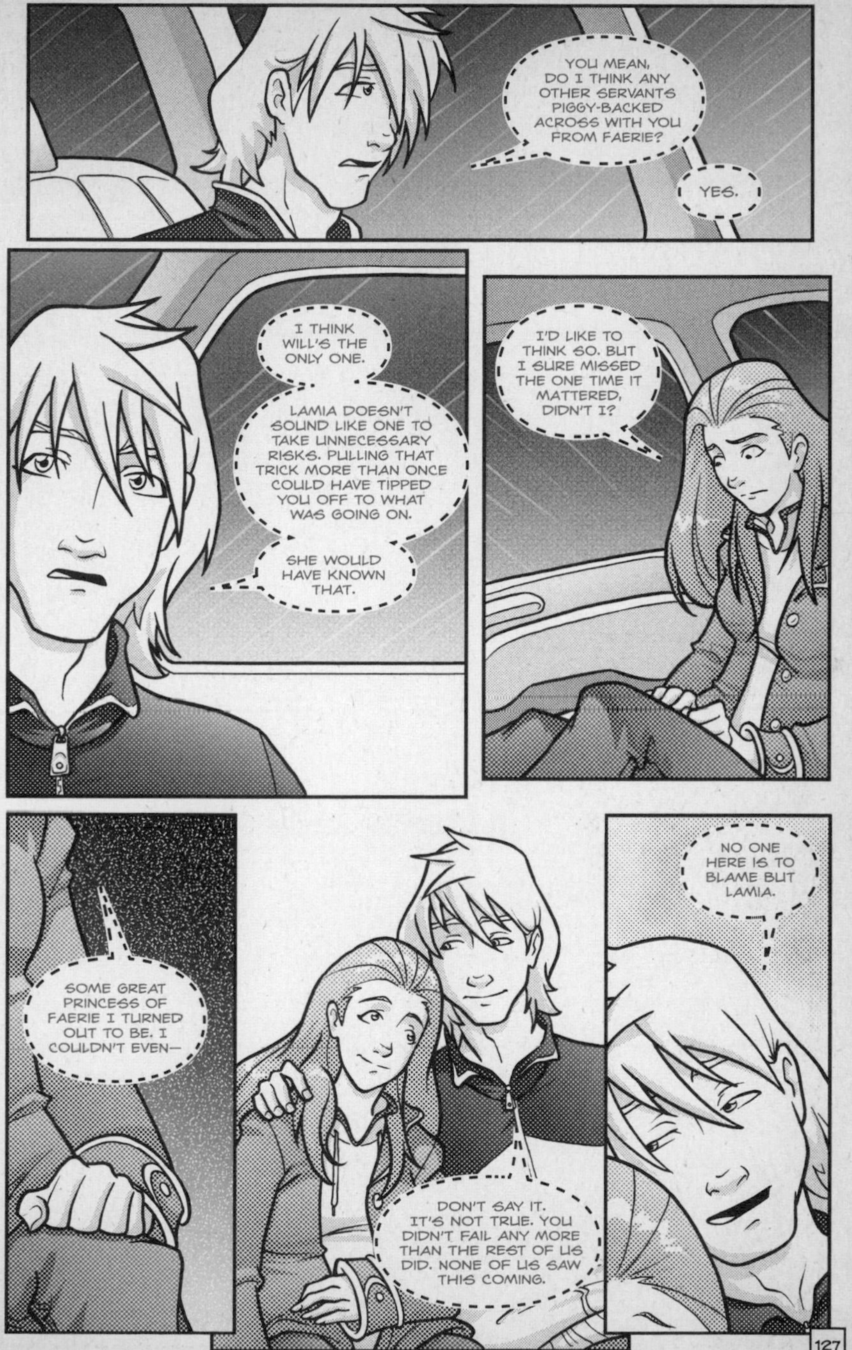
YOU MEAN, DO I THINK ANY OTHER SERVANTS PIGGY-BACKED ACROSS WITH YOU FROM FAERIE?
YES.
I THINK WILL'S THE ONLY ONE.
LAMIA DOESN'T SOUND LIKE ONE TO TAKE UNNECESSARY RISKS. PULLING THAT TRICK MORE THAN ONCE COULD HAVE TIPPED YOU OFF TO WHAT WAS GOING ON.
SHE WOULD HAVE KNOWN THAT.
I'D LIKE TO THINK SO. BUT I SURE MISSED THE ONE TIME IT MATTERED, DIDN'T I?
SOME GREAT PRINCESS OF FAERIE I TURNED OUT TO BE. I COULDN'T EVEN—
DON'T SAY IT. IT'S NOT TRUE. YOU DIDN'T FAIL ANY MORE THAN THE REST OF US DID. NONE OF US SAW THIS COMING.
NO ONE HERE IS TO BLAME BUT LAMIA.

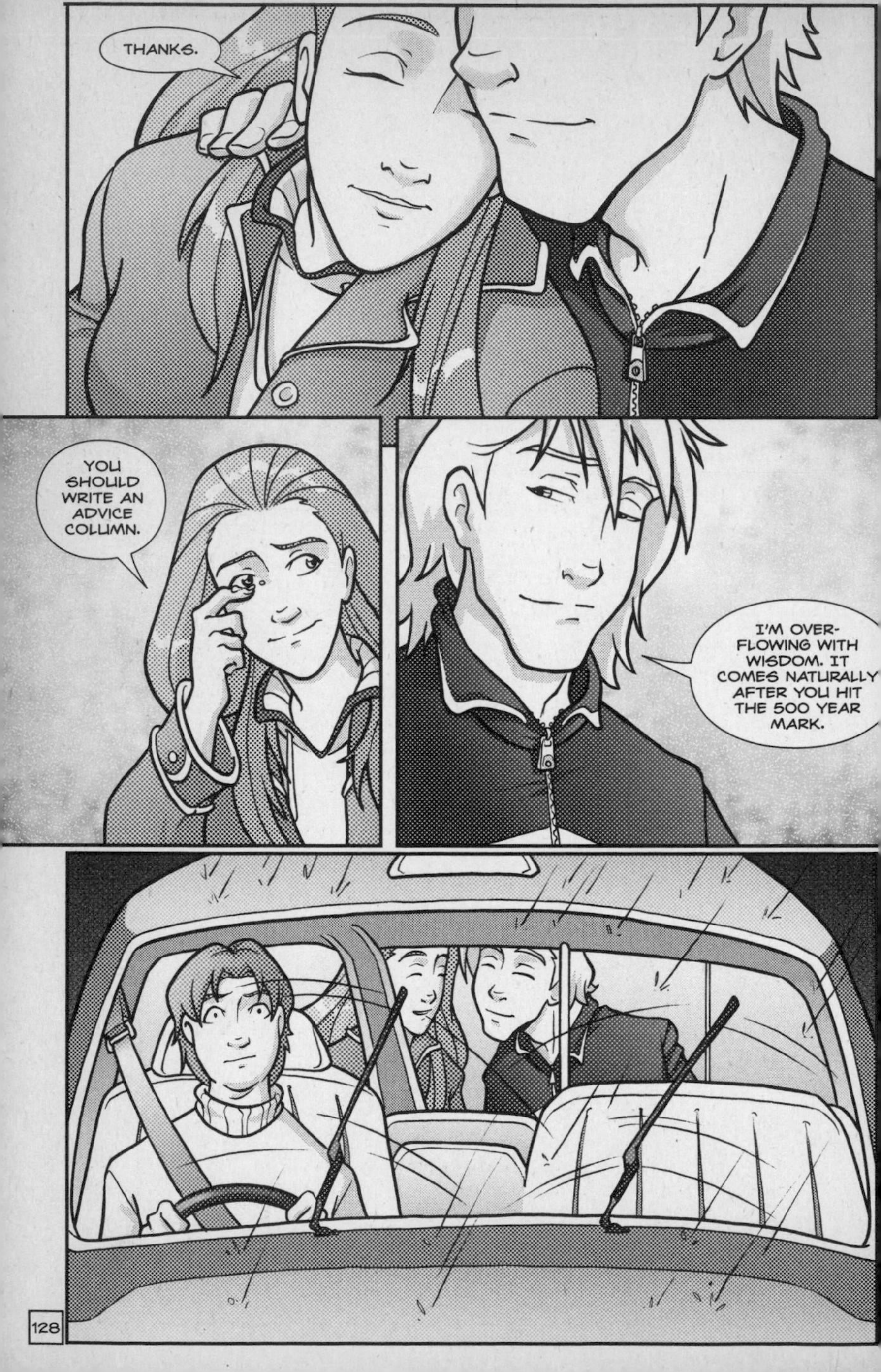
THANKS.
YOU SHOULD WRITE AN ADVICE COLUMN.
I'M OVER-FLOWING WITH WISDOM. IT COMES NATURALLY AFTER YOU HIT THE 500 YEAR MARK.

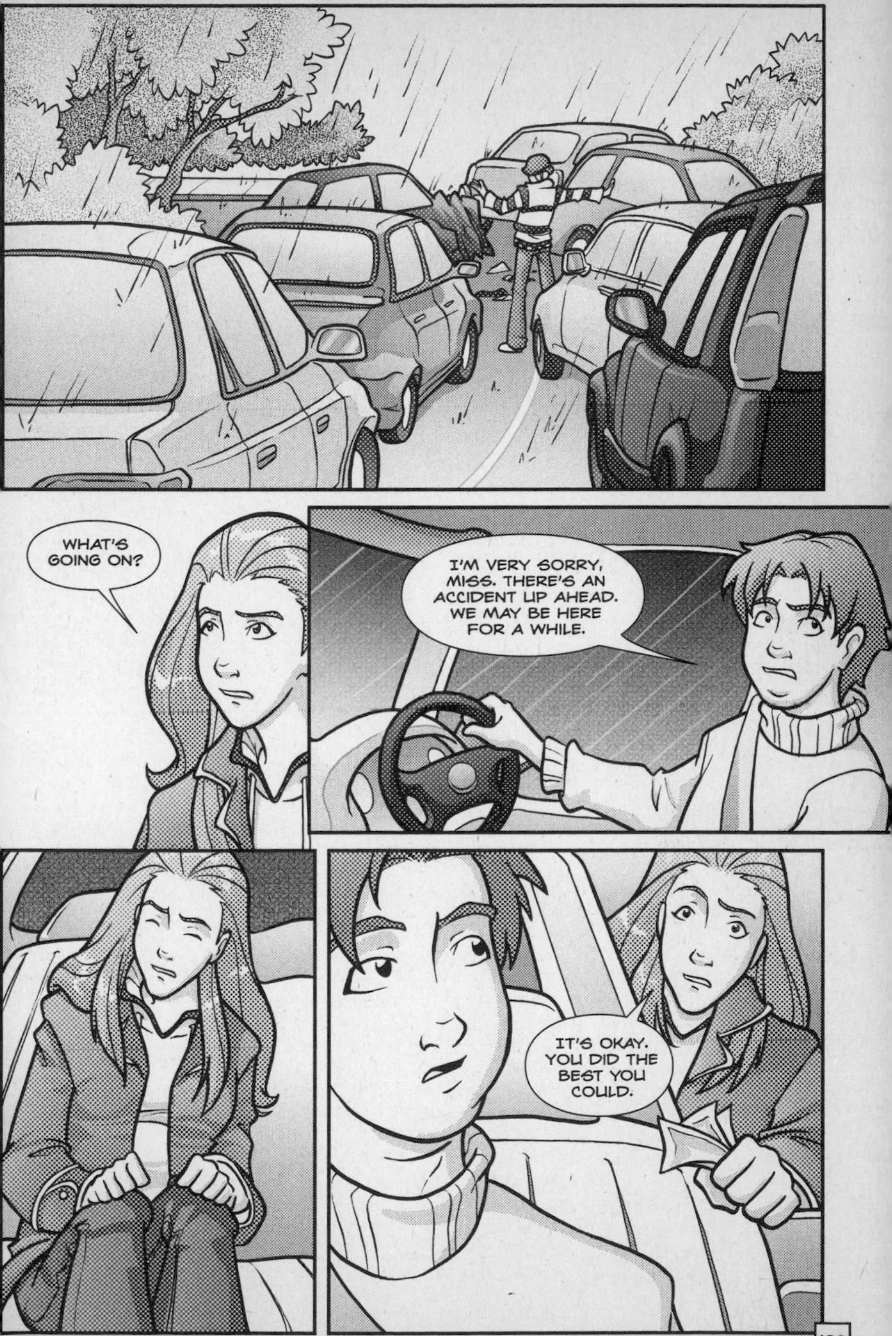
WHAT'S GOING ON?
I'M VERY SORRY, MISS. THERE'S AN ACCIDENT UP AHEAD. WE MAY BE HERE FOR A WHILE.
IT'S OKAY. YOU DID THE BEST YOU COULD.

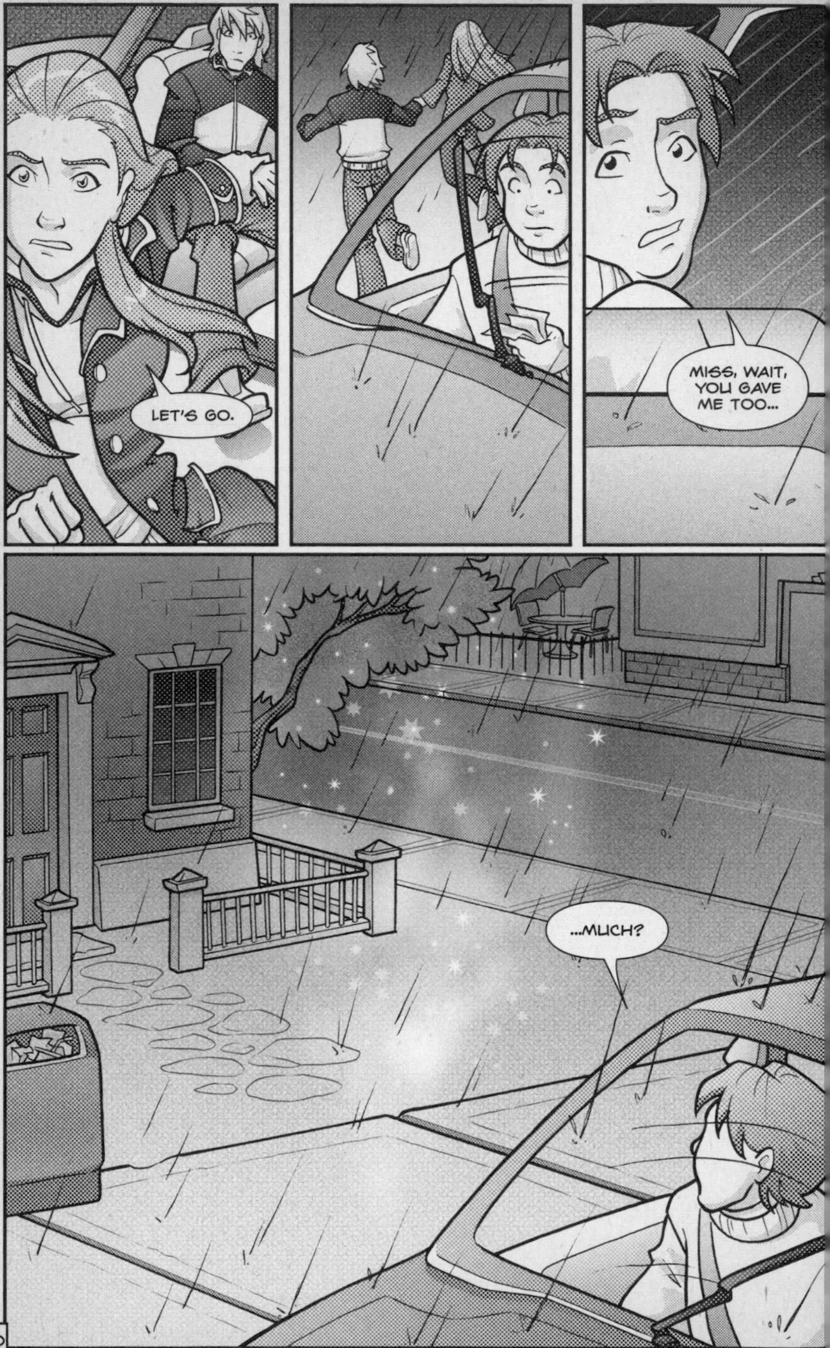
LET'S GO.
MISS, WAIT, YOU GAVE ME TOO...
...MUCH?

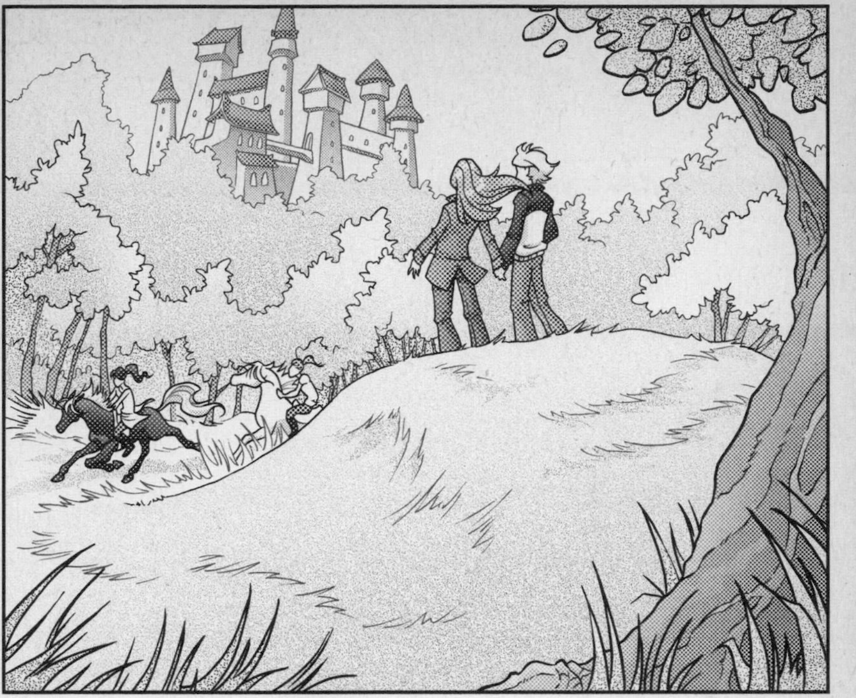
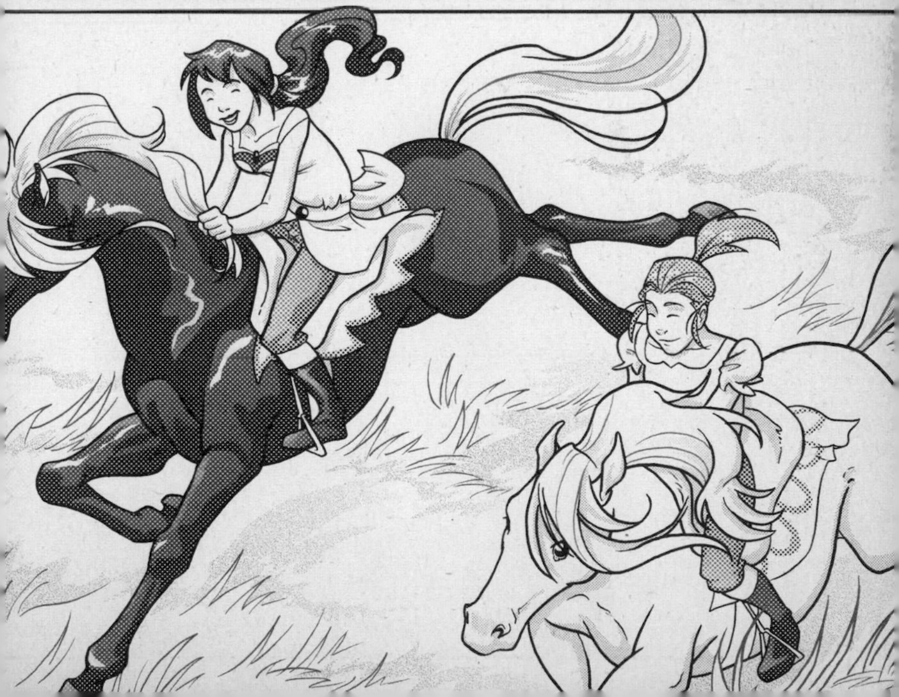

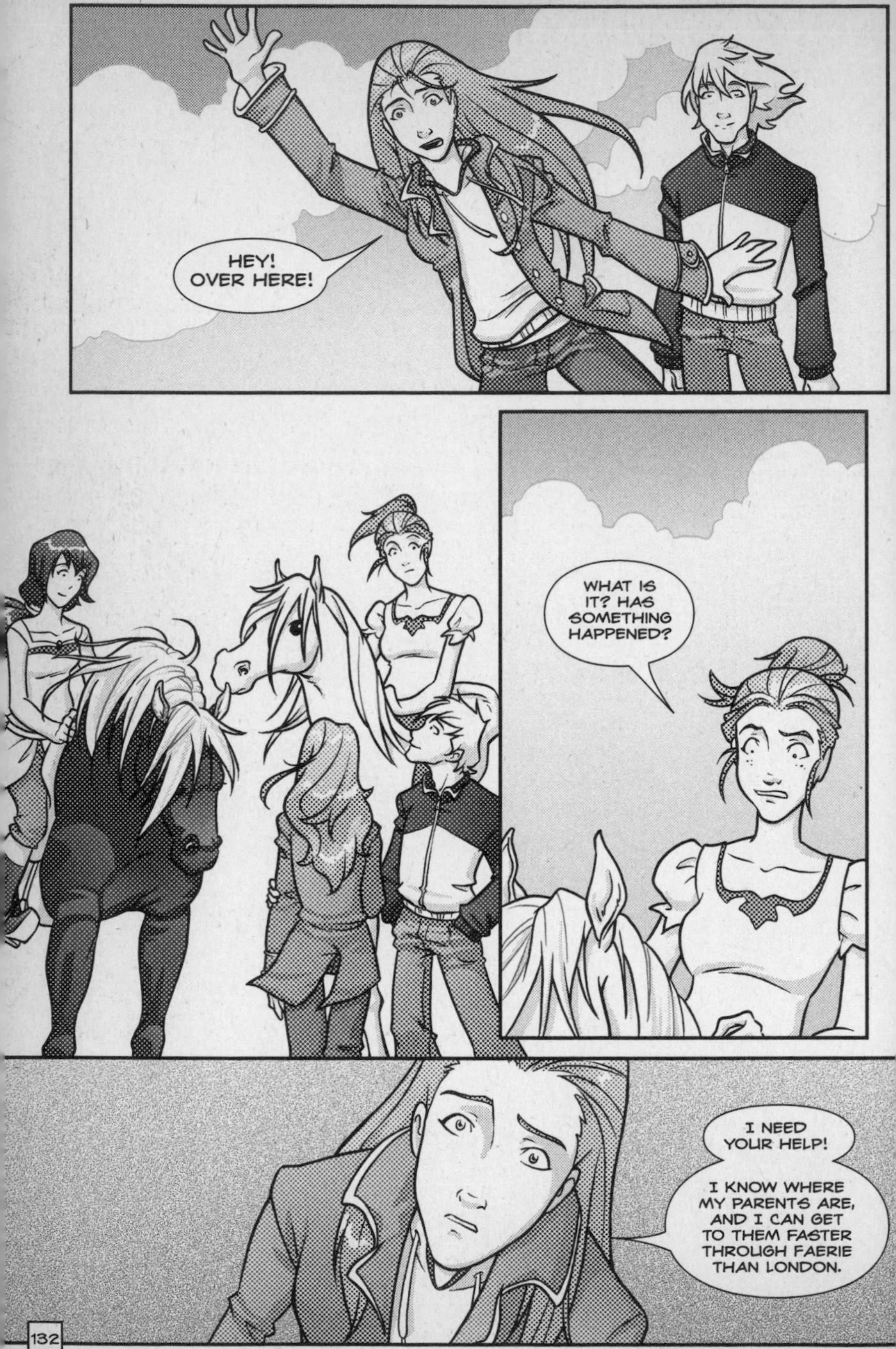
HEY! OVER HERE!
WHAT IS IT? HAS SOMETHING HAPPENED?
I NEED YOUR HELP!
I KNOW WHERE MY PARENTS ARE, AND I CAN GET TO THEM FASTER THROUGH FAERIE THAN LONDON.

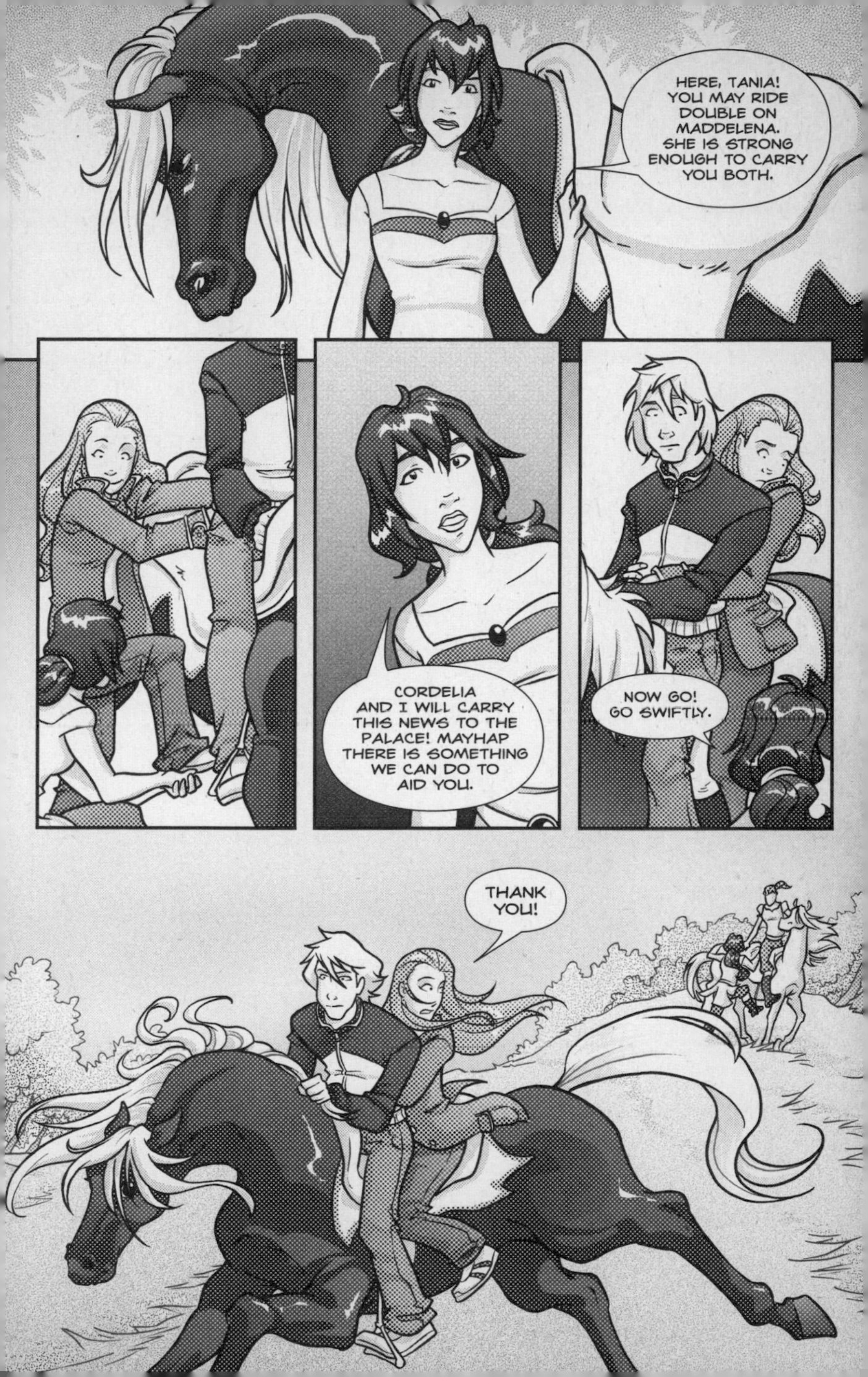
HERE, TANIA! YOU MAY RIDE DOUBLE ON MADDELENA. SHE IS STRONG ENOUGH TO CARRY YOU BOTH.
CORDELIA AND I WILL CARRY THIS NEWS TO THE PALACE! MAYHAP THERE IS SOMETHING WE CAN DO TO AID YOU.
NOW GO! GO SWIFTLY.
THANK YOU!

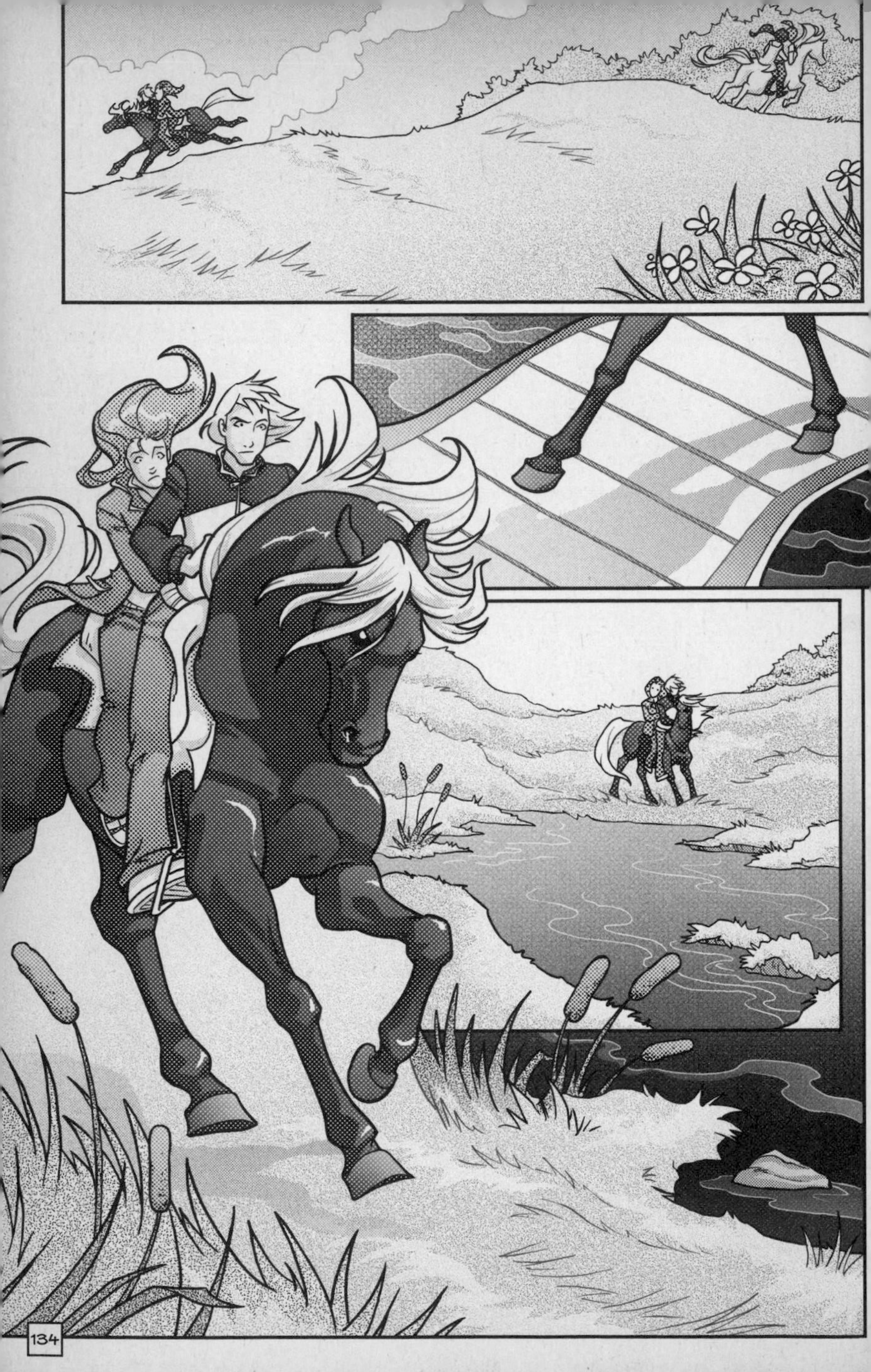

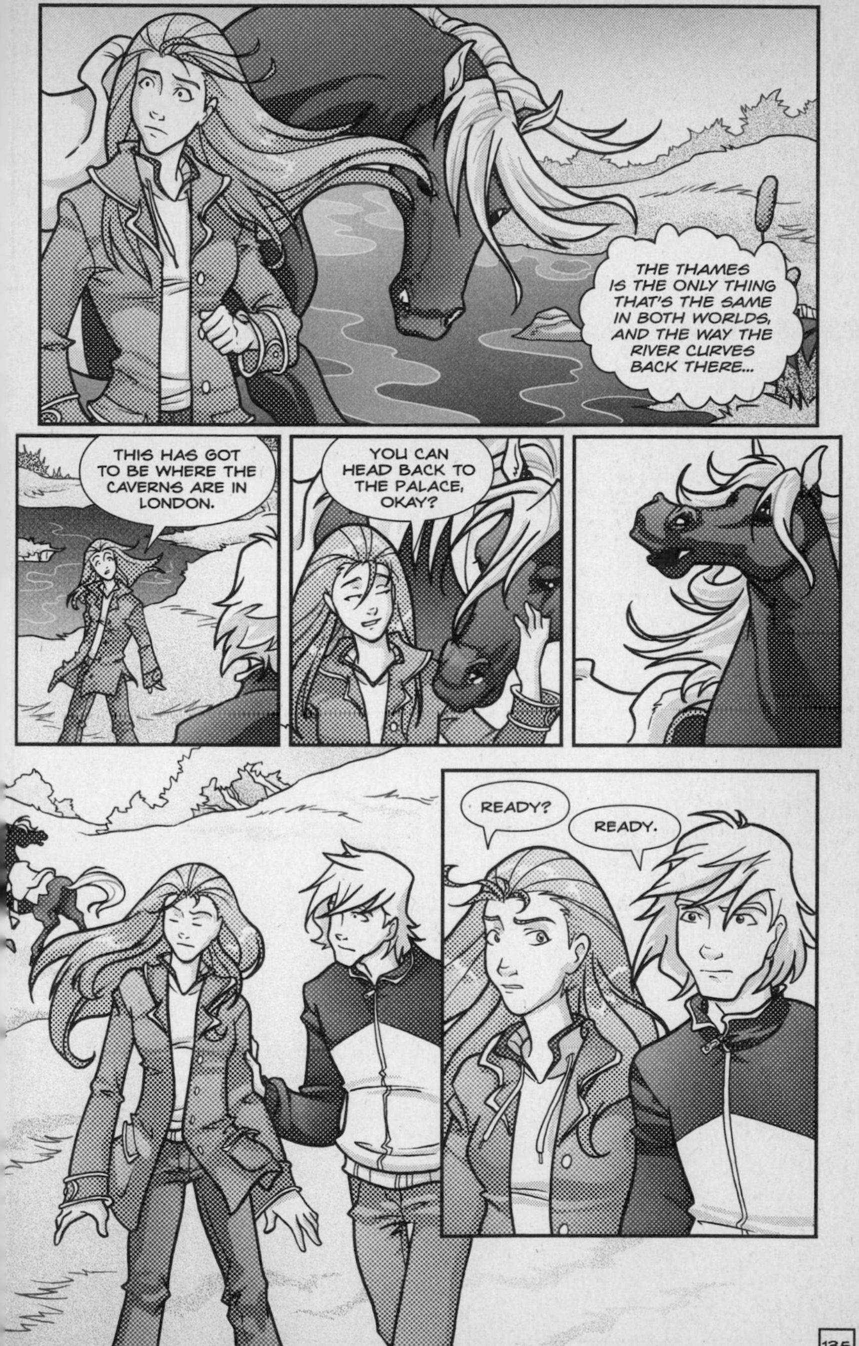
THE THAMES IS THE ONLY THING THAT'S THE SAME IN BOTH WORLDS, AND THE WAY THE RIVER CURVES BACK THERE...
THIS HAS GOT TO BE WHERE THE CAVERNS ARE IN LONDON.
YOU CAN HEAD BACK TO THE PALACE, OKAY?
READY?
READY.

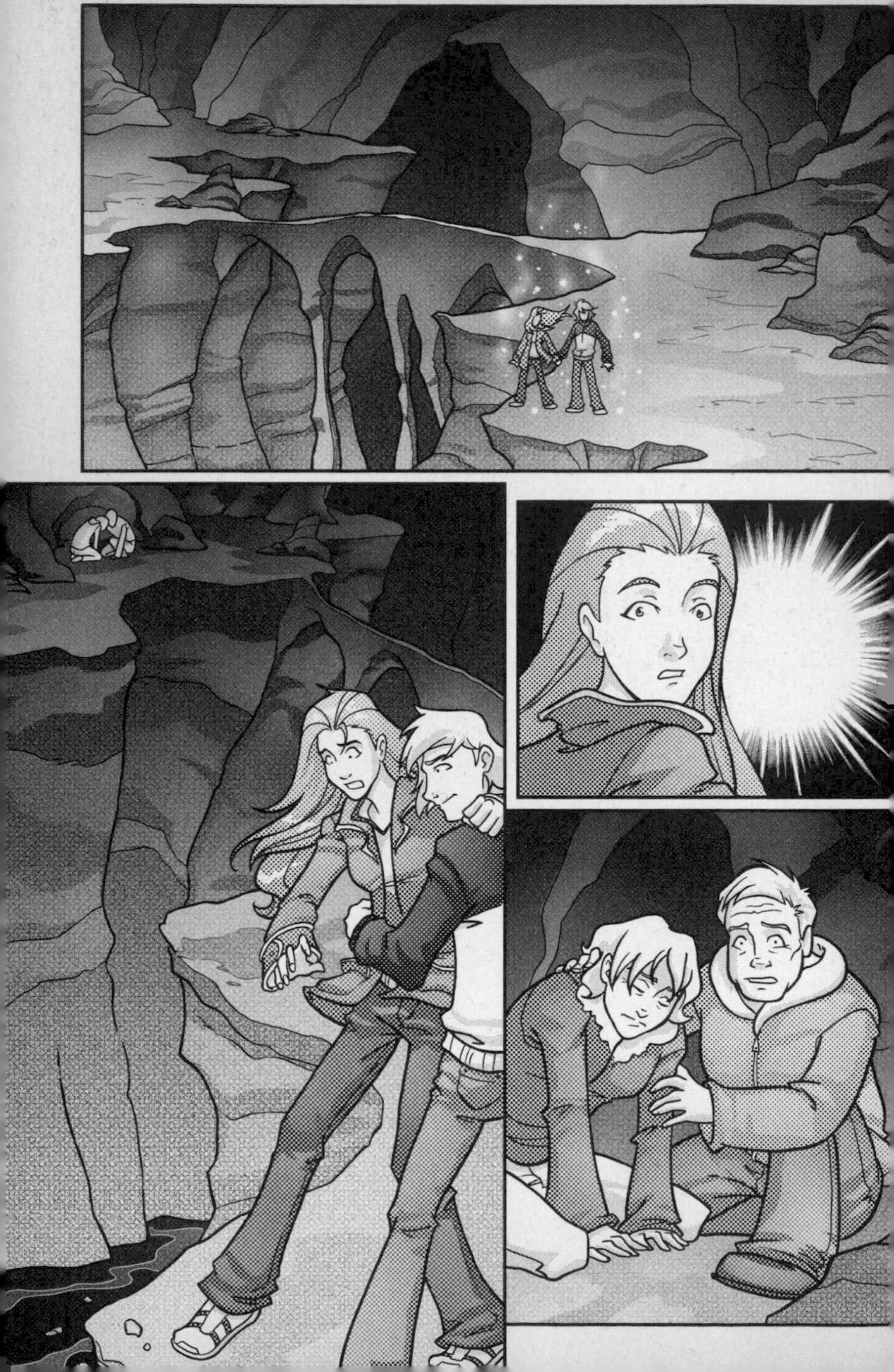

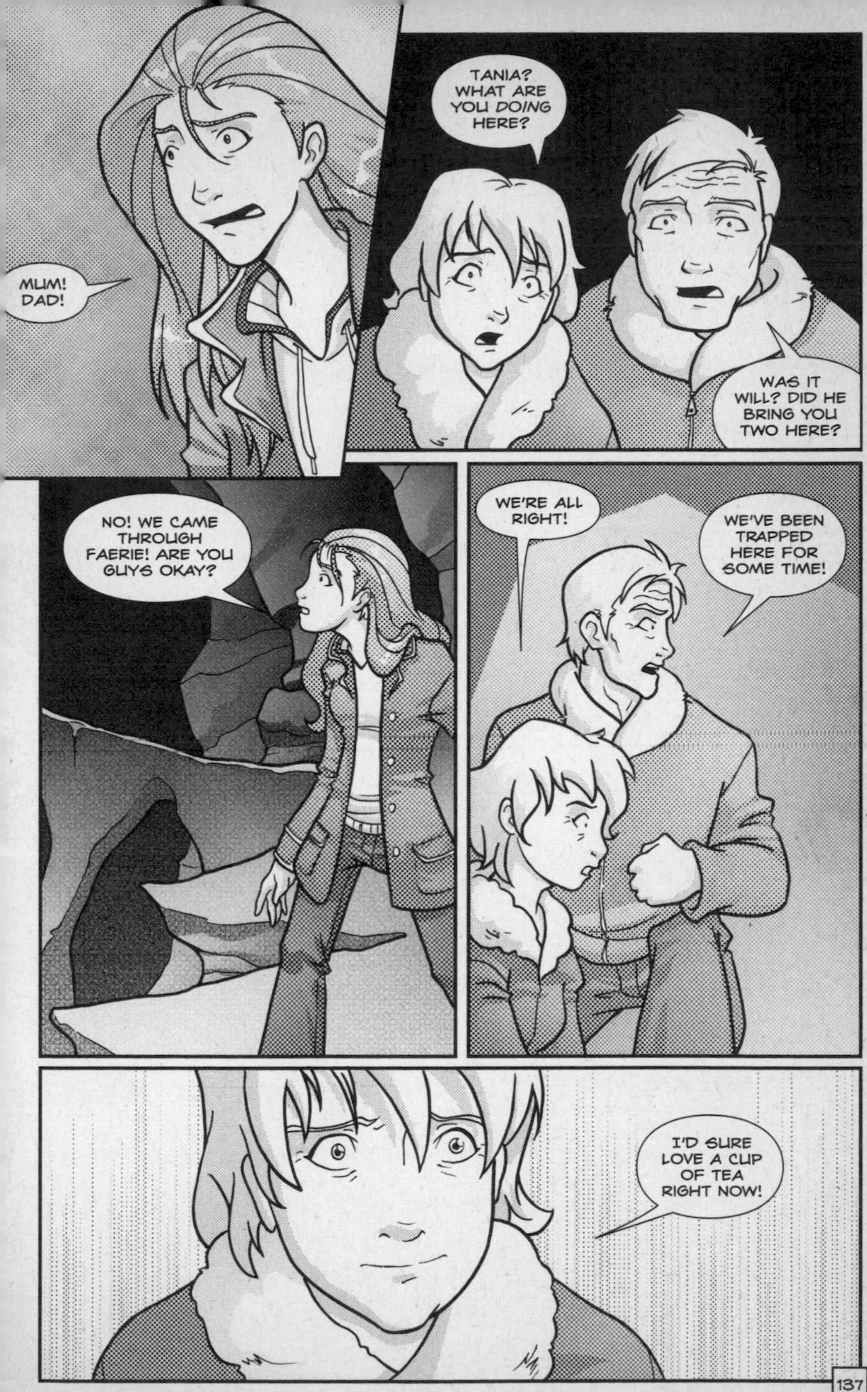
MUM! DAD!
TANIA? WHAT ARE YOU DOING HERE?
WAS IT WILL? DID HE BRING YOU TWO HERE?
NO! WE CAME THROUGH FAERIE! ARE YOU GUYS OKAY?
WE'RE ALL RIGHT!
WE'VE BEEN TRAPPED HERE FOR SOME TIME!
I'D SURE LOVE A CUP OF TEA RIGHT NOW!

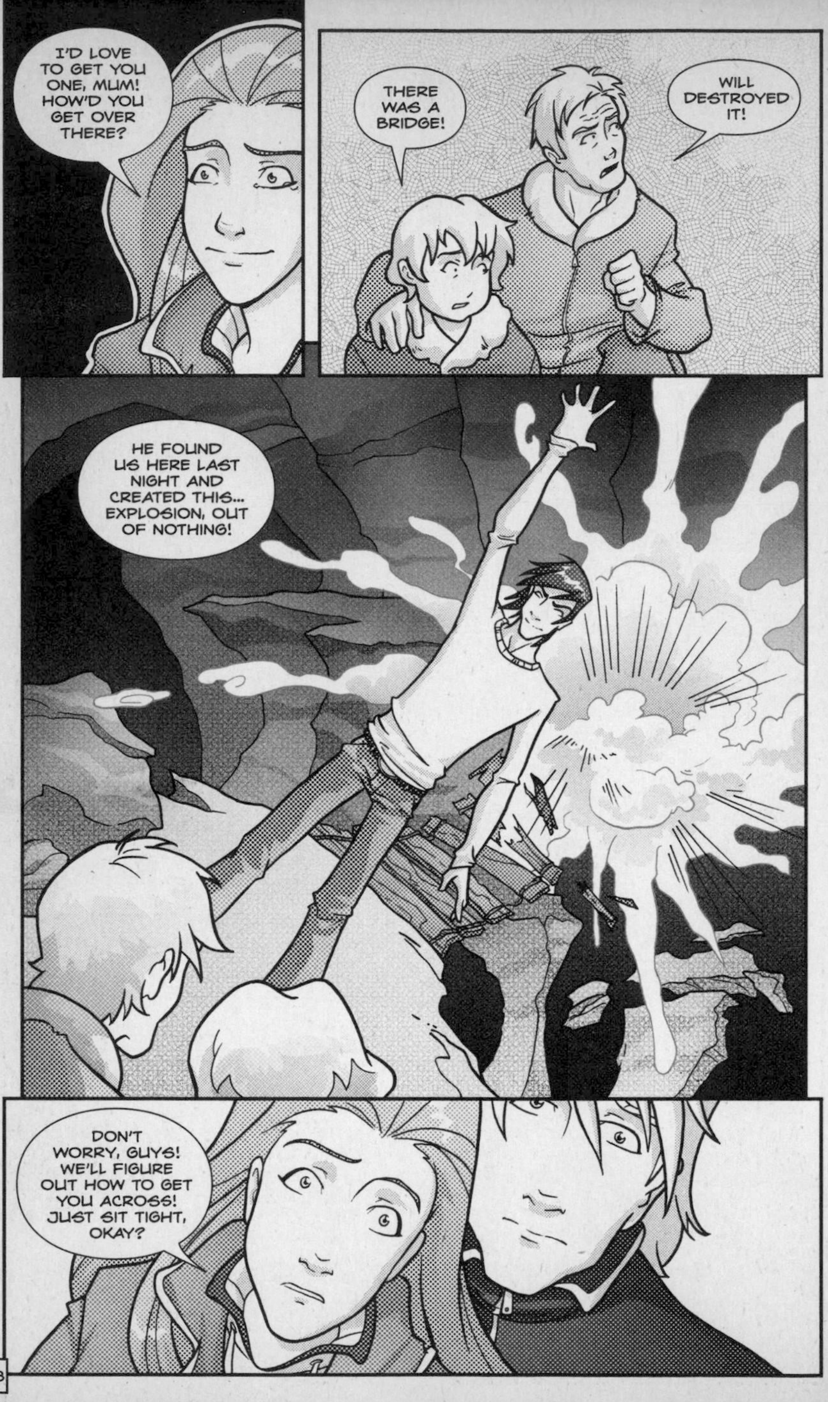
I'D LOVE TO GET YOU ONE, MUM! HOW'D YOU GET OVER THERE?
THERE WAS A BRIDGE!
WILL DESTROYED IT!
HE FOUND US HERE LAST NIGHT AND CREATED THIS... EXPLOSION, OUT OF NOTHING!
DON'T WORRY, GUYS! WE'LL FIGURE OUT HOW TO GET YOU ACROSS! JUST SIT TIGHT, OKAY?

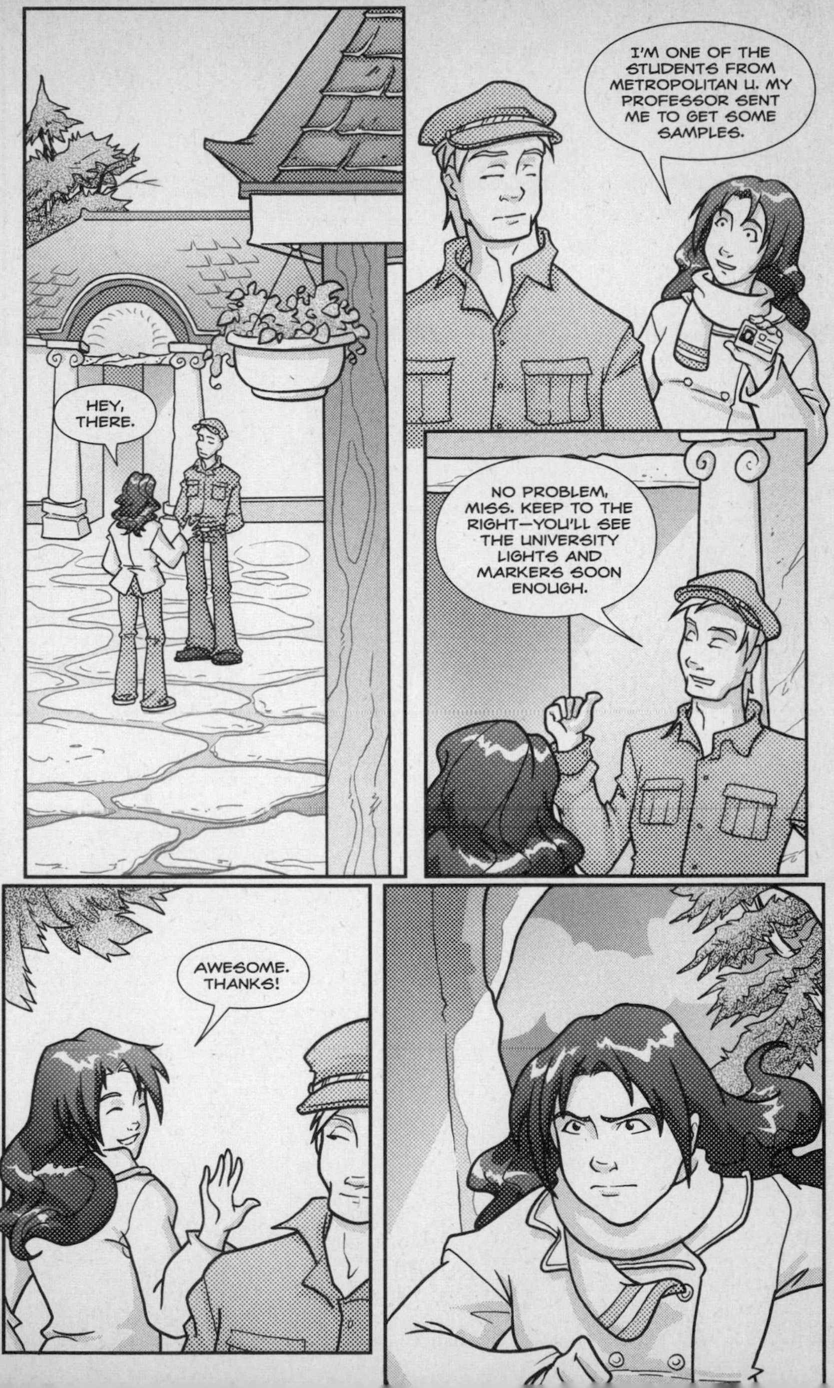
HEY, THERE.
I'M ONE OF THE STUDENTS FROM METROPOLITAN U. MY PROFESSOR SENT ME TO GET SOME SAMPLES.
NO PROBLEM, MISS. KEEP TO THE RIGHT—YOU'LL SEE THE UNIVERSITY LIGHTS AND MARKERS SOON ENOUGH.
AWESOME. THANKS!

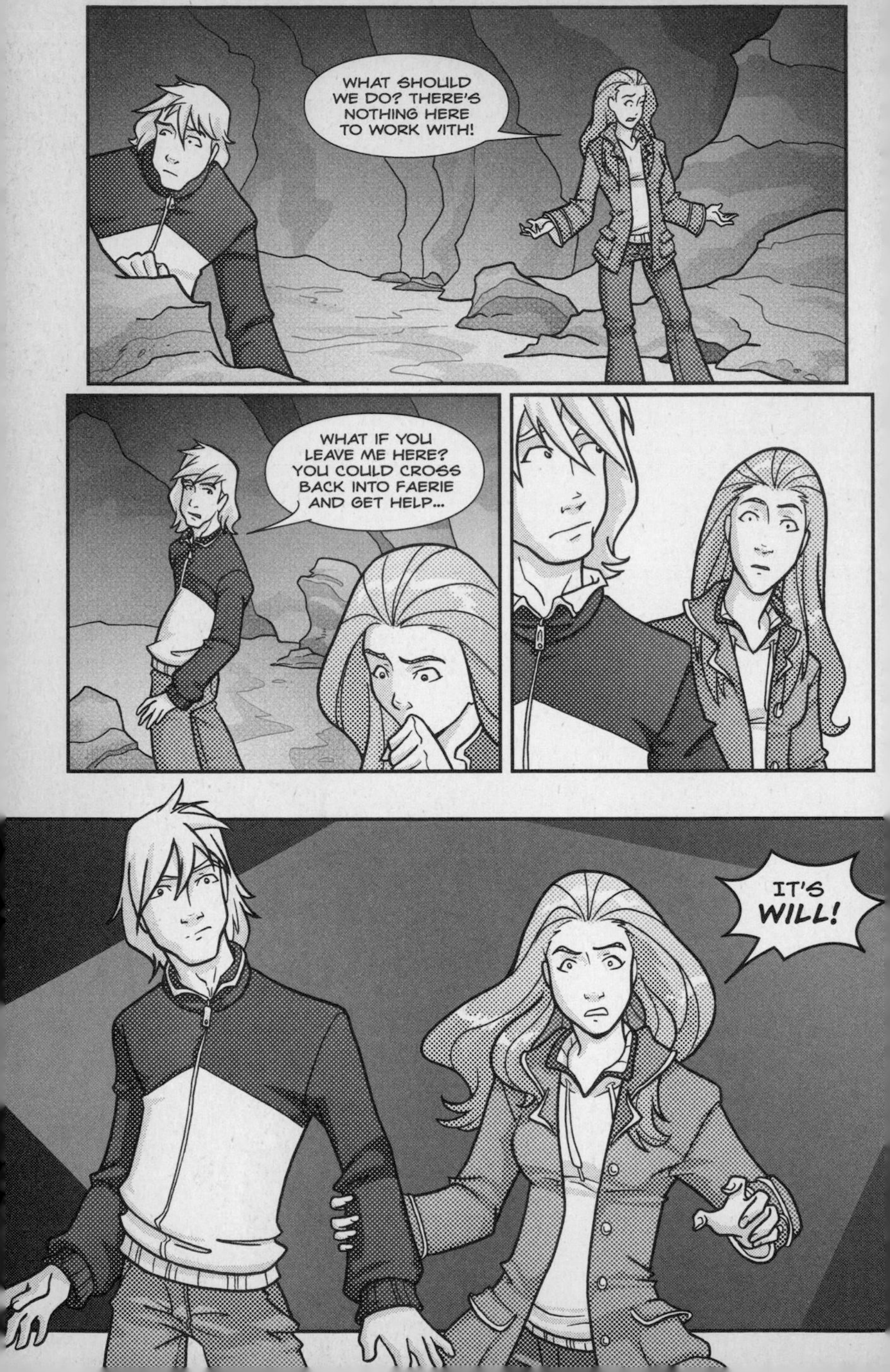
WHAT SHOULD WE DO? THERE'S NOTHING HERE TO WORK WITH!
WHAT IF YOU LEAVE ME HERE? YOU COULD CROSS BACK INTO FAERIE AND GET HELP...
IT'S **WILL!**

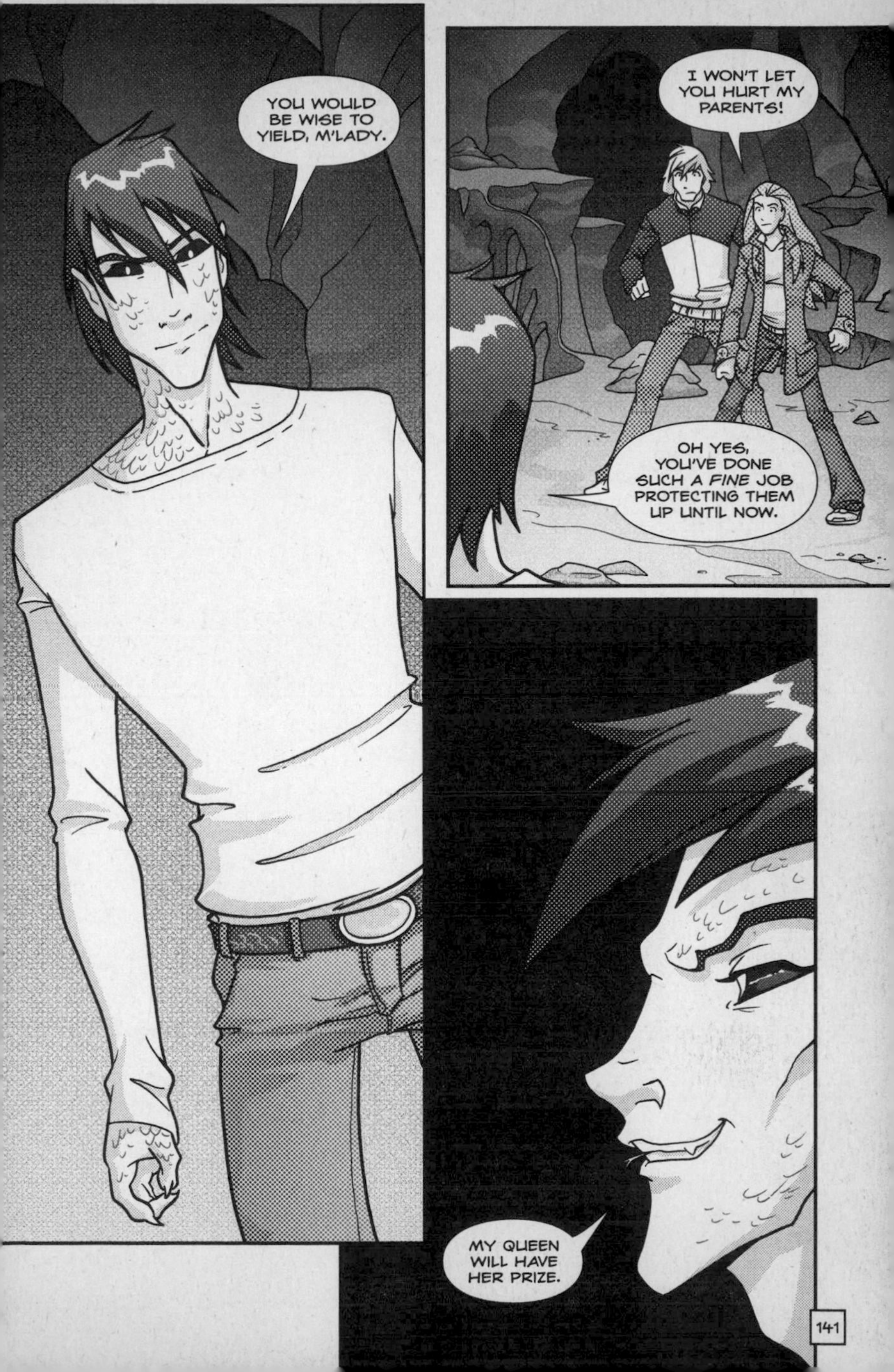
YOU WOULD BE WISE TO YIELD, M'LADY.
I WON'T LET YOU HURT MY PARENTS!
OH YES, YOU'VE DONE SUCH A *FINE* JOB PROTECTING THEM UP UNTIL NOW.
MY QUEEN WILL HAVE HER PRIZE.

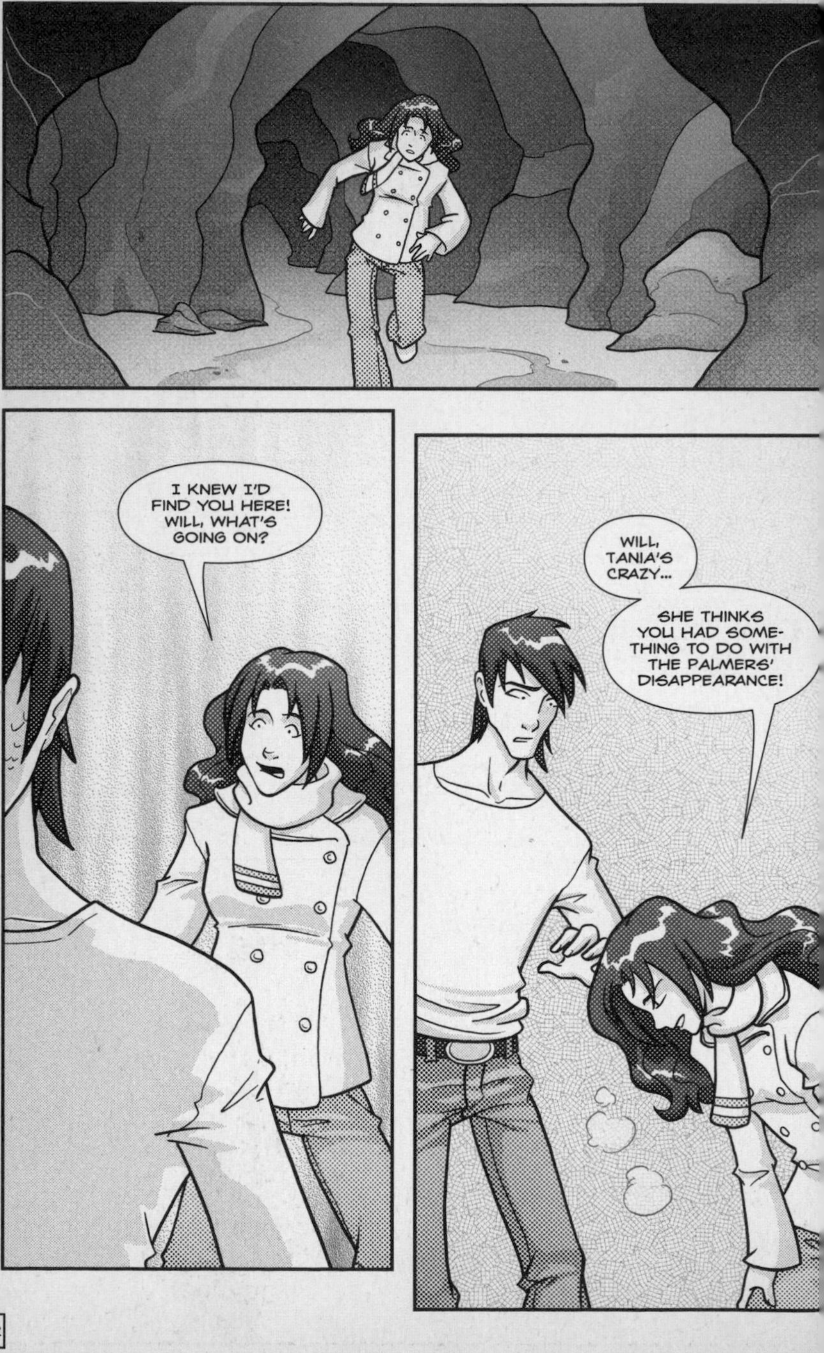
I KNEW I'D FIND YOU HERE! WILL, WHAT'S GOING ON?
WILL, TANIA'S CRAZY...
SHE THINKS YOU HAD SOME-THING TO DO WITH THE PALMERS' DISAPPEARANCE!

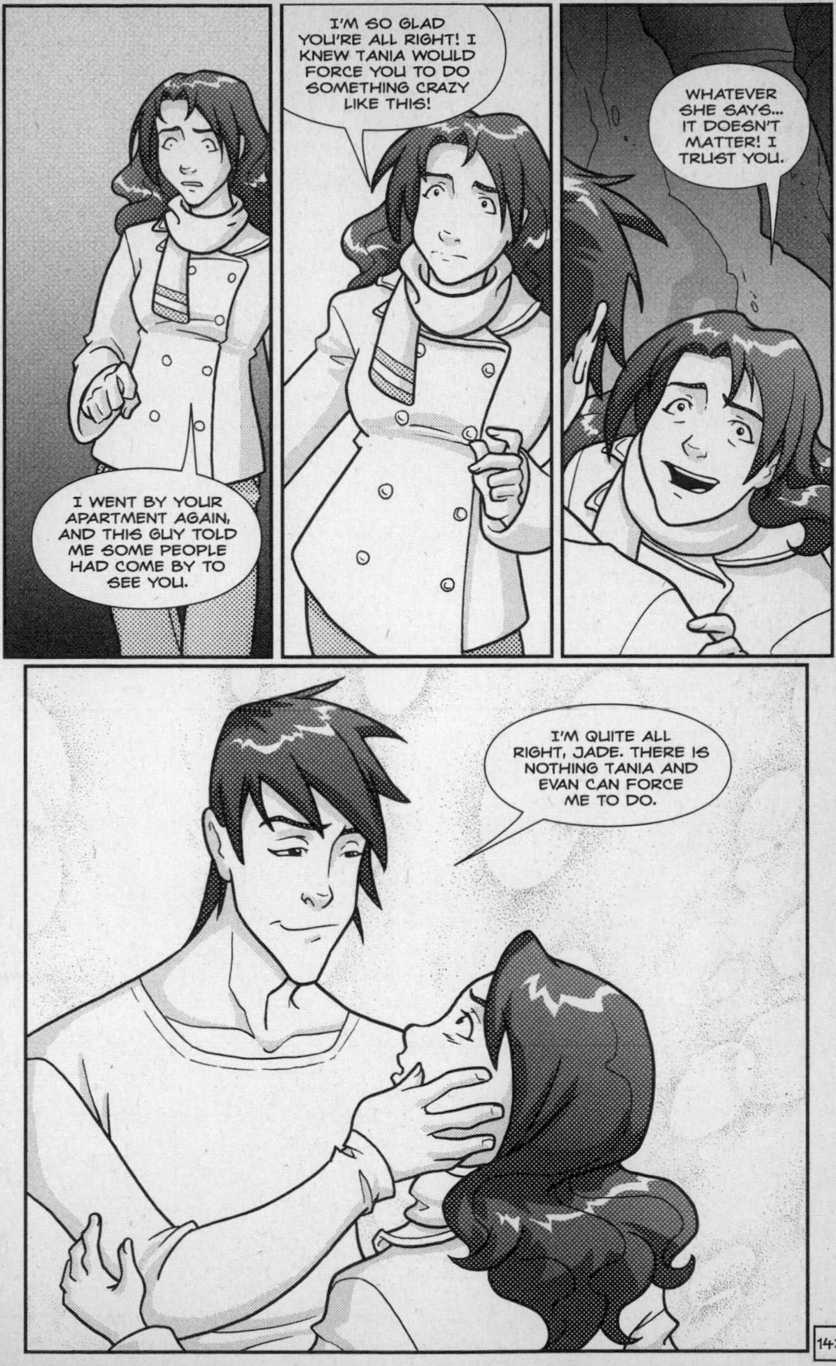
I WENT BY YOUR APARTMENT AGAIN, AND THIS GUY TOLD ME SOME PEOPLE HAD COME BY TO SEE YOU.
I'M SO GLAD YOU'RE ALL RIGHT! I KNEW TANIA WOULD FORCE YOU TO DO SOMETHING CRAZY LIKE THIS!
WHATEVER SHE SAYS... IT DOESN'T MATTER! I TRUST YOU.
I'M QUITE ALL RIGHT, JADE. THERE IS NOTHING TANIA AND EVAN CAN FORCE ME TO DO.

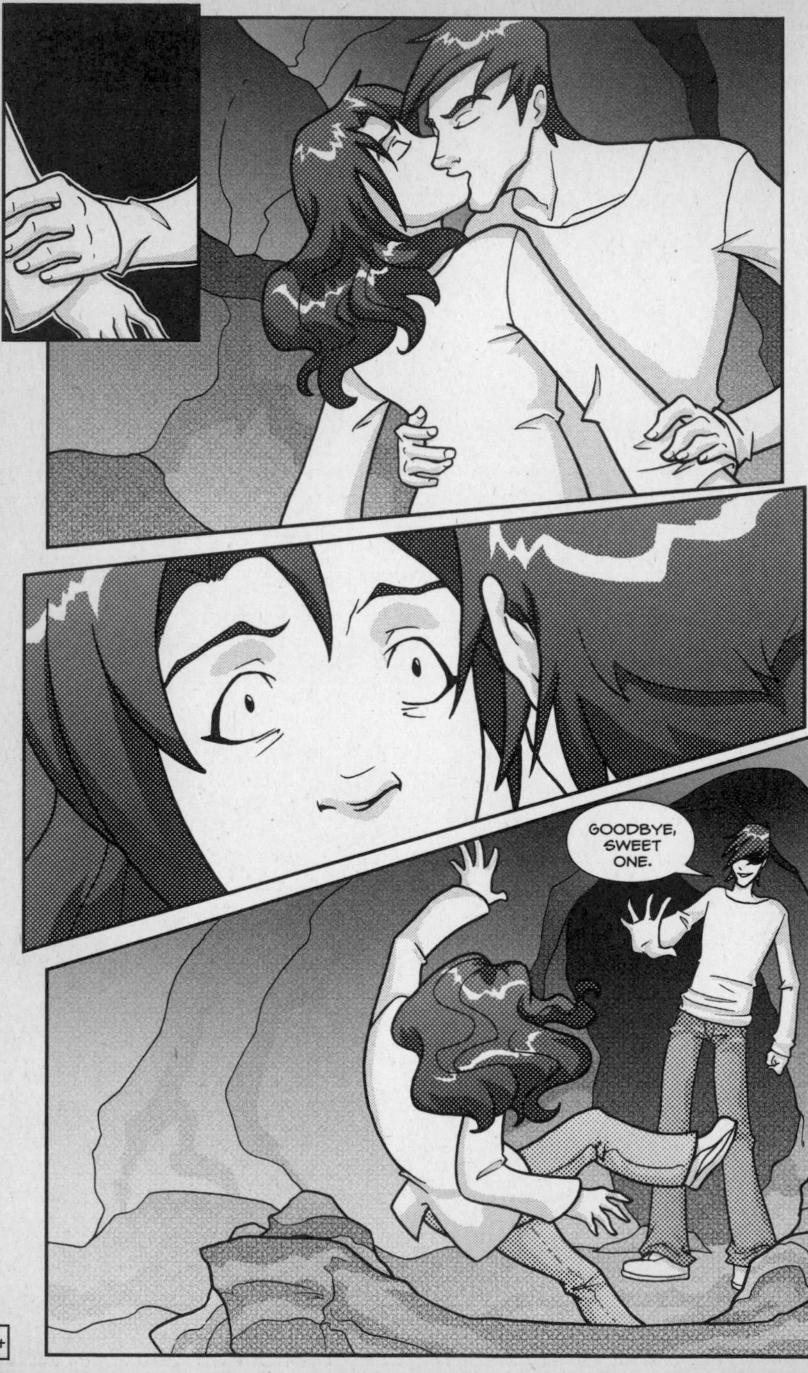
GOODBYE, SWEET ONE.

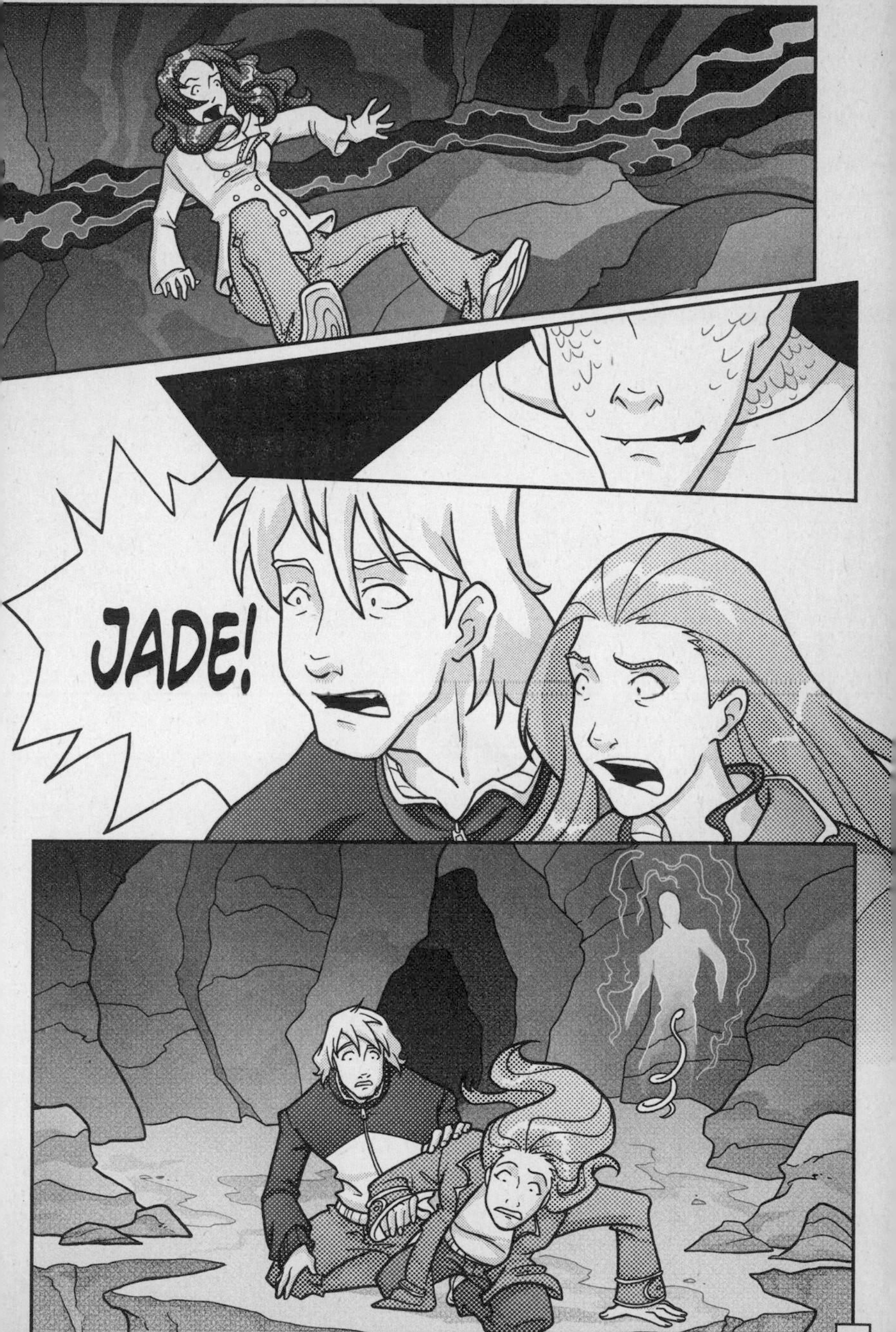
JADE!

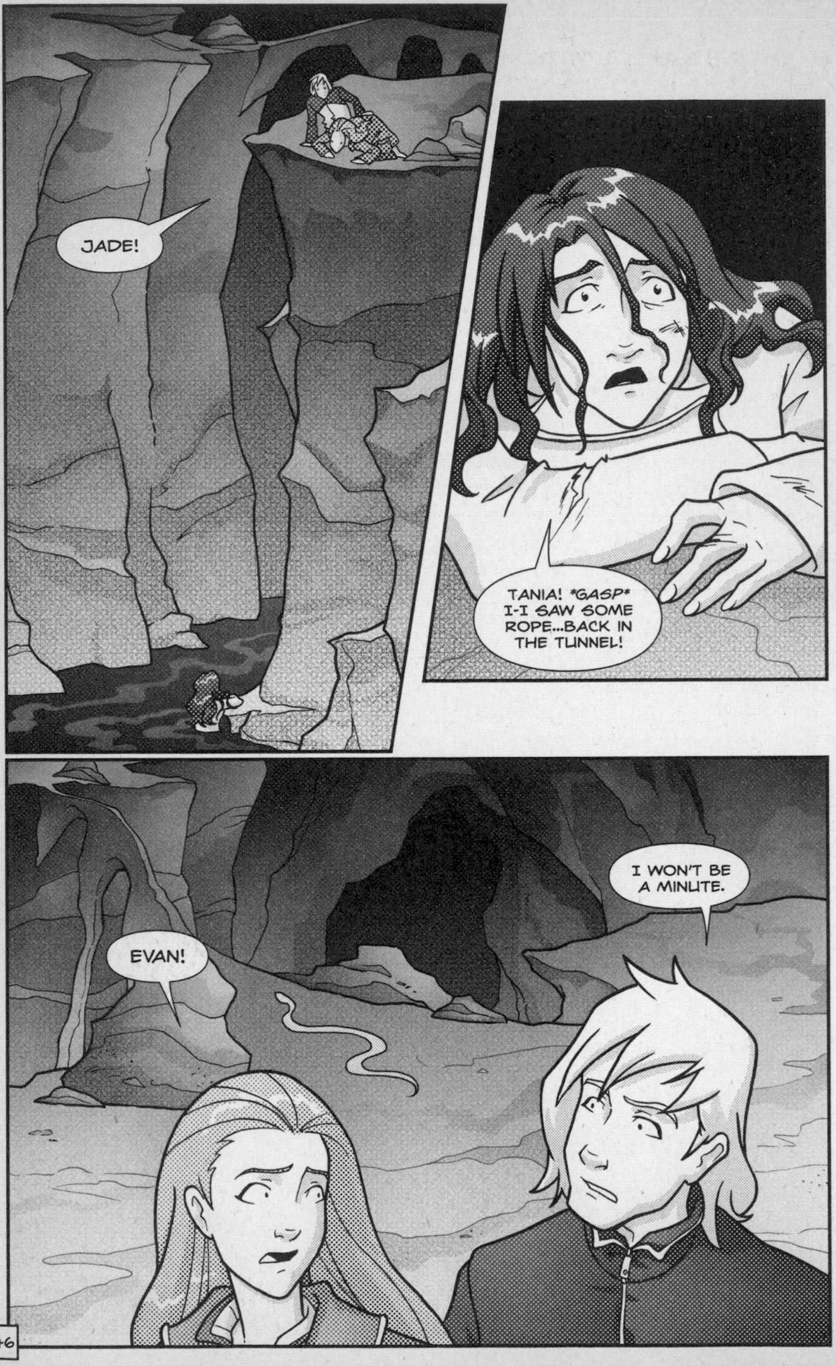
JADE!
TANIA! *GASP* I-I SAW SOME ROPE...BACK IN THE TUNNEL!
EVAN!
I WON'T BE A MINUTE.

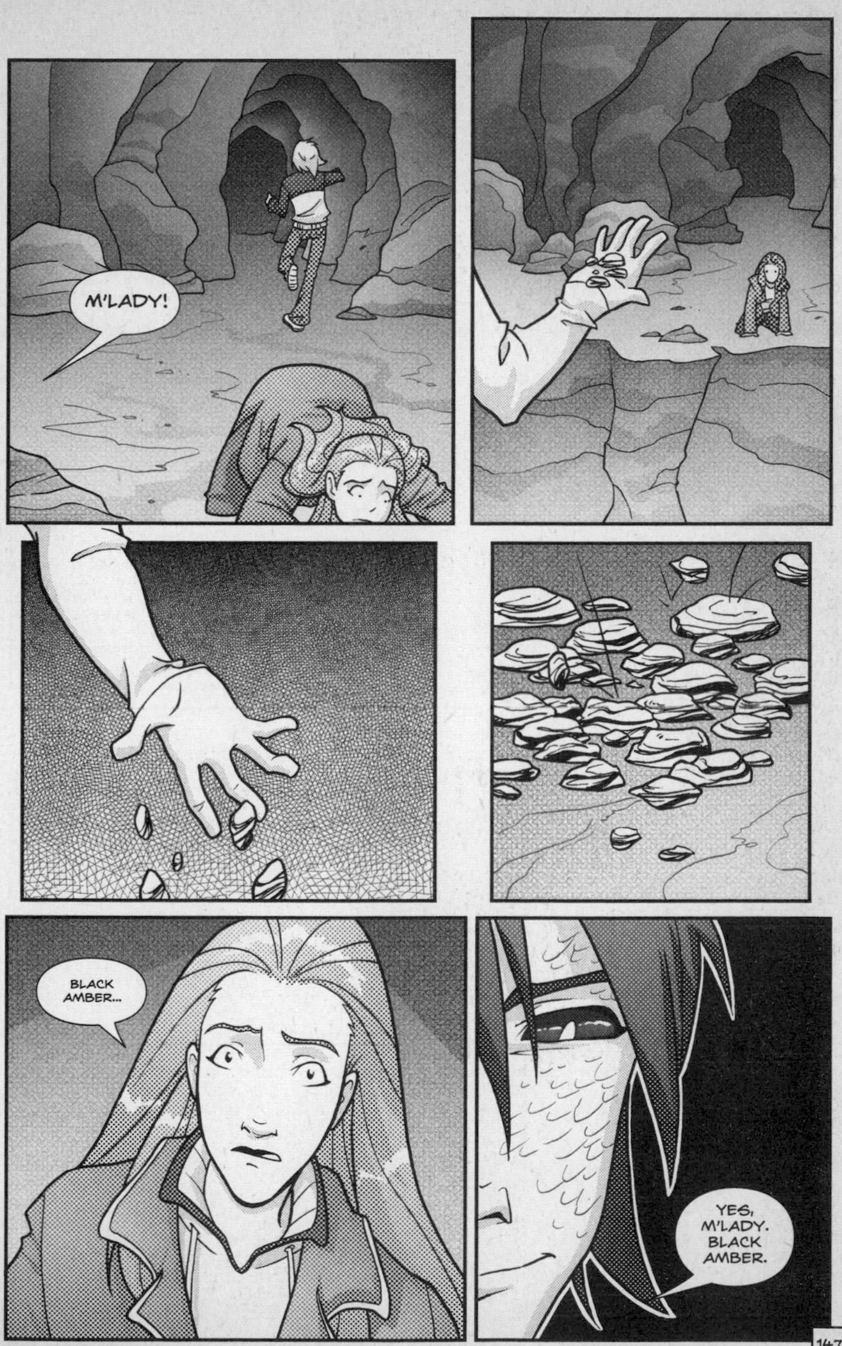
M'LADY!
BLACK AMBER...
YES, M'LADY. BLACK AMBER.

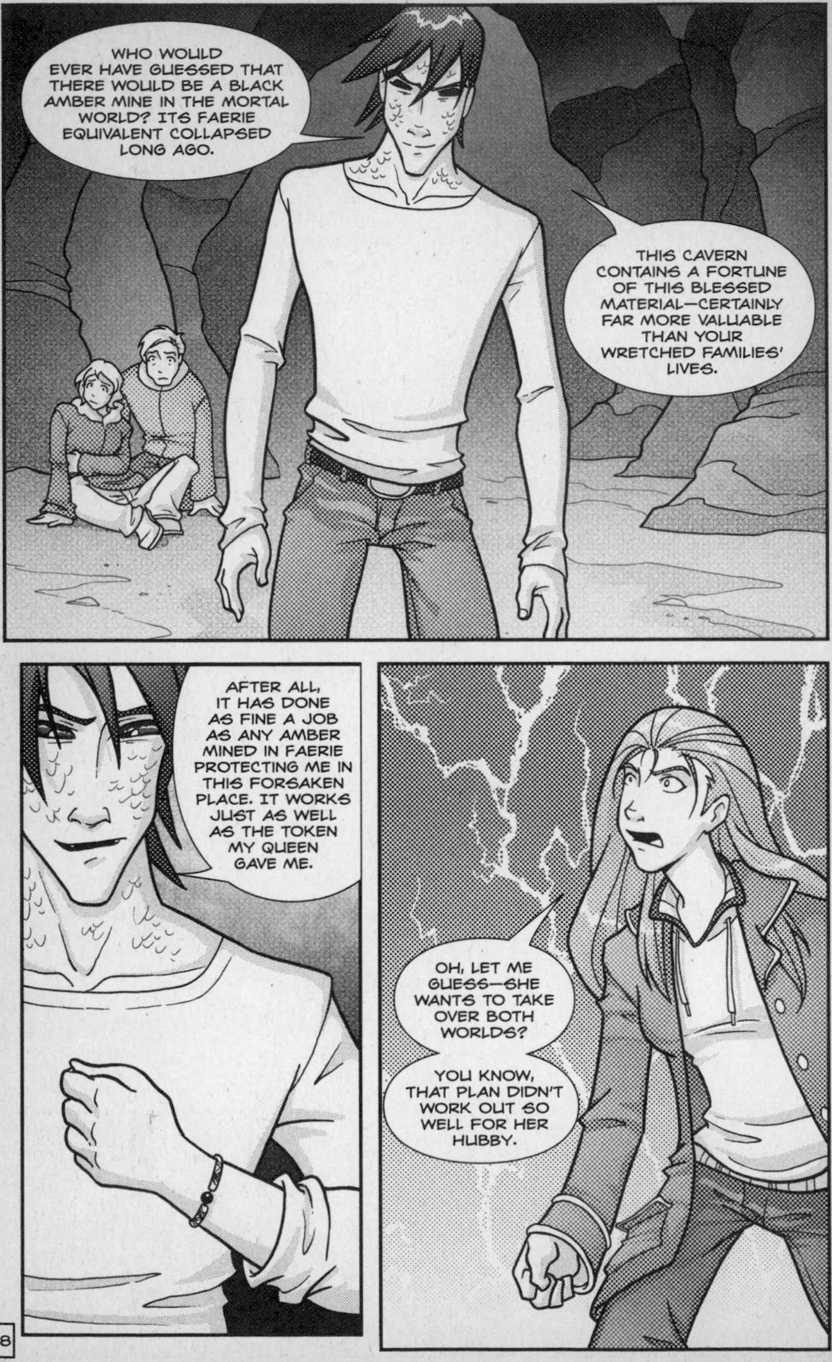
WHO WOULD EVER HAVE GUESSED THAT THERE WOULD BE A BLACK AMBER MINE IN THE MORTAL WORLD? ITS FAERIE EQUIVALENT COLLAPSED LONG AGO.
THIS CAVERN CONTAINS A FORTUNE OF THIS BLESSED MATERIAL—CERTAINLY FAR MORE VALUABLE THAN YOUR WRETCHED FAMILIES' LIVES.
AFTER ALL, IT HAS DONE AS FINE A JOB AS ANY AMBER MINED IN FAERIE PROTECTING ME IN THIS FORSAKEN PLACE. IT WORKS JUST AS WELL AS THE TOKEN MY QUEEN GAVE ME.
OH, LET ME GUESS—SHE WANTS TO TAKE OVER BOTH WORLDS?
YOU KNOW, THAT PLAN DIDN'T WORK OUT SO WELL FOR HER HUBBY.

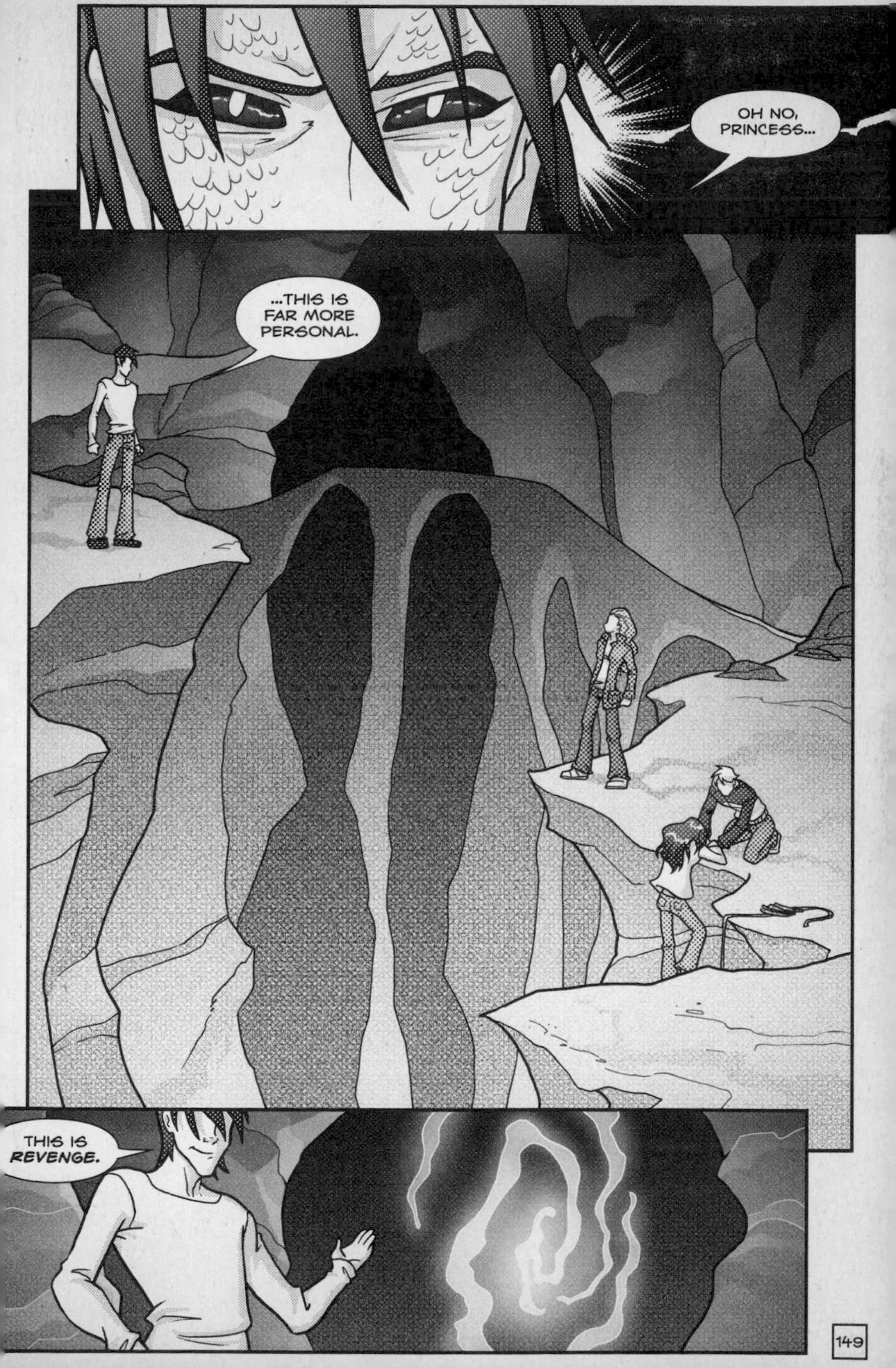
OH NO, PRINCESS...
...THIS IS FAR MORE PERSONAL.
THIS IS *REVENGE.*

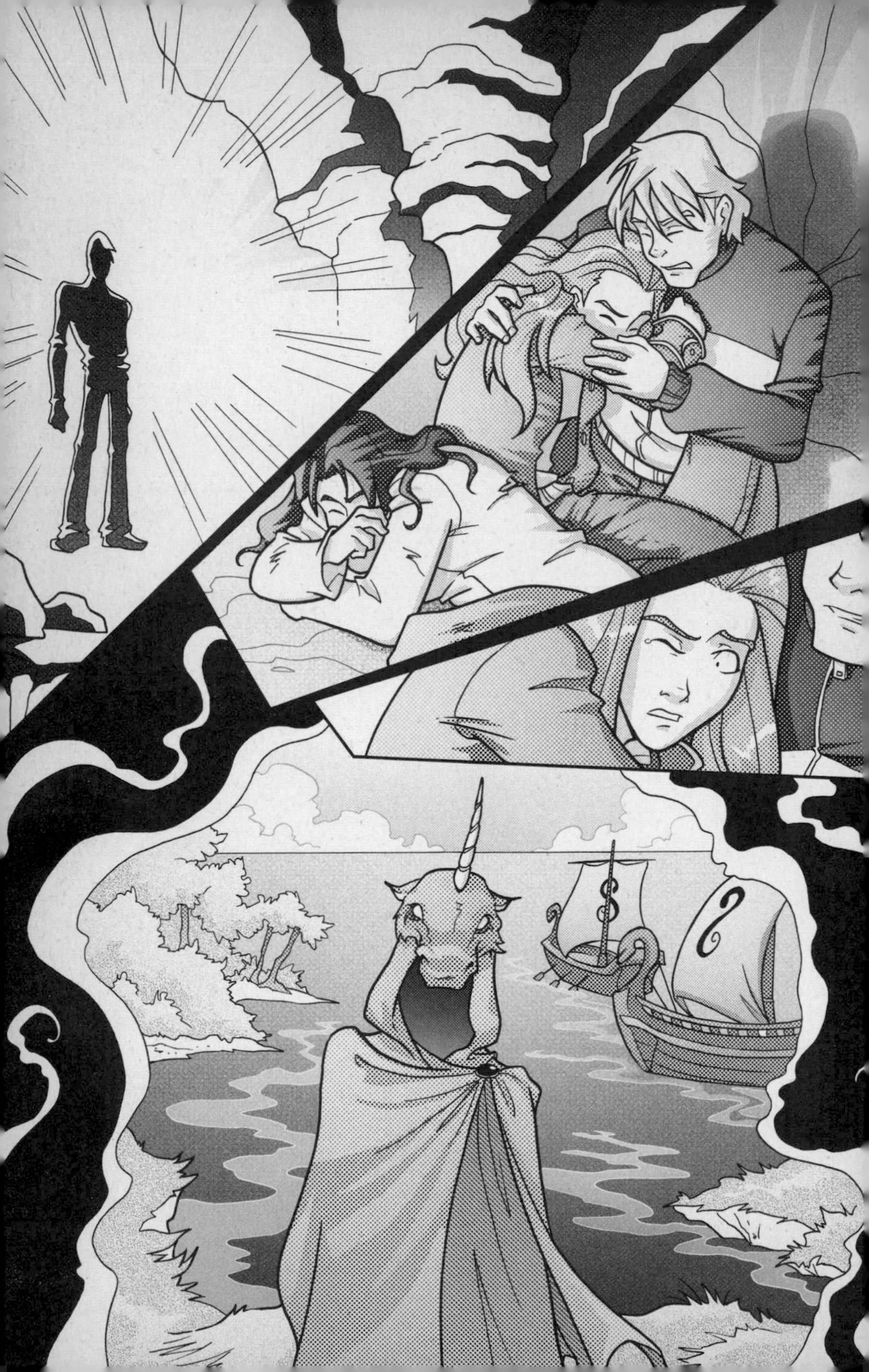

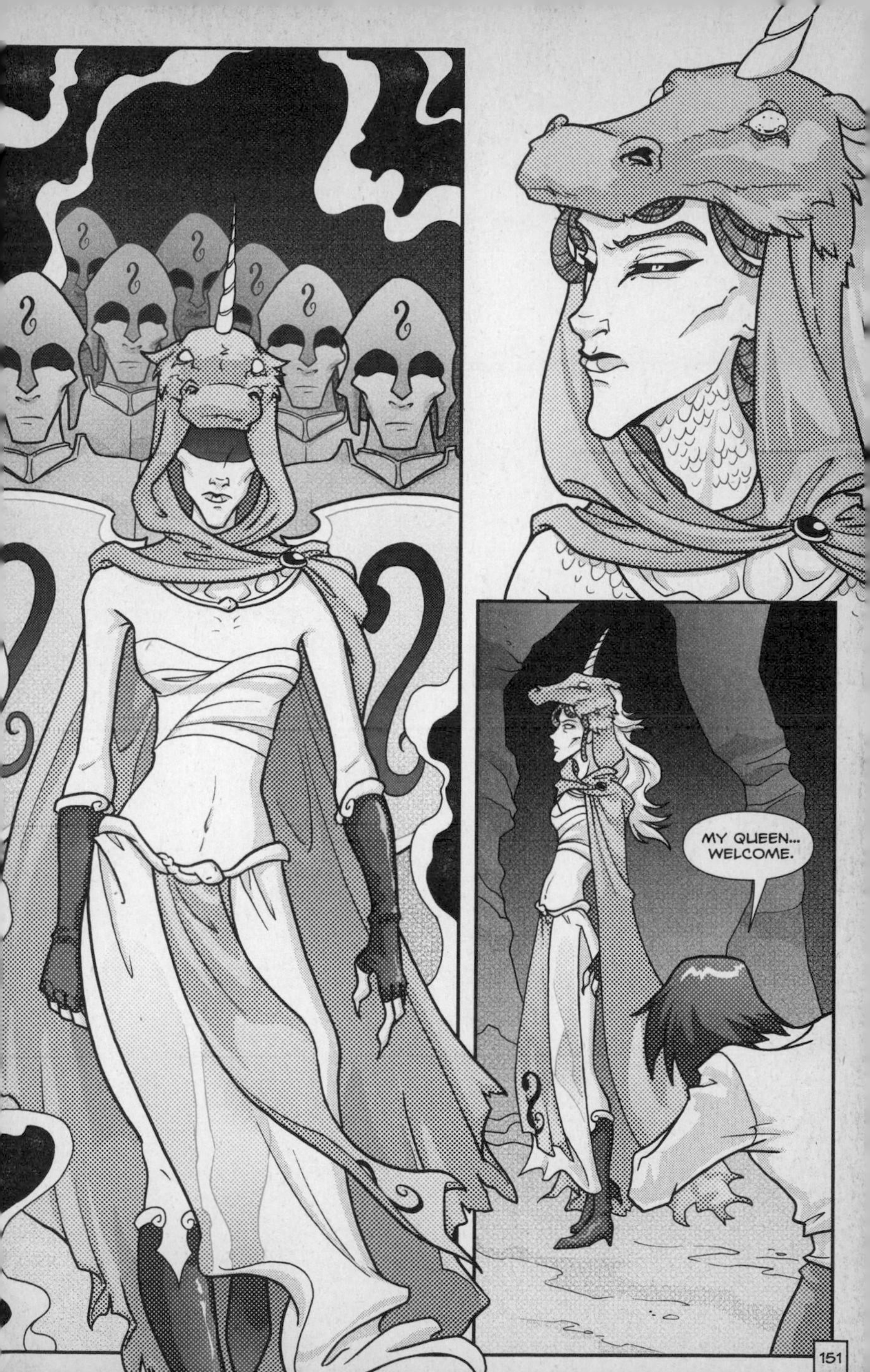
MY QUEEN...
WELCOME.

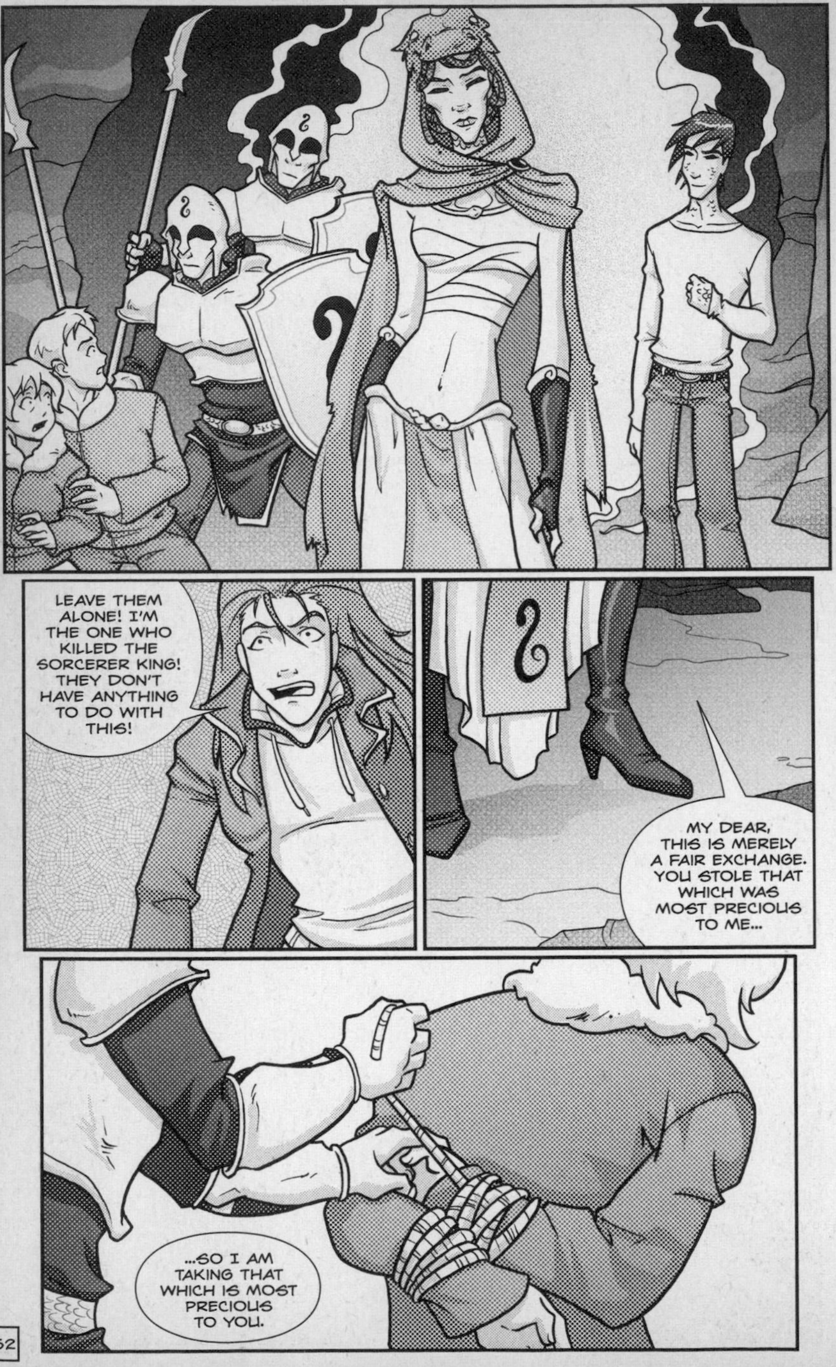
LEAVE THEM ALONE! I'M THE ONE WHO KILLED THE SORCERER KING! THEY DON'T HAVE ANYTHING TO DO WITH THIS!
MY DEAR, THIS IS MERELY A FAIR EXCHANGE. YOU STOLE THAT WHICH WAS MOST PRECIOUS TO ME...
...SO I AM TAKING THAT WHICH IS MOST PRECIOUS TO YOU.

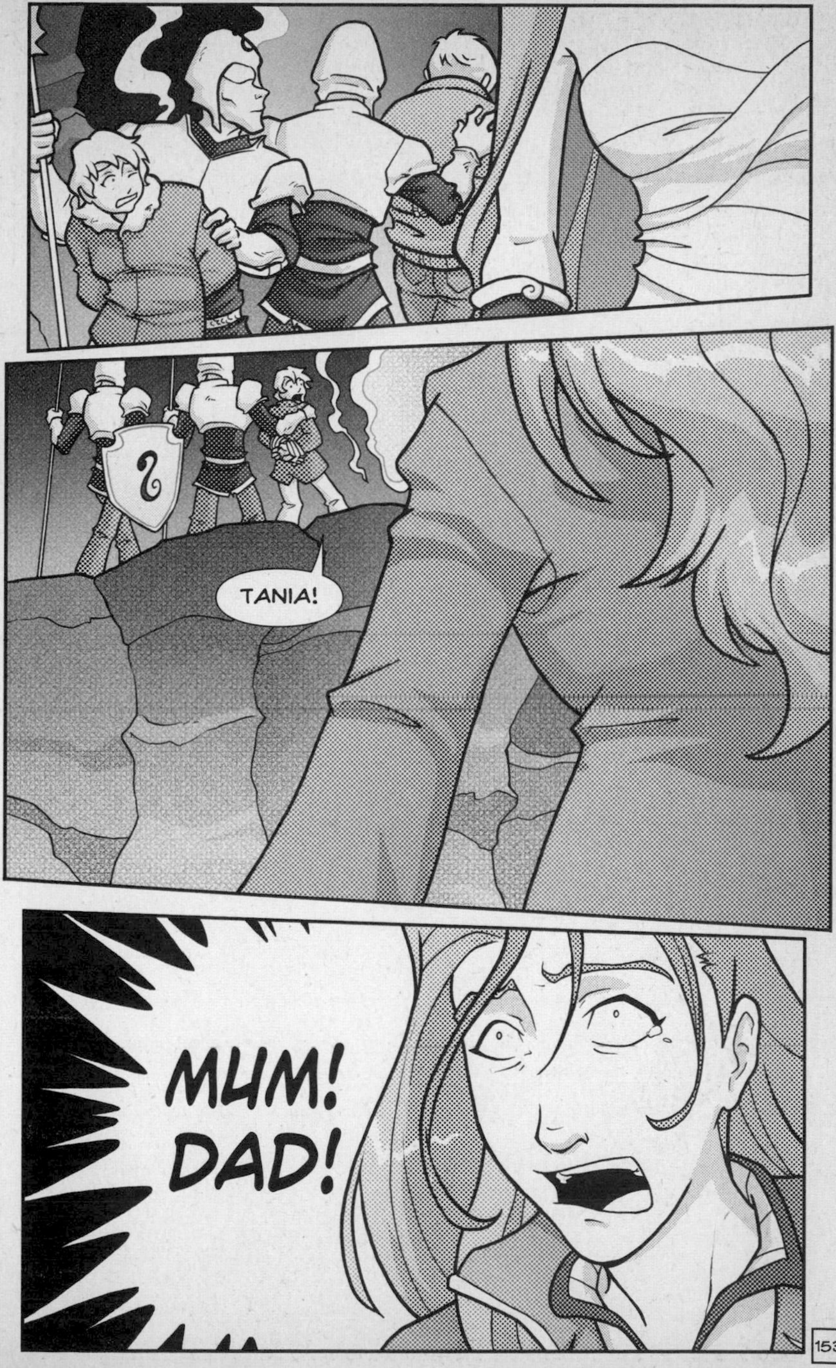
TANIA!
MUM! DAD!

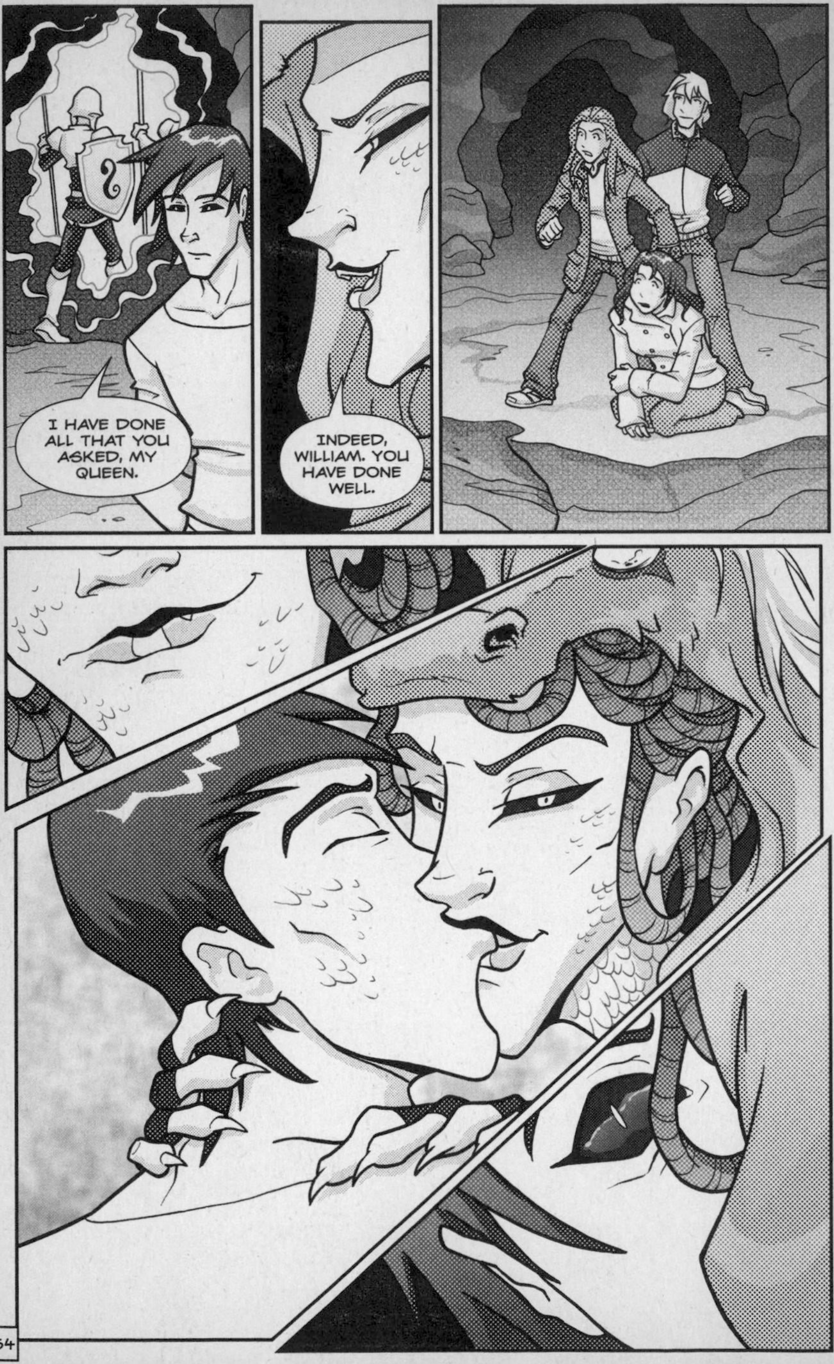
I HAVE DONE ALL THAT YOU ASKED, MY QUEEN.
INDEED, WILLIAM. YOU HAVE DONE WELL.

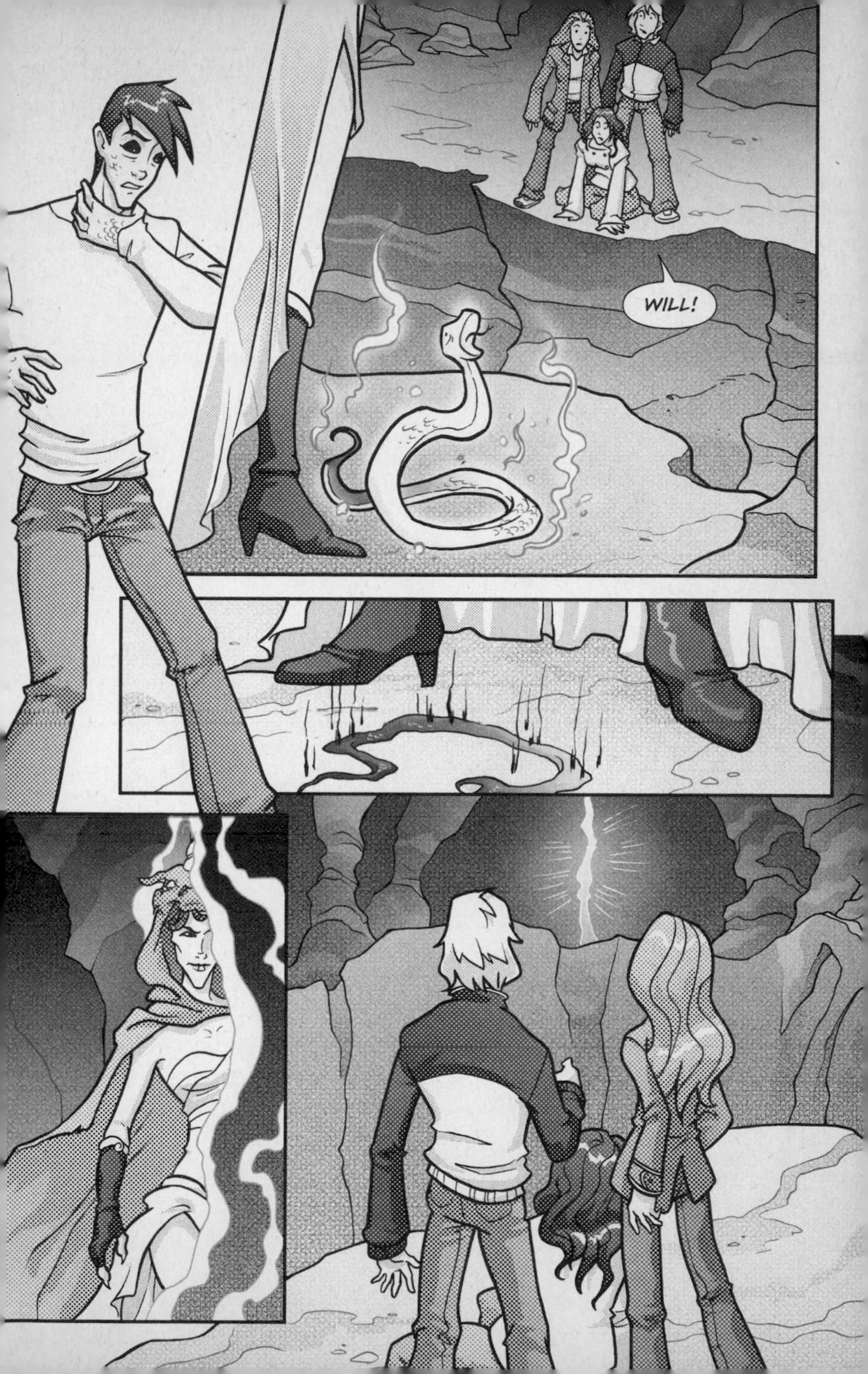
WILL!

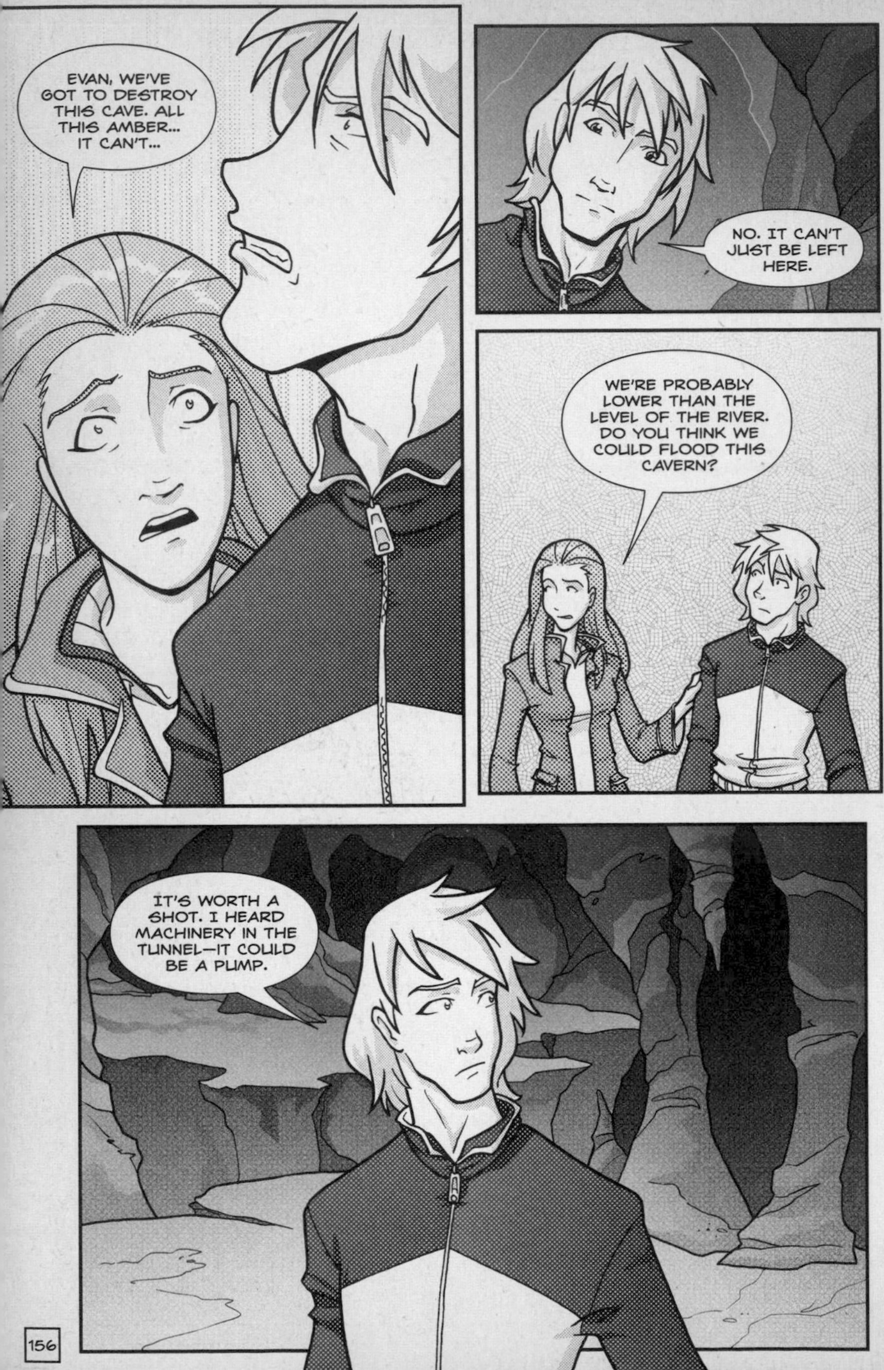
EVAN, WE'VE GOT TO DESTROY THIS CAVE. ALL THIS AMBER... IT CAN'T...
NO. IT CAN'T JUST BE LEFT HERE.
WE'RE PROBABLY LOWER THAN THE LEVEL OF THE RIVER. DO YOU THINK WE COULD FLOOD THIS CAVERN?
IT'S WORTH A SHOT. I HEARD MACHINERY IN THE TUNNEL—IT COULD BE A PUMP.

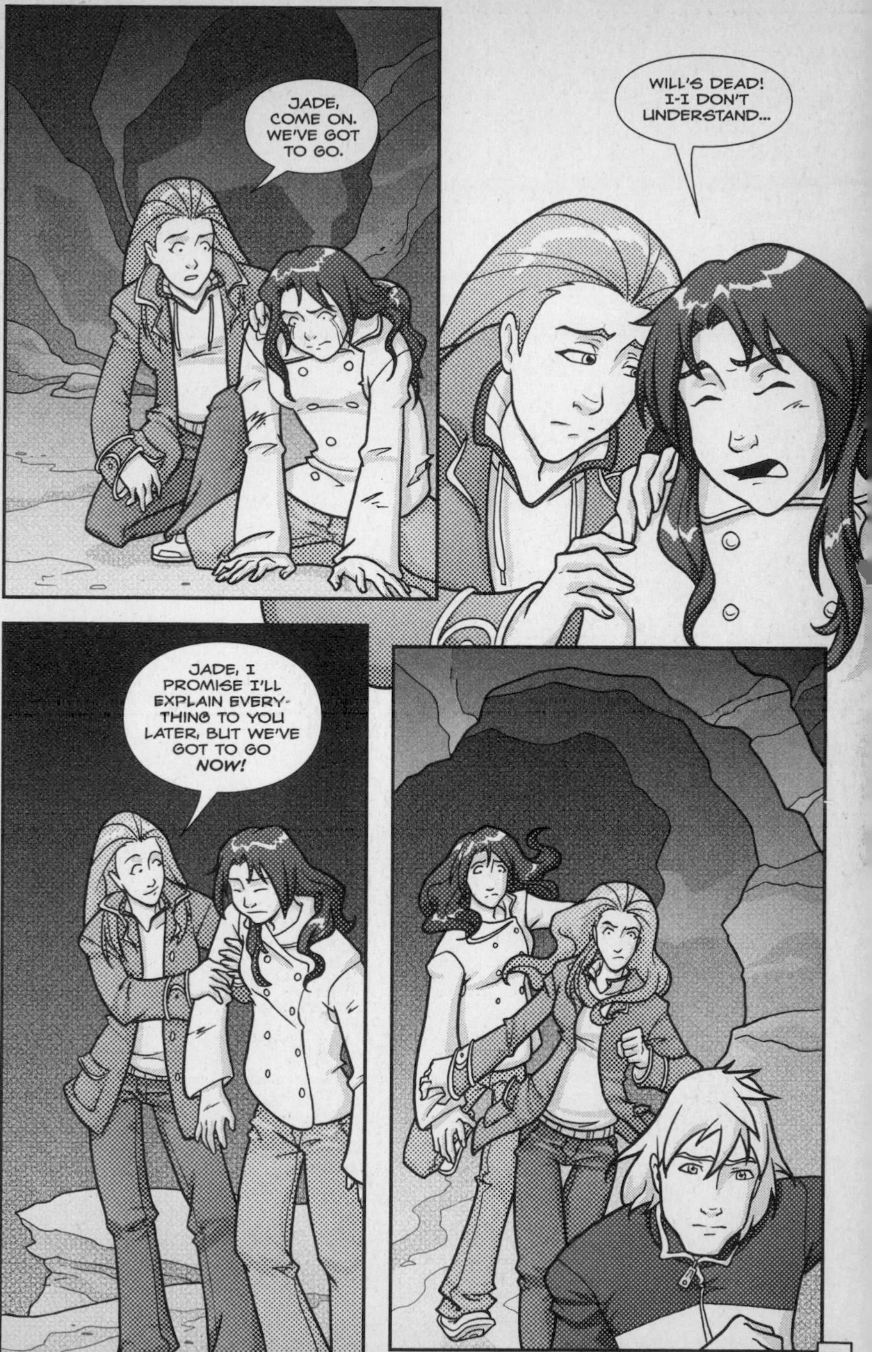
JADE, COME ON. WE'VE GOT TO GO.
WILL'S DEAD! I-I DON'T UNDERSTAND...
JADE, I PROMISE I'LL EXPLAIN EVERY-THING TO YOU LATER, BUT WE'VE GOT TO GO NOW!

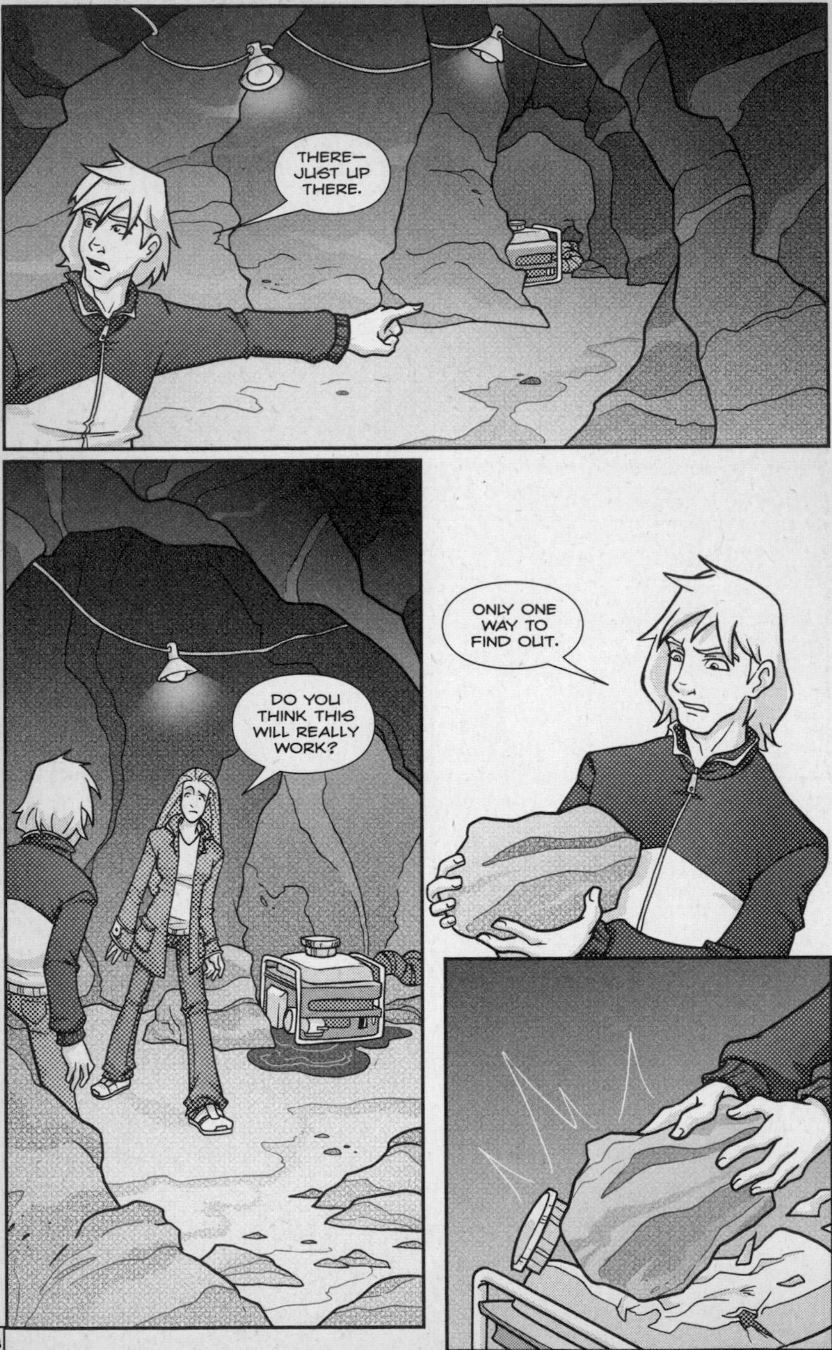
THERE— JUST UP THERE.
DO YOU THINK THIS WILL REALLY WORK?
ONLY ONE WAY TO FIND OUT.

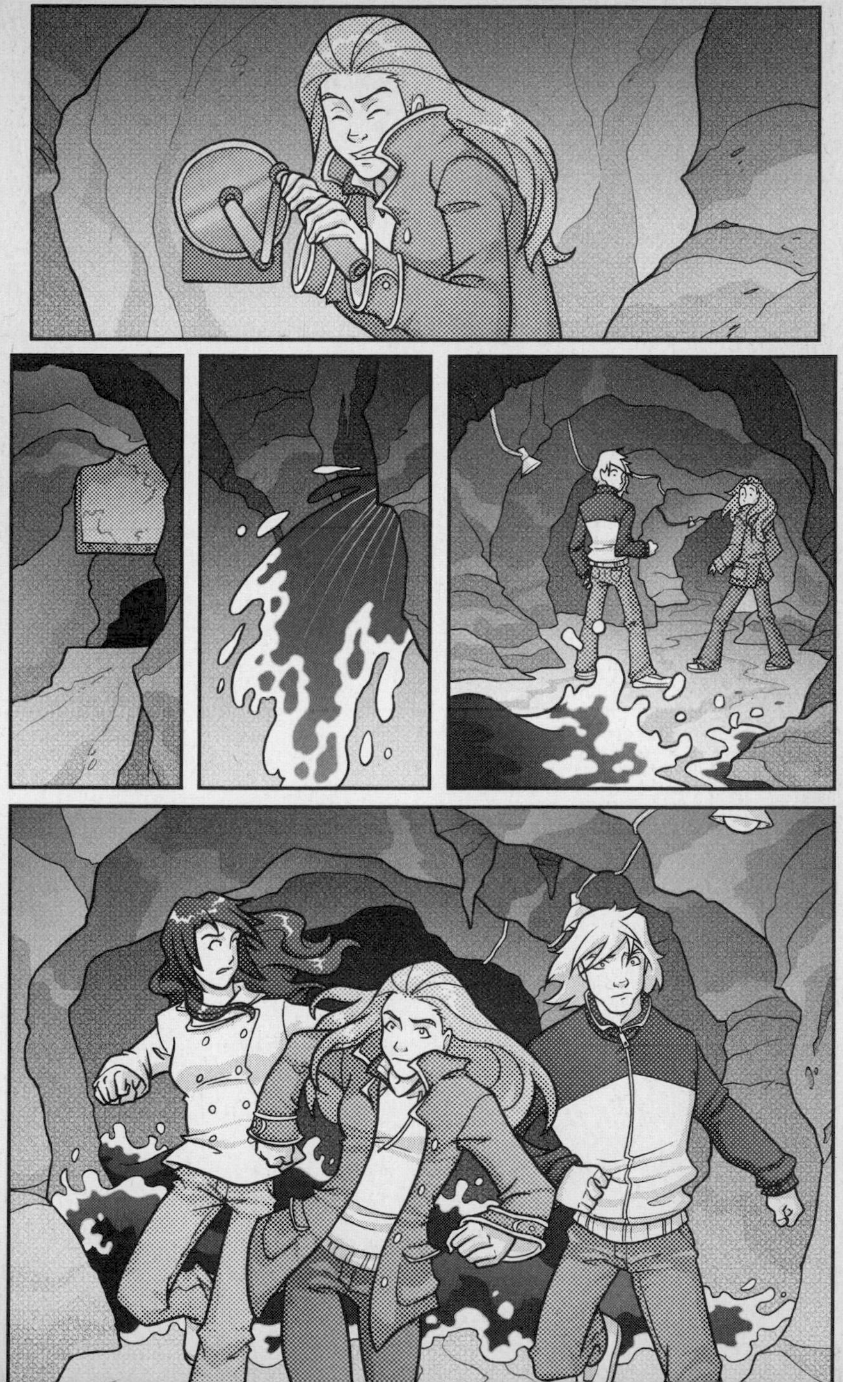

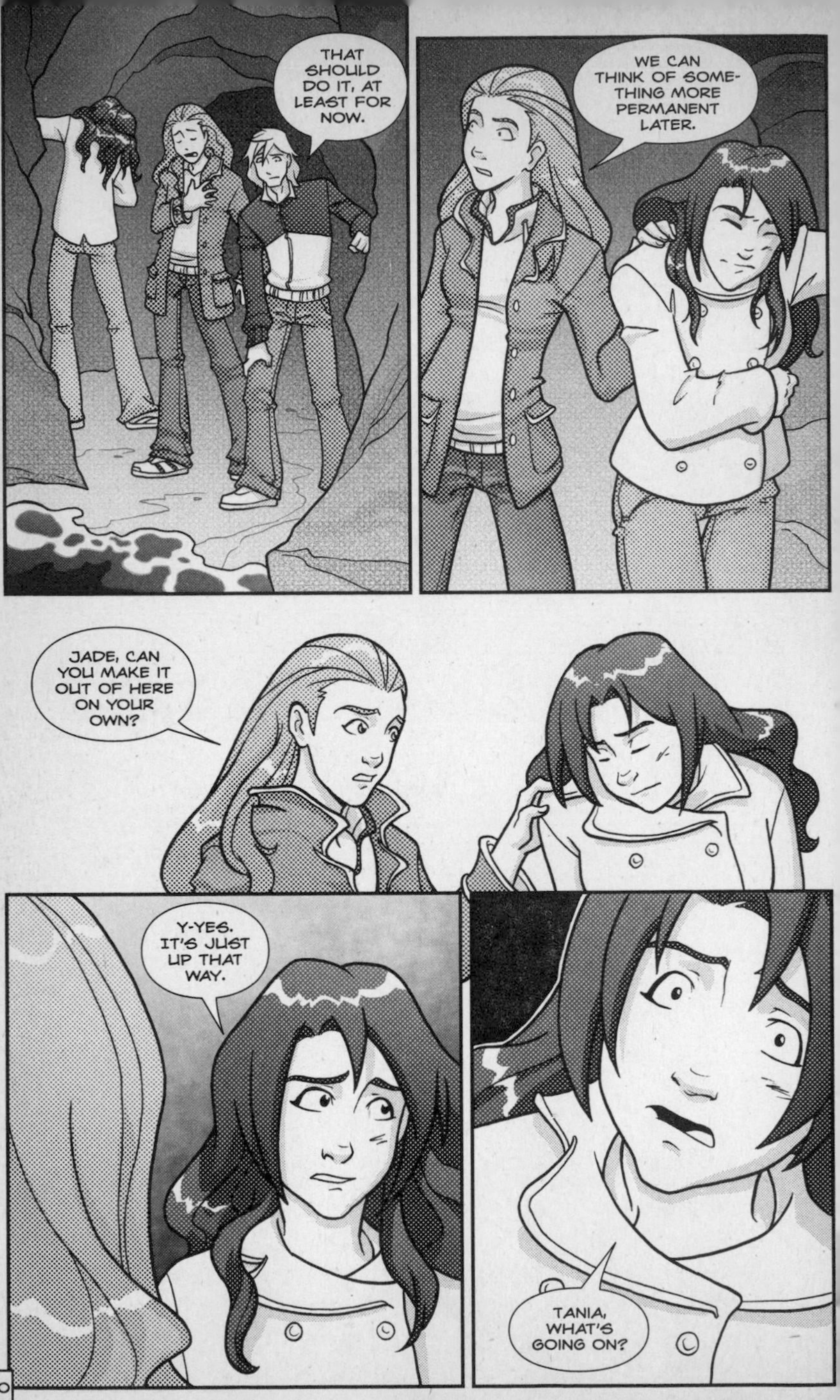
THAT SHOULD DO IT, AT LEAST FOR NOW.
WE CAN THINK OF SOME-THING MORE PERMANENT LATER.
JADE, CAN YOU MAKE IT OUT OF HERE ON YOUR OWN?
Y-YES. IT'S JUST UP THAT WAY.
TANIA, WHAT'S GOING ON?

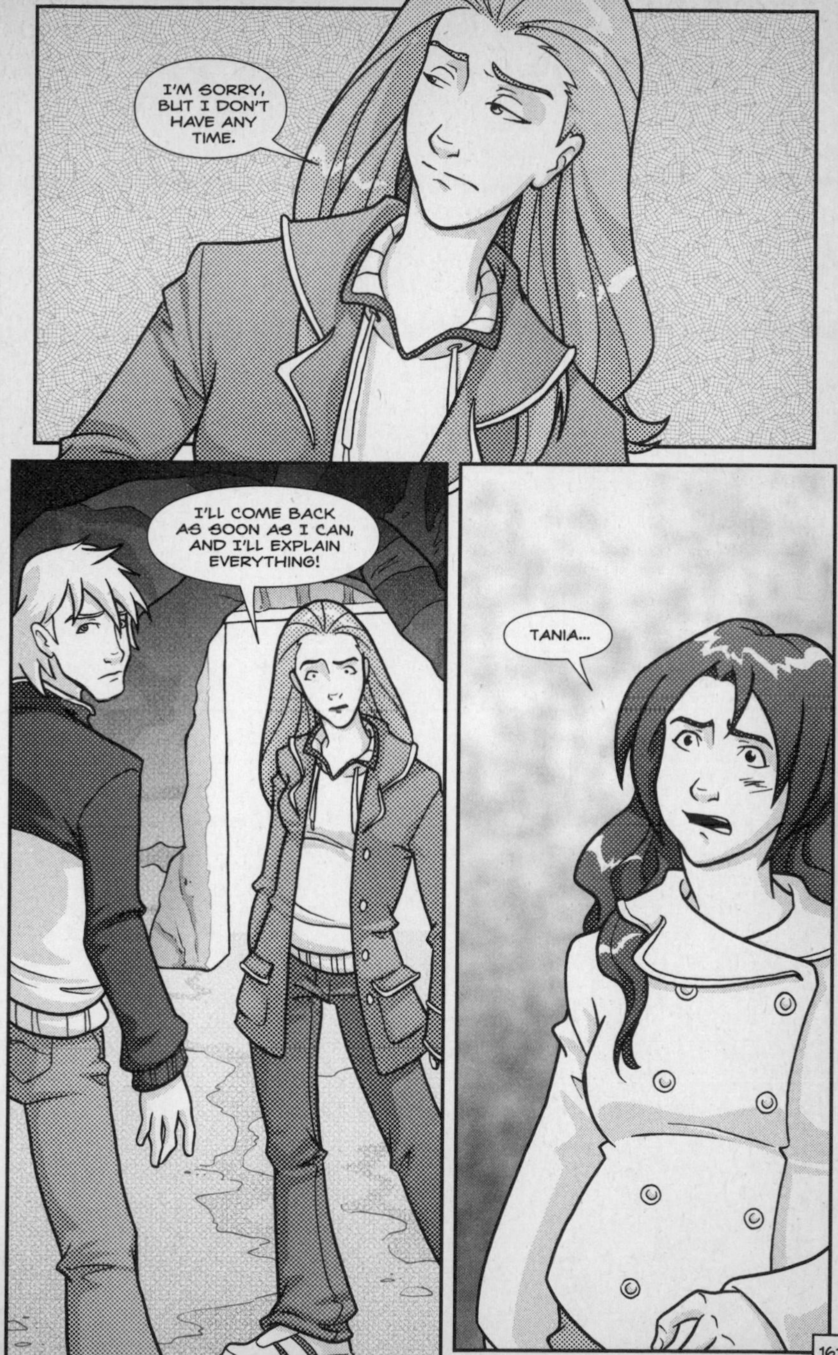
I'M SORRY, BUT I DON'T HAVE ANY TIME.
I'LL COME BACK AS SOON AS I CAN, AND I'LL EXPLAIN EVERYTHING!
TANIA...

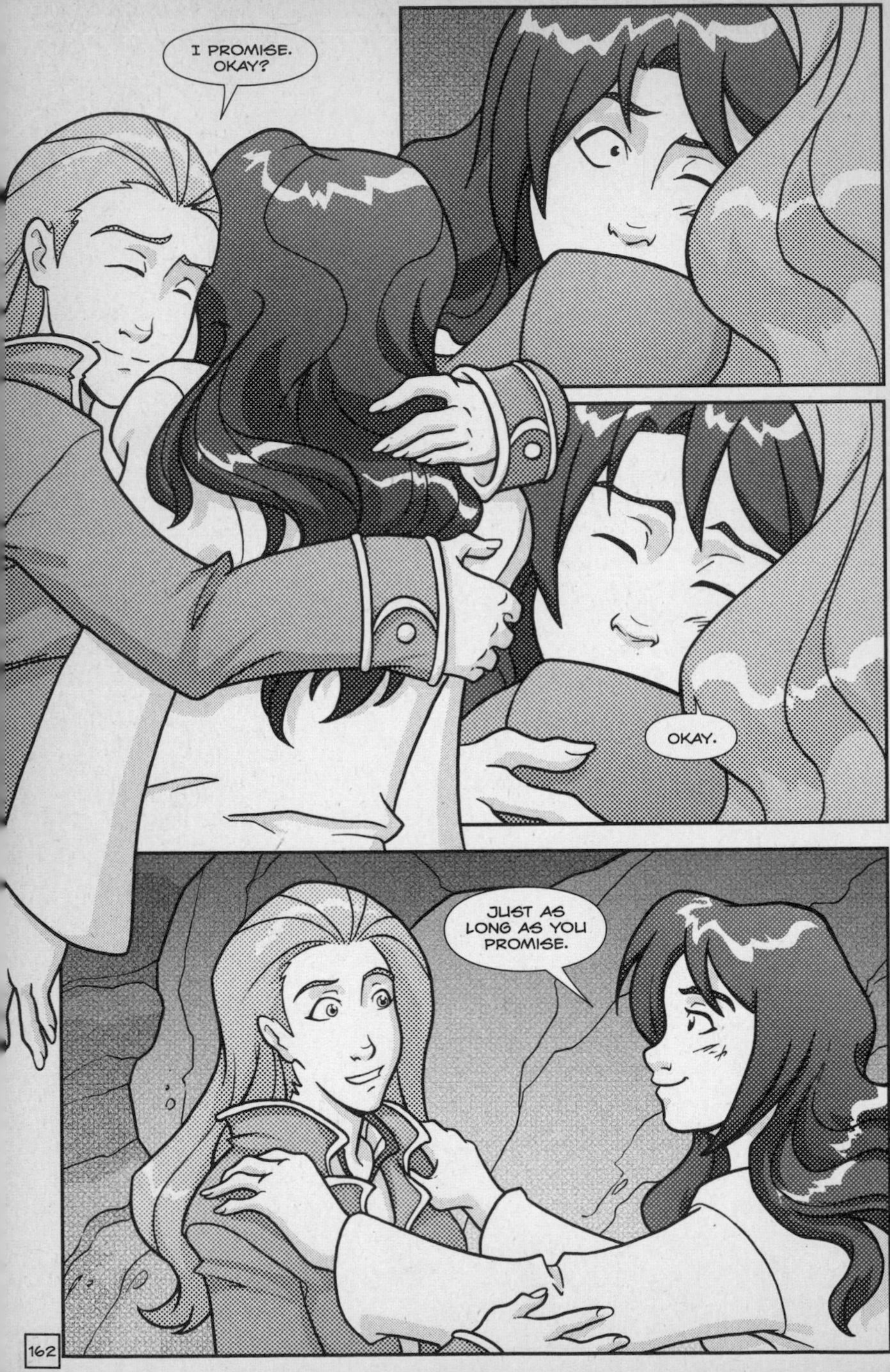
I PROMISE. OKAY?
OKAY.
JUST AS LONG AS YOU PROMISE.

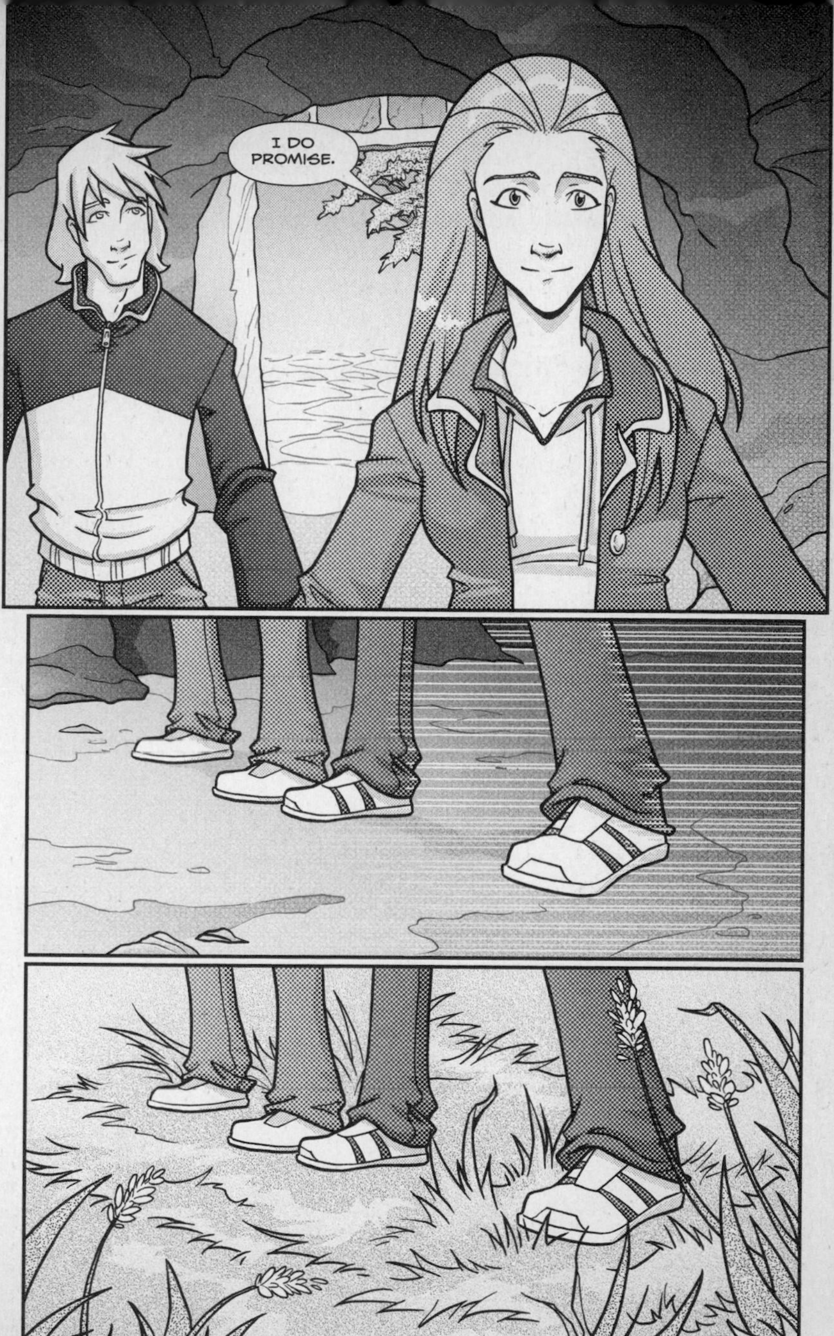
I DO PROMISE.

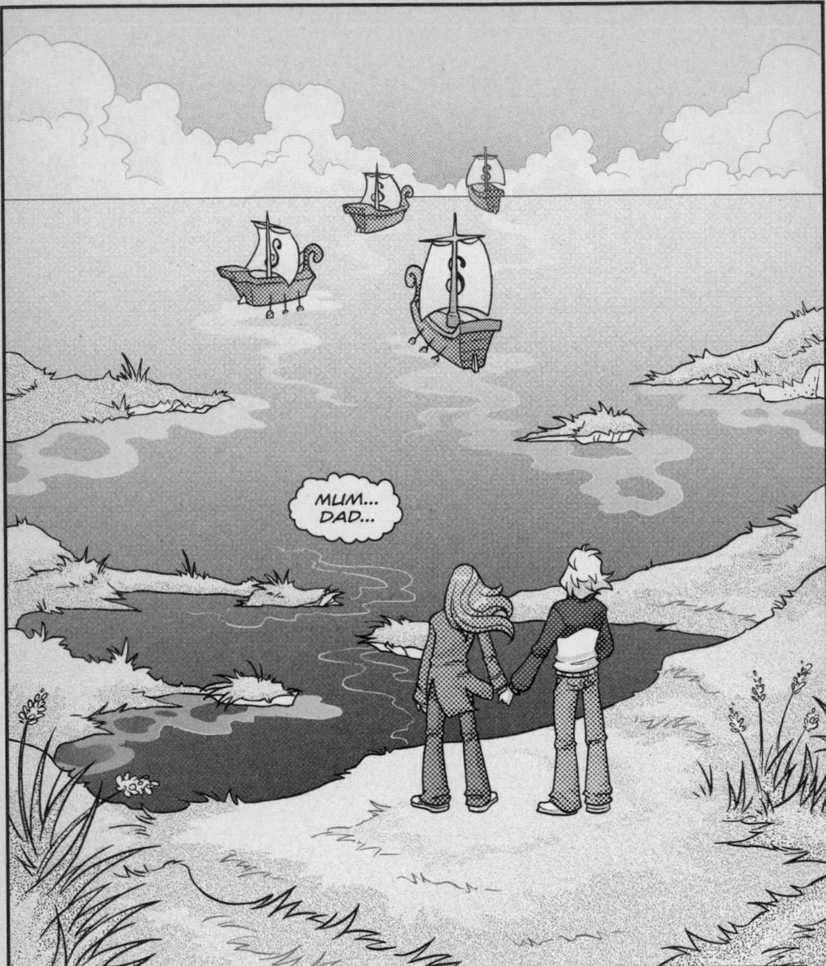
MUM...
DAD...
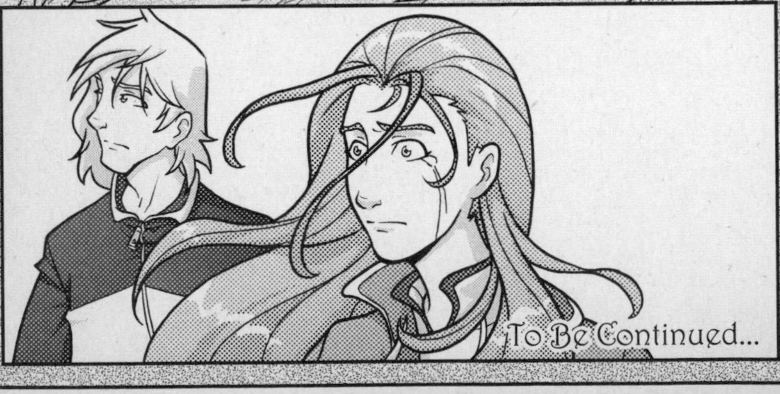
To Be Continued...

We hope you're enjoying
Tania's adventures in
manga form!

It's a real challenge for an
artist to bring characters
to life who are already so
familiar to readers through
the printed word. But
Alison Acton did a great
job developing designs that
reflect the personalities of
those friends and foes from
The Faerie Path and Frewin
Jones's subsequent novels.

It's exciting to see how
Alison's early character
designs evolved into the
manga you've just finished
reading. Take a look!

TANIA

In Faerie form, Tania takes on a more regal look, with long flowing hair and a more polished appearance—except for her bare feet!

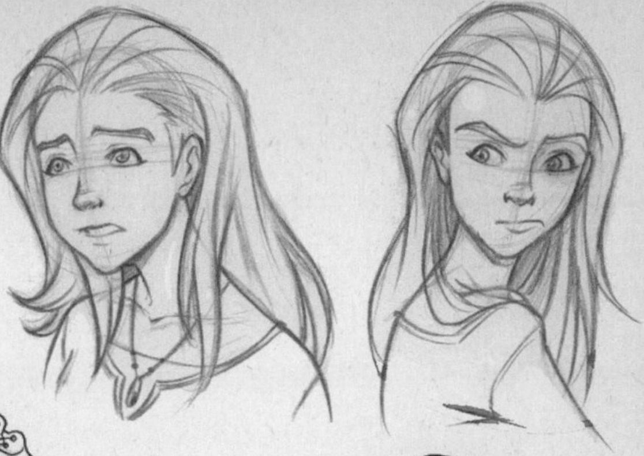

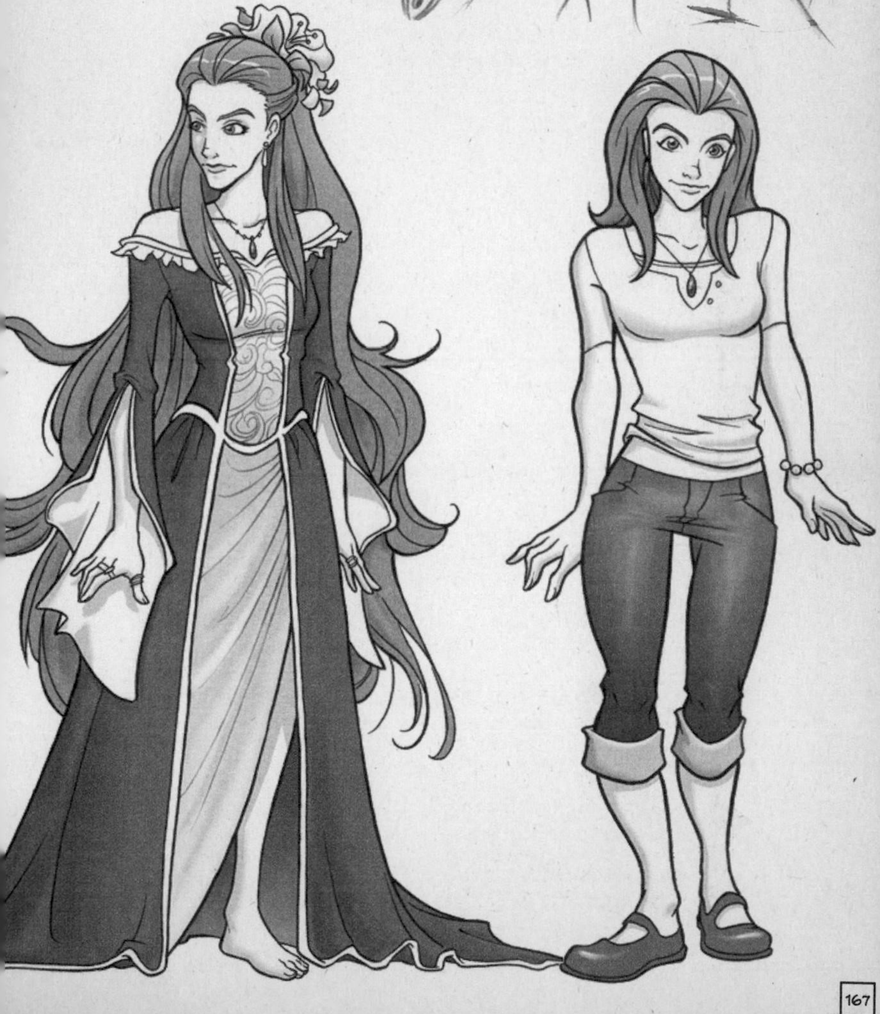

TANIA'S SISTERS

Each of Tania's sisters has a very distinct personality, and it's important to portray that in their appearances.

Eden

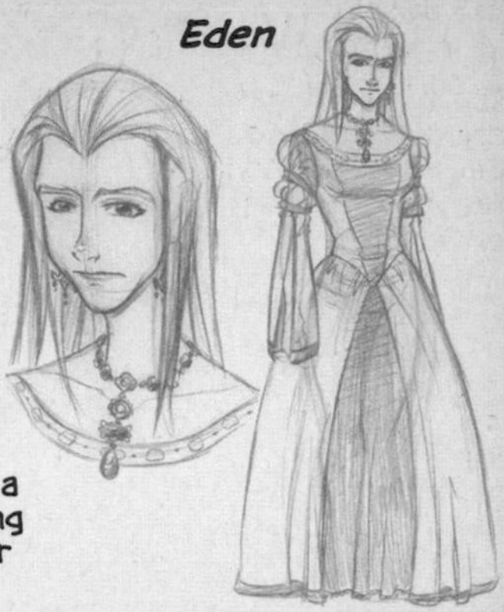

Hopie

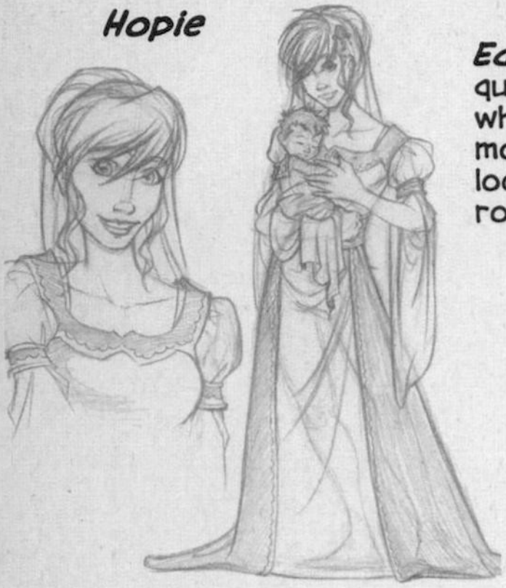

Eden, the eldest, is quiet and serious, whereas ***Hopie*** has a more open, nurturing look, which suits her role as a healer.

Sancha

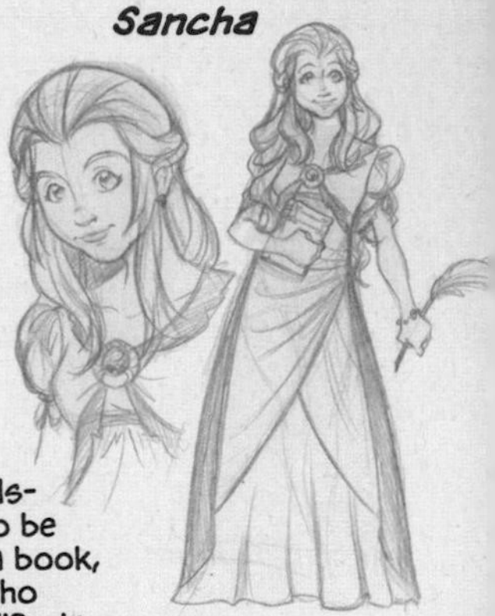

Cordelia

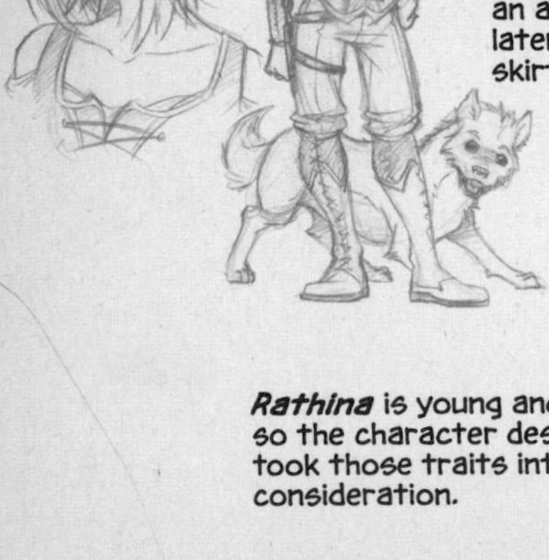

Sancha, the records-keeper, is unlikely to be anywhere without a book, just as ***Cordelia***, who can speak with wildlife, is always accompanied by an animal. Her pants were later swapped for Faerie skirts.

Rathina

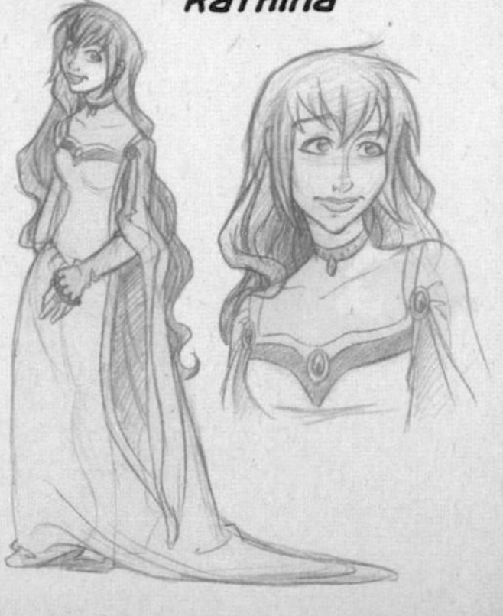

Rathina is young and naive, so the character design took those traits into consideration.

TITANIA AND OBERON

Tania's Faerie parents are as majestic as can be, and Titania looks like an older version of Tania.

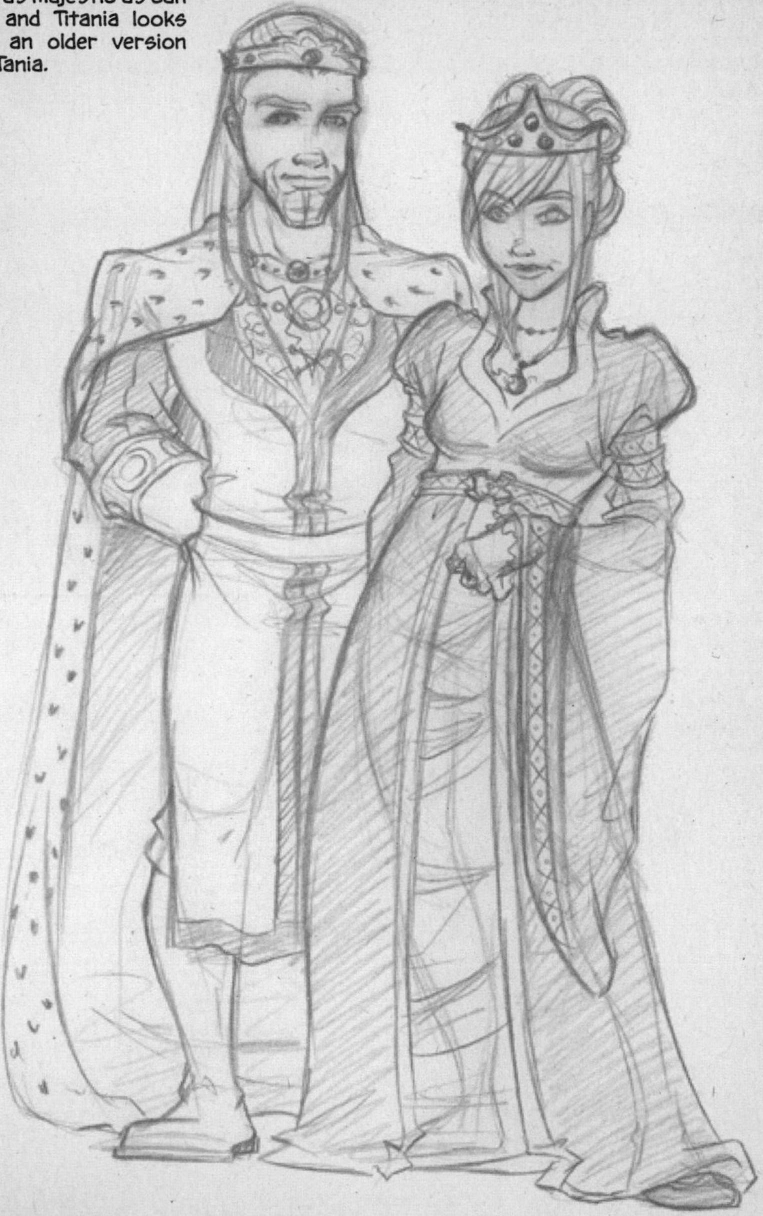

MR. AND MRS. PALMER

Tania's human parents look more like typical parents, and are meant to appear very approachable and kind.

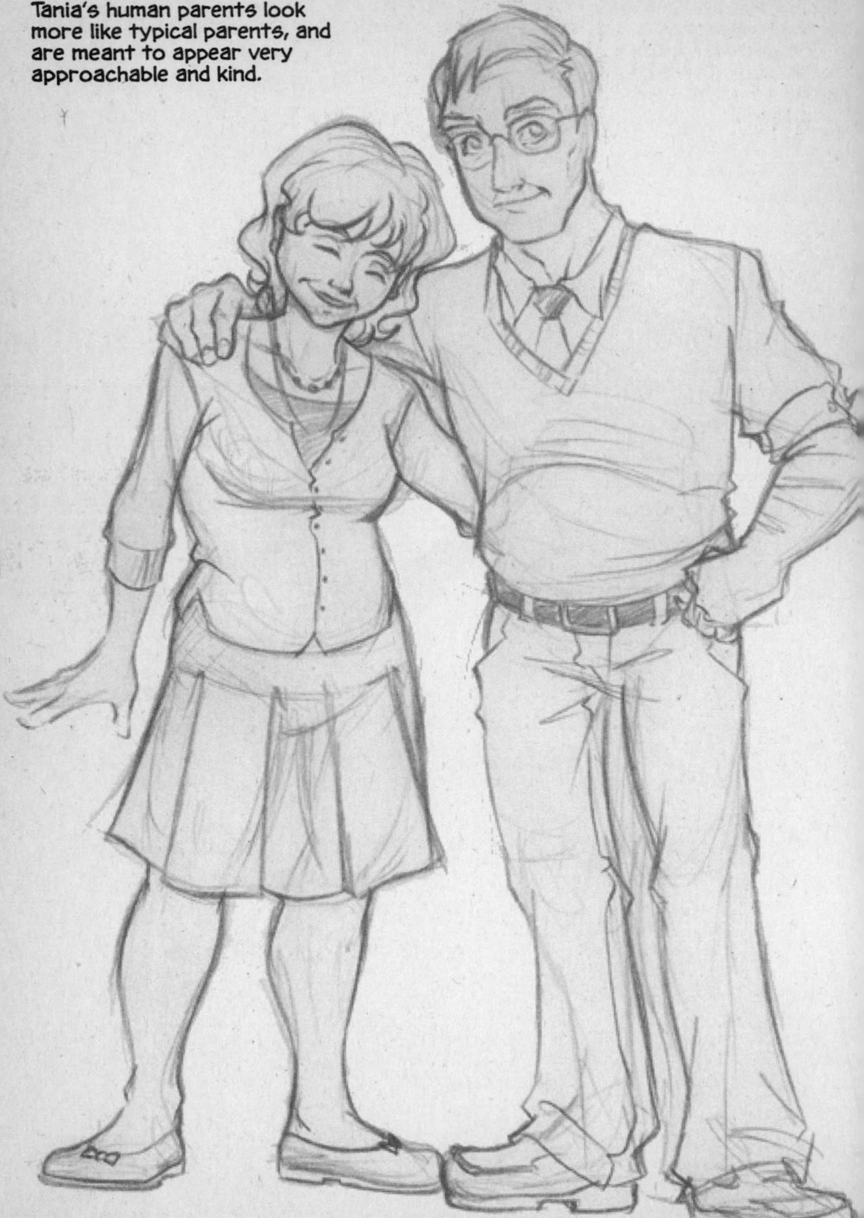

EDRIC/EVAN

Evan looks like a classic teenage heartthrob, whereas Edric has the royal air of a messenger of the court. In either form, he is confident and cool.

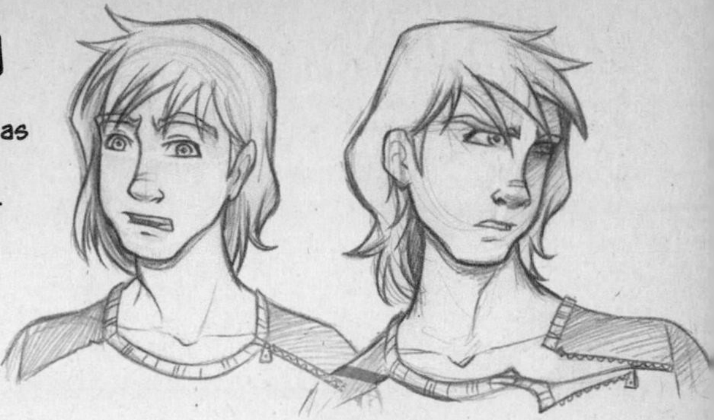

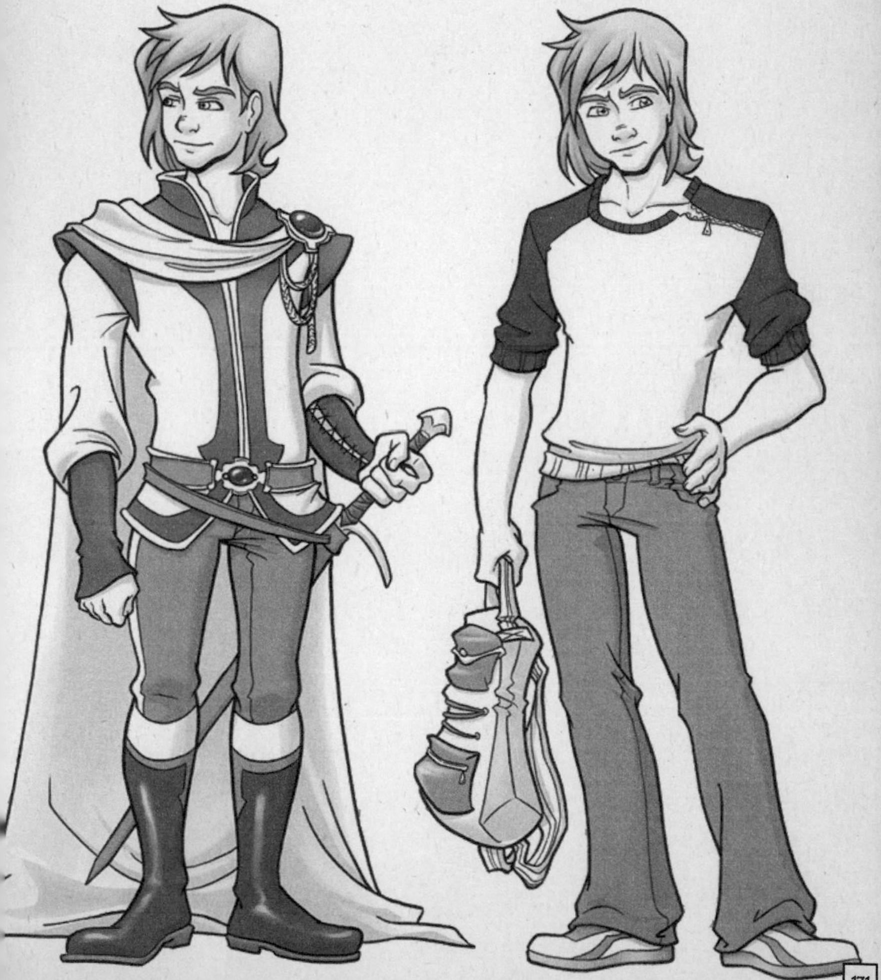

WILL

Will has to come off as a little slimy—after all, he is reptilian—but he still must be attractive (and human!) enough to interest Jade.

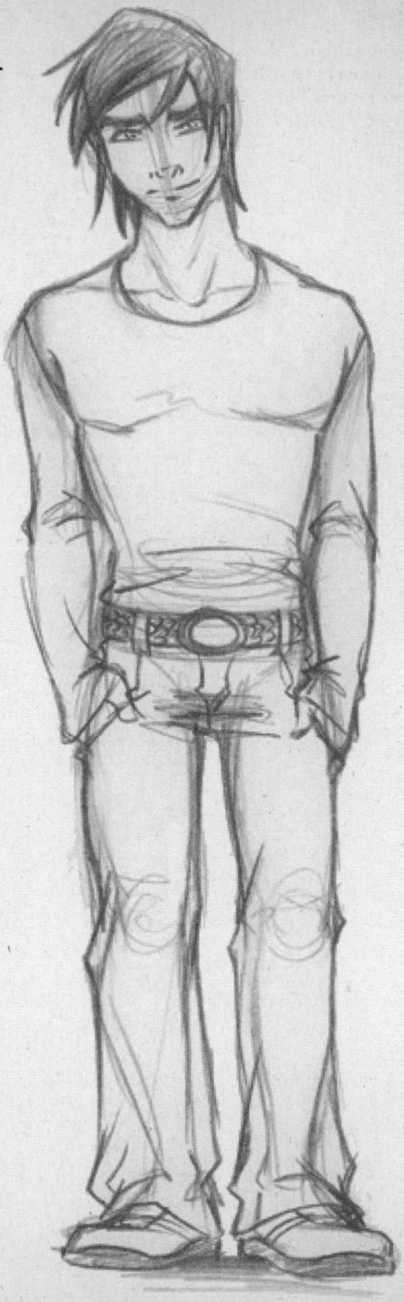

LAMIA

Lamia is more obviously reptilian, but still beautiful nonetheless!

LOOK FOR THE CONTINUATION OF TANIA'S ADVENTURE IN:

The FAERIE PATH

LAMIA'S REVENGE
VOL. 2: THE MEMORY OF WINGS

Tania's hopes for peace in Faerie were dashed when one of the Serpent Queen Lamia's evil servants lured her parents into a deadly trap. Now, she, her boyfriend, Edric, and her Faerie sisters must embark on a quest to save them and defeat Queen Lamia, who seeks revenge for the Sorcerer King's death. But when an ancient prophecy suddenly becomes a very real possibility, Tania realizes that walking between the worlds might not be the only thing that makes her different. Can she use her mysterious new strength to save her parents?

READ THE NOVEL THAT STARTED IT ALL!

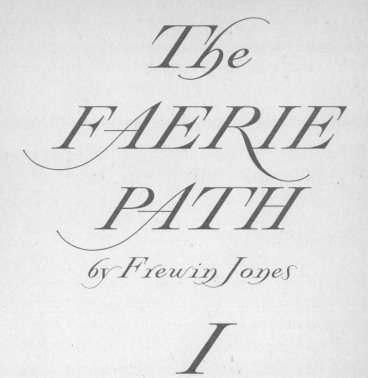

The FAERIE PATH

by Frewin Jones

I

Anita Palmer stepped out of the shower and reached for the bath towel. Wrapping it around herself, she padded over to the mirror. She lifted her hand and swept a clear path across the misted glass before leaning forward to look at her reflection.

Her long red hair clung to her head like seaweed to a rock, framing her heart-shaped face with its wide mouth and high cheekbones. She leaned closer, staring into her mirrored eyes. The irises were a smoky green. Nothing particularly remarkable about them.

Or was there?

She leaned even closer.

Gold flecks deep in the green irises—that was what she was looking for.

Evan had said that if he looked into her eyes for long enough, he could see gold dust in them.

Anita grinned.

Gold dust in her eyes.

Sometimes when she was with Evan she could almost believe she had gold dust in her eyes.

She frowned.

It was quite scary—the feelings that Evan Thomas was stirring up in her.

Were they real? They felt real enough. Over the past few weeks thinking about Evan had somehow become the default setting of her brain. And she kept seeing his face—in the swirls of a freshly stirred cup of coffee. In shadows and light. In clouds. In the darkness behind her closed eyelids.

She recalled lines from the play they had been rehearsing for the end-of-term performance. Shakespeare. *Romeo and Juliet.*

She could hear Evan's voice in her head.

"But, soft! What light through yonder window breaks? It is the east, and Juliet is my sun!"

She'd said to him, "That's not right, Evan. Romeo says, *'and Juliet is* the *sun'* not *'my* sun.'"

He'd smiled and said, "No—you're Juliet, and you're definitely *my* sun."

And the way he had looked into her eyes right then

had made her feel like the whole world was turning upside down and inside out all around her.

She laughed into the mirror, shaking her head to dislodge the memory. Still grinning, she threw the towel up over her head and rubbed vigorously at her wet hair. She didn't want to be late meeting Evan today—*especially* not today.

She winced as the towel scraped against the two itchy points on her back. She lowered the towel and angled her bare back to the mirror, craning to see over her shoulder. Something had bitten her. Twice. There was an angry red point on each shoulder blade. They had been there for a few days now. Very irritating, and in such an awkward place to scratch. She'd have to wear something that covered her back—the last thing she wanted was for Evan to think she was crawling with fleas.

She looked into the mirror again.

Did she really love Evan, or was she just getting tangled up in the fact that she had to *act* as if she loved him in the play? No, she was sure that it was much more than that. She had felt a strange, thrilling flutter in her stomach when she had been chosen to play Juliet opposite his Romeo, and over the weeks of rehearsals, as she had gotten to know him better, that thrill had just kept getting more and more intense.

She thought back to the auditions. Everyone had been surprised that Evan had shown up at all. He had only been at the school for six months, and he had always seemed so reserved and self-contained, not the type of person who'd want a major part in the school production. He was amiable enough in class, but he hadn't made any close friends and the other students mostly thought of him as something of a loner. No one had ever been invited to his home, and he didn't hang out with them on weekends or go to any parties.

Anita could remember exactly when Evan had first turned up. It had been on the same day as the school trip to Hampton Court.

It had been a weird day. She knew it was called déjà vu when you have vivid memories of a place you've never been to, and that's how she had felt from the moment the bus had driven up to the parking lot and she had first set eyes on the sixteenth-century palace at Hampton Court—the feeling that she'd been there before. The sturdy red-brick Tudor towers and buildings with their cream-colored stone battlements and ornamentations, and the cobbled courtyards and wide, formal gardens—they had all seemed strangely familiar. But when she mentioned this later to her parents, assuming she'd visited the palace when she was much younger, they said they'd never taken her there.

The strangest thing of all had been the world-famous maze. It was a large triangular block of tall hedges, grown close together to create a warren of narrow winding corridors. Pretty much every visitor to the palace wanted to put their sense of direction to the test and find their way to the center. Everyone from the school bus had bundled in there, the boys boasting that they'd get to the middle first. It had been total chaos—most of them got hopelessly lost and had to be guided through by the people shouting from the wooden viewing platforms.

At first Anita had hung back. The green tunnels of the hedges had given her a creepy feeling that she couldn't explain. But then her best friend, Jade, had grabbed her arm and dragged her in—and once she was in the maze, the oddest thing had happened. Somehow she had known the path, and made her way to the little statue in the center without taking a single wrong turn. "How about that?" she'd said to Jade, laughing. "Am I a genius, or what?" But Jade had said it was just luck.

That same afternoon, she had seen him for the first time. The most gorgeous boy she had ever set eyes on in her entire life, standing outside the school gates when the bus pulled up. Evan Thomas—a new student who had just moved into the area.

And here she was, six months later, not only playing Juliet to his Romeo, but—more stunning yet—with Evan as her first-ever boyfriend.

At the early rehearsals, Anita had been nervous about getting the complicated words wrong or falling over her feet, but Evan had been friendly and helpful to her. And he turned out to have a great sense of humor. In the death scene at the end, she had to throw herself across him as he lay on the floor, but he kept giggling, which would start her off, and often the rehearsals would end up with the pair of them laughing hopelessly.

That was really when they had started to bond—that,

and lunches together in the school cafeteria to discuss the play. Except that the more they met, the less they talked about *Romeo and Juliet*. After a couple of weeks, it had seemed perfectly natural for them to go to a café together after school. She could still vividly remember sitting across the table from him that first time—just sitting there gazing into his eyes and not hearing a single word he was saying.

She had found it so easy to tell him about all her secret wishes and desires—things she had never told anyone else. Like the fact that, if she did well in her exams, she planned to fill a backpack and tour Europe or America. Then go to college, and maybe have a career as an investigative journalist. And afterward— well, the rest of her life. Traveling the world. Having adventures. Always with a home to come back to, of course—a white house perched on high cliffs overlooking the sea. A husband. Children.

And she had wanted to know every detail of his life. But he would just shrug and say it was too boring to talk about. He had relatives in Wales, but he didn't really get on with them. He had come to London to escape—and he'd found her! And that's when his life had really started, or so he had said.

"That's just silly!" she'd told him, but it had made her feel special to believe he really thought that way.

He always wore a broad leather strap around his wrist, tied with two thin leather cords. Set into the leather band was a small, flat black stone. He told her it was a family heirloom, the only part of his family that he would never part with. "Why's that?" she had asked, intrigued. "What's the significance?"

But he had just smiled. "I'll tell you one day," he'd said. "Not now, but soon. I promise." Very mysterious! Anita liked that—the feeling that there was so much more to find out about him.

Of course, Jade and the others wanted all the details of her private time with Evan—what had happened? Did he walk her home? Had he kissed her? Were they an item? *We talked, that's all, and he bought me a coffee. Yes, he walked me home. No, we didn't kiss. Not then, anyway. Are we an item? I don't know . . . yet.*

Anita looked into the mirror. Their first kiss had been pretty amazing. That was when he had told her about the gold dust in her eyes—and at that moment she had believed him.

A couple of days ago he had revealed that he had arranged something for her birthday. She was going to be sixteen tomorrow. A lunchtime barbecue with all her friends had been organized at her house for tomorrow, but Evan said he wanted to do something really special the day before, just for the two of them. When Anita asked him what he had planned, he told her she'd have to wait and see.

Maybe he would take her to some romantic place and tell her he loved her.

She gazed at her reflection. How would she feel about that? No one had ever said anything like that to her before. The idea of Evan saying that he loved her was huge and kind of scary—but it was pretty exciting too.

And she had the overwhelming feeling that she'd want to tell him the same thing right back.

She stared at herself in the mirror and mouthed the words silently: *I love you, Evan.* Her eyes widened. She didn't know whether to yell with laughter or scream in panic.

A sudden flare up of itchiness on her shoulder blades broke into her thoughts and she opened the bathroom cabinet to look for some antihistamine cream.

It was half an hour later that she ran down the hall, shouting good-bye to her mum and dad as she passed the open living room door.

"You're late!" her father called. "Evan will probably have got fed up waiting. He'll be long gone by the time you arrive."

"Thanks for the vote of confidence, Dad!" Anita called back, grinning. "I think he'll be a bit more patient than that."

She bounded down the front steps, swinging on the railings and running down the pavement toward the Camden Town Underground Station. All that effort to look good for Evan, and now she was going arrive sweaty and breathless and late.

Now is the sun upon the highmost hill of this long day's journey . . . it is three long hours—yet she is not come . . .

Anita let out a yell of exhilaration as the speedboat skimmed the water and the wind whipped her hair against her cheeks.

"What do you think of your birthday surprise so far?" Evan shouted over the roar of the engine and the slap and smash of the keel on the water. "Like it?"

"Like it? I *love* it!" She let out another yell as the prow dipped and rose, cutting the rippling surface of the river like a hot knife. Fine spray stung her face. "This is the best present I've ever had!"

He smiled at her, lifting one hand off the wheel and reaching out to stroke her hair. Trembling a little at his touch, she took his hand. She kissed it and pressed it to her cheek. She was so happy that she felt like she was about to burst right out of her skin. She looked at Evan, her heart pounding. His dark blonde hair was flying back off his face. His wide chestnut brown eyes were narrowed against the wind, his lips spread in that gorgeous smile.

Evan guided the boat under one of the curved arches of Westminster Bridge. They were in shade for a heartbeat, then they shot out into bright sunlight again. To the right, Anita could see the Gothic spires of the Houses of Parliament, backed by the office blocks and towers of London, glittering against the clear blue sky.

"This is just the start of it," he went on. "We're going all the way up to Richmond. We can have something to eat and hang by the river for a while. Then I'm going to bring you back to town for some heavy-duty clubbing." He smiled at her. "Are you up for that?"

"You bet!"

Evan had not said a single word of complaint when she had turned up half an hour late at Monument Tube

Station. He had simply kissed her hello, then taken her hand and led her down to the river. They had walked along a bobbing jetty and down to the small, sleek speedboat that he had hired for the day.

A few minutes later they had been speeding along the Thames with their curved wake lifting like a swan's wing behind them.

"Where did you learn to drive a boat?" Anita called.

Evan grinned at her. "Are you impressed?"

"Very!"

Evan laughed. "I'm multitalented—didn't you know?" He wiggled the steering wheel from side to side and the boat did a little jig on the water.

"Don't!" Anita gasped. She grabbed the metal rail. "Ow!" she exclaimed, snatching her hand back.

"What's wrong?" Evan called.

Anita rubbed her fingers. "I got a shock from the metal rail."

"It's your electric personality," he said, slowing down the boat as they passed a water taxi.

She frowned at him. "Don't make fun—it stings!" She was able to speak at a more natural level now that they weren't moving so fast. "It's been going on for a couple of weeks now. Every time I touch something metal, I get a shock. Dad says it's static electricity."

Evan shrugged. "So stop touching metal things."

"That's easier said than done," Anita pointed out. "How do I eat if I can't hold a knife and fork? It's very annoying. If it carries on, I'm going to have to start wearing gloves all the time." She shook her head. "It would happen to me!"

"Do weird things often happen to you, then?" Evan asked, looking at her sideways with an amused gleam in his eyes.

"Not weird, just awkward," Anita said. "Mum says I'm accident-prone. Dad says I was probably born under an unlucky star."

"I don't think that's true," Evan said.

Ahead of them, Lambeth Bridge was getting rapidly closer.

"I certainly don't feel unlucky right now," Anita said. She grinned.

"Good." He glanced at her again, suddenly looking more serious. "Anita? There's something important I have to tell you."

A buzz of nervous excitement went through her, and her stomach seemed to flip right over. She looked at him, half scared and half thrilled by what he might be about to say.

Call me but love, and I'll be new baptized . . .

But before Evan could say anything, a chill shadow swept over them, as if a dark hand had covered the sun. Anita looked up—the sky was cloudless.

Evan's head turned quickly and his eyes widened. A look of alarm twisted his face.

Anita gazed across the river, trying to make out what it was that had startled him. For a split second, she thought she saw a long, heavy dark shape wallowing low in the water.

"No!" Evan snarled between gritted teeth. "He can't have found us. Not now, of all times!"

Anita stared at him in confusion. What was he talking about?

He spun the wheel. The boat turned sharply, tipping on the water so that Anita staggered sideways, falling against Evan. Cold water dashed into her face, making her gasp for breath.

"Evan! Stop!" she shouted.

"No!" he howled, his voice wild and cracked. "He'll know we're here. He'll take you away from me!"

"What are you talking about? Evan, *please*!"

From the corner of her eye, she saw something huge and dark looming toward them. She just had time to turn her head as one of the stone pillars of Lambeth Bridge filled her vision.

A moment later, a violent impact sent her hurtling forward. Her ears filled with a brain-shredding noise. The sky whirled like a kaleidoscope. Then there was the deadly, freezing embrace of deep water. Red flames rimmed her sight and everything went black.

MAGIC, ADVENTURE, AND TRUE LOVE...

What happens when an ordinary girl is torn between two worlds?

Don't miss any books in The Faerie Path series!

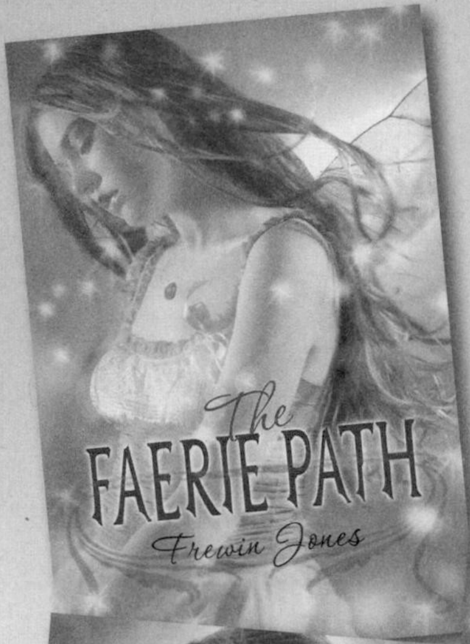
The
FAERIE PATH
Frewin Jones

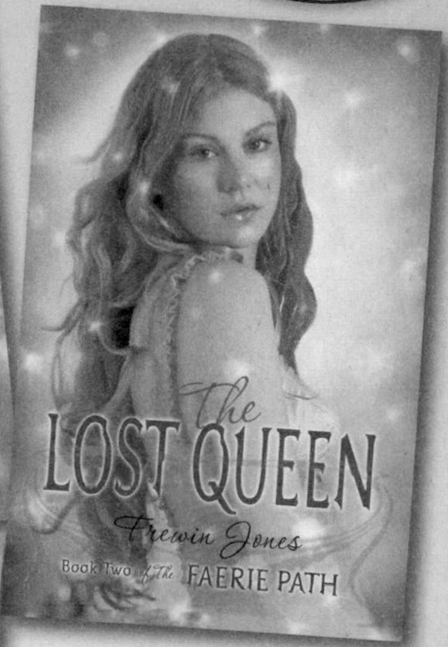
The
LOST QUEEN
Frewin Jones
Book Two of The FAERIE PATH

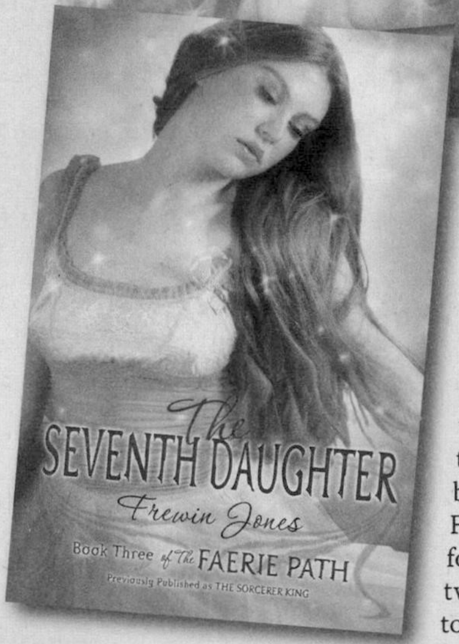
The
SEVENTH DAUGHTER
Frewin Jones
Book Three of The FAERIE PATH
Previously Published as THE SORCERER KING

The Faerie Path

Anita was living an ordinary life, until an elegant stranger pulled her into another world. There she discovers she is Tania—the lost princess of Faerie, and the only one who can stop a sinister plan that threatens the entire Realm. Torn between her duty to the throne of Faerie and the Mortal World she can't forget, Tania must choose between her two worlds, and two loves, as she begins to understand why she disappeared from Faerie so long ago.

eos
An Imprint of HarperCollins*Publishers* • www.harperteen.com